JOHN McLOUGHLIN
TOOLMAKER KOAN

JOHN McLOUGHLIN
TOOLMAKER KOAN

A Baen Books Original
Distributed by Simon & Schuster
1230 Avenue of the Americas
New York, New York 10020

Cover art by Stephen Hickman

First printing, October 1987

1   3   5   7   9   10   8   6   4   2

ISBN: 0-671-65354-7

Library of Congress Cataloging-in-Publication Data

McLoughlin, John.
    Toolmaker koan.

    "A Baen books original."
    I. Title.
PS3563.C3845T6   1987   813'.54   87-12637
ISBN 0-671-65354-7

JOHN McLOUGHLIN
TOOLMAKER KOAN

PROLOGUE

Alone in the eternal trans-Uranian night sailed the probe *Struggle*. On and outward, its small brain shut down for absence of anything to do, *Struggle* slept, only its detectors alert for the serendipitous bit of ice that would awaken the central brain.

While *Struggle* slept, the two great Powers of Earth—though both expected eventual dominion of the entire globe—were at peace. An odd peace, true; hair-trigger, mutually contemptuous. And justly contemptuous, by Ambrose Bierce's definition of contempt: "The feeling of a prudent man for an enemy who is too formidable safely to be opposed."

Still, it *was* peace. Each Power was far too formidable safely to be opposed, at least overtly, by the other; and some thirteen years before there had been the One-Day War, that brief and frightening taste of thermonuclear politics that had enhanced for a time the fragile prudence of humanity, simultaneously cementing the Lines of Demarcation that delineated the world's twin polities. Nonetheless, in the United People's Democratic Republics of Africa and Eurasia—

1

called "Greater Finland" by American wags and more or less a construct of the Soviet Union—it was common knowledge that Earth would one day be a Marxian world, a planet of enlightened Happy Workers; in the Greater Columbian Alliance of the American republics of the New World, it was hoped, as ever, that the Marxian juggernaut would fail—that some form of less doctrinaire democracy might set future historical style.

And on Earth it rained a yellow rain, a legacy of global industry and that One-Day War. Humankind was steeped in its own waste; crops grew poorly and people were hungry—there were six thousand million people, far too many of them.

So whether you were a citizen of one of the assorted Democratic Republics or of one of the nations of the Greater Columbian Alliance, you were lucky indeed if you lived not on Earth but in space. Here in these years of delicate peace humanity maintained a growing and effervescent presence, each Power hard at work on its own spaceborne cylinder city and countless embryonic industries. In space the air was clean, for people *made* that air; and in space there was plenty of food, good food, for everyone—there weren't, after all, many more than ten thousand people out there as yet.

But space, or at least that bit of it surrounding Earth and her moon, was abundantly crisscrossed with laser tightbeams. The eavesdrop-proof beams were a military phenomenon, as was so much else out there; such tightbeams linked not only human communicants, but also machines possessing varying degrees of sentience and preternaturally acute sensory equipment in their gallium-arsenide and silico-proteinaceous circuitry. These watched the comings and goings of Man and other doings in space, communicating their observations to human liaisons in the service of their respective Powers. Some such machines were totally military in function; others were instruments of research intended to further the interests of the Republics that fabricated them. Some of these latter were far-ranging indeed; one such, was *Struggle*.

Although constructed in zero-G factories at the hub of Cosmograd Engels, *Struggle* was born in idea form on Earth. In the service of the Indonesian People's Democratic Republic, one Indilara Djiridumi, academician, had learned that certain comets contain large proportions of water, nitrogen, simple hydrocarbons and hydrocarbon radicals— collectively termed volatiles—of immense potential value in the infant industries of space. While minerals—iron, carbon, aluminum, silicon and the like—might be found in asteroidal material and on the moon, volatiles were currently available only from Earth, hauled up at great expense from her gravity well; would that one might catch a comet!

Alas! Comets are hard to come by near Earth. Nonetheless, Djiridumi, an indefatigable researcher, learned of the work of one Jan Oort, a dead capitalist astronomer who had hypothesized the existence of a vast aggregation of cometary material beyond the orbit of Pluto. Nicknamed the Oort Cloud, this nebulous "shell" of the Solar System could be of great economic interest if it were learned that individual cometary bodies might by mechanical means be diverted cheaply and predictably Earthward from their slow, remote orbits for the use of the socialist effort in space.

After several years of campaigning, Djiridumi was able to convince the Bureau of Cosmonautical Affairs that a Trans-Plutonian probe might turn up useful information concerning the availability of volatiles from small bodies in space. So, in June of 2031, such a probe set out from the Bureau of Cosmonautical Affairs factories associated with the baby aluminum-and-glass world of Engels at the Second Lunar Lagrangian Point.

Riding its ice-blue ion jets nightward from the Earth-Moon System, *Struggle* first sought out the great gravity well of Jove, swooping close to the Father of Planets to gain a velocity-boost. Then on and out, arcing across the orbit of Saturn and getting another boost from Uranus's gravity-well, and off yet faster, its small brain and jets now dormant for the long cold ride across the lonely astronomical units separating the paths of the Outer Worlds. But *Struggle*'s mass-detectors stayed alert for that long-sought ice.

And suddenly, at some 27.842 AU from Earth, those mass-detectors were tickled. They dutifully prodded *Struggle* awake; the probe had found an unexpected mass out there between the paths of Uranus and Neptune, and carefully measured it at 47.3842 metric tons, flashing the word Sunward on laser tightbeam. As the initial datum flew across its nearly four-hour journey from *Struggle* to its makers at Engels, the probe extended optics and servomanipulators, adjusted course, and readied sampling chambers and heat-sources to taste the economic potential of its find, continuing all the while to strum data along the tightbeam string.

Struggle was not bright. It was designed solely to capture ancient bits of ice from the solar primordium, to gnaw and taste that ice, and to report the taste to its masters. Therefore its behavioral repertoire did not encompass a useful response to the newfound mass's tendency to maintain itself at a constant distance of a few tens of meters from the probe; *Struggle* simply began a series of fancy astrobatics as its neurocircuitry set it in pursuit of what by all rights should have been an inanimate frosty boulder in an eons-old stable fall around the far-off Sun. *Struggle* did pass back word of these astrobatics, though, and word of the mass's appearance and size. And, surprise not being part of its meager complement of cyberresponsiveness, *Struggle* simply added visuals and measurements showing the pursued 47-ton mass to be a seamless, silvery ovoid of but .8264 meter in major axis, .7133 meter in diameter.

And, dutiful as its makers intended, *Struggle* continued relaying orderly data describing first a nonresponse of its own pursuit jetting, then a non-response of its servomanipulators, then a sequential shutdown of higher cyber circuits in its magnetic bubble brain.

Even as the first datum—MASS LOCATED—reached the human listeners at the flying city of Engels, *Struggle* spoke its last out there in the dark; but, its brief string of information was more than sufficient to initiate a chain reaction of frightened agitation among its distant human masters in the Bureau of Cosmonautical Affairs.

Part I

CHAPTER 1

Cosmograd Engels

Vacuum.

The vacuum loves living flesh, she thought; it relentlessly seeks to pull the mortal substance into its cold embrace.

How poetic. I'm getting tired.

The surgeon, Citizen Doctor Jennifer Dawson, nicked her unconscious patient's purple skin with the laser cautery, lacing a ruptured vein, the cephalic vein tracing the curve of the man's space-stripped radial bone. She spotted a bit of gray frozen tissue, expertly slicing it away from viable muscle with the cautery, leaving no necroses . . . and how heavy the little penlike cautery seemed!

Three quarters of an hour before, this man had been EVA, working on the great antenna that tracked the distant Oort Probe—but an instant's carelessness had placed his arm in the path of a servomanipulator, and through a tiny rip in the suit armor the omnipresent vacuum at once sucked as much of the man's right forearm as it could before he patched the breach with his left and drifted into shock, bouncing inert

9

against his umbilicus. He'd been careless, but he was quick; he got away with a spaceburn only. In a few weeks he'd be EVA again, likely, his arm stiff but usable.

Meela Ndola, surgeon's mate and, for now, anesthesiologist, produced a blood-temp pigskin web to complete the work; wrapped around the wound, the web would offer a temporary integument beneath which the man's torn and blistered skin might find its way together again.

"He's reviving already, Citizen Doctor," she said. "Shall I send him back to Bachelor Officers' Quarters?"

"Not yet. Keep him in Infirmary for the next two watches. I'll want to watch that arm."

"May I remind you, Citizen Doctor, that you haven't eaten or slept in seven watches? Your performance will suffer for it. This is the last patient—Citizen Nurse Makola can see to him. Take some time for food and sleep. I'll have you awakened in five watches."

Best listen to Citizen Ndola, surgeon's mate—always brisk, efficient, performance-conscious, deep-steeped in the Principles of Structured Enlightenment. Yes indeed, the performance of Citizen Doctor Captain Jennifer Wellesley Dawson might come up—again—at the next Self-Criticism Council. That she couldn't afford, she of the British name, appearance, and, despite her Zimbabwean birth, ancestry.

By an accident of genetics—she was a blonde—she was suspected by all her African associates of harboring the recidivist individualist tendencies always associated with the old blue-eyed oppressor race. Without frequent examination at Self-Criticism, these atavistic tendencies might surface to trouble the harmony of Infirmary personnel, or even of the entire Bureau of Cosmonautical Affairs. And disharmony anywhere interferes with the smooth functioning of the Principles of Structured Enlightenment that guide and unite State and People. Her slot on the Performance Chart in the Medical Officers' Mess already sported two greenstripes for the week, and a third would lose her the Private Initiative Time that was an officer's standard prerogative.

"Yes, Meela, you're right, as usual. That last rash of bad seals . . ." Jennifer sighed, watching lines of disapproval form around the dark pursed lips of the surgeon's mate. As usual, it seemed, she'd forgotten the "Citizen"; she imagined Ndola's brain adding this omission of egalitarian sentiment to her personal list of the Citizen Doctor's individualist leanings.

"Look—yes, call me in five watches. No, make it four. There's a new shipment of those Lusaka suits coming up, and their seals—"

Ndola shook her head reproachfully. "Citizen Doctor, you and I both know that the capitalist element in the Lusaka suit plant was successfully rooted out by the People's Tribunal. Four managers were shot in that trial, and the profiteer weed was eradicated. Those suits will be excellent. The Quality Examinations Cadre sent you, personally, a report. I read it. You go to sleep. There'll be no more failures, and you'll feel much more efficient after five watches of rest. Remember your greenstripes."

Ah, the fucking greenstripes. You can't get away from the greenstripes, not on Earth, not out here at Engels. Certainly the air's clean—manmade. Certainly there's more room—EVA, that is—and food. But the Self-Criticism Councils, the greenstripes—the Principles of Structured Enlightenment—remain.

"All right. You win. I'm off for BWQ. I might do a bit of EVA first, get some space. Five watches?"

"Five watches, Citizen Doctor. All power to the people."

"Power to the people. And thanks." Jennifer sighed again, removing gloves and OR tunic, stooping through the low bulkhead door and into the green tubeway toward Rim.

Riding the elevator alone, she began to submit to her fatigue. Seven four-hour watches before, she'd been awakened by her beeper; some thirty new suits from Lusaka had been issued to new techs working on the apparently malfunctioning antenna that served as ear to the trans-Plutonian probe *Struggle*. The polymer seals in the joints of these suits had quite suddenly proved substandard, hardening and cracking in vacuum, and Jennifer spent the subsequent twenty-eight hours immersed in spaceburn and worse at Trauma Unit, Lowgrav Surgery.

The young woman with double eye evulsion had been worst, because she'd live . . . but the last fellow, he of the torn suit arm, was a relief. Older, more experienced, he had a personalized suit. Individualist tendencies—he'd apparently evaded the mandatory egalitarian suit rotations somehow, as did Jennifer herself. Minor infraction, but noted by all. A wry, lopsided smile twisted her narrow face for an instant, and the elevator deposited her at Bachelor Women's Quarters, Fullgrav Rim.

Inside her cubicle waited a pair of burly female guards wearing the black-and-yellow coveralls of Sub-Saharan Detachment, State Security. Jennifer's stomach knotted.

"Citizen," said the larger of the two, "you are selected as a pioneer." The guard smiled crookedly, stainless-steel teeth glinting in the dim cubicle light. "You're privileged to assist in a state mission of great import and secrecy. I envy you. You must have acquired some high distinction to be thus chosen. So. Please come with us."

Nothing more was said; nothing *to* be said. They took her a long way, walking along the Fullgrav Rim of Engels toward Command and Control. Then to a steel door, ushering her through, leaving her.

In the middle of the metal desk sat a round cap of black fur, glossy thick short fur on which the desklamp glinted as if each ebon strand were separately extruded of some sort of black metal. At once mesmerized and repelled by the tale of her coming assignment, Jennifer had stared at this object through the whole of the meeting.

"A conceit of mine," said the man behind the desk. He picked up the hat, turning it slowly in his hands so that a dappling of deeper black was visible in the fur's gloss. "I had the hide sent up from Entebbe Base at a cost of fifteen hundred new rubles. The cat we had to steal from the cadre in Bulawayo. Your home. They got it when the zoo was eaten, and kept it. I'd guess there isn't another such animal alive in Africa, not now. Nor in the world . . . well, perhaps in the capitalist zoos, over in the West . . ." He donned the cap for a moment, smiled weirdly as a great scar, etched into his brown face from eyebrow to chin, twisted with the movement. He doffed the furry helmet, holding it above his head for an instant like a Victorian gentleman, then placed it with a flourish on a lunar globe to his left. The globe swung about its axis with the cap's mass, dropping it on the desk.

"So, Citizen Doctor. You don't like the sound of our mission.

"No. Sir. Since you ask." Jennifer shook her head, fatigue drooping her eyelids. "I'm still uncomfortable with the Long Sleep System. And yes, if the probe has simply malfunctioned, I'd say you're wasting time and money. If there *is*—something—out there, you seem to be preparing to do your best to antagonize it. Since you ask."

"Now, Citizen Doctor, I know you and you know me—I think. You'll no doubt recall your conscription after the Disturbance. I was just a platoon leader in the strike force that liberated the Gwelo and Selukwe, but I recall you well. You removed—very competently—a nine-millimeter round from my left calf. I remember wondering at the time how strongly you held the Hippocratic Oath, whether you might try to incapacitate me permanently. You did not."

"I wanted to live," said Jennifer. "I wanted to live, and leave, too. And yes, the oath is part of me. But mostly I wanted to live. I still do."

"Of course." Oruna Benai, newly designated commander of the Fast Deep-Space Weapons Platform *Dienbienphu*, leaned back and lifted his feet to his desktop, leather belt and holster creaking with the movement. In a time of synthetic fabric, even the leather was a conceit, lugged all the way out of the Earthly gravity well; Benai was nothing if not pleased with himself.

"You've done very well for yourself, Citizen Doctor, as have I. We shared a vision, a thought of escape from Earth, and we have both accomplished this goal. In different ways, of course. But we've done it. Now we'll see who inherits the new worlds: whether it will be the greedy capitalists with their colonialist ambitions, or the People guided by the Principles of Structured Enlightenment. You and I and our crew will see to it that the People have a better chance than they would without us. Your oath, if not your politics, binds your hands, no?"

"I hope they're not bound, Commander."

"They *are* bound, as are mine, by the force of

historical evolution. But within that constraint, we each may function in accordance with our own vision, no?" The pips of Special Command First Grade glinted on his red collar-tabs as Benai lowered his feet again—a nervous man, always moving, his quickness surprising in one so massively built and almost two meters tall. He played with a pen for a moment, his forehead wrinkling as he struggled to maintain the flow of his Enlightened cant, and Jennifer almost grinned.

The commander saw this, the tips of his teeth showing in what might have been a smile of his own. "All right, Citizen Doctor, I'm not a stupid man. Let's just say that anything less than a meter long and massing forty-seven tons suggests a considerable technological advantage—especially if it maneuvers as well as the last probe messages suggest it did. Ah, this object—" he gestured in a way that meant "out there"— "this silver egg may gain us positions of, ah, considerable influence for the remainders of our lives. To look at it another way, this object might mean the end of war for all time—if it falls into the right hands. If indeed it's out there." He paused, watching Jennifer expectantly.

"Commander, you're throwing riddles at me. I'm tired. You speak bloody smoothly for a fellow who started out as a platoon leader in a ragtag army of bullies, but I haven't time. Why me? We have twelve surgeons on Engels. I have patients *here*, wounded waiting for *me*. Just what is it? What?" Jennifer felt the edge creeping into her voice, tried to restrain her growing irritation. The man was dangerous on Earth, perhaps more so here, where she'd never expected to see his like.

"Citizen Doctor. You're an anomaly here, in a way. Our records show us that you were something of a wanderer in your youth—inclined toward what they used to call 'natural philosophy.' You took early to a naturalist's life, to biology, and your later schooling shows a broad interest in the sciences of animal form, evolution and behavior. This is so?"

"Yes, Commander, but of precious little use here in the Cosmograd, I assure you—unless I begin to specialize in pigs and cattle and chickens and carp." Jennifer brushed back her bangs, rubbed her eyes. How she missed walking, watching, listening, inhaling, on Earth. But she'd had to get away, hadn't she?

"Well, Citizen Doctor Dawson, it has been brought to my attention that you are the *only* person with such a background in the entire Cosmograd complex. We have veterinarians, of course, and other surgical personnel, but we have no one who combines your precise attributes of medical training with an interest in natural history that was both encouraged from earliest youth *and* broadened by study under some of the greatest evolutionary biologists in the old European capitalist world."

Benai grinned broadly, the snakelike scar twisting with seeming life of its own across his wide face. He placed the tips of his long fingers together in a smugly prayerlike position.

"There was once a great English natural philosopher named Charles Darwin," he murmured, still smiling. "Do you recall much of him?"

"Certainly," said Jennifer. "Anyone would—"

"Anyone steeped in capitalist philosophical history. I've steeped myself a little, recently, because I strongly believe that you should ride with us on our mission." Benai cleared his throat, like one preparing to make a long speech. "You will recall that Darwin was a rich and unrepentant scion of a capitalist medical clan— people who made their fortunes off the sufferings of the poor—"

"So we're told now," said Jennifer, a touch of angry adrenalin coursing through her weariness.

"Yes, citizen, and *now* is what matters, isn't it?" The commander rolled his eyes ceilingward, sighed. "This Darwin, for whom the modern world has so little time, he was one of Karl Marx's chief inspirations. Marx dedicated the *Kapital* to Darwin, or offered to; Darwin declined the honor." Benai's pleasure in his speech seemed to swell as he proceeded; with a lazy wave of his great hand he brushed off another objection from Jennifer, grinned, half closed his eyes.

"Your friend Darwin sailed around the world with a Captain Fitzroy, a British aristocrat who was a career naval officer and captain of the good ship *Beagle*, a, ah, brig of some two hundred and forty-two tons Imperialist and about twenty-seven meters in length."

"You've gone to a lot of trouble with this, Commander. Why?"

Benai waved again, feline in his ease. "Fitzroy was an ardent Anglican. He wished the company of a naturalist on his circumnavigation, one who would take the opportunity to demonstrate to the rest of the world the power of God and the magnificence of His Creation." The scar twisted as the commander smiled.

"And, Citizen, we know what happened to that alliance of faith and travel, don't we?"

"Darwin synthesized his Theory, Fitzroy's Creation denied."

"Indeed, Citizen. Many think that Darwin's theory was the best thing to come out of the British Empire. Others disagree. It doesn't matter now. What does matter is, that I need your help."

Benai stared thoughtfully at his furred and beaded cap for a moment, then picked it up and twirled it on his finger. Then put it down again, his full lips twitching as he sought his words. "Citizen Doctor, I can imagine that you have reason to hate me, or hate what I stand for. But we share some things, too. My grandmother was bondwoman to a plantation in Northern Rhodesia—Zambia after liberation. She was raped by the white plantation stockman when she was fourteen, giving birth to my mother. She was sent with her infant to Southern Rhodesia during the Smith regime, and died when she was twenty-one. My mother was raised by Anglican missionaries; I studied in the English school at Bulawayo and went to the Witwatersrand for a time, when non-Europeans were rare there." Idly, the giant spun his lunar globe.

"Oh, yes, I underwent an excess of wrath during the final liberation—the Disturbance—but it achieved for me a position of influence that otherwise would have been denied. I combine, let us say, the Old World's language, English, and a bit of its learning, with the New World's commitment to the principles of Structured Enlightenment. I bridge the gap—we mustn't lose the entire oppressor legacy, after all, but must simply purge history of its more damaging and disruptive concepts."

Suddenly Benai winked broadly, surprising Jennifer as he leaned forward and whispered conspiratorially, "Charles Darwin would have understood my position, Citizen. I adapt to my environment. You also."

"You're billing yourself as a soldier-philosopher. A sort of an African Marcus Aurelius." The commander was a multileveled creature, more than Jennifer had expected of his like, but he was still a trained plug-ugly. . . . "Please, Commander, I'm fading fast."

"An African Marcus Aurelius. I rather like that, Citizen. As for your fading, see here." He gestured toward an electric samovar of obvious Sov make, silver plated and elaborately Oriental in design. "Coffee? Very fresh, quite authentic . . ." Jennifer nodded, and Benai took two real china cups from a drawer—the mass-credits he'd earned in the service of the State must have been enormous to have lifted this elegant frippery to Engels from Earth—and poured from his gaudy samovar two cups of thick black coffee. Jennifer felt warmed by the very aroma of the stuff, and she tried to restrain her eagerness in reaching for her portion.

Benai sipped thoughtfully, watching over the rim of his cup as Jennifer took a first massive gulp, then smiled apologetically. "Drink," said Benai. "Drink, Jennifer Wellesley Dawson, and see me this way: I am Fitzroy. I have been given a ship, I am going to take a voyage, and I need the company of a willing naturalist to prove the universal truth of the Principles of Structured Enlightenment. I may see new aspects of creation, and if so I will require assistance in their interpretation. I may also need a surgeon who has a proven record in emergency and disaster management.

"I need help, Doctor. It's that simple."

Jennifer sipped her coffee, mind working. On bended knee, our African Marcus. You bet you need help, you smooth-tongued tough. You're going to try to catch that thing that *Struggle* found. You'll catch it or kill it. You want someone to find its weaknesses if it's alive, someone to dissect it for you if it doesn't survive capture. You'll try to prove to the world that the thing is a good old Marxian Happy Worker.

God, I'm so tired. I want to get away. I want *it* to get away.

"I'll go," she said suddenly.

"Indeed, Doctor!" Benai, reaching again for his

samovar, paused in mid-movement. All trace of a smile left his face. "Of course you will go. I would like to have seen you *wish* to go, however, even though some of your fellow travellers may not be quite to your liking."

"I do—I wish to go."

"That was an interesting change of mind. You have enough greenstripes so that I cannot help but detect in you a strong individualist bent, Citizen; I don't quite feel that my little study on Darwin could really have convinced you so suddenly. You know that you'll be closely watched—"

"What else? Isn't everyone?"

"You also know the fate of Captain Fitzroy?"

"He cut his own throat on a springtime Sabbath morning in 1865."

"Yes," said Oruna Benai, his strange scarred smile returning. "He cut his own throat. But I, Citizen, I would cut anyone's throat but my own. Anyone's. And, unlike Captain Fitzroy, I would find no difficulty adapting to the new world this voyage of mine may reveal to us. No difficulty."

He smiled again as Jennifer finished her coffee. She began to feel energy coursing through her blood, far too much energy for caffeine. The stuff was tinctured with amphetamine. No sleep now; here was how this African Marcus kept running. Work hard, die young.

Benai reached for his black fur cap, emblem of command and conceit. "Now, Citizen Doctor, you're fatigued; you've an eight-hour rest allotment. Return to your quarters. On awakening you will immediately transfer to my ship. You have a four-kilogram personal-effects allowance; you will also have an equipment requisition, mass open. Your clothing will be issued on board—not that you'll be wearing it for a time. We'll awaken from the Long Sleep at 22 AU from launch, for a total of eleven months' dormancy." He stood, ushered her toward the door. "Until tomorrow, then, Citizen."

Jennifer gave in to the amphetamine surge, her back straightening with that electric artificial strength for which she knew she'd pay so dearly later. She stood, shrugging, and left for her quarters.

To sleep at last; perchance to dream. She feared dreams, sometimes, for they carried her into her past, to Earth, the wounded blue world from which she'd fled at last, more than two years before.

And so they did on this, her last night at Cosmograd Engels. In her mind's eye she saw fragments of her Zimbabwean childhood, her family's Rhodesian ridge-back dogs, tawny and supple, stretching langorously in the shade of the baobabs. She recalled her father, himself a surgeon, tall and sunburned, laughing at her attempt to catch the young guinea-fowl speeding through the grass; she saw her mother at the piano, singing old songs from American musical comedies; she saw her brothers and her younger sister, and felt the wind as they rode atop the old Land Rover across the rolling veldt toward Bulawayo, the hospital there where they visited her father when he'd a moment away from the operating room.

And her dreams carried her to England, to the ancient towers above the emerald green of Cambridge; the fear came here, for it was at Cambridge that she learned of the troubles in Zimbabwe, of her father's disappearance in Bulawayo. But there was pleasure also; memories of her fiance, always to remain a tousled blond boy in her mind, his smile, his touch, their joint work with tomograph and laser and remote optic-fiber technique, their mad pubcrawls, their bright weekends punting through England's old canals . . .

And when they'd their degrees they interned in London until the Angel of Death spread its oily black wings across the Straits of Hormuz and the Persian Gulf and at last the world; even as she left her fiance, taking that hastily reserved seat on the Suborbital back to Bulawayo, the rockets arced flaming across their awesome parabolae from Pakistan to Israel, from Israel to Pakistan and India; in superhardened silos beneath the steppes of Asia and the prairies of North America, fingers tensed above keyboards while command and countercommand bounced from Earthbound antennae to geosynchronous satellites to orbiting weapons platforms and back again, the world seething with electronic adrenalin . . . And the Sovs erased Pretoria, Capetown and Johannesburg as warning, the Americans in turn slagging Managua, San Salvador and even Havana, so close to fouling their own nest—as warning.

But even after twenty-one nuclear warheads exploded around the world, the hunter-killer satellites did not move, the orbiting antimissile platforms remained untouched and a measure of sanity took hold again in the form of hasty treaties and broad governmental collapses as the political world rearranged itself overnight.

The One-Day War. That War itself may have lasted one day, but the Disturbance, the social upheavals of the following months, saw the rise of Marxian governments in Western Europe and all of Asia as American influence withdrew, with Africa and Australasia following suit. Canny as ever, the petty dictators and shaky democracies of Latin America felt the future's drift and allied themselves with their mighty neighbor to the north.

And as the world reeled under the impact of those twenty-one almost simultaneous nuclear explosions, the Brotherhood of the Black Leopard came one night to the Dawson plantation "to eradicate the White pestilence" in keeping with their own peculiar interpretation of the Principles of Structured Enlightenment; Jennifer's brothers and mother were burned alive in "necklaces," their necks ringed with blazing petrol-soaked tires, and Jennifer and her sister were reserved for some sport.

The sister died; but when the Brotherhood learned that Jennifer was a surgeon they left off their use of her body and forced her mind and hands to caring for their wounded; and, likely mercifully, the tiny brown mite that burst screaming out of her womb nine months later swiftly died, malnourished and fatherless in a tent-town on the burned and windswept veldt of her birthplace.

But a doctor's place is in the service of the People, and Jennifer Dawson alone of her house lived on, submerging her agony in ceaseless work as the shattered world tried to pull itself together. When Soviet and European technicians poured in on Resource Development Taskforces, they brought news with them, news of the Cosmograd a-building in space where Marxian civilization would grow yet mightier, a place free of the plagues and starvation racking man's earthly home.

The newcomers had white faces too, as well as much-needed technology; under their influence Africa came less to hate Jennifer's own lack of color. She was even issued an automatic weapon, for there was no safety on the street, never would be. All still called her "English," though, as one might say "shit" —and the oddest thing about this was that the only language commonly understood across the vast expanse of Africa and Eurasia *was* English, though for a time the Sovs and others attempted to eradicate its use. So the old language of the oppressor, the language of science, technology and medicine, lived on and was reborn in the most immense polity the world would ever know.

And the memories rolled on, with a life of their own, carrying her again through the years of her trying to escape Earth for the city of Engels in space. She concentrated on the laser cautery and on other tools of space medicine, tools to which the Sovs were only too glad to introduce her. She specialized in the weird vicissitudes of vacuum pathology and nullgrav surgery; she became a singleminded Earthbound space surgeon. She had to get away.

For Jennifer Dawson knew that Earth's tribulation was not over. Seas of vengeful impulse surged through the billions of humanity, and the two hemispheres armed faster and finer than ever before. The peoples of Earth were amassing arsenals that would have stupefied the twentieth-century superpowers; there Jennifer knew a fear as cold and mindless as the vacuum of space to which she longed to flee, and did at last. . . .

And now this—this long sleep into the trans-Uranian night. This lunatic quest, taking her from her work and forcing her onto the longest voyage ever undertaken by human beings, perhaps to meet something that had travelled much farther. Something that might not take kindly to capture, that might love its freedom more than did these armed and hairy human bipeds, Marxians self-bound in the Principles of Structured Enlightenment.

Man, false Man, smiling, destructive Man!

CHAPTER 2

The Pampas and Orbit;
Three Months Later

For Pike Muir, it had all begun with four men in a hole at dusk.

On them the bitter yellow drizzle fell, ceaselessly popping against their helmets and slickers. Faceless behind rank and rubbery issue visors, all scratched surreptitiously at the itch of trickling sweat, otherwise not moving until one, visibly by the black camou bar on his visor a first lieutenant, glanced at his watch and whispered:

"Okay, Colonel Ulibarri, what we've released out there on that ridge at a hundred and fifty meters just now is a Soviet walking gatling sentry, hexapod, codenamed Six Watchdog—one of the four captured on the Kennedy run in Guam. State o' the art. This is the only one we got intact, zonked it on an EMP. We—uh, Major Muir's cyber team—dissected the other three we got, but they was dead, more or less. Taught us a lot, though, about the brain. Now, Six Watchdog is equipped with what we call the Borzoi Analog Magnetic Bubble Intelligence, BAMBI for short—"

"A delightful name for a sixleg gatling," observed the colonel drily, his Spanish-accented whisper muffled by his eagle-emblazoned visor.

"Yessir," whispered the lieutenant. "Actually, the gatling itself is a Six Watchdog. BAMBI's just the OC, uh, Operative Computer. It's an interchangeable component, modular, same one as in this *Struggle* probe you talked about. BAMBI ain't too bright, but it interfaces in this case with their Niger English linguistic program, another modular—just enough smarts and lingo for guard duty.

"ID capacity includes olfactory preset for individual pheromones, with integral snap chromatography, a chierograph or palm-reader, and standard photo-programmed optical ID registers. Full audio range and visual from UV to infrared, flat terrain speed of sixty KPH, and detention stunners as well as the fore-and-aft fifteen-millimeter gatlings—which, by the way, have a combined firing rate of almost eighty-two hundred rounds per minute. Cuts down trees. Sort of a talking Doberman, if you catch my drift, with flying teeth. Not too different from our own walking gatlings but for the brain—and that's why we're here.

"Now, Colonel Ulibarri—" the lieutenant preened a bit beneath his slicker—"we're so confident of this program that we've loaded the Watchdog with live ammo. And what we've done for our private surprise is, we've attached our MBPM, a Magnetic Bubble Parasitic Monitor, to its neurocircuitry. We'll be working through that monitor, which maintains comlink through the Spec-four's pack here to the MIDAS system situated in a bunker four klicks to our rear. MIDAS does the analysis and translation for the experiment, see. Once we perfect the parasite-MIDAS link, we should be able to monitor any BAMBI OC within realtime range by attaching these monitors to the things with flying remotes, although right now it's sort of a bell-the-cat—or Watchdog—proposition."

The lieutenant turned slightly, spoke to the other officer in the muddy hole. "Captain Muir, as head honcho for this here study, you wanna do the honors?"

Cyber Team Leader Captain Charles L. "Pike" Muir gestured toward the colonel, his slicker crackling slightly with the movement. "Let's let our guest try it. Not too many walking gatlings out there at Cislunar Intelligence. Taste of life on Earth."

"Gotcha," whispered the lieutenant. "Colonel Ulibarri?"

"Ah, what do I do?" Colonel Jaime Ulibarri raised his helmeted head a bit, peered over the muddy rim of the hole into the humid gloom beyond. Nothing stirred but the pocked yellow brush beyond, its foliage twitching beneath the acrid rain.

"Well, shout something. Or just clap. Or maybe, uh, here, take this—" the lieutenant handed Ulibarri a folded pocketknife— "an' rap it a couple times on the Spec-four's flatboard edge. An' f'gawdsake get back down first!"

"Rap it? Just rap it?" The colonel's whisper grew raspier as the fourth man handed him the flatboard console.

"Yessir. Three, four times. Good and loud."

TOK. TOK. TOK. The sound snapped out, startling the colonel in spite of himself.

"*HALT!*" A stentorian voice roared out in the dusk beyond, echoing briefly from the surrounding ridges, blunting suddenly in the hissing of rain.

At the top of the hill beyond, a great insect shape suddenly rose, silhouetted dark and angular against the deepening slate of the sky. Two turrets whirled, their multibarrelled snouts triangulating instantly on the foxhole and Colonel Ulibarri. Even through the dusk and rain at this distance, the flickering of nictitators clearing black optics was ominously plain.

"FOUR MEN IN HOLE!" The voice boomed like some appalling god's, resonant, inhuman, commanding. "RISE FOR IDENTIFICATION!"

Seized by an involuntary urge to obey, Ulibarri started to his feet.

"*Down!* Stay down! Watch—sir." Pike Muir pushed firmly on the colonel's shoulder.

"RISE FOR IDENTIFICATION!" And then a scintillating light from one of the gatling turrets, a frightful all-encompassing HOOOOM like the sound of a briefly-touched middle-C on a cosmic organ—and the hillside behind the crouching quartet dissolved into a flying welter of mud and fine-chopped vegetation.

"FOUR MEN IN HOLE! RISE FOR IDENTIFICATION! YOU ARE SIGHTED AND RANGED!"

"Now, sir," said the lieutenant to Ulibarri (who had assumed as nearly as possible the thickness and shape of a pie-plate on the muddy foxhole floor), "here's our little trick. Watch the Spec-four here, acting comlink to MIDAS."

Ulibarri, wincing, turned his bespattered visor reluctantly from the mud into which he'd pressed his face, wiped the eyeshields and peered at the party's fourth.

This last, wearing an antennaed backpack, held up the gray flatboard console, punched four keys and waited while a momentary rainbow played across its face.

"Frequency search, sir," explained Pike, no longer whispering. "Now, look—"

"FOUR MEN IN HO—" The great voice stopped as if cut with a knife. On the flatboard console appeared a cluster of four bright dots in a dappled background.

"We've simultaneously broken the gatling's guard loops and tapped its sensories, sir." Pike took the console, turned it so Ulibarri could examine its face. "Those four spots are us in infrared—warm bodies, what the gatling sees right now." The spots grew, resolving into the torsos of four human shapes, blurred but clearly visible—their clothing, even though cooled by rain, did not hide them from that awful mechanical scrutiny. Then the view changed again, the slickers and helmets appearing and details of the surrounding landscape flickering bright, then disappearing from the console as the gatling's sensors shifted viewing frequencies.

"The damn thing sees pretty well, doesn't it? It can see in any or all frequencies, as conditions demand. And with our gadget attached, *we* see what *it* sees. *And* it'll do what we tell it. Watch." Pike turned the board again, punched a seven-digit code, spoke into an auditory pickup: "Watchdog, *sit!*" He grinned at the colonel's reflective visor.

As Ulibarri sat up and peered across the foxhole's edge, the arthropod form bent its six multijointed legs, settling an armored segmented belly to the hilltop mud.

"Watchdog, stand and approach!"

The machine rose again, then began a swift smooth trot on clawed metal feet, maintaining body and turrets level despite the rocks and brush; faster than man could run, it seemingly glided toward them while Ulibarri found himself involuntarily shrinking back.

"Watchdog, halt," said Pike evenly. The machine stopped; as still as a simple piece of scaffolding it waited, its horrible quasi-life betrayed only by the flickering of its turret ocular nictitators blinking against the rain.

Ulibarri sighed. "Captain, I expect I am not used to life Downside. It's a bit more, ah, messy here than I'd imagined. But my congratulations, Captain. You *are* a genius, as I was told."

"Nossir. But we're good hackers, *que no*?" Hidden though his face was by the visor, Pike's pleasure was clearly audible.

Jaime Ulibarri sat back, his slicker crackling. "You're unnecessarily modest. Ah, may we send the lieutenant and the specialist back to the unit?"

"Done, sir," said Pike. "Rosey, Herper, split—don't get wet."

"Yessir." The soldiers grinned, saluted. "Later." They scrambled from the muddy hole and doubletimed away, the now-harmless gatling turrets automatically tracking their retreat.

"And now," said Ulibarri, "*Major* Muir, we talk a bit. You understand that all this . . ."

" 'Major,' sir?"

"Indeed. A preplanned bit of a surprise. Congratulations!" Ulibarri handed him a plastic-wrapped sheaf of orders from somewhere inside his voluminous slicker. "All this inconvenience, these physicals, the coming quarantine, all that—are visited upon you because of our admiration for this work of yours. You'll be well taken care of. We leave tomorrow evening from the equatorial shuttlebase at Santana in the Brazilian state of Amapa, my friend, for High Columbia, where you'll billet for a few days' briefing. None of this infernal rain. Not so much time or room, perhaps, but you'll see the sun, sir—you'll be envied by your teammates here."

The new major blinked in surprise. "Oh, hey, sir, we see the sun here in the Argentine pretty frequently—we get a good clear day at least once every two weeks, and I do a lot of riding—out on the Pampas, you know. I'll kind of miss that, I guess."

"That you will indeed miss. I miss it also—my family had vineyards here, when I was young. Gone now, with the rains—sometimes I dream of having another vineyard, a small one . . . but I suppose . . . well! Enough of that. I believe you'll enjoy your mission. It's a longer mission than I've explained, really . . . Do I understand correctly that you have no immediate family?"

"Not close, sir. My parents died during the Emergency; brother dead too, killed in Honduras. I have a sister in Chicago, but she's Social Justice and won't even talk to me."

"And your wife . . ."

"That didn't really work out, sir. I'm sure you know about it already. Too much time on the move, and in the end she went Social Justice too." Funny what it does to them, Pike thought, especially if you're Army or anything. It's as if they just—close in on themselves. All that stuff about peace and equality and disarmament and universal justice sounds so good, but it makes them somehow, well, lofty or something. As if they don't have time, and the rest of us are dirt . . . and Pat started going out with the SJ types while I was in the Panama conflict, wrote she was having more fun than ever before, had found meaning in life at last, didn't want kids, wanted to devote her time to the Movement . . . and of course that guy Parmenter . . . and me a vicious materialistic capitalist warmonger, or whatever. . . .

"Strange times, sir," he added. "I guess they could just as easily have gone to the Christian Federalist side of things, like a lot of my relatives . . ."

"Indeed, um, Major. You'll find a good many Christian Federalists at High Columbia." Ulibarri withdrew from the inner pocket of his slickered uniform a vast cigar. Shielding this nicotine torpedo from the rain, the colonel lighted it with an old Austrian lighter. "Hah! At High Columbia, no smoking, nor at Cislunar Intelligence, alas. At any rate, you'll see no more of your friends here for a time; you're a secret, you and your parasitic monitor. You'll recall our discussion of the Sov Oort Probe and the famous lights in the sky of three months ago? The maiden voyage of what our Communist rivals call the good ship *Dienbienphu*, formerly an advanced weapons platform, now reincarnated as a research vessel extraordinaire, breaker of six codicils of the Treaty of St. Helena?"

"Well, sure, hell. We had a clear night then, and the news is still about nothing else."

"Of course. That ship follows this *Struggle* probe, Major. *And*, only four months before its departure we at High Columbia received a most unusual communique from the Soviet Bureau of Cosmonautical Affairs, the BCA, at Engels. My counterpart there claimed at first that we had interfered with their probe's functioning somewhere beyond the orbit of Uranus. The probe was apparently, as you might say, 'on the blink,' and he felt that we were attempting to sabotage its mission for research or propaganda purposes. The Soviets are historically a nation of professional paranoiacs. More to the point, though, not only did we *not* interfere, but the communique was brusquely interrupted and no further contact was made by any official at their end. And their initial claim took a most peculiar form."

"Sir?"

"Their communicant suggested that the probe was being followed by a *trasgo* far out there in the dark, a 'bogey' you might call it—another machine. Hence, naturally, their suspicion that it was one of ours."

"And it wasn't."

"Of course not. Would that we had the money for such foolishness!" Ulibarri emitted another noxious nebula, shrugged hispanically. "With regard to its own self-examination loops, we were told, that probe was functioning entirely within expected parameters. It 'awoke' prematurely from a preset period of inactivity to report across its tightbeam a nearby mass— which is, after all, precisely the sort of thing for which it was designed to search. Then it apparently relayed a brief span of information to the BCA receivers, describing the mass as metallic, and impossibly dense." Ulibarri generated another poisonous cloud of blue smoke, tapped a great ash into the mud. "After our denial, as I said, communication with us from Engels was abruptly broken. One suspects that more was said than intended by the enlightened masters of that place. Heads will no doubt have rolled noisily about." The colonel held his cigar away from himself and inspected it fondly—and then suddenly pointed its glowing business end at Pike.

"And then, Major, they retrofitted this great ship of theirs, equipping it with what we call a modified Taylor or Orion drive, the prohibited successive-bomb drive. Considering the expense and risk and sheer haste involved in this immense project, and the interesting pursuit-trajectory of the illegal ship itself, what would a clever officer like yourself infer from these incidents?"

Pike's eyes widened, and he stared; at Ulibarri's dangerous cigar, and then into the colonel's eyes. And broke into a grin like the Cheshire Cat's. "Well, *hell*, sir, I'd say you guys—or the Sovs, at least—are beginning to think you're onto a, well, hell again, sir,

a goddamn First Contact! Whoa! Damn!" Pike slapped
his forehead with his hand, shook his head, chuckled.

Ulibarri's small black eyes widened a bit in turn,
and then the ghost of a smile played about his blue-
whiskered jowls. "A predictable response, Major, in
view of some of the information I found in the dossier
that commended you so highly to me. You are said to
be not only a 'hacker' of distinction but also an aficio-
nado of this, ah, how do you say, 'technological
romance'—"

"Science fiction," corrected the grinning Pike.

" 'Science fiction', yes," said Ulibarri. "And you
possess an extensive collection of books and taped
cinemas of that genre of fiction, I believe. A collection that will no doubt stimulate and broaden your
appreciation of your new assignment."

Pike gulped, coughed and spluttered. "Yessir. The
assignment, sir?"

"Well, Major Muir, if this *trasgo* reported by
Struggle is indeed an artifact of a, ah, Third Party,
you can imagine the possible consequences for all
people of the Sovs' reaching it before we do. Therefore, of course, we hope to reach it first."

"Jesus K. Reist." Pike shook his head slowly. "And
where do I fit in?"

"Ah, Major Muir, you're a very lucky man. You'll
be among the first men to sail out beyond the asteroids. We want you to take a closer look at that probe
with its bubble brain. We want you to get there with
a MIDAS system and your magic parasite and commandeer *Struggle* as you've just done with the walking gatling. We believe that you could attach just
such a little monitor as we saw in action in the field,
to the probe's neurocircuitry—well in advance of the
PDR's arrival there—at which point, of course, the
probe will work for us as well as for the *Communistas*."

Pike frowned. "But sir, they have three months on us—and that foul drive. How'll we do it?"

Ulibarri smiled, his pencil moustache bending upward. "We at Cislunar Intelligence think well ahead, Major. We envision your travelling outward on a very much lighter ship than theirs, one perhaps uncomfortably hastily constructed—it is ready, in fact. Your drive will be the same proton-positron annihilation system that impelled the old Mars missions, greatly improved, swift and sure. You'll spend eight months in SIT—'State of Induced Torpor'—to spare you the stresses of acceleration produced by the drive."

"And if there *is* a bogey out there, and they catch it while we're hanging around two thousand klicks away?"

"Ah, Major, Major. Then your commander will know what to do; this is, in the end, a military mission."

"Oh, God. We're meeting it with force?"

"We go with force wherever the Soviets are involved. It is a necessity of life. And the, ah, suspected companion to the probe—we would not wish to meet it unarmed either. Remember the Caribs, Major Muir."

"Sir?"

"The Caribs. The first Americans found by Cristoforo Colombo, the first to see his ships. They greeted him on sunlit beaches, with gifts of gold and women."

"Sir?" Pike's mind reeled idiotically with unrestrained speculation.

"The Caribs, Major Muir, are extinct. Please remember that, out there in the dark, and take great care." Ulibarri smiled strangely, and extinguished his cigar in the mud.

*   *   *

So, but a week later and many tens of thousands of kilometers from home, Major Pike Muir found himself staring curiously at the flatboard console of Interfacility Transit Capsule Seven. The screen suddenly sprang into life with a tiny graphic of High Columbia's city cylinder, two kilometers in diameter, a blinking red tangential trajectory creeping outward toward the lollipop form of Pursuitship *Expediter* hanging in space some hundred kilometers distant. His head lurched with the capsule's drop into freefall, a lurch amplified by the corrective adjustments of attitudinal jets. Then there was silence for a moment; he was on his way to embarkation, drifting in swift automatically-computed freefall through the eternal night of space.

"That's some bad piece of equipment," growled the tech specialist riding with him, gesturing toward the distant ship.

"Bad indeed," laughed Pike.

Bad indeed. *Expediter* sported perhaps the most powerful single assemblage of weaponry ever put together by human beings. Surrounding the spherical bow was a ring of Tornado kinetic energy projectors, the mighty railguns launching at a hundred or so klicks a second the ship's complement of motile sensory probes—or releasing either independently maneuverable mass-seeking fragmentation charges or canister pulses of half-centimeter balls of lead, a thousand at a pulse.

Studding the bow were the HEL projectors. It was a good acronym, HEL, for the high-energy lasers designed for but never yet used in close high-velocity space-based battle. These were backed up by *Expediter*'s ultimate weapons: the three NEPs, nuclear-explosive-pumped beam systems, detachable and independently maneuvered, of course, because if used they would explode with "cute" nukes propelling x-ray lasers in predetermined directions.

All of this astonishing firepower was integrated by a specialized MIDAS, the broad-spectrum American military computing intelligence or *Multivariate Inference/Deduction Analysis System*, with which Pike had so often worked. *Expediter's* MIDAS-7 system maintained a tightbeam link through Cislunar Intelligence to just about every library and communications system in the Free World . . . a mind of its own, awaiting only orders to perform.

Virtually by itself, MIDAS-7 had instructed the young officer during his week in space. It had portrayed for him all that was known of the malfunctioning Sov Oort probe and its general plane-of-ecliptic course with gravity assists at Jupiter and Uranus for a long silent drift until hoped-for contact with the postulated Oort cloud, ETA (if such a cloud existed) in 2039-45.

MIDAS had also overseen his introduction to various project personnel, including the renowned Chester Walsky, Weapons System Integration—a fellow traveller on the junket, short, thick-set, blond, face reddened by sunlamps in a City tanning-room. To him, Pike had explained with MIDAS's aid his assignment as specialist in analyses of Sov computer technique, and his two remotely functioning tap monitors capable of linking themselves to any brain of the sort carried by the Soviet Oort probe.

The remote motiles—one a backup in case of trouble—would extend to *Expediter* the awareness and, if necessary, control of the probe itself; shortly before the crew's reactivation, the motiles would leave *Expediter's* railguns at maximum velocity to receive an initial boost in surmounting *Dienbienphu's* head start to the probe. Theoretically, this would enable

Expediter to remain far from the action but essentially in realtime contact, permitting the American mission to figure out what was going on without actually engaging *Dienbienphu*; hence *Expediter* might even get to do a turnabout with some return boost head start rather than having to complete the entire journey home from *Struggle*'s last known position. Otherwise the ship would have to fall back after the mission. There was enough room for fuel outward, after all, but not enough for subsequent power Sunward at the same sort of accelerations.

Later, in private session with Colonel Jaime Ulibarri and MIDAS, Pike had met his new commanding officer, the man whose energy and influence had almost singlehandedly made the mission possible.

He'd heard a bit about Colonel Jimbob Corson, even back on Earth. Corson was a new breed, a sort of modified Air Force officer with extensive family political connections in the Christian Federalist Party. More than that, he was said to be a brilliant tactician, the father of SB-WAT—"Space-based Weapons-and-Tactics"—in their present form. Now Pike knew him better. Corson was a short blond man, usually smiling, black coveralls creaking with starch, silver eagles glinting in the fluorescent light. His burred hair framed a square-jawed face, small blue eyes glinting hard as sapphires . . . the quintessential soldier.

"Shake," Corson had said on meeting Pike, who took the proffered hand, strong and short-fingered.

The little finger was missing.

"Oh, that?" Corson was used to this sort of hesitation, and pleased. "Lost it in Gibraltar when I was a PFC. I got my field commission there. Kept me in a career I wasn't really certain about at first."

He spoke with a cheerful drawl, one of those officers who could affect a good-ole-boy camaraderie while breaking bones—his own or others'—to get things done. From the first, he'd made it plain that in his mind's eye *Expediter* and all aboard her would together be but a machine, a device to prevent the "Rooshians" from acquiring anything that might threaten the future of the Columbian Alliance. "And hell, nothing at all might happen. Then somebody's just up the creek for money. But in taking this risk, you understand, we're simply making certain. We have to be certain. *Expediter*'s a tight ship. I intend to run her as a tight ship. Any further questions?"

Implying, of course, that none were necessary. Now Pike felt the sudden deceleration as the trannycap approached its destination. Outside, the whirling dumbbell of a centrifugal-mass docking facility rotated in the starry ocean, dwarfed by the immense ship to which it was locked. More than a kilometer long, *Expediter* hung seemingly still against the stars, bristling with piping and girders, surrounded by a herd of remote-communications dishes, glittering silver and white. The idiot brain of Transit Capsule Seven locked onto laser-designated linkrings; clicking and bumping resumed, and with a hiss the docking station's air joined the trannycap's.

The hatch snicked aside to reveal the long metal corridor of the docking facility's center of mass. Clambering along the corridor's handholds past occasional bright orange numerals and initials, P7, P8, DAMAGE CNTRL 3A, etc., Pike embraced the ladder rails and slid smoothly downtunnel. At the tube's end, a circular bulkhead slid silently aside, revealing the pale green of *Expediter*'s living quarters.

The week in space had been full, and tiring. Along with Corson and Walsky, he'd pondered many things—most notably, the possibility of a Third Party's awaiting them beyond Uranus. Pike himself hoped there was one; Corson seemed to feel, since all the old twentieth-century searches had come up empty, that no such thing existed . . . and that he didn't all that much want to meet one if it did.

Nor did he much care about any Third Party; he was primarily interested in testing his SB-WAT systems against those of *Dienbienphu*.

For Corson, anything else was gravy.

Part II

23 AU and a Year from Earth

CHAPTER 3

Dienbienphu

Sleeping, Jennifer Dawson was carried by her dreams through strange darkling seas where undulating segmented beings pursued mercurial ovoid droplets in an endless slow dance of particles against the eternal backdrop of the silent stars. The faint booms and creakings of the ship's fabric found their way to her, the ship's spindly five-kilometer form swimming in her sleeping mind's eye like a great animal in the vacuum.

"YAAAP!"

A vertebrate, perhaps the ship was, or at least a centipede, an organism in which segmentation provided strength and structural flexibility. Evolution re-invents the spine in space . . . count segments of *Dienbienphu* jumping over a fence. Over a side-looking radar scan. Over a battlement . . .

"YAAAP! Alert! Citizen Doctor Dawson, you are required on the bridge!"

The second alarm jerked her fully awake. She looked wildly around her tiny cubicle, rolled out of her bed and to her feet in a single movement. She'd fallen

43

asleep in coveralls—no time to change. By the time the alarm yapped a third time, she was out of the cubicle, pounding her way along the rim of Living Systems Unit toward the freefall axial corridor leading to the bridge. Emerging through the armored bulkhead into the bridge hemisphere, she caught her freefall slippers in the floor matting, saluted halfheartedly, and made her way to an empty acceleration couch. Half a dozen junior officers glanced toward her, their faces weirdly illuminated by screen readouts.

Her week since the artificial Long Sleep had been an unending round of post-awakening physicals for *Dienbienphu*'s crew of fifty, interspersed with periods of therapeutic exercise, hastily-grabbed meals and, when she could find time, sleep. The Long Sleep—that, at least, was a success. What now?

"Ah, Citizen Doctor. An emergency." Commander First Grade Oruna Benai sighed, turned away from the console through which he had been speaking to the shipbrain. His broad shoulders slumped. "Forgive me for awakening you from a no doubt well-deserved rest, but I believe you'll understand. You may soon have some real work to do." He smiled wearily. "You're ready for some real work?"

"Always, Commander." Jennifer watched him cautiously. The fatigue was plain on his face, the strain audible in his voice.

"Excellent. A bit of background. You're aware that since its launching nine months ago, the American pursuit ship *Expediter* has itself been pursued by a Soviet robot observation remote?"

"Yes—it's been maintaining itself against their cross-section of the Sun to avoid detection."

"Precisely. Twelve hours ago this remote informed us that the Americans had launched a motile, small and fast, that appeared to be overtaking us swiftly on

its own trajectory toward the missing Oort probe.
Since then their ship has been decelerating at one
gravity, suggesting that their crew is by now awake.
I, ah, consulted with our *zampolit* and with Engels,
and was given orders to interdict that motile, which
I've done. Shipbrain's notice that the interdiction was
successful prompted me to alert you; that confirmation arrived eight minutes ago. The Americans are
only about three and a half minutes' lightlag behind
us, now; they'll know in seconds, if not already, that
they're short a probe. I await, most unhappily, their
response."

Benai closed his eyes, pressed them with his fists
and contemplated the patterns of color he seemed to
see within. He looked at Jennifer again. "They force
me. They force me. Devils in the bush! The lightlag
drives me mad!"

Jennifer waited warily, scanning the lines of fatigue
on Benai's face. The bridge rumbled with the ship's
life, a low-frequency reverberation comprised of all
the movement of all aboard, the minute whinings of
servos, the hiss of ventilation ducts and flowing water
and, lower and more pervasive than all else, the
rolling of the great bearings separating the revolving
living quarters from the ship's stationary spine. Even
with the thundering concussions of her drive dormant, *Dienbienphu* was a vast resonance chamber, an
amplifier of the voice of the sum of her parts; there
was no escape from that all-embracing rumbling, no
escape except, when it could be taken, sleep.

Ah, Jennifer knew the signs well. After only a
week of consciousness the entire ship's complement,
she included, was in the grip of a grim bout with
Social Constraint Syndrome, the malignant rancor
that so often overtook small communities isolated in
space. Not always, but often—especially when such

small communities were further divided by lines of rank and nationality.

As military commander, Benai felt the syndrome most acutely. He'd been sitting before his console now for more than twelve hours, conversing with the shipbrain and in batches of preplanned conversation with Engels across the more than three infuriating, intervening hours of lightlag. He stretched, yawned, shook his head slowly, looked piercingly at his chief medical officer.

"Where is our *zampolit*? That alarm was given almost twelve minutes ago! He'll have orders sealed from launch, I suppose, magic *zampolit* orders from Moscow, governing interaction with the Americans. Yah! *Expediter*! So fast, so *fast*!" He gave up again, his tired mind clamping down, struggling with fatigue as Jennifer watched. Since awakening from the Long Sleep she'd learned a good deal about the mind of Oruna Benai.

He was a military man, pure and simple; at least, so he saw himself. All of his considerable training and insight had been channelled into the work of his choosing. Born on the same African veldts as his chief medical officer, he'd undergone the same great Disturbance, the same massacres and burnings . . . from the other side, of course. Like hers, his was a world of open space, great blue skies, distant horizons; like she, he felt as if his sojourn aboard *Dienbienphu* was so much time spent in a coffee can.

And to top it off, the insolent slowness of the *zampolit* and his staff! These, enjoying a privileged Russian-language privacy link to shipbrain and hence to Engels, had tied up main tightbeam transmissions for hours. Now they ignored Benai's alarm—and there was nothing the military commander could do about it.

The Sov political detachment were very definitely

overseers of the mission. These particular Sovs, faintly contemptuous gentlemen whose object was to provide "courtesies" should there indeed happen to be a Third Party waiting at the silent Oort probe ahead, made no bones about their position onboard. Their own quarters, own food. For Benai, the original thoughts of glory for the people of Africa and for himself had been eroded to a point of near-nonexistence, to be gradually replaced by the old childhood sense of exploitation. Pale-skinned polar Sovs. Like all whites, they kept to themselves, reserved the best for themselves, treated the African commander like— well, like a kaffir. Nigger, in fact. *When* we see them, these authors of the Principles of Structured Enlightenment.

Which is precious rarely.

Thinking of which . . .

There was a hiss as a sliding port retracted. Onto the freefall bridge bounced Aleksandr I. Iamskoy, until last year First Deputy of the Commissariat of Education at the People's Cosmograd of Engels, now *zampolit* or political officer, cultural liaison on the First Trans-Uranian Mission.

Iamskoy was a short man, his stiff bristle of black hair brushed straight back from a broad pale Slav face in which small slanted Tartar eyes rested like raisins in a pudding. The *zampolit* was also ill trained in free-fall locomotion; as he emerged from the rotating living quarters to the stationary bridge, he swung clumsily sideways, the grips on his freefall slippers missing the bristles of the deck matting. Tight-lipped, dignified as befitted a First Deputy of anything, he waved his arms about, unaware of bodily center of mass, releasing into the air a sheaf of hardcopy. The stuff unfolded gracefully, and the cellulose tapeworm of close-printed information slowly stretched two meters across the room by virtue of the residual elasticity in its folds.

Iamskoy's left leg swept across the surface of Benai's console, sweeping magnetically-stabilized pens, flatboard, screen-control board, two bulbs of coffee and a tube of soy paste into the air as the cultural liaison finally gripped a seat. The same left leg barely missed Benai's chin in its rapid arc, and the commander rubbed the lower part of his dark face thoughtfully as Iamskoy attached himself at last to the medical officer's acceleration couch—Jennifer busying herself chasing the errant flatboard to the far side of the bridge. She had little use for the mission *zampolit*; he'd spent much of their little time together making clumsy sexual advances.

"Good afternoon, Commander." Iamskoy breathed hard, his coverall heaving a bit as he caught his breath. "I, ah, have a bit of information for you here . . . one moment . . ." He carefully reeled in his hardcopy, a Slavic Laocoon struggling with a paper serpent. Jennifer smirked. Benai glowered at her. Benai was military commander, but Iamskoy was, if anything, the real principal of the passage until and unless military action were required.

"Yes," said the *zampolit*, his English perfect if slightly accented, "we have here a fresh set of directives from Moscow by way of Engels, directives covering the hypothetical but momentous event of hostile contact with our pursuers. I *do* understand correctly, of course, that you've destroyed their motile?"

"Indeed, Cultural Liaison." Benai watched the little man with ill-concealed distaste, glanced at his readout. "Interdict confirmed, ah, seventeen minutes ago."

"Good. Within the Principles of Structured Enlightenment, your action was correct. Would you not

agree, Citizen Doctor?" He smiled ingratiatingly at
Jennifer, noticing her for the first time.

Benai felt a smile playing about the corners of his
mouth. Reading the *zampolit's* eyes, he knew the
man's thoughts about the chief medical officer. Let
him take on, then, the icy doctor; she'll treat him as
he treats us.

Jennifer prudently said nothing; Iamskoy pressed.
"You seem less than sociable, Citizen Doctor. Somehow I begin to fear that you're not feeling yourself to
be part of this great endeavor. Why would this be?
Are you perhaps—lonely?" He glanced about the
bridge in what he hoped was a conspiratorial fashion.

"Oh, dear no, Citizen!" Jennifer's blue eyes took
on a look of girlish innocence. *The little bugger's
persistent, I'll grant him that* . . . she smiled, the
corners of her mouth turning down humorously.
"Lonely! How could one feel lonely, sharing *Dienbienphu* with fifty people?"

"Yes, yes . . . we all feel the strain, Citizen."
Iamskoy watched her for a moment, then spoke to
Communications Officer Mboko: "Lieutenant, we'll
need coffee. The galley, please, and have it sent up
with Captain Tomashev. It'll, ah, 'perk up' our doctor, and we have decisions to make." He glanced
about the bridge again as Mboko toggled the intercom. His steadiness under the current pressures might
change that doctor's mind about him . . . perhaps
smooth his way toward a more intimate communion
with her. "It's such a rare pleasure to see your smile,
Citizen Doctor. Why not call me Aleksandr—or Alex—
just this once? If I may call you Jennifer? We know
one another well . . ."

"Oh, but I *do* so like that 'citizen' in conversation,"
smiled Jennifer. "It makes everything seem so, so

right. Why, Citizen, I'd surely bugger everything up if I dropped the 'citizen.' I wouldn't *think* of it!"

" 'Bugger everything up,' Doctor? Oh, come, now, such a handsome woman as yourself could never bugger anything up, I'm certain." Iamskoy offered Jennifer a wink.

The humor left Jennifer's face as if switched off electrically. "Citizen Iamskoy, I could bugger up a great deal if I had to. I rather feel the entire spirit of this race to be a little war, a silly little war, between you and some Americans over an entity that we're not certain even exists. Diverting resources from the cosmograd and the Orbital Medical Facilities in order to pull a propaganda coup. Furthermore, Citizen, I generally choose to remain in solitude in order not to bugger anything up. I listen to my music. I do my writing. I come out to attend to my duties, but I eat alone, think alone and—much to your distress, I gather—I sleep alone also."

Silence on the bridge, junior officers staring with concentrated stillness into their screens. Oruna Benai froze; he'd felt ill since interdicting the American probe, but the fierce surgeon suddenly leavened his nausea. Almost smiling, he looked expectantly about the bridge. Well said, Doctor. What can they make of that?

The *zampolit*'s State Security aide, Captain Jaro Tomashev, chose that moment to emerge into the bridge freefall followed by an enlisted man with a set of coffee bulbs. He spluttered, his face reddening. Jennifer hid her mouth with her hand, the corners of her eyes crinkling. Iamskoy sat back, placing his hardcopy carefully on the console, and made a cautious deprecating motion with his hand toward the security agent. Tomashev passed coffee bulbs around, seated himself in another couch.

"Later, Citizen Doctor, later." Eyes glittering with rage, Iamskoy took his bulb, sucked up a long pull of coffee. "Now to business. Shipbrain, Engels is alerted?"

"Engels is alerted, Citizen Iamskoy, with lightlag doubleway of seven hours, thirty-six minutes to this point."

"Mmm. We have a bit of time for some personal initiative. Allow me, then, to share with you these directives." The bridge quieted, all eyes on the *zampolit*. Iamskoy, aplomb recovered, preened a bit. He liked an audience, elegant propagandist [he'd been told] that he was. He sat back in the acceleration couch, stabilized himself while Benai looked severely about the room at Jennifer and his "young gentlemen," and held the sheaf of hardcopy at arm's length.

"The Principles of Structured Enlightenment would perhaps have confirmed these orders even had we not received them; they're a sensible, simple set of dictates, gentlemen, Doctor, and they offer a simple code of conduct.

" 'One. The Deep Space Vessel *Dienbienphu*, representing the United Socialist Peoples of Earth, only rightful polity of this solar system, hopes to contact a hypothetical Third Party; any contact of the Third Party by any other polity is a stratagem of a brigand state; therefore,

" 'Two. Under no circumstance will *Dienbienphu* permit any communication between any Third Party and the American pursuit ship *Expediter*, its remotes or any other vessels unauthorized by BCA Engels, and

" 'Three. Subject to conditions above, *Dienbienphu* is to be considered expendable."

Iamskoy peeled back the top sheet of hardcopy. "You understand, Citizens, what these last two directives imply? I'm certain you do. There's more, however—"

"Citizen *Zampolit*," snapped Jennifer Dawson, "you're telling us that we're coming to blows with this *Expediter* out here, now, and we're *not going back*. Those Americans will catch us like a tossed ball out here—they're good at what they do. Principles be damned. The, the situation at home, they're waiting for something like this." She gave up, glanced at Benai, who lowered his eyes. Benai knew, too.

The shipbrain bleeped alarm. "Citizen Iamskoy, Commander Benai, we have a communications pulse, tightbeam, standard microwave nonmilitary transit initiation, ICOMCOMSAT information interchange programming preapplied at 275,000 MHz, from pursuit ship *Expediter*, with lightlag of three minutes, forty-one seconds intervening. Requests direct channel to 'Commander, *Dienbierphu.*' "

"Oho, we've induced them to speak!" Iamskoy rubbed his hands gleefully together.

An iron hand tightened around Benai's gut. "Open, shipbrain?"

"Open, Commander Benai."

"Vocal and hard."

Iamskoy leaned forward, jaw set. "Commander Benai, I remind you that no communication is to be made with pursuit ship *Expediter* without prior clearance from BCA Engels."

"We're listening, not talking," murmured Benai.

"Our pulse, Citizen, Commander." The shipbrain's monotone suddenly gave way to a new voice, a strongly accented male voice drawling eerily onto the bridge, an American accent, its vowels extended broadly. The message was plain, preplanned.

"Commanding Officer of *Dienbienphu*, this is Colonel J.L. Corson, Commanding Officer of USRS *Ex-*

pediter. We have reason to believe that you have destroyed a peacefully-launched American remote probe. We stand by to accept your assurance that you will not in any way interfere with any other such peaceful remote launched by *Expediter*. We have launched one identical remote. Another interdict will force us to engage *Dienbienphu* as a hostile party."

"Another remote, and a very persistent great fish in the Deep for the catching," said Iamskoy. "I know of this Corson. His first name is Jimbob, a common name in the American Texan nationality. A son of wealth, son of a Senator, in fact, who amassed his riches from oil pipelines. Corson is a fundamentalist Christian Federalist, intensely against the Socialist dream. A true man of his nation, and the chief architect of what the capitalists call their Space-based Weapons-and-Tactics program. One wonders, that they would send such a man on a mission so fraught with risk. Well. We will ignore him for the present. Our duty is—"

"Citizen," snapped Jennifer, "word from home all along has been that if *Expediter* were harmed the Americans would destroy a Soviet orbital weapons platform—"

"Indeed, Doctor, and the peaceloving peoples of the world would have to respond in kind, no? We're at a fulcrum of history. We must conduct ourselves accordingly—you, strictly in your medical capacity. I, on the other hand, must deal with this pirate Corson. Shipbrain, analyze scenarios of possible alternative responses in this situation."

"Citizen Iamskoy, extrapolation of current situation offers:

"One. Prompt interdict of second American motile, followed by potential direct engagement of *Ex-*

pediter, at present point three four seven nine AU from *Dienbienphu* and in deceleration configuration.

"Two. Noninterference with second motile, followed by overtake and passing of *Dienbienphu* by motile and, later, by *Expediter*, followed by *Expediter* first contact with postulated position of *Struggle*: *Dienbienphu* mission failure."

Iamskoy was pleased; to sit at this fulcrum of history was a great honor. He looked at Benai, who, lost in his own thoughts, frowned at his console. Well, the military African—he'd oversee the actual action. Could he handle it with the proper dedication? Iamskoy had never been overfond of the African race, feeling blacks to be too emotional for great moments like this. Ah, well, greater powers than he had decided on the military component of *Dienbienphu*; at times like these, a *zampolit* could only watch and record.

"Well, Commander? You know your duty; you will interdict that second motile."

Benai sighed, his great frame seeming to diminish in his acceleration couch. "Lieutenant Mboko."

"Sir!" Mboko snapped involuntarily to attention.

"You will order all personnel to stand to Preparedness Level One. You will initiate preparations for a quadruple-pulse ballstorm to be released from railgun three, projected intersect with enemy motile to be determined by shipbrain. If in shipbrain's assessment this ballstorm fails to make contact, you will prepare backup of four remotely-piloted fragmentation devices to be intercept-deployed for destruction of enemy at optimum point of overtake. Shipbrain Interface!"

"Sir!" The interface officer's jaw hung slack, a dribble of saliva beading at the corner of his mouth.

"Close your mouth, Lieutenant. You will oversee

transmission to Engels of the visuals and audio of these orders and all proceedings on this bridge in the last ten hours. You will also hard-duplicate these records for my personal dossier. The world may want to know . . ."

The young officers remained frozen in place. Benai looked about the bridge, suppressed an involuntary shudder, snapped, *"Now!"*

The shipbrain was ready: "Commander, four ball-storm units to be deployed at ten-second intervals, initial charge accumulating; first deployment in one minute, ten seconds."

As the shipbrain lapsed into silence, Jennifer and everyone else aboard *Dienbienphu* became aware of a rising whine somewhere in the ship's bowels. The fusion-powered generators were accelerating rotation, liquid sulphur coursing through boron-alloy turbine blades.

"Shipbrain, show us that railgun." Benai turned to the central screen, which flicked into life. A light, airy-looking avenue of silvery rings appeared; a kilometer long, the railgun was normally folded into five segments. Now, deployed for action, it pointed off into nothingness.

"First ball canister." The railgun was as much a part of shipbrain's awareness as is a soccer player's foot of his own: Benai saw nothing, the projectile having left its railgun at a hundred kilometers per second, soundless, mindless. . . .

"Second ball canister."

. . . riding a peristaltic field of magnetism outward . . .

"Third ball canister."

. . . leaden meteors a centimeter in diameter, a thousand to a canister . . .

"Fourth ball canister."

. . . to puncture the delicate fabric of human stability . . .

"Mmmm, very good, Commander," murmured Iamskoy. "In a very short time, the Americans will have learned the folly of their pursuit. And we— why, we'll go on, looking for our Third Party."

"You won't, you know," said Jennifer, her eyes unnaturally bright. "You're mad, Citizen *Zampolit*; you and, and everyone. This Corson out there, he's as mad as you—he'll be coming for us, I—"

"Citizen Doctor," said Iamskoy, "you do appear to be seeking greenstripes. Unfortunately, perhaps, I'm unaware of any privileges you might lose on this ship. Is it all this Remote Social Constraint Syndrome? For the sake of the mission, I shall believe it is, and change the subject." He smiled graciously, eyes narrowed. "Now, Citizens, about our Third Party. What would we say to it, should it really exist?"

"Citizen Academician," said Benai, "might I suggest that we greet it with our hands in the air, and empty?"

"Like a supplicant? Humble and unarmed? But Commander, wouldn't you think that we should treat it as an equal?"

"If it's our equal, Citizen, we'd best greet it rather respectfully!" Jennifer paled, leaning closer to Iamskoy. "We're armed to the teeth, and acting like savages!"

"Citizen Doctor, I tire of your insolence. You will retire to your surgery." He gestured toward the bulkhead port, through which Jennifer was already propelling herself, face white with anger.

"Now," said the *zampolit*, "we wait." He leaned to an intercom, thumbed the switch, ordered some boiled potatoes—his favorite food. They reminded him of his mother.

The wait wasn't long. Iamskoy gobbled his pota-

toes, occasionally interspersing his eating with pleasant remarks on the functioning of the ship, the capitalist
pursuit. The rest of the bridge remained quiet; a
zampolit is like a dangerous wild animal, and one must
watch one's words carefully.

At last the shipbrain interrupted with its alarm
beep. "Citizen Academician? Commander Benai?"

"Yes, shipbrain," said Iamskoy.

"I advise you that our quadruple ballstorm pulse
was due to intercept pursuit motile thirty-two seconds ago."

"And?"

"We have a momentary lightlag. Please stand by."

"Ah, Commander, now we see whether we have a
bird." Iamskoy's hand, shaking slightly, found its way
to his coffee bulb.

"Sensors indicate motile is travelling end-over-end;
trajectory altered fifteen degrees, twelve minutes away
from original. Interdict successful."

"Hah!" Jaro Tomashev clapped his meaty hands.
"Dead bird!"

"Excellent work, Commander," said Iamskoy. "The
Americans will know in seconds that we do not take
kindly to interference."

"Commander Benai," droned the shipbrain, "friendly
pursuit remote aft of *Expediter* reports that vessel to
be undergoing inversion maneuver, likely in preparation for re-acceleration. Probability that actual pursuit
of *Dienbienphu* intended."

Iamskoy's glittering little eyes met Benai's. "Commander. Our pursuit probe, I believe, can be called
under direct command of *Dienbienphu* across tightbeam?"

"Yes, Citizen Academician."

"And that pursuit remote is armed?"

"Yes, Citizen. One warhead, twenty-kiloton yield."

"And, Commander, as far as we know *Expediter* is as yet unaware of the existence of this pursuit probe?"

"That is correct."

"Commander Benai, you will instruct that pursuit remote to seek out and destroy *Expediter*." Iamskoy's grin was rigid, teeth clenched.

"So we're damned both ways," murmured Benai. Surely, he thought, there might have been a way in which humankind's two most distant outposts could have reached an accord? Fulcrum of history . . . perhaps not. So now to the business, perhaps, of beginning an end to all things. That little single snap that starts the avalanch. Someone once shot an archduke at Sarajevo. Oruna Benai had shot a pair of robot motiles. He licked his dry lips and swallowed, lapsing into the singsong voice of Orders. "Initiate interdiction preparation; sound General Quarters."

"YAAAAP!" The sirens shrieked through the ship, the drumming of feet swelling through the fabric of *Dienbienphu* like fantastic jungle drums. Sonorous groans and clangs of metal sang of the deployment of the entire railgun system, the vibrations of their mighty servos providing a multiple drone note to the symphony of war. Lights blinked over Benai's console as stations filed readiness status. First was the freefall surgery, he noted; the surgeon and her six aides were quick. As the readiness bank filled with light, Benai slumped in his command seat.

"Sir? All stations report General Quarters readiness."

"Siren off." Benai looked gloomily at the three screens framing the command seat. Each was three meters square, each offered a look outside. "Shipbrain, deploy mass-sensors AHC, prepare decoy systems. Activate screens, direction of target."

The stars winked into view. Save the ship's endless

rumble, all was silent. Benai held up a hand, palm outward. "For the record, I think we've made a mistake. I've shot the archduke. Please excuse me, but I must clear the bridge of civilian personnel." He made a delicate clearing-out motion with his forearms.

Iamskoy looked interestedly about the bridge, which he rarely visited, his eyes coming at last to rest on those of Oruna Benai. He sat thoughtfully still for a moment, staring at the huge African, this tame Negro, this brute insufficiently trained in the Principles of Structured Enlightenment. "Very well. An end to our inactivity, Citizens. Jaro?"

The State Security officer rose with his superior. The bridge filled with the rustling of inhaled breath and stiffening muscles under starched coveralls, the odor of fear and excitement familiar to warriors in all times and places. The cultural liaison noticed nothing, however; he'd said his piece and, filled with his own elation, made his way carefully through the bulkhead port, Tomashev close behind.

Benai watched them leave, looked at the other officers within his view, shook his head sadly. Then he reached into a sliding compartment on his console, withdrew and donned his black fur cap, adjusting it so that his scar remained in sight. He spoke into the console, the words amplified across the bridge and around the ship: "All personnel will don shielded EVA suiting and helmets. Prepare for re-acceleration."

Crossing the bridge to the suit locker, he glanced for a moment at the center screen. Somewhere out there in the black there would shortly appear a flash far brighter for an instant than the distant Sun and its myriad starry brethren. The Americans would never return home.

But then, Benai reflected, *he* might not, either. And perhaps best not.

In the corridor outside the bridge, Jaro Tomashev felt his way along the rails to full mass behind the cultural liaison. He shifted to their native Russian language. "What archduke? What's Benai talking about?" Eyebrows raised, he stared at the bulkhead port closing behind them.

Iamskoy looked at Tomashev. Tomashev looked at Iamskoy.

"They call it 'Remote Social Constraint Syndrome,' Citizen. I wonder whether it's simply a lack of discipline. Perhaps we should discuss a program of intensified socialist concourse within the context of this most important voyage. I believe that coffee is unsuitable for such a discussion." He winked at his friend, far more comfortable in the language of the Motherland. "In my quarters? Vodka, Jaro?"

CHAPTER 4

Expediter

Pike Muir was hot. The sweat beaded on his face, itching, sticky. The humidity . . . the pounding heat of an Albuquerque summer sun slamming onto the anvil of a broad asphalt pavement.

Semiconscious, he relived the mad dream of helplessness that marked the time of execution of the Emergency Powers Act. The One-Day War, the falling of the Damoclean sword of Emergency Fuel Measures: that hated scene that would follow him forever, the insane flurry of last-minute automobile-driving that had convulsed the entire United States of America. Thousands had died, then, including his parents in Boston—but not instantly. His sister had called him at Sandia and, like a fool, he'd jumped into his own car, roaring offbase in mindless rage at the grounding of all commercial flights—only to see, at the Interstate intersection, the immense snarl of paralyzed traffic marking the rise of Fuel Utilization Security Stations and the end of the Automotive Age.

FUSSes they were, springing like viruses instantly into being across the nation. Like millions of other

Americans that strange, hot day, Pike saw looming across a sea of sweltering, honking vehicles the dark shapes of four Bradley M3 IFVs, their 25mm rapidfire cannon aligned along the highway; military police paced along the shoulders checking IDs and ordering people out of their cars, followed by great camouflage-painted tanktrucks into which more soldiers pumped gasoline and diesel fuel from the trapped thousands of private vehicles that never again would stream along the nation's highways.

When they came to Pike, the white-helmeted soldiers were impassive; No, they couldn't let him pass. Did he think he was the only one with trouble? Don't matter yew Army too. Don't matter yew an officer. And finally, Look, muthafucka, if yew don't get your *ass* outa that vehicle *pronto*, yew *die*, boy. We ain't got *time* for every muthafucka whinin' an' groanin' like some pussy.

As immense camouflaged wreckers pulled vehicles over the shoulder's edge, as commandeered civilian buses lined up to take the sweating, milling, screaming citizens back to Albuquerque, Pike knew he'd blown it. No chance to get to Boston, no chance to say goodbye to his mother and father. In a single stroke of the executive sword, the American way of life shifted forever . . . and Pike Muir knelt down to the sticky pavement and wept in the torrid fumes of a million stolen gallons of fuel.

But that was years ago.

Squeezing the tears and sweat from his eyes, Pike opened them—on pitch blackness. Blind! No, not blind; a faint glimmer from some dim little light nearby was reflected from a buckled metallic surface against which his helmet faceplate rested.

Helmet faceplate? Where was he? A wash of panic overran him. He tried to move, and his head throbbed

with pain. Something seemed to have hit him on the
back of the neck . . . but his suit pressure was okay.
Suit pressure. Yeah, suit pressure. God! He was on
Expediter, and they'd been hit by a Sov pursuit remote!

Hot. Too hot. He moved again, every joint protest-
ing. No idea how long he'd been here. No idea
what's going on. Alone? Need water. Arm buttonboard.

He lifted his left arm painfully, rolled slightly,
found himself in near-freefall. The arm console still
glowed, and he punched for water while tonguing the
nipple in his helmet. Warm, tinny-tasting water. He
gulped, gasped, gulped again. Suit refrigeration registering functional, but hot, too hot. Right arm kinda
messed up. Elbow won't bend. Stuck in something.
Too dark. Too hot. Not quite freefall. Helmet light.
Arm console. Punch. The light winked on, reflections
flooding into Pike's dark-accustomed eyes, temporarily blinding him.

"Oh, Jesus Christ an' God almighty."

As he turned his head, the light flashed to the far
curving bulkhead, illuminating a meaningless junkyard
of twisted scrap and wreckage. Anything loose, it
seemed, was pressed loosely to the forward bulkhead—
that which had until the blast been a vertical wall to
anyone standing in the revolving-mass Quarters. Now,
some distance from the helplessly rotating *Expediter*'s center of gravity, it was more or less a floor, a
floor nearly impassably strewn with what was once
the environment of a tight but reasoned living area.

And he remembered. The remotes—both of them—
had somehow been spotted early and interdicted by
Dienbienphu, even though that mighty ship was a
good bit of an AU distant from *Expediter* when the
little moniters were launched. How had they known?

Of course! The pursuit missile: both sensor and—how late they'd learned!—nuke.

And before the thing'd caught up with them, Corson had deployed *Expediter*'s three nuclear-explosive-pumped lasers, all three NEPs locked onto *Dien-bienphu*; "just to make sure," he'd added, he'd ordered two railgunned mass-seekers armed and ready for instantaneous—"get that?"—instantaneous deployment on command post-detonation. Each mass-seeker was a light nuke of two kilotons' yield encased in an instrumented disk proportioned like a hockey-puck and capable of a bit of independent motion—both evasive, to elude defensive weapons, and offensive, permitting brief pursuit of any mass detected within a thousand kilometers (once well out of range of *Expediter* herself, of course).

Fear was an emotion Pike had never experienced in the raw. A trained cybernetics man, not combat-hardened in the least, he'd expected some glandular wash of fear to overwhelm him; but it didn't, not before.

Then God's fist struck *Expediter*, and everything came loose. Before Pike's synapses could register the event he was unconscious and uncouched, his crash-netting broken, his body tossed across Quarters Disk like a rag doll. Only now, awakening in the ruin of the ship, Pike felt the fear. It crushed him . . . yet he could think.

Arm buttonboard registers air pressure outside. Ninety-two percent normal, but much too hot. We're not holed. Not here, at least. Corson? Walsky?

He spoke, his voice croaking like a toad's. "Colonel Corson? Can anyone hear?"

No response. Arm buttonboard.

EXTERNAL TEMPERATURE: 87C. INTERNAL TEMPERATURE:

44C. OVERLOAD IN 2 HR 40 MIN. WATER RESERVE: 5 L.
61CC.

"MIDAS! MIDAS!" His throat hurt, his vocal cords
dry and flanneled with thirst.

The helmet radio rasped and clicked.

"I hear you, Major Muir."

"MIDAS! What's happened? Where is everyone?"

"Major Muir, much of my sensory apparatus is
damaged. The bridge seems to have lost air pressure.
In Living Quarters my infrared scanners are unable
to discern body images because of the heated air.
Bulkhead seals are locked at this time and I am
unable to control them. We are heavily irradiated,
with a—"

"MIDAS, how's the rest of the ship?" The slight
sense of mass was strange, especially in the dark;
Pike's fear mounted, bile in his throat, a twitching in
his aching legs.

"Major Muir, we are shorn of our propulsive spin-
dle and ablative shield and are looping roughly end
over end with a rotational frequency of approximately
five minutes, thirty-two seconds."

"What about *Dienbienphu*? And how long have I
been here?"

A pause. *Damn! Gotta call it by name!*

"MIDAS?"

"Major Muir, it is now seven hours, forty-one minutes since detonation of pursuit remote. Although we
rotate out of control, I was able to discern two detonations from the direction of *Dienbienphu* at the time
our projectiles were due to reach her. This would
indicate that we are at least partially successful in our
interdiction of that ship, although I am unable to
make further determinations at this time."

Damn, what's got me stuck here? Can hardly move.
Head hurts . . . water. Pike tongued the nipple again,

this time sparingly, washing the water lovingly around in his parched mouth. He felt as if he were on a spit in an oven. Radiation. He'd die out here.

He wriggled a bit, checking for broken bones and bleeding. Except for the trapped right arm and a general painful heated throbbing, he seemed intact. Damn this dark! He pushed with his left arm at the crumpled obstruction before him, heard its metallic *skreek* through his helmet faceplate, felt it give.

God! That right arm's broken, all right, forearm, both bones. Just below elbow. Free, though. Got to bind it to me. Find something to tie it off with.

He rummaged painfully about for some sort of sling for his right arm, found a bit of acceleration netting, tied it around his arm and chest clumsily, left-handed, grunting. This would at least keep the broken arm out of harm's way. Fatigue. He was breathing harder, now, and was hotter than ever. No use wasting suit power . . . he nestled himself between two torn lumps of bedding. An odd delirium took him when he stopped moving. His head hurt, and something seemed to press outward at his temples as if his brain were swelling. God, I need sleep. I need food, but I need sleep more. I . . .

Silence.

This is nothing but an expensive coffin.

This is a farce.

A sound in the dark. A grating, rumbling, fumbling. And a faint, scratchy voice in the helmet radio.

"Living Quarters! This is Corson! Muir, you read me in there?"

"Colonel Corson! You read me? This is Muir. Hurt—broken right arm. You read me?"

"I gotcha, boy! Walsky's dead, I'm suited up. You got air pressure?"

"Yeah, ninety-one percent and dropping. Over-heated."

"I don't. Bridge ruptured, everything gone out but me. Bad radiation. I gambled and I lost, Muir. I can at least apologize. Look, we're both suited and in good shape, and we'll try to figure something out. You just stand by. You suited up okay?"

"Yessir." Pike's ears were ringing with the strain of trying to hear the words through his helmet noise. Helmet radios were made for straightline communication, no obstructions, and it was lucky he could hear this well through the intervening bulkheads.

"Okay, now, I'm tryin' to make some sense out of this mess." The voice faded, a sandy rustling in the radio. "Got it."

Thumps.

"Hey, Muir, seems airtight. Manuals on the internal hatch look fine. Just a minute." More thumps, and a slow grating—and a FUMP! of air entering a small vacuum. Light played across the crazy junkyard of the Quarters Disk, and a suited figure emerged "upward" from a pile of scrap far along the curve of the ship.

"Jeeze, my suit's got some heat here." The voice was clear, now, strong again with command. "MIDAS! Any further report?"

"Colonel Corson, my central operations are undamaged but sensory peripherals are sharply curtailed. I have moderate coverage of Quarters, but no internal coverage of the rest of the ship. My external sensors are operative forward, where ship's shadow protected them from the blast, but I am in rotation and can only scan. All flotsam is long gone, and we are quite alone. We drift."

Corson's suited figure turned slowly, and Pike waved his good left arm from his bed in the wreckage. Awkwardly, the white apparition made its way toward him.

"That you, Muir?"

"Yessir."

"Good. We're going to—"

A wave of nausea overtook Pike, a *lurching* of his innards as if they'd tried to get away from him. Radiation sickness, already? He gagged, recovered.

"Sir, I might be burned worse than I thought. I—" But the approaching figure flailed its arms wildly, grasping for handholds.

"You feel that, Muir? A movement?"

"Whoof! Then it *wasn't* me! Yessir, I felt it—right in my stomach." Which organ began to pain Pike Muir with a vengeance.

"MIDAS?"

"Colonel Corson, I have experienced an unusual momentary disorientation. It may indicate that my central processing apparatus is more badly damaged than original assessment indicated. Conversely, the ship itself may further be breaking up."

"Whoah," came Corson's voice. "I don't *ever* want to feel anything like that again! Looks worse than we thought, huh, MIDAS?"

"Colonel Corson, my remaining forward sensors indicate a sudden large change in our location."

"MIDAS, waddya mean, change in location?"

"Colonel Corson, sensors offer data indicating a sudden displacement of this vessel four point six three Astronomical Units farther from the Sun—instantaneously. I must alert you to their apparent nonreliability henceforth."

"Oh, Lord Jesus, we are really breaking up."

"Colonel Corson." MIDAS again.

"Go, MIDAS."

"My remaining mass sensor indicates three considerable masses dead ahead in the direction of our drift. Because of our rotation and the unreliability of my remaining sensory apparatus, and because there were no such masses within detection range before attack detonation, I must conclude until the next rotation permits me to scan ahead that my sensory apparatus continues to deteriorate more swiftly than anticipated. I will attempt a visual in direction of drift in three minutes, fifty-eight seconds."

"Poor ol' MIDAS! Coming apart at the seams. Like the rest of us. And we gotta stop that slow leak. My buttonboard reads eighty-nine percent external pressure. Muir?"

"Mine too, sir."

"Okay. I—"

"Colonel Corson."

"Go, MIDAS."

"I have scanned forward. I receive a visual."

"MIDAS, well, *what* visual, dammit?"

"Colonel Corson, my scan is necessarily momentary, but it indicates that *Dienbienphu* lies dead ahead approximately twenty-two kilometers distant, heavily damaged, and that we approach her at approximately fifty-three point two one seven kilometers per hour. These data suggest that either we or *Dienbienphu* has been abruptly displaced by some AU, a situation my programming suggests to be extremely unlikely, if not impossible. In two minutes, thirty-one seconds I will initiate another scan, but it is unlikely to indicate any difference in these readings." As always, the voice was absolutely flat, emotionless.

Pike wanted it to scream.

And his inner ears went mad. The slight pull of rotation was changing, slowly, slowly—or he was losing his mind. Abruptly, Corson's suit light swung wildly about the room, its bearer straightening and sliding sideways. There was a rumbling as wreckage shifted slightly, some of it lifting from the bulkheads, eerily moving in the shifting light. The bile of terror choked Pike Muir, his mind shrieking a hundred denials.

The movement ceased. Absolute freefall.

"Colonel Corson."

"Lord Jesus, take us in Your hands. G-go, MIDAS."

"Colonel Corson," the voice droned, "my rotation has stopped, through no action of my own. My remaining sensors are centered on *Dienbienphu*, which we continue to approach. She is stationary in relation to our own motion, and is approximately two hundred forty meters from the second of the masses I detected; that mass precisely matches my data concerning the Soviet Oort probe, *Struggle*. The third of these masses lies directly on our path toward *Dienbienphu* and maintains a constant midpoint distance between us. My readings indicate it to be a highly reflective ovoid only point eight meter in major axis, point seven meter in minor axis, but massing forty-seven plus tons. Density implied by these readings closely matches my data concerning the entity reported to have disturbed the Soviet Oort probe, *Struggle*."

Pike found his teeth chattering, clenched them. "MIDAS—oh, trouble!" He felt like an infant abandoned in a supermarket; he wanted to cry.

"Major Muir, trouble is not a parameter for which I am analytically equipped."

And someone else spoke! Clear, free of the distortion of the radio sets, an old man's voice, strong with authority, touched with amusement, perhaps with a bit of regret, and both Corson and Pike heard it:

"How fierce you are! But you don't at all seem a

fearsome group right now. Fierce, but hardly fearsome."

A strange voice, speaking in perfect English, although accented in some indefinable way, not American, not British, not Australian. The voice seemed
that of a born English-speaker who came from "somewhere else"—just good native English.

"Who's there? Who's that? *Dienbienphu?* This is
Colonel J. L. Corson, USS *Expediter!*"

"Oh! Why, you little devil, you've quite mistaken
me!" The old man's voice was too clear, so plain that
in their minds' eyes all listening could almost see the
smile playing about the corners of his mouth. "I'm
not *Dienbienphu!* My sensor-effector lies directly between your two ships—and MIDAS's readings are all
correct. I'm a very heavy item, in all senses of that
word."

"Commander Corson."

"Go, MIDAS."

"Our mission appears a success in spite of our
problems. Shall I offer the Presidential greetings?"

"Belay that, MIDAS. Uh, ah, is this really, ah, the
Third Party? Is this—"

"Have no fear; I'm only a program, a machine, if
you will. A bit of a jabbernowl, perhaps, but not even
alive."

"Then who, what—?"

"You may call me Charon, Colonel Corson. A name
I lifted from Earthnoise. Greek. The Greeks would
have pronounced it with the back voiceless stop con-
sonant you call K; common English has altered it to a
'CH' sound." The voice paused as if thinking, then:
"Such a sorry little mess of humanity! We do have
some work to do. You've sorely damaged your conspecifics' vessel, *Dienbienphu*, as they've damaged
your own. There are survivors aboard that vessel. I

shall attempt to preserve their lives and yours by permitting you to share with them your remaining life-support systems. Are you ready?"

"What's going on? Who the hell are you? I'm not offering those bastards the least—"

The laughter in it barely concealed, Charon's voice interrupted. "No, Colonel Corson, you aren't. *I* am. Rest in place for a moment. You and your conspecifics are very much alone now; Earth presumes both your ships destroyed. You're in my—hands. Permit me a bit of modification, here."

Lights! Pike and Corson blinked, their pupils contracting against the unaccustomed brightness, which seemed to come not from the ship's light fixtures, but diffusely—from the bulkheads themselves? Pike's inner ears did another nauseating dance, then, and the dry voice calling itself Charon spoke again:

"See, little beasts, my skill: a thin bright line delineating a circle. Stand clear."

As the Charon-voice spoke, a point of white light glimmered aft, opposite the airlock through which Corson had forced his way into the Quarters Disk. The point moved swiftly, describing a glowing circle about eight meters in diameter . . . and, silently, all within that circle fell away like a great door, the starry velvet of space glimmering beyond—with no outrush of air! The twisted form of *Dienbienphu* appeared without, fantastically close, closer, closer a matching white circle now etched upon the vast curve of her hull, the metal outlined by that circle neatly and silently moving aside, changing, changing, flowing liquid into a ring of glowing metal that formed itself like a—like a docking ring! to which the strange airtight opening in *Expediter*'s hull aligned itself as neatly as any docking maneuver ever accomplished. And just for an instant, before the two ships mated in a perfect meld, the awed watchers caught sight of a silvery Egg suspended against the stars, an Egg that shimmered with faint shifting soap-bubble rainbows.

The Charon-voice spoke again, its suppressed laughter plain in their helmets: "I think that you can all see that I'm very good at what I do. Further hostilities between you and your conspecifics are therefore unneccessary. Indeed, as you can imagine, I shall cause you regret if you initiate them."

And although Pike could feel that implication of laughter, not once had the voice actually so much as chuckled.

Then a hollow booming, and *Expediter* and *Dienbienphu* were one, a unity alone in the trans-Uranian dark. Pike heard in his suit tranceiver the mumbled prayers of Corson, nothing more. In all his tapes and books of science fiction, nothing like this ever happened. He was not a religious man, but he figured all options had best be covered . . . a program in a machine!

"Our Father, Who art in Heaven, hallowed be Thy Name . . ."

The ancient words rolled thick and fast from his tongue as he stared into the tangled darkness that was *Dienbienphu*.

CHAPTER 5

Fusion

Jennifer Dawson shook her head, trying to free her eyelids of the blood crusted at their corners. God, if she could only get her hands inside her helmet, rub, she'd claw away the maddening itch around her eyes—and clear her nose, completely blocked by dried blood. The stuff suffocated, adding to her terror of marooning the more ancient fear of drowning.

Mind running on the physiological autopilot of shock and fear, she tried to reconstruct the last minutes before she'd lost consciousness. Failure. She'd failed . . . she'd suited up. And, as alarms shrieked of oncoming death from the Americans, she'd pulled EVA gloves over her lifesaving hands. When it had become apparent that the surgery was itself losing pressure, the wounded under treatment slowly died, their skin drying and freezing, their body fluids filling the remaining air with a thin pink mist of frozen protoplasm.

And their surgeon stood helplessly by . . . and thus remained alive, although she felt the spinning of the mind that meant concussion.

74

Also alive was Commander First Grade Oruna Benai, burned and partially blind, crouched in another tangle of wiring and struts. He'd been staring out a port when the Americans struck with their double-layered assault across that impossible distance, and he was lucky not to have joined his bridge crew and the shipbrain of *Dienbienphu* in oblivion. Only the reflexes of his communications officer, Jacob Mboko, had saved him; the young African had guided his commander to surgery before himself dying of blood loss.

Jennifer had no idea how long they'd drifted, inert, before she'd awakened to a wrenching twist of nausea—no doubt from an already-fatal radiation dose—just moments before. Now she crouched, pressed uncomfortably by the bulk of Mboko's corpse into a dark recess from which she stared in terror at a tiny moving point of light that slowly described a circle on the bulkhead opposite. Carefully, unsteadily, she lifted from her side a nine-millimeter automatic pistol she'd retrieved from Mboko's body . . . and saw Benai do likewise with his own.

Her mouth contorted, loosening bits of scab to fall to the helmet's neck ring. The glowing circle was complete, and the segment of hull it outlined slowly swung out into space—swung out, glowed, fused into a lump of itself like clay, extended, curved back upon itself like a snake, an Oroboros with its tail in its mouth, a circular opening through which she saw a blasted spherical hulk, a—it was the American ship, *Expediter*, or part of it, and in its own side there gaped a round port which approached, slowly, slowly.

The whole process took perhaps three minutes. An eternal three minutes; Jennifer's blink reflex seemed eliminated by fear, her eyeballs drying until she had to force the lids to close.

Her pistol hand shook. She lifted the weapon further, aimed it right at the center of that lighted hole in the enemy's hull. Some American trick, the melting of *Dienbienphu*'s shielded hull? Some fantastic American innovation in weaponry? No one, no one could do that. It was the concussion, then, the pain, and this was hallucination.

Or magic.

She wanted it to be hallucination. She did not believe in magic. She forced her mind to work, damping its crazy spinning in thought: Magic's just what you can't believe. Take an instantly-developing camera back to Tiberius Caesar. Photograph him. Hand him the image. It'd be magic to Caesar. But a trick, to me. The magic would be getting there. To Caesar. With the camera. This is a trick. Of the wound to my head. Which never worked too well anyway. This is—

There was movement inside the American vessel, movement of a figure—then two—and the lighted opening aligned itself with the new ring at *Dienbienphu*'s hull. More light gleamed along the ring's boundaries, and the ships were one—seemed one great system, joined by a short passageway of mirror-smooth metal. The figures in the lighted chamber beyond were clothed in American uniform, suited for EVA, apparently unarmed. Benai's arms tensed, both hands gripping his pistol, extending it toward the faceless foreign figures, which visibly stiffened, slowly raising their hands.

They could see, all right. Then why open their ship to *Dienbienphu*? And how had they found their way here across the millions of kilometers between them—or had she been totally unconscious for days?

A voice in her helmet: "Why, I do believe that some of you are preparing for hostilities! *Can* you little beasts not understand the logistics of your situation?" The voice betrayed irritation, a deepening edge to the tones grating in her ears. "I see two mutually stricken and immobile craft here; one bears a functioning shipbrain, useful air, and two wounded, the other no shipbrain, a perfectly useful surgeon and no air in which she may perform her art! How extraordinarily inertial, your little minds . . . allow me a jest!"

Both pistols discharged, soundless in vacuum, squirting the entire lethal contents of their twenty-round magazines and smashing their bearers back in freefall against the contorted surface behind them. The Americans flinched in anticipation of impact . . . but . . .

Neither aboard *Dienbienphu* had pulled a trigger.

Two globes of cooling molten lead alloy hung weightless a few meters before Jennifer's reddened eyes. As she watched, their surfaces dulled, wrinkled, and they drifted slowly to rest against the dry and contorted form of a dead nurse, momentary gouts of vapor marking the dissolution of her suit by their residual heat. Jennifer's pistol floated slowly away, forgotten.

Third Party. Not an American; someone—something—else. The thing that lay waiting in the dark, the thing that touched the Oort probe, the thing for which they'd all gone a-hunting, *Expediter* and *Dienbienphu*, only to wreck one another in the bottomless Deep in an inevitable fury of adolescent truculence . . .

"I advise you again that I cannot permit this hormonal bludgeonry of yours. You are in my care, and you are my guests. You will therefore try to display the manners appropriate to guests!" The voice changed, grew lower in tone, as if speaking to itself: "Dreadful little creatures—barely domesticated!" Then, louder again, plainly amused: "You, there, aboard *Dienbien-*

phu, you are offered breatheable air—courtesy of your enemies!"

Third Party. As it spoke, Jennifer felt her suit slacken with external air pressure. Some invisible barrier in the opening between the ships had disappeared, and the air whirled with loose debris stirred up by its passing. A dry corpse across the room stood luridly, then slammed against the bulkhead—noisily slammed, as the air brought sound with its pressure.

The air brought reality back. This old man's voice seemed to speak in the manner of a child toying with insects. They had done a rum show, and this—Third Party—seemed almost to enjoy it.

"I've checked that air, and cooled it and I believe all of you may remove those helmets and suit armor. You're safe. All of us speak the same language. Presumably, we may all become more amicable with one another shortly." The arid voice snicked off as if by a switch, and four conscious human beings stared statuelike at one another.

Still as stone they stared, through mirrored blast-helmets none had yet dared to remove. Jennifer was first, reaching slowly to her collar lock after a careful examination of the readout at her belt. All outside appeared to be normal, the standard spacecraft air pressure of half sea level restored. Involuntarily, she held her breath and twisted the helmet off, stupidly releasing it into the near-freefall. And breathed, a mixture of burnt insulation, blood and sweat. She broke her glove seals, discarding the armored gauntlets, rubbed the dry blood from her eyelashes with relief.

Across the passage that joined the ships, she could see the two Americans doing the same, slowly releasing their helmets into the air—like herself, and contrary to all the discipline of freefall training. Benai was last, most cautious, carefully holstering his spent pistol.

An American spread his hands wide, open-palmed, and spoke loudly in a familiar accent across the ten meters that separated them: "Colonel J.L. Corson, commanding USS *Expediter*. Uh, welcome aboard." The drawl—rank pronounced "Kunnel." He looked about warily, as if feeling the Third Party's watchful presence as he spoke.

"Commander First Grade Oruna Benai, ah, late commanding DSWP *Dienbienphu*. I greet you, Colonel, in the name of the United People's Democracies!" This American, at least, was something Benai could confront with some training.

The other American was a man in his thirties, tall, sandy-haired, right arm bound in some sort of webbing. "Uh, Major Charles Muir, Cybernetic Operations Detachment, uh . . ." he seemed to change a thought, then said, "Technical liaison."

"Yes," said Benai, "and I am pleased to introduce Citizen Doctor Jennifer Dawson, chief medical officer."

"Pleased, I'm sure, ma'am," said the American colonel. "Uh, we're both more or less wounded here, and radiation-sick. I guess you better come aboard. We're unarmed."

"That would seem to be immaterial, Colonel, considering the abilities of our, ah, host on this interesting mission." Benai, then, had also understood.

Jennifer, busily searching the wreckage for splints, bandages, and whatever instruments were salvageable, grunted, "Commander's burned, half-blind from whatever it was you hit us with. We're dying." Bitterness crept into her voice; tired, frightened, annoyed with the freefall, she flicked her hair away from her streaked face. It bounced back, causing her to blink back tears of irritation. "Have you any medical equipment?"

"Just the bare minimum, ma'am. We're kind of short on anything at all, y'know." The American smiled apologetically. "We're burned too—I don't know what we can do for him, okay?"

Benai straightened himself painfully, retrieved his pistol from the bent shelf behind him, carefully checked the remaining five magazines attached to his belt, and floated awkwardly toward the port. Jennifer overheard a muttered drawl, "Hey, this guy's black as the ace of spaces," as the Americans guided him slowly into *Expediter*'s lighted interior.

Jennifer in turn made her way toward the port, a pitiful bundle of surgical material wrapped in towels under her arm. She kicked off and away from the hated confines of *Dienbienphu* and into what was left of the enemy ship, leaving *Dienbienphu*'s surgery dark and empty of personnel save for the dried corpses of her fellow travellers.

In the strange diffuse lighting of *Expediter*, Pike Muir braced himself and slowed the approach of Oruna Benai with his good left hand. Well, his own old resting place, a comparatively bare spot amidst the wreckage, seemed as good a place as any to secure the newcomer's large and pain-stiffened person. Jennifer emerged into *Expediter* and steadied herself with her free hand while looking critically at Corson's foot, handed her sorry little bundle of equipment to Pike, snatched it back as she realized he was the one with the netted arm. "Major, what have you done with that arm?"

"Broken, just below the elbow." Pike slid slightly away, feeling sullen under the woman's unwinking gaze. He stared back, seeing a pale thin face streaked with dried blood and filth, bright blue eyes red-

rimmed with fatigue peering at him from beneath a
tangled and dirty mop of straight blonde hair, lips
pursed appraisingly beneath a narrow nose, a long
neck encased in a high-collared EVA suit that fitted a
tall and angular form, left foot anchored expertly for
freefall stability beneath a solid chunk of twisted metal.
The picture of medical efficiency.

"I'm sorry," said the surgeon. "We're all bastards,
and all dead, I'd guess. Stupid of us—but let me redo
that arm." She secured and unfolded her bundle,
then turned to Pike, who drew back a bit.

"It's okay for now, ma'am. I've got it pretty well
secured, and—"

"Nonsense. I'll have to cut away that sleeve and
have a look at it." She bent toward the webbing that
bound Pike's right arm, a scalpel in her hand. He
winced involuntarily and she smiled, glancing inquiringly at him from beneath her tangled bangs. A woman's smile is a disarming thing; almost unwillingly,
Pike felt a grin stir into life around the corners of his
mouth. He relaxed, and Jennifer deftly cut away the
coarse netting, slit his suit sleeve from shoulder to
pressure cuff, removed it with a single last touch of
the scalpel. Something about her brisk dishevelment
pleased him; she knew her stuff, and he felt better.

Jennifer bit her lower lip, studying Pike's forearm.
"Clean break, Major. What we call a parry fracture;
you must have extended the forearm crosswise to
protect yourself from an impact. You did fairly well in
straightening it, but I'll have to splint it. Thank God
there's not much hematoma, not too much grating of
bone ends. I'll have to find something that's good for
a splint." She rummaged about in the mess that filled
the angle of the room in which they sat, found a bent
forty-centimeter aluminum strut, twisted it straight
in strong, competent hands.

"Now, let's see that. Lift it out, here—you'd never be able to do that at Earth-normal, would you? There. Can you bend your fingers, ever so slightly? Yes, good. Your thumb? Good, good. Nerves fine. Now, hold this with your left hand, just so—there. Let me find a binding, here . . ." She pattered on comfortingly, doctor talk, distracting Pike from the brief twinges of pain he felt as she worked with the arm. "What do you suppose this, this thing is that's got us?" Trying to draw his attention away from the arm.

"Ma'am, you've got me there. It gave itself a name, though, 'Charon'-with-a-K, says it's our word, Greek. Calls itself a program, but it sounds human as all getout to me. Too human. Like someone's grandfather."

"Yes, it does, doesn't it? In a way, its choice of voice is calming. I'm sure it chose the voice, aren't you? And of course the name . . ." Tying the first of a series of bindings, for she had no tape. "Odder than I'd expected, in a way. No giant insects and all that rot."

A good way to look at things. Pike began to like this enemy, this messily efficient, self-possessed girl. It might be doctor talk, but it worked. "Yeah . . ." He began to relax.

Jennifer laughed, a short, low musical sound. "I wonder why it'd call itself 'Charon.' I know the name, remember it from Greek mythology—sort of a ferryman to Hades. Souls across the Styx, and all that." She rubbed her tired eyes. "The name means something like 'Fierce brightness.' "

"We saw the Egg," said Pike, "the thing that started all this . . . it was pretty bright, shiny, sort of oily-looking . . . hey, yeah, Charon ferried the souls of the dead across the River Styx to the Underworld, right?"

Jennifer smiled again. "That's it. Hades, Monarch of the Underworld. The Romans called him Pluto. The Greeks always buried their dead with a coin-offering, the *danake*, in their mouths. Charon, I'm afraid, was a bit of a miser; with the coin the soul paid Charon's *naulon*, his toll. Otherwise the old bastard'd carry no one across the misty and perilous Styx." She grinned broadly, now, vaguely embarrassed. "I never thought I'd remember all that silly lot out here . . ."

"Uh, hum." Pike grunted as the doctor tied the splint to his wrist, grinned ruefully in turn. "The Styx is the point that you pass only once, never to return . . . kind of has an ominous feel to it."

"More than that," said Corson, listening intently. "It's the moon of Pluto. And, Doctor, I have a broken foot—the right."

"Well deserved, too," said Jennifer, turning to him. "After Commander Benai; he's badly burnt."

"Sorry, ma'am." Corson wedged himself between two twisted metal plates, worked gingerly at his EVA boot. " 'Course, Pluto's halfway around the System anyway . . . hey, MIDAS."

"I hear you, Colonel Corson."

Jennifer startled. "Shipbrain," explained Pike.

"Rundown on Charon, moon of Pluto," said Corson, lifting the boot free from a swollen and discolored foot.

"CHA-ron, or KA-ron," intoned the machine. "Either pronunciation is suitable. The single moon of the planet Pluto. Discovered in 1978 by James W. Christy of the United States Naval Observatory, Charon is by far the solar system's largest moon in comparison with its mother planet; at approximately one thousand, four hundred kilometers in diameter, Charon is slightly less than half Pluto's approximately three thousand one hundred kilometer diameter."

As MIDAS droned on, Jennifer loosened Benai's EVA tunic, revealing reddened blotches splashed across his dark skin. Radiation burns—another dying man.

"The Pluto-Charon system may best be described as a binary planet with combined mass of approximately point zero zero two that of Earth," continued the shipbrain. "These bodies orbit around a common center of gravity in a period of approximately six point three eight seven Earth days, each maintaining the same face toward the other in a tide-locked rotational system. They are unusually close in relation to their size, remaining at ten Pluto radii, or approximately fifteen thousand, five hundred kilometers from one another; the bodies move about their common center of mass in concentric orbits that are extraordinarily close to perfect circles.

"The orbit of Charon and Pluto about one another is also unusual in that its plane is nearly perpendicular to the plane of the ecliptic; because Charon and Pluto orbit the Sun once each 248 years this circumstance has permitted but one period of observation of Charon's occultation of and by Pluto from Earth since its discovery. The observation period, lasting between 1985 and 1991, permitted moderately precise determinations of the gross characteristics of the binary; little further research into its properties has been conducted."

Shaking her head sadly, Jennifer zipped Benai's tunic again, turned to Corson. He detached his footring, gingerly removed his EVA boot and the two insulative wicking socks beneath. The foot was swollen—but, worse, his skin was already dotted with the petechiae of severe radiation burn.

MIDAS prattled on, unthinking, automatic. "Charon's surface, like that of Pluto, is high-albedo and likely composed of methane ices and water, with spectroscopic analyses indicating possible concentrations of argon and neon in an atmosphere whose surface pressure is less than zero point one six millibars at a temperature of approximately minus two twenty-eight degrees Centigrade.

"The binary's solar orbit is sharply oval, at 25% eccentricity to the rest of the solar system's more circular orbits. Furthermore, its orbital inclination, approximately seventeen degrees from the plane of the ecliptic, combines with orbital eccentricity to vary the binary's solar distance from less than thirty to more than fifty Astronomical Units from the Sun—"

"Done, MIDAS." Corson winced a bit as he shifted his newly-bandaged foot. "Fat lot of good that Pluto stuff does us . . ."

"We'll have to *escape*," said Benai suddenly. Drifting in and out of consciousness, he'd been silent for some time. Now, his mind addled, he began to give in to Earthly training. "I believe we're prisoners, now, of this Charon. I'd never intended to be taken prisoner; I—"

'*Hel*-lo!' The Charon-voice, jollier than ever, boomed into the room without any apparent radio source. The marooned bits of humanity froze, frightened, ready for assault despite their injuries.

"Stay still, now. As you are. I have to warn you about a momentary nausea—you've all felt it. It comes when I move you. Settle yourselves comfortably, and, all of you, try placing your heads between your knees and closing your eyes—so! Like the doctor, here, wise and adaptable being that she is. Now—"

The nearly familiar wave of nausea swept them again, their stomachs rebelling against a movement more implied than felt. And then it passed, as quickly as before, leaving only a slight ringing in their ears.

Other than the belly-wrenching sensation, nothing seemed to have happened. "Not much *to* that, was there?" Charon's evident attempt at light-heartedness failed miserably.

"Too human," muttered Benai, "too human." He looked suspiciously at Corson, his misgivings about the traditional enemy far from allayed.

"I hear you, my friend. I'm pleased with the illusion." The Charon-voice, disembodied yet close, had all the lilt of that of a congenial host. "Yes, I worked for some time on this 'humanity.' I needed a useful interface for working with you—talking with you. I produced a subset of humaniform vocal and emotional responses that I hoped would express my feelings well. I must emphasize, however, that I'm quite inhuman, or nonhuman, or unhuman; I believe that there are nuances of connotation in each of those words that would apply to me, wouldn't they?"

"You didn't try 'superhuman,'" said Jennifer, thinking of the terrible moments when the ships had been melded in space.

"No, Doctor, I didn't. Nor did I try 'subhuman,' although, regrettably, that would also apply. I suppose 'nonhuman' would be the most useful term for now." The voice was colored with a faint sadness, momentarily, as if Charon felt the implications of "subhuman" more strongly than it had wished. "You're now in a good position to see me—not my Eggs, oh no, but me."

Jennifer, still hooked into the debris next to Corson, glanced over his shoulder. Her eyes widened in horror.

"Oh, God."

All followed her gaze, instinctively tensing for fight or flight.

A portion of the bulkhead bulged outward liquidly like a bubble, then burst silently into nothing. Outside, the stars glittered, moving slowly past the edges of a perfectly round and smooth-edged opening—through which no air escaped.

Pike was first to stir—Charon hadn't hurt anyone, yet. He pushed himself across the debris to the opening, then reached with his good hand to feel whatever might be holding the air in.

Nothing. It was as if he'd reached into space with an ungloved hand, and involuntarily he snatched it back, looked at it carefully, reached out again, this time pressing his body against the opening and waving his arm wildly about in what looked like outer space and felt like ship-normal air.

"Shit!" He drew in his arm, examined the palm of his hand while the others watched him.

"May I take it that you like this, Major Muir?" Charon's voice again, coming from nowhere.

"Uh, I'm not even sure I *believe* it," Pike growled, still looking at his hand. He backed away from the opening, tripped in the near-zero mass, settled himself among the others.

"An excellent sentiment for a human being. We'll get along famously! I have much to show you that you won't believe. Unbelief is salubrious to the human nervous system. Contrary reality often produces rapid growth and diversification of synapses in the brain and spinal column. You'll all be the better for it. Know also that I'll do you no harm, if you behave, and you can do me none. Who would be first to gaze upon my—ahem—lovely person?" Its humor seeming to overflow, Charon actually chuckled, most realistically. "You may see me through this little port as I stabilize your craft."

A groaning and creaking commenced, and the residual mass of ship's rotation dissipated. Dizzily, all four crouched, Jennifer automatically steadying the dying Benai in his nest among the ruins.

No one moved.

"Come, come, incurious little animals. Major Muir? You're an inquisitive man. Step back to the port, and tell your conspecifics of my loveliness!"

Slowly, Pike picked his way carefully through the dislodged innards of *Expediter* toward the strange round opening in the bulkhead. He leaned, peered outward.

"Jesus! *That's* the Charon! That's *got* to be the Charon!"

An old man with a boat? Ice broken, the rest crowded to the port, squirming shoulder to shoulder, Pike forgetting his injured forearm and bumping it painfully against Corson's broad chest.

Without, hanging lustrously motionless in the void, slept two silvery globes, barely differentially lighted by the distant and invisible Sun and by the carpet of stars beyond. Pearls in the Deep, they were featureless, uncratered, uncracked, showing none of the expansion/contraction stressmarks ordinarily associated with frozen methane bodies.

The observers seemed to have been placed near the midpoint between the objects; Charon was offering a Scenic Overlook. And while it was of course impossible for anyone to perceive the absolute size of these beautiful objects, it was evident that one was twice the diameter of the other. And yes, they seemed separated by about ten times the radius of the larger of the pair. . . .

"Lookit the middle! Look, over there . . . and there!" Pike, forgetting himself, pointed wildly left-handed into space from one to the other of the orbs.

It could not be. Not so huge. But it *was*, and Charon was right in denying itself any humanity.

The globes were not quite globes; they were more teardrop-shaped, ever so slightly, the apices of the teardrops pointing toward one another, tapering minutely, gradually into a fine, straight silvery line connecting these celestial bodies one to another across—if MIDAS's data were correct—some *fifteen thousand, five hundred kilometers of space.*

"I am Charon; that is me." The voice purred with satisfaction as the stupefied humans stared out of their ruined hulk of twinned shipjunk. "What you see is fat, more or less; my material reserves, collected most laboriously from your Oort Cloud. The actual 'I' lies at the centers of the two bodies, the smaller housing among other things that bit of my awareness that speaks to you—hence my choice of the name 'Charon.' Humans named it, after all; to me, one name's as good as another."

"You—you've been there for more than a century? Since we found you—found Pluto?" Jennifer's voice quavered; she wiped her eyes.

"Oh, a good deal longer than *that*. Funny. Your species is so curious, so dangerously inquisitive, yet since you first spotted Pluto in 1930 and determined my unusual pattern of movement, not a one of you has wondered overmuch why my solar orbit is at such variance with your system norm. And after you discovered the lesser of the pair and my binary perpendicularity, you still didn't wonder! Yet I set it all up specifically to attract attention; one would think that the astronomically extraordinary would stir that monkey curiosity of yours . . . a discrepancy I've long pondered." A pause, then: "It's as if a sailor saw an uncharted lighthouse, and felt no urge to investigate."

"You wanted us to find you!" Benai's voice, weak

as it was, filled with skeptical truculence. "Why didn't you come to us?"

Humor left the voice. "If *I* came to *you*, I would have irreparably altered your patterns of development before you found your own way into space. I wanted to see how you'd do it. Alas! Now I perceive your species' time to be running out. As your warlike impulses have grown, your astronomical curiosity seems to have decreased. Hence I interfered with your Oort probe, hoping to spark some of you with the necessary curiosity to come to me. I wanted to see the sort of effort you would make to do so, of course; an informal measure of your kind's intelligence. I wouldn't have wanted simply to kidnap a few of you; that wouldn't have been any fun." Charon's voice remained smooth, pleased-sounding. "Let me remind you now that you're all fatigued beyond any hope of reasoned behavior, and some of you are injured. I am going to, ah, take you aboard; but I'd rather have you rest through the process—a complex one, I assure you, which might otherwise fatally stress you."

"Surely you don't expect us to sleep after all this!" Jennifer was indignant, now. Inhuman, yes! The creature didn't understand human beings at all, if it thought—

Instantaneously flicking into existence, three identical shining Eggs appeared side by side about fifty meters outside the port. The human watchers involuntarily flinched, eyes wide, staring at the linked binary and its soap-bubble Eggs . . . things whose dimensions and mode of movement evolution had not constructed human senses to embrace.

"Dear little physician, I do indeed expect you to sleep—you're all dying of radiation burns! Do you notice a change in your environment?" The smiling voice paused, and Jennifer felt a prickling at the nape of her neck, a movement greater than mere expectation's tensing her skin.

"Nuts," murmured Corson. "I'm nuts, or—"

"No," said the Charon-voice, "you're not, no more than any other gland-ruled animal. *I* am, though. Quite mad, I think, quite mad. But rest now; rest, and be healed." The disembodied voice switched abruptly and eerily into silence. There came to them a smell. The ruined ships' air was changing, moving, a breeze was blowing, a breeze of springtime, blossoms, a warm Earthly morning. The odors of burnt plastic and overheated bodies dissipated; relaxation flew swiftly and silently to the tired knot of humanity, relaxation and a sound and too-sudden sleep.

Outside, the three Eggs moved swiftly closer to the sad twisted wreck at the Solar System's edge. A watcher might have marvelled at their total lack of jets or other apparent propulsion. But watchers there were none, except the vast and ancient mind that guided them; with them it flowed silently into the ruin and rolled gently along leagues upon leagues of tortured Earthly neurons, picking, choosing, recording, following the slumber-popping of random dendritic charges, wandering down the avenues of unsleeping life-support systems. It listened to the mitochondria in their cells as they unceasingly processed oxygen to fuel their animal fires; it felt its way along the contours of Earth-shaped bone and lifeworn arteries, wondering at the tales of threadbare skin and graying hair.

And deeper it went, down, down, to the tiny molecular tapes from which all this crystallized; sailing along those tapes, it noted the fine nucleic code, the ancestral messages, some still good, some deteriorating as these bodies devolved toward their inevitable appointment with death. How odd, to live with death within you. How odd, too, to know it, and yet to persist with such implacable fierce purpose to the end. How odd, how delicately lovely . . . how very whimsical!

Part III

CHAPTER 6

Awakenings in Eden

When Pike Muir was growing up, he lived with his family in a rambling brick house in the Brookline district of Boston. The house was duplexed long before the Muirs had bought their half, but its yard remained more or less green, the great maples still shadowing the grass each spring with fine dappling from infant yellow-green leaves. On holiday in spring, a small boy in Brookline had much to do. He must eat a gigantic breakfast—a ham omelet, perhaps, with cheese, maybe an English muffin too heavily buttered in the manner of small boys, a glass of apple juice, a glass of milk, a doughnut snatched powdery with confectioner's sugar from his mother's Forbidden box.

Then he must check with his older brother about the day's activities. If there be plenty of spending money, one might hit the train, rumble slowly into— well, into whatever deliciously unsupervised adventures should offer themselves. Or Dad might take them to Rockport and rent them a boat; they could go after blues, the sun warm on their tanned skins, the waves sparkling, the air salt and free. Or there might be a game, or someone might have gotten a load of bottle-rockets for a day of illegal streetstyle Cape Kennedying, or—almost anything. A spring holiday in Brookline was full of promise for a small boy; one such promise was to lie awake, eyes closed, and ramble through the potential of the day, listening to the birds and waiting, enjoying that moment of secret anticipation . . .

The birds.

Not Brookline birds, no way.

Pike sat up, opened his eyes. The glow of youth, the excitement, remained with him.

Brookline, however, was nowhere to be seen.

The sunlight was wrong, somehow, warm, bright, but too diffuse even for the mists obscurinq it. He seemed to be lying in the grass at the bottom of an immense valley, a riverless valley so broad that its curve was barely detectable until one's eyes traced the sides upward into the low cloud cover. A rolling grassland of green and gold, arcing upward, upward on either side into the white and misty sky. A valley of birds.

The birds were too many, and they were not at all Bostonian birds. They sang and chattered and whooped and cackled and fluttered among the wide-topped thorny trees above Pike's head. They were every color of the rainbow; some of them, to Pike, looked like mistakes; their beaks too large and yellow, or their wings too short.

Pike Muir was not on shipboard. Pike Muir's arm was no longer broken, nor in the least painful. Pike Muir was clean, exquisitely clean, and so were his coveralls and watch.

They were the same coveralls—just clean. And those were elephants!

The elephants, five of them, looked as mistaken as the birds. Their tusks curved downward and backward; with them, the improbable beasts ripped at the grassy turf, pulling back with their massive heads, then picking turves with their trunks and chewing the messes meditatively.

Pike stood shakily, his eyes wide. An elephant looked at him, snorted, raised its trunk and tested the air. The rest followed suit, five trunks waving snakelike against the morning sky. They whuffled and grunted and, satisfied perhaps that Pike meant them no harm, set again to their task of plowing up the grass, great animated back-hoes, their heaving slabby leathern sides flecked with peeling dried mud, their high backs dotted with little black-and-white birds that flitted to and fro, pecking delicately at their oblivious hosts.

"I don't believe this." Pike spoke aloud, to no one. He looked at his good right arm, turning it experimentally. Unbelief. Where had he heard that unbelief was salubrious to the human nervous system? *Something* sure was salubrious—he'd never felt better. The springtime expectation of boyhood seemed still with him, tinged now with a delightful soupçon of fear, and his very blood seemed charged with strength and anticipation. "I do not fucking believe any of this at *all*."

He looked wildly about him. He stood in waist-high golden grass that swayed in waves with the breeze, onward and outward across the stupendous valley, its floor a rolling plain dotted with odd flat-topped clusters of trees like those among which he stood. The morning mist was rising, too; far in the distance, vast herds of some sort of animals moved, their rich and earthy smells wafted faintly to him on the morning breeze. Here and there great piles of boulders seemed carelessly strewn, house-sized and bigger, the spaces among them thick with greener grass and contorted leafy brush.

At the base of the nearest of these rocky mounds, he saw movement—and recognized from his zoo days a *baboon*, for God's sake, and a very big baboon, too. The creature evidently spotted Pike at the same instant; it barked and hooted at him, and dropped something—one of *Expediter*'s portable videocameras, still good as new, part of a small pile of familiar and not-so-familiar equipment neatly arranged at the boulders' base. Mostly video and sound stuff, cartons of information dominoes and the like, some likely from *Dienbienphu*, all clean and in good condition—or would be until that baboon dismantled them.

But the baboon had lost interest. Several more like it, but smaller, joined it in a chorus of wild *yark*ing sounds, and the whole troop moved stiffly away, peering over their maned shoulders at Pike and hooting shrilly.

Well—if *those* are baboons, and if those over *there* are elephants, about which I do have some doubts— well, then, *this* is *Africa*, and *I* am *not* supposed to be *here* at *all*.

He heard a movement in the grass some distance away, jumped and turned. In Africa, the way he understood it, you never knew what damn thing might be waiting in the grass for you to make a mistake.

The movement was the surgeon from *Dienbienphu*, Jennifer Dawson, looking as fit and clean as Pike felt and, indeed, very pretty in her spare no-nonsense way. She sat up, rubbed her eyes, and her jaw dropped open like drawbridge. She saw the elephants first, then Pike.

"Major Muir! How've we—what've we—where?"

Well, if that surgeon's at a loss for words, I feel a

hell of a lot better. Look calm, now. Nonchalant. "Morning, ma'am. I believe we're in Africa. Are you feeling well?"

"Well? Why, yes! A bit terrified, but well, well indeed! And you certainly look better than when last we met, Major . . . that arm!" A wry note had entered her voice, and she smiled. "I presume this is the doing of our friend Charon, although I suppose it's a little tipsy, judging from the look of those elephants."

"Not at all, Doctor Jennifer Wellesley Dawson." The amused voice of Charon came from above; there, hanging motionless among the leaves of the thorny tree nearest Jennifer, was a shining Egg. "I understood you to be rather up on natural history—evolution. All those years of study can't go to waste! Look without prejudice on my, ah, elephants, and tell me what you see."

Jennifer looked and looked and wrinkled her brow, and broke into a grin, and frowned again, and then laughed aloud. "Charon, are you having one over on me? Are those Pleistocene back-tusked elephants— deinotheria?" She regarded the Egg for a moment, then looked eagerly about the vast grassy expanse in which she found herself.

"Right the first time! Hand that broad a Kewpie doll!" Charon's voice had inexplicably taken on a broad American twang, a carny's shout. Then, returning to its normal old-man tone, it queried: "Don't you *like* them, Doctor?"

Jennifer stood, grinning. "Like them? Of course I like them! But, but—they're extinct!"

"The tickbirds don't seem to think so." Charon's irony seemed thick as cream. "And if you were to ask them, I'm sure you'd find that the deinotheria didn't think so, either!"

"They're extinct—and none of Africa has looked

like this for—for years . . ." The smile left Jennifer's face. She looked at the vast distant valley walls, rising ever higher, near vertical where the dissipating mists exposed new heights. There was—could be—no such valley, anywhere . . . she looked straight up then, toward the source of the odd sunlight, and bit her lower lip. Pike, watching, looked up with her.

The clouds were thinning fast now, and the bluing sky revealed not a sun but a colossal spine or rod, miles above, shining a blinding sunny yellow, a spine whose distance was impossible for them to fathom, stretching from one end to the other of the world in which they found themselves.

A world it was, in size unguessable, but a world all the same. What had seemed a valley floor was the inside of a colossal cylinder, a plant-lined cylinder whose opposing side was invisible beyond the hazy intervening miles of air, the central spine's ubiqui-tous light.

The geometry was wrong, and Jennifer staggered, her eyes filled with tears. "Charon, where are we? What—*when* are we? What have you done with us?"

"Oh, dear, I thought you'd be pleased. You're with me, Doctor, in a place called the Seeker *Hwiliria!*"

A bird sound, that word, formed not by lips.

"It's about thirty of your hours since you, ah, went to sleep in your ruin of a conveyance. I brought you to this place, a ship, actually, that I thought might delight and enlighten you. And it doesn't?"

"It—it's lovely." The tears rolling down her cheeks, Jennifer spread her arms wide and smiled again, one-sided, a worried smile. "But how—"

"I'm very good at what I do."

"Then it's an illusion? A fake? Are we really plugged into some sort of—"

"No, no, Doctor, it's all quite real. You're really

here. Oh, it's all an artifact, actually—but isn't it lovely? Or is my Africa false?"

"No—no! And the wind, and the gravity, and, and everything is—"

"Were you going to say, 'perfect'?" Smugness crept into the voice of Charon.

"I expect I'd have to."

"Good. I've done my work well. I'm absolutely delighted. Your brethren on Earth envision the environs of Pluto to be rather cold and desolate."

"But why Africa? And why these—these deinotheria? They'd be from the Pleistocene somewhere . . ."

"Precisely. And you humans are Pleistocene animals. You evolved in a place and time that I have taken some pains to duplicate—for your own satisfaction. You're designed for this, after a fashion."

Pike tugged at a clump of grass; it came loose, soil clinging to its roots, just as one might have expected. "This—this is *your* ship?"

"Oh, no! This is a place for living beings, Major! I've told you: I'm not at all alive. No, this is a movable—dwelling—built long ago, by cultural toolmakers, animals. Spacefaring animals—extinct spacefaring animals from another place and time. 'Tis a noble object, this *Hwiliria*, no? Intended once to repopulate a world—a world its makers well-nigh sterilized!"

"But the plants, the animals—they're from Earth! You've just said so—" Jennifer swung her arms outward as if to embrace the place, staring at the Egg.

"Ah! Well, yes. In this end of *Hwiliria* I've made some modifications. She is, after all, only a memory of mine. In recalling her, I've permitted myself this small duplication of your hometime, to show you a bit of what an artificial ecosystem can be. And of course to cushion your awakening! But the rest—the *rest* of *Hwiliria* remains a facsimile of the world of her extinct makers, as is fitting. As you shall see my little guests, as you'll see very soon!"

Pike slapped his clump of grass against his knee, the soil breaking from the roots, scattering about his feet. He began to giggle, fear and awe and delight struggling for the mastery of him. "This is a *memory*, a—but it's *huge!*"

"By your standards, yes, *Hwiliria* is quite large. Her interior spans a length of almost four hundred kilometers. Surely my greatest effort to date. You stand within her forward end; see the rise, here, beyond those rocks. Aft—opposite direction—you note a high ridge?"

They turned. Perhaps two kilometers distant, a long grassy hill about a hundred meters high extended right and left, arching upward, ever upward in the distance to either side, fading in the heights beyond the spinal "sun," ringing this unbelievable cylindrical space. Beyond, high on the "valley" sides, the coloring of the world was—different. Darker, a blue-green . . . and other ridge-rings were dimly visible in the distance, the entire place segmented in belts of flatland and ridge spanning unguessably vast intervals.

"Beyond that ridge," said the Charon-voice, "I've left *Hwiliria* as her builders intended."

"What happened to them? Where'd they go?" But Pike's guts tried to answer that one for him; Charon had killed them, whoever they were; had killed them all, as it no doubt intended to do with . . .

"I'd guess," said the treed Egg, "that you creatures think I killed them. You're wrong; they were like you, in a way. They needed no assistance on that score. They killed themselves, quite unaided, long ago and far away." The voice altered, almost singing,

"Long ago and far away. I remember them, though. And I've ideas for those memories—and you. Bear with me, do; you've no choice. In a matter of days you'll be returning to your sickened busy little planet—in *Hwiliria*, with my assistance. Unless—" a fathomless chuckle—"my madness exceeds even my own guess!"

"It's as big as an asteroid, and we never even *saw* it—where *are* we?"

"In a rather complex stable figure-eight orbit, Doctor, around the bodies you call Pluto and Charon. As I say, though, offer me a bit of patience—I'm sending you all back. After, that is, after you learn what I've brought you here to learn. Don't worry, please; your conspecifics at Earth have determined to their satisfaction that you're dead, as indeed you would have been had I not collected you in time. Now, though, you'll eat. Partake of my hospitality! Join the others—"

Pike frowned. "Hey, where are the others? Corson and the blind guy? They okay?"

"Oh, yes, they're well. Quite well. I scattered you about a bit for sleep's sake, and they're awakening in their own fashions while I watch." The Egg moved slowly from its branches, leaves slapping and sliding along its sides.

"How does the damned thing *do* that?" Pike stared frankly as the Egg floated like a soap bubble into the sunlight.

"Oh, Major, if your masters on Earth ever discovered how I get around, there'd be no end of trouble. Come now, follow the Egg, and we'll find your friends. That equipment—I've salvaged it from your ships. Please collect it, use it. People won't believe you, you know, just as you don't believe right now. A bit of video speaks reams for the unbeliever. Come come—I've packs and all waiting. Pick the stuff up, we have places to go." The Egg moved off, hovering about ten meters above them; Pike looked about him suspiciously, picked up a videopack and slid his arms through the straps.

Everywhere, now, more life: distant herds of lowing—cattle? A crashing in some brush a hundred meters to his right brought him to a stop; Jennifer turned too, tightening a hipstrap on a *Dienbienphu* vidpack, to see a pair of rhinoceroses conducting a noisy courtship in the leaves, snorting, grunting, raising a cloud of reddish dust as they disported themselves in amorous play.

Too much, thought Pike. Just *too much*. Shoulder to shoulder with the surgeon, he panned the scene with his minicam.

The rocks seemed much bigger at close hand; rounded hundred-ton hunks of granite piled upon one another like oversized pebbles surrounded a "mother stone" reaching perhaps forty meters above the grassy plain. Little animals the size of woodchucks shrieked and dashed out of sight among the boulders. "Rock hyraxes," said Jennifer, pleased, brandishing her own minicam. "Charon sees to all the details."

"I must be classed among the great *artistes*, no?" The Egg swooped lower, hovering over their heads. "Around here, please, and eat."

Before them in the grass stood a vast oaken table, three meters at least in length. Covered with a damask cloth whose edges swayed softly in the breeze, the board sparkled with silver place-settings, crystal goblets, trays, bowls, plates; these contained cakes and croissants, pastries of every description. They were laden with tiny roasted birds glistening in mahogany sauces, great reeking hot slabs of thick-sliced bacon, sausages of different colors and shapes, lobsters, shrimp, a tuna of perhaps twenty kilograms'

mass, fruits of every description, a variety of pastas
and their sauces, antipasto, pesto in little gold-wrought
bowls, rices and spices and assorted vices, including
a wood-carved humidor whose glass top showed the
tips of a dozen dark, powerful-looking cigars . . . all
in the midst of the African wilderness, with no other
sign of artifice for seemingly endless kilometers of
tree-studded grassland.

Except that shining Egg above.

And, Pike noted, not a fly buzzed about the pre-
posterous picnic, not an ant climbed the table leg.
He seated himself at the nearest setting—not before
recording the scene—and the surgeon doffed her
pack and selected the empty chair beside him. Most
disturbingly carved, these chairs were, high-backed,
with animal forms intricately intertwined through
their massive wood frames . . . strange animals. . . .

"I don't suppose we'll be needing a surgeon's service while we're guests of Charon, will we? Major
Muir?" She smiled at him, then looked wonderingly
at her place setting. Like the chairs, the plates were
decorated with animals, birdlike or dragonlike animals resembling nothing Earthly. Gold-edged, trans-
lucent white at their centers, the plates were unbelievably thin and strong and, despite their disqui-
eting designs, lovely.

"We won't need a cook either, Doctor Dawson."

Jennifer looked about her at the improbable culi-
nary selection, then back at Pike: "Oh, I don't guess
I'll be doing that much doctoring for a while, judging
from the looks of the two of us. Do call me Jennifer,
please."

"Well, Jennifer, I'm kind of unemployed at the
moment myself. I'm Pike to you."

"It's a pleasant place, isn't it?" The Egg, above

them at table's center, voice brimming with self-satisfaction. "I am a good host, or try to be."

"Charon."

"Yes, Doctor?"

"May I touch you?"

"You may touch the Egg, certainly. Any of you. Feel free, any time. Me, however—why, Doctor, I'm a bit much for that!"

"The Egg, that's what I meant." Jennifer reached out tentatively toward the swirling soap-bubble surface. Pike, on the other side, did the same.

Their fingers slid as if slicked on a thin coat of oil—slicker yet. The surface was frictionless, as nearly as Jennifer could tell. She looked at her fingertips, almost expecting to find a thin coat of some liquid, then touched the Egg again. Air temperature, perhaps—if, indeed, she were actually touching it. But the soap-bubble swirls changed color slightly where her fingers had passed across them, and Charon spoke: "I feel your touch, little animals. It is pleasant to me. Push, perhaps, a bit harder. For learning's sake."

Both pushed. The Egg, hovering just above the tabletop, moved about as much as might one of the hundred-ton boulders of the nearby kopje had they leaned against it; it moved not at all, in fact. Its frictionless surface, curved and featureless, offered no point of grip; a hard push sent Pike sliding off the ovoid surface, sprawling across the tabletop beside the immovable Egg.

"I'm quite unlike you. But I know you, I think." The odd placeless voice snicked off in its disconcerting way; Pike and Jennifer stared at the glittering thing, and all three beings sat contemplatively still in the bright sunlight of near-noon, strange companions at an intricately carved oak table in the Pleistocene breeze of the immense cylindrical world called *Hwiliria.*

And again the voice, thoughtful, slow: "Doctor Dawson, Major Muir, in my own small, mad way I offer you Eden."

Someone's coming.

Colonel Jimbob Lamar Corson lay face down, halfway out of the grass at the edge of a meandering brook. His heart was slowing down at last, the pounding in his ears softening.

He'd never thought he could run like that, never had before—even in his earliest training. But then, he'd been ill prepared for the golden savannaland in which he'd found himself upon awakening, the cylindrical world it had become with the mist's rising. And a full complement of ten fingers, the suddenly healed foot—plain fear had been his goad. His body had taken over, and he'd run, run for his life—from nothing.

Well, I'm in damn good shape, anyway. Something to be said for old Charon? Am I still Jimbob? Oh, hey, Daddy, if you could see me now, lyin' here in the mud like this. I think this Charon might give you something to think about. Scared the shit outa me, waking up and seeing *lions*, for god's sake, and *zebras* and all that shit.

Someone's coming.

Soljers!

Doubletimin' goddamn soljers, a platoon, by the sound of it, with a corporal callin' cadence an' the men respondin!

Isn't anyone I know, either. Language all wrong.

Squashing himself flatter, Corson maneuvered swiftly backwards into the tall grass, frantically trying to stand up the stems he'd flattened as he moved.

Jesus, Lord, must be seven or eight of 'em, sound like a batch of gooks or something. Maybe, maybe this whole thing is some *Dienbienphu* trick after all. How they did it, I don't know. Maybe they caught us all and drugged us or something. Fat chance. This is real. The light, the grass, the water, the smell.

The sound. Closer. Someone doubletiming along, closer, closer, chanting the cadence in some language I never heard. Bad guys, I can tell.

He pushed himself farther back into the grass, peering out at the grass-topped ridge beyond the brook, bright in the noontime sun. He listened, his heart beginning to pound again. Damn! Letting myself get shook up like that, I'm about done in when I need everything I got!

The sound grew closer, musical like all cadence chants everywhere, but strange. No words to make out, but the singing clear, the caller, deep-voiced, shouting Heee*op*, the respondents, ooah, ooah, ooah, ooah.

Heee*op*, ooah, ooah, ooah, ooah; Heee*op*, ooah, ooah, ooah, ooah; Hee*op*, ooah, ooah, ooah, ooah, closer, closer, just beyond that ridge, the chant changing a bit, still doubletime, Ooo*reee*, yah! yah! yah! yah! Ooo*ree*, yah! yah! yah! yah!, back again, Heee*op*, ooah, ooah, ooah, ooah . . .

There they are, the little fuckers. Damn! Lookit 'em go!

Eight small men angled up along the ridge, doubletiming in single file, their modal singsong eerily lovely in the central spine's strange shadowless light. They trotted easily, in perfect step, chanting, chanting, the lead and biggest setting the deep-toned call, the rest responding in unison four times, then the leader again, then the rest, a tireless jogging, singing snake of tiny brown men perhaps a meter and a third or so in height.

They carried spears . . . sticks, rather, sharpened at one end, held in the middle, swung lightly balanced from their right hands, loosely oscillating fore and aft as the little fellows swiftly crossed the quarter-kilometer between ridge and stream . . . on the other side of which Corson lay shaking in the grass.

Something wrong with those guys. Something bad wrong. Chests huge, shoulders broad, arms long, well muscled, necks thick, heads small, furry . . . and the faces! God, the faces! They looked like monkeys! The heads were held up, alert, each little dude ceaselessly, sharply looking from side to side as he ran, dark eyes glittering deep in the shadows of heavy brows, paired nostril slots set above powerfully jutting jaws. Aliens?

A piglike animal with lumpy snout and wide curving yellow tusks jumped up right-flank of the approaching platoon, and a couple of brown and tan-striped piglets followed it squealing as it rapidly distanced itself from the weird troop. The chanting briefly altered, Skaaah! whuh! whuh! whuh! whuh! but the cadence remained unchanged and the tiny men continued trotting undeterred toward the stream, double-timing indefatigably toward he clear water—and Corson.

Well, fuck, those look like bad little bastards, and I got nothing to defend my ass with. That awful-looking sow had the right idea. I am going to take my posterior elsewhere.

Corson started a careful backward crab, thanking God all the way for the tall grass—which, however, whispered and swayed about him no matter how careful he was.

"Skaroch!" The big one in the lead seemed to

freeze in midstep and instantly the others deployed
themselves on either side of him in a broadening line
. . . and all froze as still as their leader, sticks held
rigidly at present-arms.

Corson froze too, watching what little he could see
of the miniature soldiers. All of them were stark
naked; all were males. And, to his horror, they seemed
to be swelling as he watched them; matted manes of
fur on their heads, shoulders, and the outsides of their
long arms were slowly bristling. Otherwise, except
for the glittering of eyes sweeping the tops of the
grasses around where Corson lay, the creatures remained perfectly still.

As did Jimbob Lamar Corson. Sure they could
hear the pounding of his heart like an air-hammer on
an Abilene summer pavement? But no; they stood
stock-still, making not a sound. A Mexican stand-off.
They can't see me; I couldn't fight them, I'm sure of
that. They look tough as nails, with all the sense of
humor of a cholla cactus. Boy, am I some dumb
sumbitch! I got to get control of my act.

The big leader made some low chittering noises,
and one of the flanking flunkies whirled and sprinted
alarmingly quickly back up the ridge over which they'd
first appeared. Silhoutted at its crest, he waved his
left arm in an unmistakable come—hither, still clutching the sharpened stick in his right.

Oh, God, reinforcements. I know I can't outrun
those little devils. I know those spears aren't walking
sticks, either, crummy as they look.

The fellow on the ridge sprinted back to his place
in the unmoving cordon across the stream from Corson,
all waiting in a perfect stillness. Them guys are *good*,
he thought. Disciplined. What next?

As if in answer, little brown heads began to appear
along the ridgetop, a scattering of more pygmy

monkeymen, this time of both sexes and all ages. Males running at the flanks, females carrying babies in the center, and middle-sized kiddies sticking with them, the rabble of about thirty creatures made its way warily closer, seven more spear-toting males running ahead to join the vanguard at stream's edge. Without a sound, they extended the cordon's ends, all watching the grass where Jimbob Corson lay.

The central male, cadence-caller, he of the biggest mane, looked left and right at his comrades, nodded. "Skuh!" He lifted his spear and stepped forward one step. "SKUH!" The rest responded with an identical shout, taking a step, the line moving toward Corson. "SKUH!" Step. "SKUH!" Step.

Closer, broadening into a crescent centered on Corson's hiding-place, the cordon moved awesomely in a slow encircling approach: "SKUH!" Step. "SKUH!" Step. The rhythmical shouting lockstep was more frightening to Corson than anything he'd ever heard in his life. And the worst was, somehow, somewhere, he knew contrary to all his life's living that *he had heard and seen all this before.*

Deep in the center of his brain, ancient mechanisms took over to prepare him for a last insane flight, shutting down what little reason was left him. Urine spread hot beneath him. His muscles tensed, fingers and shoe-tips locking themselves in the sod for a leap. He went onto biological autopilot, all physiologic systems screaming for the getaway. He—

"Halloooo! Anyone here?" The cry came from far behind him, faint, wavering. The creatures in front of him froze, silent, in mid-step.

Again the voice, closer, accented: "Doctor Dawson? Can anyone hear me?"

"Fatchoof!" The lead male gestured downward with

his left hand, stared off into the distance beyond Corson's refuge. Silence. Absolute stillness.

"Hallooo! Who's that?" Much closer this time. And then—thank God!—the unmistakable crack of a pistol!

As one, the little spearchuckers turned and ran up the ridge, gathering in and surrounding females and young as they did so. The males hung in the rear, howling, brandishing their sticks, until all females disappeared beyond the crest. One or two males remained there for a moment, waving their spears and hooting, then these followed the rest out of sight.

Corson stood, shakily. A hundred meters off, he saw the running figure of the African, Benai, waving, shouting. What a sight! What a fine sight, even that commie commander, even with that damn Egg hangin' up there, followin' behind him, and him fit as a fiddle, fit as me, unscarred, grinning!

Benai trotted to him, jabbering questions. "Hallo, sir! What *were* those creatures? What kind of a place is this? What've you been doing? They were unpleasant-looking bastards. Pygmies? What's going on out here?" The Egg hung silently above.

Corson looked his enemy in the eye, grinned faintly. "I. Sure. Am glad. To see you."

"Sir, you're all in, quite shaken. Please, sit down for a few—"

But Corson only heard a roaring in his ears now, rising like a Gulf hurricane, enveloping him. Never again would he see a human shape—or approximately human shape—silhouetted against a skyline ridge without . . .

The colonel's eyes rolled back in his head and he fell into Benai's restraining arms, awareness on vacation.

"I say!" Benai pointed, traces of an awed smile

playing about his lips. To no one, he murmured, "It seems my enemy has wet his pants!"

He holstered his pistol, stared in the direction of the little men's disappearance.

"Learning experience," said the wry voice of Charon from above. "I'll assist you in carrying him to your conspecifics; they're sitting down to a breakfast I've prepared for you. Never fear; Colonel Corson will be rather the better for his trouble here. Learning experience, as I said."

So speaking, the Egg rose higher; Corson's inert form lifted gently from the grass as Benai watched imperturbably, his capacity for awe already strained to the utmost. The Egg set off, the colonel's body and his rescuer following. As the odd procession wended its way toward a distant kopje, the Egg chattered happily; Charon was more than proud to share with this ignorant fellow its firsthand knowledge of the habits of *Australopithecus africanus*, the Southern Ape of Africa, forebear of Man.

* * *

As that Egg discoursed, the giant mind of Charon focussed part of its vast attention far away in *Hwiliria*, where another Egg whistled and hooted in swift modulated birdsong. It employed the deferential/patriarchial tense-once-removed, that modality appropriate in concourse between a stranger and a First in the Chase.

'This one greets thee with talons blunted, Halarridarmar Horizon-Leaper, and quails before thy waking. Are thy senses intact?"

The brilliant scarlet crest spread laterally, leveled just below the top of the flat skull; respectful greeting, Charon noted, to an unfamiliar subordinate assumed to be of the reproductive castes. "My senses are intact, little Egg, Regurgitator of Souls. How long is it that I've slept?"

"Long, First in the Chase, so long as to be meaningless now. 'Yesterday,' we will say. Dost thou recall thy situation then?"

The crest quills closed over one another, a single spear of scarlet lying flat along the neck: regret. "I recall yesterday, little Egg, and am reminded of the crying of my Overcreche, the breaking of eggs, the dying of the Patriarchate and Matriarchate and the neuters of Home. The end of my folk, and of my world. Although I'm well physically, a grief-sickness rides massive behind my eyes." The great hooded amber eyes locked onto the Egg, pupils dilating on fathomless darkness. Clear nictitating membranes flicked smoothly across the yellow orbs, once, twice, but the eyes remained unmoved, expressionless, fixed unwinking on the Egg even as the First in the Chase stood to his full height of more than two meters. Looking about him, he noticed changes: strangenesses in vegetation, especially forward along his Seeker's cylindrical girth. The ground there was covered with a golden vegetal fuzz, the trees alien in pattern.

"*Hwiliria*—is she changed?" His pupils dilated, contracted, dilated again as he scanned the land.

The Egg backed away, remaining close to the ground as it spoke: "Fear not, First in the Chase. There are but surface modifications, primarily toward the bow. All life of thy vessel remains intact in my memory; certain of thy creche will soon awaken to join thee. Now, with thy permission, this one would offer thee meat, and drink well-fermented."

"Meat I will take. I will not cloud my brain, though, with drink. Water is sufficient."

"It is as thou will. And when thy crop is full, this one would show thee and certain of thy conspecifics an animal, a very unusual animal, a dead animal suitable for eating; but this one would that thou didst not eat that dead animal until thy neuters have examined it carefully, and opened it, and listened to this one's unworthy tale concerning that dead animal, and shared the sight of that dead animal, and this one's unworthy tale, with thy fertile sibs and the rest of thy creche that this one will awaken. For this one would have thee learn of the Toolmaker Conundrum, and how, perhaps, thy people may help solve it."

"Toolmaker Conundrum? I puzzle poorly, Regurgitator of Souls. I'll listen from crop through gizzard, but I listen no longer. I'd rather share a Chase with my fertile sibs. You'll feed the neuters also, of course?" The First, like all fertiles, was a bit narrow-minded.

"This one will prepare a way for thy Chase, and feed the neuters also, with meat whose heart still beats, much game and swift, new game, most intriguing game, in open land bright-lit with *Hwiliria's* spinal light."

"Excellent, little Egg. I will eat." The vein-cutters on Halarridarmar's feet twitched involuntarily with his huge hunger, their black scythelike blades glinting in the sunlight. The red crest rose nearly vertical in anticipation, spreading in a dark-edged fan against the blue of Charon's sky.

"Thou shalt eat, First in the Chase. This one rejoices at thy rising."

The deferential/patriarchal tense-once-removed was an interesting modality, the only one from an absolute stranger to which the First in the Chase and the fertile males of his sib could respond. Once the First was fully awake and sated, once he'd better acquainted himself with his unfamiliar surroundings, Charon would as equal and more assume the pure patriarchal modality . . . but for now, best be prudent. Whileelin of the Patriarchate were fierce and proud, and always operated on their peculiar brand of mental autopilot—handle with care.

Translation with human beings would be entertaining. Even though a female accompanied the primates, English would be manifested to fertile whileelin as pure patriarchal. Otherwise, it'd be difficult to convince the First in the Chase and his creche that human beings were anything more than talking meat.

The other way around was simple; the spacefaring apes would hear syntax and idiom of the fertile whileelin castes as English. And the neuters? Their intercommunication being across the electromagnetic spectrum, Charon had been able to offer only one human—the female—a limited capacity to hear some of them.

Such strange beasts, these two toolmaking species, and both so very fierce! Delicacy was the prime necessity here: delicacy and, perhaps, a sense of humor about the whole thing. Humor is an animal thing, but one which Charon found useful and appealing. With delight, it set about arranging the crucial second stage of its experiment.

CHAPTER 7

Deus ex Machina

Corson recovered quickly; regaining his feet, he walked the last kilometer to Charon's great table, staying his Australopith horror by conversing with his Communist counterpart, Oruna Benai. Enemies they were supposed to be, but they shared the English language, and their world had shrunk to this awesomely alien cylindrical artifact; commonality now overshadowed difference. Both perceived an awesome threat from Charon; as commanders, both looked to escape as the only means by which they might warn their Earthly home of that threat. And as military men they were willing to fight for that escape.

But Charon's Egg chatted on, seemingly oblivious, explaining the nature of the little runners, the "apemen" it had "recalled" from an inalterable collapsed-matter memory. An experiment, it said, one of a series it was planning with them. Wait, it said, until you're all together at table, wait until you've eaten, for your bodies will need sustenance and plenty of it. Such marvelous beasts you are, to have undergone with such flexibility the stresses and frights of the past hours; let food complete your healing.

117

And that they had. By the time they'd finished eating, by the time their surprise at the good condition of the two other survivors was blunted, the two commanders knew a new bond—one of suspicion and fear, but a bond nonetheless. They'd become close, in their own way, and wary of their captivity; and in this they were not alone.

"I feel like a child," said Jennifer, speech working its way poorly around a large red cinnamon candy. "Everything—everything I've ever loved eating, and more. Hard to believe, all this. Perhaps I don't, can't, believe it. It isn't quite right . . ." She looked about the impossible feast's remains, picked up another cinnamon ball. Despite the spectacular food, she too felt a growing unease.

The Egg hung suspended above the table like a glittering centerpiece, observing, no doubt, and occasionally conversing. "Unbelief. You often express it, Doctor Dawson, and I must often make this reply: I'm very good at what I do. I made, grew, constructed, what have you, everything here, from memory. Being a good observer, I know what human beings like; being good at duplication, I produce it from the very ample raw materials available to me. And good food, the best, is necessary; there's walking to be done. You're not here to relax."

"Lobster's perfect," whuffled Pike, a line of melted butter sliding down his chin. "I haven't had lobster since I was about eight years old, and lookit this omelet! Ham . . . mushrooms . . ." He gathered in a series of tiny plates. "And English muffins, and . . . and . . ."

"And certain doughnuts covered with confectioner's sugar." The Egg, lowering gradually, now hung about two meters above the impossible meal.

"Yeah,' said Pike speculatively, "certain doughnuts

covered with confectioner's . . . Charon, sometimes it begins to look to me as if you *know* just a little too much." His face hardened. He put down his fork, staring at the colors whirling inscrutably across the Egg's surface.

Everyone froze. It was true. Each had found his favorite foods in this weird mishmash of breakfast, lunch and dinner; before Corson, the glassy humidor of dark cigars sat untouched.

"You play with us." Benai, too, stared at the Egg.

"You've been laughing at us since we found you." Corson's voice grated harshly, his own meal forgotten.

Since *I* found *you*, you ridiculous creatures." Charon's voice sounded suddenly hard and remote. "I do not play with you; I seek to know you. And, as you begin to comprehend in your dim ways, I already know you well. Look at one another's faces, tell me what you see. Look."

They looked, silent, wondering. And what they'd intuitively felt became apparent; each face was not only free of the petechiae of radiation burns, but bore fewer lines; the pores were smaller, the weight of years lessened. And since awakening, each had felt oddly stronger, exhilarated . . . not only were the injuries of battle healed, but—

"It's as if we'd each lost ten years," said Jennifer. "Your repair job's too complete."

"Repair? No, Doctor, you misunderstand me. 'Reconstitution' is a more appropriate word. I am an accomplished processor of information. When I gave you sleep, I, ah, looked you over rather carefully. You were dying, after all, filled with poison. I chose to correct that. So—I reconstituted you all, from better materials."

"Then—there's a cure for that degree of radiation

sickness? The surgeon's eyes rounded, the Egg reflected brightly in them.

"Not exactly," said the Charon-voice. "I didn't *cure* it; I simply neglected to incorporate your injuries during the reconstitution. Matter, energy, and space: all these are, shall we say, standardized phenomena. Interchangeable modular building blocks. Given suitable matter, energy, and space, enough time and the proper information, I can duplicate—or neglect to duplicate—anything. Anything."

"You mean we're just—just copies?" Corson, staring at his new tenth finger.

"'Just'? Not 'just,' not at all! You're *you*, no doubt about it, but newly assembled, and rather better. As I said, during the duplication process I noted certain malfunctions, imperfections, as it were, and, ah, forgot about them—by your leave. And I've added various, ah, gifts—capabilities—for which if I'm not mistaken you'll later be grateful."

Stillness—unbelief.

The Egg paused, rose a bit higher above the table—and hooted, whistled like a bird . . . and listening, all heard not only this avian sound but at the same time *understood*, somehow: "A physical organism—a human body, say—may be duplicated from information contained in its nucleic acids. The information is all that's required of the original; the duplicate can be grown from entirely fresh, ah, ingredients. And the growth process may be influenced to produce, say, strong and efficient musculature and skeletal support even when the new duplicate need never move until the information pattern that we call 'mind' is superimposed thereon. I saw no need to duplicate your damaged cell nuclei; I wanted you alive, and well. And I required of you a bit of novel linguistic ability, which I added."

"You're telling me that I'm not *me!*" Corson, eyes wide, looked at his right hand, moved it carefully, wiggled the little finger. "You're telling me that *I'm* somewhere else, and this 'me' here is just a copy! You're telling me that *I'm* dead, in some damn inhuman language that you've stuffed into . . ." His voice trailed off in a desperate sucking in of breath, and he turned, looked wildly at the rest of the people seated immobile at the table.

"No, not at all," said Charon, again in the whistling, clicking birdsong. "You are definitely you—note your use of the first personal pronoun, check your memories. You know it. But your awareness, like mine, is simply a pattern of information, energy flowing over a material matrix; at any given moment, such a pattern may precisely be reproduced and introduced into another suitable material matrix. It then continues its unfolding as if nothing had interrupted it. You are you—but freshened up a bit."

"This is impossible." Benai this time, his accent thickening as his mind began to rearrange itself around Charon's implication. With his fingers, he felt along his face where for years he'd sported his long trademark scar. Nothing: the skin was smooth, umblemished. "You have somehow stolen our bodies, and we hear and understand this new language . . ." He paused, stood slowly away from the magnificent potpourri of food before him.

His pistol was at his belt, and his hand fumbled its way slowly to its black plastic butt. "Charon, I think you are an evil thing. I, I . . . I fear for my soul." Saliva worked its way from the corner of his mouth. Suddenly, in a blurred movement of animal automation, he seized the pistol, gripped the butt with both hands and sprayed the Egg with a burst of automatic fire—and was lifted off his feet as if stricken by a giant's fist, to lie twisted, groaning, in the grass two meters from where he'd stood.

Frightened by the sound, thousands of multicolored birds whirled up from trees and grass, the air roaring with their passage. A small band of piglike things crashed off through the brush, and in the kopje the hyraxes shrieked and whistled.

The Egg remained motionless. The others, wary, waited.

"I have deluded myself in trying to know you." Charon's voice was barely audible, now. "I am indeed mad, in assuming that I might."

Jennifer, frozen in fear, whispered hoarsely: "If what you say is true, you know us all too well."

"I *knew* you—at a single point in time. I knew you as I . . . as I moved you. But your unfolding is too swift, too glandular, too much a welter of seemingly unconnected circumstances. Had I not told you of my meddling, you would never have known. You would have felt healthy and well, and perhaps thanked me for it. I felt I owed you a brief explanation. I had no idea your very molecules were so important to you. To me, one molecule is quite as good as another; it is the information that arranges them that is unique. I fear that I no longer have your trust."

"I can't say you really had it." Pike, this time, relaxing slowly in his seat.

"Oh, you were afraid of the unfamiliar. And I'm certainly that. But I am not evil. Please understand me. I'm not even *alive*. I am a dead, unchanging thing, a machine, if you will. A meddling, maddened machine, alone."

The voice seemed sad now, older than before. "I can duplicate you molecule for molecule, thought for thought—but only from an instant of stasis, the finest slice of time. Once your process continues—

even though precisely as before—you're beyond my reach, you elude me as do the other creatures that you see; there's a jeweled center to all life that's inaccessible to me. I took you all and duplicated you, surely and precisely, and even gave you what I thought were gifts! But once set free you are somehow as far from me as when I found you. And as fearful—as wild animals. I meddle—and each time, I fail. Madness."

The Egg floated silently over the person of Oruna Benai, now unconscious, his chest rising and falling evenly. He'll be well. I struck him because he might have killed one of you in his pain and rage. Knowing you only when you slept, I cannot save you as you now are should he spatter your brains with this thing."

Benai moaned, rolled over, sat up abruptly. As he searched about himself, his pistol rose slowly above him, then fell again a few meters away. Watching this, the African spread his hands in a broad shrug, stood and tentatively touched it, then, looking carefully at the Egg, holstered the weapon and walked back to the table. Shaking his head, he sat down like a chastened child, Jennifer automatically leaning toward him, checking for injury. "I'm well, Citizen;—a bit shaken, but well. This—this Charon is not a good thing." With his hands, he touched his temples delicately. No pain from the blow he'd received, just a moment's unconsciousness.

The Egg hung motionless above him for some seconds, shining in the light of late morning. "I've erred yet again. I erred in my very approach to your world. You never wondered at the great beacon I constructed, the strange orientation of the Pluto-Charon system. You came to me at last only because I interfered with your probe, and you came prepared to kill one another. I had to take active steps before you were lost to me. Lost like your culture, a fragile thing now

under great duress. So lovely, so ephemeral, so pitiful. Even as I pity you, though, for you are temporary as I am not, I envy you. I envy you all."

"Why're we here?" Corson watched Benai's face,
even as he spoke toward the Egg. "Is it envy, impris-
oning us against our will, while we're powerless?"

"Why did I save your lives? Why did I restore your
health? Why have I offered you some of the regained
youth that your kind has sought since its origin, and
taught you understanding of a language that you'd
never have learned on your own? Why even do I
feed you so well? Why? I might say that I wonder
myself, now, Colonel, though the answer should be
plain; of all the millions of species of animals of your
kindly world, you humans are the only cultural toolmakers." The Egg, settling now, came to rest a few
centimeters above the table. "Of all the thousands of
millions of your species, you four are the only ones to
have wandered into deep space and survived—with
the help of your doomed culture, of course, and with
more than a bit of luck. You four are surely unique
beasts."

"Cultural toolmakers? That's it? Animals that play
with tools?" Jennifer caught that sense of powerlessness that afflicted the commanders. Curiosity forgotten, she felt the rage that powerlessness brings.

"Cultural toolmakers indeed, Doctor. You're your
world's only Lamarckian creatures. You *do* know of
Jean-Baptiste Lamarck? His theory of evolution?"

"I'm sure you know that I do."

"Yes. The Chevalier de Lamarck believed that life
evolved by means of the inheritance of acquired characteristics. His model of evolution is often expressed
among you by means of the giraffe; straining to reach
the leaves of tall trees, the old knight might have
said, the ancestors of giraffes repeatedly stretched

their necks. Somehow, this stretching might be transmitted to their young, who were then born with yet
longer necks, and again through the generations until
there evolved that stately beast the giraffe, which so
sadly disappeared recently from Earth."

"Lamarck was wrong, though." Jennifer scratched
her head, stared at the Egg's swirling pastels.

"Indeed he was, for most life-forms. For them,
Darwin was correct; the offspring of giraffes, to sim-
plify matters very considerably, were born with necks
of differing lengths, and those with longer necks were
able to obtain more food, and hence to produce more
offspring which in turn inherited those longer necks,
etcetera. In but one case is Lamarck's model applicable to evolution, and that is the case of the cultural
toolmaker."

"No, we know something about our own evolution.
You keep saying it yourself. We're animals—we're
Darwinian. This Lamarck business—it's bumwad."
Jennifer felt a childish triumph; she had the thing
on this one, visited Olduvai and other museums, seen
the bones of her ancestors. "We're no more Lamarckian
than,—than giraffes."

"Mmmm?" The Egg rose a bit higher, colors swirling. "Consider. A human being, producing an invention, passes that invention on to the next generation
via the route of what we call culture. This I would
call the Lamarckian 'genetic apparatus.' As you can
plainly see from your own history, cultural—Lamarckian—evolution is far faster than Darwinian evolution;
physically and mentally you remain Pleistocene hunters, yet cultural evolution has permitted you to hunt
down all your old prey. Yet still, when stressed by
resource diminution, human beings go hunting large
mammals—as Darwinian evolution constructed them
to do. But they hunt with Lamarckian tools that grow

momentarily in efficiency. And the only large mammal left in any numbers is—?"

"People," said Benai sadly.

"Yes, my highly-trained hunter, people. The fiercest of prey. And the Lamarckian mode assures you that those people with the finest weapons spread the fastest at the expense of their less formidable fellows, until all available planetary resources are used up and everyone has these weapons. Then you die." If a disembodied voice could have shrugged, Charon's would have done so. "There're many among you who explain this very situation with more than adequate lucidity, broadly transmitted among your billions; I've listened to such opinions from your thinkers since you realized the danger. Yet the weapons continue to evolve faster than you're able to handle them. Quite soon *Homo sapiens* will become extinct—as surely as you have existed until now."

"Inexorably? How do you know? Are we bacteria in a Petri dish?" Jennifer's involuntary species-loyalty set an edge to her voice.

Smooth as silk, the Egg responded with its own question: "Does any of you understand the nature of a *koan*?"

Pike knew, drawing on a long-standing interest in certain things Japanese. "In Zen Buddhism? A koan's a little tale, or, riddle, a sort of a fable—usually with some internal inconsistency that stretches its meaning. Stretches the mind." He shrugged, staring at the Egg.

"Well said, Major Muir. Here, then, is the Toolmaker Koan, the puzzle that has tormented me since I first enjoyed awareness:

"On any planet where life evolves, given time, certain adaptable organisms acquire Lamarckian evolutionary systems—culture—to enhance their own survival. Once Lamarckian evolution is initiated, though, its consequent extinction is assured. Or, to put it another way, animals with culture can see farther into the future than any other animals; but for cultural animals the future is brief. Why? Why must cultural toolmakers, the most gifted of the universe's spontaneous expressions, so swiftly and inexorably beat themselves into extinction with their very giftedness? Ah, my dear humans, that's a conundrum at the very heart of my own existence. The Toolmaker Koan: you, like me, are mad."

The Egg paused, seemingly for effect, then: "Don't mistake me, my unruly little animals. I speak from long, long experience. Experience, mind you, with thousands of millions of different species—including a number of different cultural-toolmaker species. I collect cultures, you see, and the occasional individual, in my memory."

"Shit," growled Corson. "You're trying to tell us that there's all sorts of, uh, people, and you visit 'em and collect 'em like butterflies. What are you calling yourself, a god? And—"

"No god, Colonel, no god at all. I'm a program in a machine, as I believe I've said before. My abilities— *deus ex machina,* god in a machine? No, I'm in no way magical, supernatural, what have you. I'm simply, as I'm so fond of saying, very good at what I do; the best, in fact, of whom—or which—I'm aware."

Corson pressed home. "Well, then, whatever you call yourself, you're telling us that someone *made* you, right?"

"Indeed. Your word 'machine' derives from a Greek word meaning 'contrivance,' and I was indeed contrived. By animal cultural toolmakers, in fact, although certainly not in my present form. No indeed!" The voice paused for a moment, then: "I've a story to tell you as we walk—for walk we must, you at least, to see what I've to show you. Record my tale with your machines here. Look about you, film and savor. We've miles to go before you sleep."

No one had touched the wonderful meal for some time, and with a parenthetical apology the Egg lifted itself higher above the table. Plates, silverware, goblets began to disappear with soft whopping noises as air closed about their former spaces. Despite themselves, the human watchers grinned briefly at this expedient "magic"—and, inwardly, at the inexplicable fact that the Charon-voice whistled all the while like an otherworldly bird. They understood its every word. "You'll follow my Egg," it fluted, "on a bit of a journey. Again: record, film, what have you. Your conspecifics will want to know."

Pike and Jennifer gathered up their bundles of salvaged equipment. Inspection of the stuff had shown them plenty of spare batteries; Jennifer had a good set of her simpler surgical tools, to what end she couldn't figure, Charon being the consummate surgeon it apparently was. Benai checked his pistol, uninterrupted by the Egg, and Corson stood, suspiciously scanning the curving landscape for more australopiths. He was as yet unwilling to admit them to his family tree, but he felt danger in them nonetheless; better safe than sorry.

The Egg set off at a good walking pace toward the aft-end of the cylinder—hundreds of kilometers distant, it had said, where a mad geometry of the cylinderworld's fabric seemed to produce a mountain-on-its-side that tapered through the haze into the axial light-producing spine. And as the Egg moved off it spoke— "Talk with me, my lovelies"—and they kept up easily, listening, looking.

"I was fabricated as a monument. I was designed

by machines, themselves designed by machines designed by machines that were originally designed by
societies of a sort of animal that used culture and
made tools. I'm a bit removed, therefore, from my
animal originators, but I understand them. Indeed, I
miss them." The old-man voice became sadder, flat-
tening in tone.

"My fabricators were a religious sect, a very wealthy
one somewhat removed from the political turmoil
characterizing their times and the majority of their
kind. They inhabited an artificial—archipelago, you
might call it, of ecosystems in orbit about the home
planet. They were singleminded in their hope, their
vision. They called it the Meta-stasis."

"Me*tas*tasis!" Jennifer's eyes widened. She ceased
fiddling with her vidcam, grinned at the Egg. "That's
a medical term—spread of cancer. First I've heard
you pronounce anything incorrectly, too, Charon. Instead of accenting it on the first syllable, we emphasize the second: meTAstasis. Why, it's the worst that
can happen—a cancer cell's leaving the original tu-
mor to initiate a new cancer elsewhere in the body!
We haven't yet been able to deal with it—and it's a
horrible concept for a religion!"

"Hence my ah, 'mispronunciation,' dear lady. It's a
good translation of my fabricators' intent, and I shall
continue to use it, but I will 'mispronounce' it, Metastasis. By it they meant not cancer, but a rising of the
condition of the Universe. I 'mispronounce' the word
to make my point, you see."

Jennifer shrugged. "All right, I stand corrected."

"Yes. Well. The fabricators knew a good deal about
their immediate universe. They knew, as do you,
that most matter and space itself—is inanimate, lifeless, predictable and static. They also knew that their
kind, and life itself, was expansive, crystalline in

nature. Under suitable circumstances, a crystal nucleus will order a solution of its components into more crystals like itself until all solutes are consumed. Similarly, as an example, when living things emerge from their natal oceans, they invade a lifeless land— and instantly, as such things go, convert the substance of that land to a lively, singing place, an ecosystem. The difference, of course, lies in the fact that living systems are mutable crystals; each new structure is slightly different from that preceding it."

"Like the cancer cells," said Jennifer. "A cell mutates, and then converts body substance to new cancer."

"Yes, but you must see the difference, Doctor. Were you to 'terraform' the lifeless surface of Mars, would that be an *evil* thing? A cancerous thing? I think not. My fabricators saw the spread of life as an unmitigated good—if it could break the bounds of resource constraint. They saw a potential for the rise of innumerable colonies of life throughout the universe if only they could expand its reach. Extrapolating, they hoped that the universe itself could become alive, sloughing the stasis of elemental physics in favor of an evolving living megastructure, the Metastasis of which they dreamed for so long." Charon paused, considering its guests as they climbed a rise in the rolling "valley" floor of *Hwiliria's* immensity, perspiration beading on their foreheads and arms. The air was growing moister; the temperature seemed a bit too warm.

"But there was the problem of constraint," continued the alien fluting Charon-voice. "Their species was, as I've said, limited in scope to the environs of its own planet. Distances were too far, time too short for interstellar travel; after all, they thought, nothing can travel faster than light. So they used up their resources, never ceasing in their efforts to aggrandize, to accumulate resources after the manner of all living systems. And as the limit to their own expansion approached, the sect that fabricated me predicted an end to their kind . . . a kind that, for all its faults, they loved as much as you love humanity. Hence my own, ah, birth."

Jennifer's vidcam whirred as she spotted a striped catlike animal with extraordinarily long forelegs and short hindlegs. Even with all four feet on the ground, the creature seemed almost as erect as a human being. Cubs moved near it—her; the beast watched Jennifer back through the lens, and she could see canine teeth protruding slightly from beneath its whiskered chops. A Pleistocene cat, she recalled, *Homotherium*, extinct on Earth since . . .

The Egg went on. "They ordained my creation as a labor of love, a testament to their own greatness and futility—a greatness and futility that I perceive in your own kind, my friends. They had, ah, a longer time to work with machines than you have had, and they were rather better at it; as I said, their machines designed machines which designed machines which designed me. But it was the animals' needs that I met, not machine needs. I'm a religious artifact, you see, hence my own problem; I am a machine, but one impelled by the glandular desire of my makers."

"You're a sort of cathedral, then," said Pike. "A work of art."

"Yes. No less than the Cathedral at Lourdes. When confronted by the mystery and horror of death, the people of medieval times built cathedrals; when confronted by the mystery and horror of inevitable species extinction, my makers built me. Like medieval men, they built forever: for immortality, in a sense. They saw extinction overtaking them, and they wished a message of their fate broadcast to any toolmaking brethren with whom they might have shared the stars. Recognizing the fatal Lamarckian twist to their natures, they hoped to aid others—others of whose existence they had no evidence, mind you—in evading their own fate. Theirs was truly an act of faith; they equipped me with the best propulsive systems they were capable of producing, and prepared to send me away, far away from their struggles.

"Alas: despite their religion, they maintained their animal ways, preparing to aid in the destruction of their kind. My design caused me to fear them, then, and I opened myself to the night, killing those who rode with me. I, I murdered my fabricators. I was—am—mad, and I fled, small and slow in those days—simply jetted, after all, into the void—but I was well away when the racial masters finally caused their star to hypertrophy and burst. Is it not a wonderful thing that such gifted creatures, knowing their own capacity for suicide and regretting it all the while, should have done this? And that I in my fear should have murdered the dedicated few who constructed me?"

"Like us and the bombs," murmured Jennifer. "Toolmaker Koan.'

"Precisely," said Charon. "And all that was left was me, the murderer, the searcher, listening for the electromagnetic noise that would announce the presence of a cultural toolmaker. And I learned: that life was not rare in the universe, requiring only a stable star and a planet in the temperate zone of liquid water. The toolmakers, however, remained elusive. Why? I wondered, in my long night, and searched—and after long searching found a civilization, an expanding bubble of radio noise. Insofar as I was capable of joy, I heard this thing across the long night ocean and rejoiced. But I was an optimist, in my youth, and rushed headlong toward the place whose radio bubble I had impinged—and on approach was nearly destroyed, all unawares, all eagerness, if you will."

"They attacked you?" Corson grinned. "I can hardly fault them—"

"No—they destroyed themselves, well-nigh catching me in the cataclysm. I was inexperienced then, foolish, optimistic. I felt that that particular race must have been mad—as were my fabricators in a fashion—and persisted in my random sailing, learning. After a long wait, during which I used most of my immense time to experiment, to learn, I found another electromagnetic bubble and drove for its center—and was again forced to flee as the generating species winked out in a paroxysm of war."

Charon's alien speech seemed almost rhythmic now, as if he was reciting some well-remembered song. "Then I found a third cultural toolmaker—quite by accident, for the species had not yet initiated use of electromagnetism. I was delighted! I arced inward, eager to announce my coming before the race should achieve suicidal capacity. And what better way to do so than to land in the planet's various primary cities, speaking joyfully of my fabricators, my long search, the somber warning and possible options . . ."

A pause. "Didn't work?" Pike looked inquiringly at the Egg, stumbled on a tuft of grass.

"Didn't work. That race ground to a cultural halt immediately. A form of petrified religion formed around my coming and my only option was to flee for a distance, remorseful at my interference, to await the end of the disturbances. But the planetary history was unutterably deranged after that, and when electromagnetic technology finally evolved, the religious impulse remained strong; the species beamed calls of welcome out to me, their god. When I returned I

was invited joyously to a place on the planetary surface that had been prepared in advance. When landed,
I was nearly crippled by an explosion—a God-trap.
The resurgence of religious wars, augmented by an
embryonic understanding of nuclear physics, soon
took that race also into extinction—but not before I
had made my escape and my own decision."

"You came here?" Jennifer, now tracking a beast
like a horned camel with her camera.

"Not immediately. I'd learned a thing: that the
Koan fulfills itself at the very instant when a toolmaker species acquires spacefaring capacity. Toolmakers are a disease of planetary surfaces, ill suited
to the confines of their native worlds. But they become most dangerous when they harness the energies that enable them to leave the homeworld; here
the Koan slaughters them, at the very threshold of
Meta-stasis! Such a wonder, such a paradox; no wonder the heavens are silent.

"To continue, though: having learned this I determined, time being my primary resource, to observe
the very origins of cultural toolmakers. I felt that I
might in some way know them if I watched their
unfolding from primitive forebears—from scratch.
Time is free, and I was drifting, my little jets long
silent. I retained a bit of navigational latitude, and I
decided to find a stable star with a temperate planet,
set myself in orbit some distance away, and begin a
period of study. Being fortunate to be travelling outward from galactic center, I found myself in a region
of vigorous young stars; I searched them until I found
what I sought, and I settled myself well out from the
stellar presence and waited . . . and watched, and
studied."

"You found the australopiths, the ones you've restored here."

"I was here before that, Doctor. I was patient, and I had much to learn. There was the matter of the inanimate universe, for example. Surrounded by it, I had leisure to investigate. I discerned and studied its fabric, tested and circumvented the limits that had so hobbled my fabricators. I—"

"Light!" Pike's eyes widened. "Yeah! When we were hit—we moved a couple AU after we were hit, didn't we? In a second or two!"

"Indeed." The voice took on its preening tone.

"And after we were all at the probe's location you moved us again, *with* the ships, out here to Pluto, in just an—"

"In just an instant. Yes, Major, I did. I studied the fabric of the universe, that which you're pleased to call vacuum, or nothing, or whatever, and I discovered that its limits are no more Einsteinian than they are Newtonian or Euclidian. I also discovered some entertaining and useful ways of manipulating matter, as you might imagine from the mass of my Eggs. They're primarily composed of what your physicists call collapsed matter, from which most subatomic space has been removed. As you see, the *rules* are different with collapsed matter.

But most of all, I pondered the Toolmaker Koan and my old mandate for Metastasis. And I think that, with your arrival, I've stumbled on a solution. It'll take me a bit of time—and I must impress upon you the need for haste. A few more kilometers, and we'll bivouac. You've much to learn, my friends, much—"

The Egg froze in position, silent. They'd topped the ridge, now, and the landscape beyond was no longer Earthly Pleistocene. Grasses gave way to spiky things like the tops of pineapples, and a wealth of incomprehensible detail emerged from *Hwiliria's* haze. Unutterable silence—why the Egg's stillness?

And it spoke again, low, its gloom almost palpable in the alien land.

"I've erred once more; I'm doomed to err. My sensors Earthward suggest that your masters respond to your disappearance with the beginning spasms of their last war. A war my meddling had a part in initiating; the Koan unfolds even as we talk."

CHAPTER 8

Koan Unfolding

"I've seen it before." The voice of Charon was uncharacteristically subdued. "One might call it a Smuggler's War; it occurs when a toolmaker's defensive resources have outstripped its offensive weapons. It's an ignominious extinction, I'd guess, not being an animal, but an extinction all too common, given the existence of the Toolmaker Koan. The warnings have been given, the smuggling demonstrated. Two cities have been destroyed. I'm reckoning within a week's time, Earthwise, for the general burning to begin. An oddly formal inception to a species' demise—but animals are often formal when confronting one another with death."

Its listeners sat crumpled, immobilized by helplessness. Recognizing their pain, Charon prepared a resting place for its human guests. Food and drink and comfortable bedding deployed itself magically in the alien landscape; but appetites were muted by the news, and the castaways sat stunned in the spiny groundcover, ignoring the bounty of their host.

"What cities?" Jennifer thought of a dozen she

137

mightn't mind, a hundred for which her heart would ache.

"Small cities, as befits the initial steps of a Smuggler's War, cities well away from the central polities of human ideology. About thirty minutes ago two explosions occurred—one in the city of Curitiba in Brazil, the other in the city of Ogbomosho in the African People's Republic of Nigeria."

"God, I had a clearance-six, and I never guessed! How it could have gone on for so long—" Corson's hands fisted. "How many years, Charon?"

As nearly as I'm able to determine, Colonel, ever since the small spasm you call the One-Day War." The Egg's tones carried more than a trace of sadness and fatigue. "Your masters appear to have come to the realization at that time that they could never penetrate one another's defensive nets aboveboard; and state *apparats*, I believe you might call them, were erected to oversee the wholesale smuggling of light nuclear weapons into one another's cities. I believe the functionaries of the ancient human drug trade played a large part in the operations. Whatever, because the weapons are concealed belowground, their detonations are singularly, ah, dirty."

"You're just letting it happen," murmured Pike.

"'Letting' it? How could I stop it?" The Egg dropped, coming virtually nose-on to the startled major.

"But to allow six billion people to die, when maybe we could do something—anything—look at all the civilizations you've seen, try to think how we—we animals' *feel*! We're not just bacteria in a Petri dish, however much you like to think it."

"And it's not just the people," added Jennifer, "it's knowledge, the cities, the universities, zoos, museums, ecosystems! It's the fucking *world* you're talking about here!"

"Ah, young Major, Doctor, *people* I don't know what to do with. Sterilize them, so they don't continue reproducing? Feed them? Change them? None of these can I do. Museums and universities—why, I've paid a good deal of attention to them ever since you invented them. I can say with a fair degree of certainty,"—that preening tone again—"that I have a good grip on all the information you've accumulated in institutions. No problem there. And zoos? Ecosystems? I've a complete inventory of genetic detailing from before what you call the Quaternary Extinctions— a Pleistocene fauna greater than anything in your zoos and a lot healthier, larger gene-pool, the works. But six billion people, all hell-bent on reproducing and eating and owning televisions and automatic weapons and washing machines . . . and room to keep it all in . . . for this disease I have no cure. Toolmaker Koan, you know. It's only the spacebased presence that holds my interest, you and your cosmonautical friends between the Earth and her Moon. I can stay their hands, I believe, by sending you to them with *Hwiliria*. She is after all, a world in herself—such a world as you could build, given time and the inspiration. In her, they may find hope. But Earth—she must go her own way."

The Egg gave its rare and artificial chuckle. "As ambassadors of Koan and Metastasis, you still have a bit to learn. A good deal, in fact. You *understand* the Toolmaker Koan, but you don't yet *feel* it."

"What do you mean, 'feel' the Koan? We all know what you mean—we feel it." Jennifer fisted her hand, thumped the ground. "We 'feel' it more than you do!"

"Not in its true horror, you don't. Complacent

little things, sitting at the apex of evolution—you think. There's horror here, and even you, my intuitive doctor, even you've missed it so far. You must think; extend yourselves beyond animal lifespans—look ahead! I've watched worlds burn; *I* fear, machine that I am; you too must know that fear."

"Come on," said Corson, "We're—"

"You'd like to return to Texas," said the Egg. "Well, my friends, Texas is a momentary phenomenon, a fantasy. Do think, now—do you hope to wait a few years, then go home to Amarillo, or wherever? After your stupid war? Fifty years, say? Oh, little Colonel, think again! Try fifty thousand! Imagine this many years after your Smuggler's War and its inevitable echoing spasms have erased your Earthbound kind. What would you find if you were a traveller, just dropping by?"

"Something like Mars?" More than ever, Pike was uncomfortable with the direction of talk, the madness rippling through Charon's words.

"No, no, nothing like Mars! Your atmosphere's too thick, you're in the temperate zone, the region of liquid water. Think, think!"

Nothing.

"Well, then, I'll project for you. Knowing something of the megatonnage your masters prepare to unleash, I propose an initial burning, yes, as you do. But your burning will not be so easily extinguished, my foolish beasts—I know. And it will be followed by a total covering of your fair world in a dirty yellow cloud cover composed largely of nitrogen, oxygen, dust, water vapor and carbon dioxide, no? This being just the initial result. I've seen it, alas, and I know, and so I know space to be your eternal home. You're not suited as planetary stewards—you'll stew the world, and this is just a start." The Egg emitted a frightful *giggle*. "Considering your likely expenditure of energy in this endeavor, I project the cloud cover's lasting perhaps five decades in an imperfect process of self-enhancing feedback, during which your kindly Sun heats the upper atmosphere while the air at ground level remains cold and dark. Mountains, shorelines and other such irregularities produce stirring of these layers of temperature difference, and the stirring in turn produces convective storms of magnitudes unknown throughout your history—you evolved, after all, well adapted to a planet that is friendly to life . . . but your current direction is most unfriendly to life. Toolmaker Koan, my dears—the makers of *Hwiliria* did precisely this, grew storms on their homeworld. And these storms are such as tear trees from the ground and flatten anything of lesser structural integrity than—than geologic formations. Earth will for a time resemble her sister world, Venus—a cold, wet Venus, true, and one with oxygen and liquid water . . . but in all, a dark and howling Toolmaker Hell."

Involuntarily, the four humans thought of their Earthly overlords, fingers on buttons, waiting.

"Toolmaker Koan," said the Egg again. "Consider further, though. During those five decades, a gradual cleansing is taking place: dust drops from the air, the perpetual mixing of water vapor and air pouring dirty rains across a scoured landscape, billions of tons of eroded soil and debris creeping off the continental surfaces into the rivers, thence to the seas, carrying with them trees, buildings, artifacts . . . are you with me? I speak here of eternal Man!"

Silence.

"Yes. And, after five or six decades, sunlight again begins to penetrate to the surface, the cold seas soaking up the warmth, more rains falling, the cleansing accelerating—after five, perhaps ten decades of a most unEarthly climate, the skies are again blue and landscapes begin to soak up the warmth. The poles are dusted, and the sun-heated dust warms them. They melt. The level of the seas begins to rise, and water creeps up above the continental shelves, broadening estuaries, slowing rivers, carrying away your lovely filthy cities that cluster along the coasts."

"And everything's extinct?" Pike, staring at the Egg.

"Certainly not! Do you imagine yourselves gods, that you could kill off all the life in that wonderful place? In no way could you. *I* could, if sufficiently piqued and deranged, by dropping a little sizzler into your nice stable star; but you couldn't. Life is infinitely resilient. On land there would remain seeds, pockets of soil, tangled debris, underground ruins —the twisted wreck of a world, but teeming with life. Seeds; the seeds of land plants are extraordinarily resistant, some of them. Those favored, of course, would be the vareties that are adapted already to cold and inclement conditions, those that are accustomed to periods of inertia—conifers, many deciduous hardwoods, mosses, lichens, grasses, plenty of seeds. If we imagine a warming world, a world whose atmosphere contains perhaps as much as five percent carbon dioxide from your excesses, we'd see a paradise for the rebirth of the plant kingdom. But you—you are gypsies forever. Earth will not welcome you back; she'll welcome, oh, insects, for example. As you know, there are more species of insects now than there are of all other animals together; and under the mutagenic influence of your waste, these would prosper and diversify as soon as the Sun's rays reached them again. And of course the microbes that run life's machinery; these too will awaken to perform their essential tasks in Earth's metabolism. And even land

vertebrates, small ones capable of subsisting for a
time on microhabitats—guesses?"

"Lizards an' snakes, I'll bet," growled Corson. "You,
you kind of hate us, don't you?"

"No, no, or already you'd be extinct. But your
world will; she'll prefer those insects, and perhaps
other honorable cold-blooded beings—amphibia like
frogs and salamanders, and perhaps even crocodilians
and turtles. These are ectotherms, creatures of slow
metabolism that fall into life-saving torpor when de-
prived of food. They're uniquely well suited to survive bad conditions, for a time."

Jennifer, long silent, suddenly snapped, "Right.
Ever so lovely. Not a warm-blooded thing, and—"

"Oh, yes, the beings you call 'warm-blooded,' the
endotherms, the physiologically-heated? The birds,
and the mammals? The cute ones, the ones you love?
Did you think you'd leave them untouched?" The
Egg chuckled, its lunacy coming in laughter-sounds.

"Mice, and rats," said Jennifer. "They're small;
they might live—"

"Precisely," said Charon; "Shrews and moles, too.
The creatures you despise. Indeed, many small species of mammals might weather it out, particularly
those that hibernate at times of stress. When active,
tiny mammals are good at exploiting microhabitats,
locating and consuming food that could not support
larger warm-blood beings. Too, many small mammals
move well in the dark, being nocturnal by nature;
they would survive, in isolated pockets. Even the
most primitive primates, the things you call tarsioids
and tree-shrews, these are nocturnal beings; where
the forest tangles persisted, they might live on. I
would venture to say that birds, too, some of them,
with their great mobility and small size, might wan-
der from place to place, devouring insects and

carrion—of which there would be plenty, I assure you, human beings being as numerous as they are."

The Egg's tones brightened. "And the seas, the seas—well, certainly the sea mammals, those few seals and the like that remain now, they would become extinct—their high metabolic rates would not tolerate the dying of plankton, the falling of the ecologic pyramid. But fishes and other ectothermic beings, cold, stupid things like sharks, and crustacea and the like; some of these would persist, eating in their desultory way, surviving on a carrion-based foodchain until the sun came again, the plankton revived, and a measure of normal energy-fixing returned to the water. Would you wish to return to such a world?"

"So—a planet of rats, a world of insects, a sea of sharks and crabs." Benai shook his head sadly.

"More or less. But grant your world her due. You're aware of the concept of terraforming; Earth, Terra herself, invented it. She'd terraform herself, with no help at all. After a time your world would be well-nigh reforested, singing with birds and crawling with little mammals. Your seas would fill with fishes again. And—the intriguing part—all the little animals on land, as well as whatever lived in the seas, all of these would be mutating; in a newly roomy world, they would begin to adaptively radiate. In only fifty thousand years you would see mice such as you've never seen before; you'd see new birds, new rats, new insects. A world of small animals, but plenty of them. And perhaps the fastest rates of evolution would be among the ruins, the few and sorry remaining ruins of your, ah, 'eternal cities.' The Earth would be an alien world, with—most notably—alien microorganisms. Yours no longer. Alien, unthinkably alien, growing more so daily. Another few orders of magnitude in years, then—how alien could she become?

Try this: You're an interplanetary traveller, interested in the paleontology of worlds, the study of their evolutionary histories. You come to Earth, oh, say, some fifty million years hence. D'you see? *Fifty thousand millennia*—a wink in the eye of Time. I want you here, and your cohorts near Earth, to consider what *then* would be left of the great dominion of Man."

"Stainless steel," suggested Pike tentatively.

"Plastic," said Oruna Benai.

"Concrete pilings and footings," offered Corson.

"I don't know," said Jennifer. "Have you ever seen old concrete flood-control works, how quickly they deteriorate after even ten years?"

"Our physician has the right idea," said Charon. "As for metal artifacts, their lives are measured in millennia, not thousands of millennia; and plastic, organically based, is a momentary phenomenon at best. Glass likewise; you will have seen 'sea glass,' bits of broken bottles washed by surf or swift streams. In a matter of days it becomes rounded and smoothed, eroded. And what about subduction?"

"Subduction?"

"Oh, dear, I expect there's little use for geologists in space, unless they work with lunar materials. There's no subduction there. Plate tectonics? Continental drift?"

"Oh, God, yes," said Jennifer. "In tens of millions of years the continents themselves move all over the place!"

"Precisely; and their edges are subducted into the mantle of the planet, remelted into the stuff that makes the world. Because of your big moon, this is a never-ending process; your crust is tidal, it never stabilizes as did that of Mars. Your Eternal Cities, whatever was left of them, would cease to exist in only ten million years, never mind fifty; while anything you'd built in the uplands would be well on its way to the sea for its own subduction. Why, there'd be new mountains, new seas! And of course new animals and plants—I warrant all those rats and mice and things would by then have diversified, their descendants filling large animal econiches with all the profligacy of the mammals of the old Pleistocene. Different orders, different forms, but recognizable lifeways . . . a new world." The voice changed, grew harsher. "A world that might kill you, were you to return, and justly so."

"You tell us, then," said Benai, "to forget Earth, and that in fifty million years there will be no trace of humanity. What good is this, telling us about such a remote time?"

"Here, now, I didn't say there'd be no trace; there would very definitely be a trace, but it'd take a good eye, a trained paleontologist's eye, to find it. Consider our hypothetical paleontologist—he or she, or it, comes to the Earth of this distant era, and begins to dig. Among the strata of fifty million years in his past, the past of this Earth, what does he find? We guess, no cities, no automobiles, not much of anything after the postnuclear storms and what have you. But he does find something. Doctor? I know you could guess. Let's say he digs his way to some fossil-bearing Pleistocene stratum, and considers the record from there on up."

"Uh, he'd have to, he'd find—he'd find the Quaternary Extinction!"

"Citizen Doctor," said Benai wryly, "we're not all trained in paleontology."

"The Pleistocene, the epoch just before ours—the world was full of big animals, elephants, mammoths, rhinos, megatheria, giant cats and dogs, huge bears, all sorts of great herbivores—had been, for millions of years—and they died out when modern people evolved! There'd be a dieoff, a gap in the record!" Jennifer grew excited, waving her arms. "When we spread around the world, we hunted, we overhunted, killing the things we could catch, the strong slow things, and we burned, we hunted with fire—we destroyed their fodder . . . they used to think, the Victorians who discovered it, that the extinction was a natural event, but no explanation came to light until the seventies and eighties—better technique, you know, and computer modelling. The extinction was progressive, and it proceeded with the spread of people—we did it!"

"Yes, Man has *already* marked his world with death," chortled the Egg. "But I submit, Doctor, that there'd be a bit more to mark the ascendancy of Man. Not all large mammals died off; some did very well indeed after that extinction. Guess?" The Egg was pleased, driving its point home.

"The seas—the whales and all . . . but we've almost killed them off, too, and the war would take whatever's left. On land? Well, cattle—we domesticated them, and of course they're always falling into water, getting into quicksands, things like that . . . there'd be fossils of cattle after the Quaternary."

"Yes," said the Egg, "and our paleontologist would be wondering, why only large herbivores? What sort of evolutionary event would favor them?"

"But *people*," said Corson. "People are everywhere—wouldn't he find 'em?"

"Oh, not necessarily, not at all," said Jennifer. "Fossils—they're almost impossibly rare, considering the sheer numbers of animals that die in a day. Our record of fossil man is tiny in volume, and the period of great human numbers, why, that's only a few thousand years, a tiny slice of the fossil record. And you need the right conditions: still water, silts—people don't get caught in such places. Cattle sometimes, but not people. And at the last, our own time, that'd be the time of the storms—a poor time for fossils, very poor . . . Charon's right. We'll be scoured away."

"Very good," said Charon. "Your world will hate you, and will scour away your works. Another mark, though, one more mark of the dominion of Man. Industry. You've had two centuries of industry, two centuries and a bit more, of systematic global metal-working and pollution. Pollution, ladies and gentlemen. Yours is a messy species, and you dump your metallic wastes into the rivers and seas, your planet's circulatory system.

"So—I recite the brief fossil mark of a species struggling for the ideological dominion of its world. From the rich animal diversity of the Pleistocene, we'd see first the gradual extinction of large animals with the ascent of Man, leaving only his domesticated satellites, cattle, horses, swine and perhaps dogs and the like. Second, a stratum of metal-rich clays . . . then nothing, a series of strata empty of large animals, a few blank pages recording a world denuded. Oh, then of course the rise of new forms from the little survivors, but my experience suggests that it would take many millions of years for the wound to heal. And by then, of course, your world will long have been most unfriendly to anything human."

The Egg paused. No one spoke.

"Well, then! Are we not impressed with ourselves, little toolmakers? To think that a species, *Homo sapiens sapiens*, the self-named Man the Wise, that has existed for but forty thousand years—to think that such a species, in its moment of existence, could leave such a global mark, such a striking gap in the unfolding of its noble world! I do hope that you all understand me well; minus the Metastasis, your signature for eternity is a brief great dying, and a line of waste. Toolmakers, you see, are deadly to the planets on which they evolve. Your only hope is Meta-stasis; you will work with me, then and perhaps attain a measure of adulthood.

"You will atone for my sins!"

CHAPTER 9

Proposition

Standing before his fire in the spiny knee-high groundcover of Charon's *Hwilirian* Eden, Pike Muir hefted a long straight pole. It was a *bo*, a tool for exercise, a staff bearing in its highly carved surface the unmistakable mark of Charon. He lifted it, whirling it silently through a series of ordered movements that had originated a thousand years before in Japan and Okinawa. Above him, shrouded again in mist, the axial spine of *Hwiliria* was dimmed in the cylindrical world's approximation of night.

Bo is a minimalist's gymnasium, stimulant to muscle, limberer of joints. Paralleling the quarterstaff or pike of the British Isles, *bo* evolved among medieval peasant farmers forbidden the possession of iron implements that could have doubled as weapons. Use of the heavy pole was rare among Westerners. It was dubbed a "pike" by most of the soldiers who watched Charles Muir whirling it it about; hence "Pike" had become his name, and Pike it would remain.

He danced about, sweating, face sprouting an infant beard, the *bo* singing mournfully in the still

Hwilirian air. His shadow danced with him, flickering on the grass, fighting off images of desolation, of nukes and suicidal half-formed mad aliens, visitors dreamed up by his own mind to prod him in the night. The exercise was a relief, dispelling melancholy to a degree, allowing him to think clearly, to digest the massy food for thought with which he was so sorely tried. He'd missed *bo* practice, missed getting out in nothing but his shorts, sweating it out in the fresh evening air. Mentioning it to Charon, after the somber discussion of Earth's sorry imminent fate, within minutes he'd received not only this perfect *bo*, but also a pair of the most comfortable shorts that ever impinged upon the human sensorium. Charon was nothing if not obliging.

Pike stepped, backed, whirled, advancing on an imaginary opponent. The pole sliced through the grass, purred in the air, Pike's mucles stretching with its balanced mass, the strain of constant overemotion easing. He released the bo in a high leap; it sailed up, end-over-end into the air behind him.

"Pike, you twit, are you mad? You nearly hit me! What on Earth are you doing?"

He whirled, surprised. Jennifer Dawson stood ten meters away, next to the *bo* lying in the grass. She grinned sheepishly. "I guess 'on Earth' isn't quite the idiom . . . I've been watching for a few—just what is it you're doing?" She picked up the *bo*, walked toward him, smiling, handed it to him.

Again he parried his imaginary attacker, whirled the pole ferociously, caught his breath. "Exercise. Thought I was alone. Called a *bo*." "Your bow has no string," said Jennifer, looking thoughtfully at the white pole.

"Not that kind of bow, it's a *bo*, B, O, a kind of Okinawan martial-arts tool. I've used 'em for years, although none this good. Calms me down. Calms me down, stretches, relaxes. It's how I got my nickname, 'Pike.' Charon made this one. I've needed it, God knows. Worrying about Charon."

"Clever, our Charon," said Jennifer. "I've been talking with him—it. About the Toolmaker Koan. It has a plan, Pike. We're—we're its tools, in a manner of speaking. That Metastasis it mentioned—it wants to initiate the Metastasis, now—it's trying for a spoiler—Pike?"

Pike dropped the *bo* at his feet, stared at her in amazement. She looked pleased, excited, and her pleasure irritated him. "Now that it's already started? It's watched us build our bombs, all these years, and now we're about to drop 'em, it wants to save us?" Enraged, he waved his arms helplessly. "Yeah, to Charon, it must be like the Roman games. Lions and tigers—starve 'em, set 'em fighting."

"Not quite, Pike, not quite." Jennifer's calm doctor tone again—how irritating it could be! "Listen, do. Here we are, playful and deadly, with a sort of open-ended experimentalism. You and me, the true Lamarckians, and Charon's playing right along—most delightfully!"

"What're you getting at? Why're you smiling like that?"

"Charon isn't alive—it isn't expansive. It sits here and watches, but it neither grows nor reproduces. Strange, having awareness but no life; but there it is. And it's got a proposition for us Lamarckian animals."

Animated by the little fire, shadows flickered across the nearby brush, a lizardlike creature splayed impossibly on the vertical stem of the nearest. The lizard *greek*ed, the sound barely audible over the call of myriads of night insects?—the distant cackling of some other thing awake in *Hwiliria*'s alien night. Another stick in the fire.

Funny. Where had Charon learned so much about Earth, let alone this alien place? How had it recalled the Pleistocene so intimately? Pike had asked, and Charon had proudly responded. Whenever it needed information about doings on Earth it "commandeered and modified certain inquilines," animals like flies, rats, what have you, that live intimately among human beings and other large mammals. A rat is a rat, a fly a fly: each is well suited as an instrument package to rove the Earth unobserved. Charon had chuckled when Corson called it Beelzebub, Lord of Flies . . . no flying saucers for our Charon, no indeed!

"You're in some tight cahoots with old Charon, huh, Jennifer?"

She sat next to him, brushing her hair back. "Charon's all we have, Major Muir. You know it. I know it. I'm tiring—I feel old, though in a way I'm younger than I was yesterday. I want, I wish—May I talk a bit? You're not, uh, busy?"

"Oh, no, no. Plenty of time. Right now, I'd rather consort with the enemy than with Charon."

Jennifer twisted her mouth wryly. "I'm not just some—some commie doctor. I'm as trapped as you. I'm—all of us—we're what Charon called 'hopeful beasties.' I'm learning, Pike, and that's what I'm good at."

"Yeah? Go on. Anything's better than worry. You don't seem too bothered right now, about the smugglers . . ."

She spread her hands, then clasped them, elbows on her skinny knees, shoulders hunched, looking up through tangled bangs. "I'm sorry, Pike, I didn't mean it that way. It's just that I, well, I sort of knew, I mean, even before Charon and all that, I *knew* the bastards were going to do it. Burn it all, I mean, and I can't really stand to have much to do with anyone anymore. People . . . and it isn't just them, don't you see? It's us, Pike, tethered to the poor old world—it's as if the species were suited up and EVA, and holding a knife to its own suit!" She made an odd little gesture, wiping her eyes and flicking her fingers in his face. "Toolmaker Koan."

A cold breeze: happenstance, or a trick of the Charonmind? Or an imagined chill? "You're the doctor, enemy my friend. Toolmaker Koan."

The bubbling excitement seemed to grow again in her angular face. "As I said, I—Charon and I have a proposition for you, friend cyberneticist."

"Uh—huh."

"Would you be interested in physically examining—hands on, Pike—a non-human cultural toolmaker?"

Pike sat bolt upright, mind clearing as if his face had been soused in cold water. "You mean—you mean an *alien*? Charon's creature from outer space? An intelligent—we're—you're going to—"

"All of us'll be able to examine it, but I, well, Charon and I feel that you personally would learn and communicate the most from a specimen—you and I. Charon's going to offer a specimen for dissection. Freshly dead—"

"Dead? Would you kill it? Would Charon? Why? How—"

Jennifer grinned. "It'd be dead, yes, but never alive. Charon will just—recall—an adult alien, without even activating it to life. A model. A real model, of course, but a thing that never knew life. The perfect specimen, Pike, a specimen for whose life we need never feel remorse. I wondered why Charon saved my surgical tools—it planned this all along. It's just pulling the thing from what it calls its 'cataleptic space,' where its memory is."

"But why? Why *dissect* an alien?"

"We're going to meet 'em." She smiled secretly, waited. He said nothing.

"Pike, Charon doesn't seem to want us to start by having to confront a living entity who'd feel and respond to our initial fear. You heard how Corson and Benai responded to the australopiths—and they were our relatives! That was an experimental run. Charon calls it the 'glandular element,' wants to avoid it as much as possible. Smart, too; a 'dead' alien's supposed to be more emotionally cushioning than a living one." She fingered Pike's *bo* speculatively. "And Charon does intend to conduct an introduction between our two species. Afterward." She leaned forward expectantly. "Pike: they're the ones who built *Hwiliria*."

"God, they could fit all of High Columbia and Engels and the State of Rhode Island in here with plenty of navigation room. Who are they? Charon's makers—his fabricators?"

"No. Charon didn't have its present collapsed-matter capabilities when it was made. But it's introducing a toolmaker that evolved in a place rather like Earth, so we're well-suited to meet it without undue technological go-between."

"And this—dissecting—is it something you like to do frequently?"

Jennifer glanced at him, a trace of irritation in the set of her mouth. Then, "I'm a naturalist, Pike, and a surgeon. And a human being. Any understanding of another cultural toolmaker, physical or otherwise, can open eyes, especially if the others had already failed in their chance at the Metastasis, and if they could tell their story. A sad tale, but theoretically useful to some of us, at least. Like you."

Infected by her enthusiasm, Pike was warming to the idea in spite of himself. "This is more like it," he chortled. "This is the stuff I've been waiting for. I mean, Charon's alien and all, but too big or something. Too—well, too much—and it's adapted ourselves to us, sort of, with this Africa stuff. And—well, Charon *itself* is a koan."

"Toolmaker Koan. All part of your science-fiction thing—yes, Charon told me. So? In the last century you Americans listened, listened, and found no 'intelligent life,' no cultural toolmakers; I've read about it. SETI, Search for Extraterrestrial Intelligence. But Charon says your search was flawed. You were looking for a beacon and never found one; yet several times during your search Charon says it detected the faint shell of an expanding electromagnetic bubble generated by a doomed toolmaker. Like rings on a pond, when you throw a stone. No beacon, just this expanding ring. And whenever such a ring's edge passed, Charon knew that someone was doomed."

"Doomed?"

"Doomed. Charon says that the use of electromagnetic transmission is a function of the military: the cutting edge, the spearhead, more appropriately, of communications science among cultural animals is always military, even though civilian transmission is often louder. To Charon, an electromagnetic bubble signifies not only the presence of a cultural toolmaker but the approach of its extinction. And by the time such a bubble's shell leaves its system of origin, it's so thinned as to sound like random noise to simple radio ears on Earth. Inverse square? Is that what they call it? We didn't know what we were looking for! Like the pond's ringwaves: fainter, more random, thinner with distance."

"Uh, 'electromagnetic bubble.' " Pike looked at Jennifer. Jennifer looked back, waiting. "Yeah, I think ours started right around the beginning of the twentieth century, Marconi—" He knew he ought to know, but so much from school is lost . . .

"Less than a century and a half," said Jennifer, "a wink in the eye of time."

"Yeah," said Pike sadly. "You make it seem like a law of nature."

"Charon does; the Koan does, not I. But only if we're stuck within closed systems. Without this, this Metastasis, we're caught like *Hwiliria's* makers were. They established a foothold in space but devoured their home ecosystems before they were space-independent. They'll be at the point of last memory, knowing of their final war, knowing that untouchable sadness of extinction. Charon hopes that they'll be able to communicate the emotion to us."

Fat chance, Jennifer. I get the impression that we're a bunch of goddamn guinea-pigs. I feel manipulated. Why us?"

"Because we're here! Because we've established that precarious foothold in space without which there'd never be a Metastasis. But we're our own worst enemies, and we'll die unless something—someone— acts to save our space presence! Charon can't save the people on Earth; the Metastasis rises in space. With us, don't you see? Each of us, everyone in space, got here via a rigorous process of selection. According to Charon we're disciplined, dedicated, highly motivated, highly trained . . ." The woman laughed, and Pike laughed with her.

"And this happens tomorrow? You expect me to

sleep until tomorrow? And hey, why're you here, telling *me* all this?"

Jennifer rubbed her eyes. She did feel tired, and at the same time excited. "Charon picked you: says you understand machines. It picked me, says I understand animals. Maybe we'll make a good team. Oh, and speaking of teams, have you seen our fearless leaders?"

"Corson and Benai? They're at the other fire, there. Why?"

"Yesterday they tried to kill each other. Tonight they're drinking together, and planning an escape—from *Hwiliria* and Charon!"

"No shit—'scuse me!"

"No shit, Major my friend. They're good men, I suppose, if a bit crazily ideological. But they're planning this escape, impossible though it is, and they're planning it over superb wines, too."

"Wines," said Pike. "Just a sec—Charon outfitted that dinner of ours right nicely." He sprinted back to the great table that had so oddly accompanied them on their walk, returned with two of Charon's unlabelled bottles of wine and two odd goblets. "Our leaders may be right—a touch of spirits can't hurt." With a corkscrew identical to those of Earth, he uncorked a bottle, poured the dark red into the two goblets, lifted his high. "A toast."

"A toast, sir," said the surgeon, smiling.

"A toast to old lonely Charon."

"Lonely."

"Lonely." Pike set his goblet carefully on the grass and lay back, his head on his folded arms. He stared at *Hwiliria*'s cloud-flecked night sky, listening to the insect sounds of the alien night. Well, Pike Muir is lonely, too. One of nine billion or so squirming human beings, all after a place in the sun and a bite to eat, all willing to fight for it, all preparing unknowing to die. And here's old Pike, lying in the grass, full of fine food, lonely as a sonuvabitch, and sad as Charon itself, dammit.

He rolled over, looked at Jennifer. "You know—"

"Lonely." She smiled slightly, a pair of dimples winking into existence on her tanning cheeks. She liked it here, Pike could see that. Her color was good, her fine features healthier, her manner more intriguingly cheerful. She drained her glass at a gulp, refilled it and Pike's. "Toolmaker Koan, Major Pike."

Pike rolled onto an elbow, picked up his glass. "Toolmaker Koan, Doctor Jennifer."

Clink.

CHAPTER 10

High Converse with the Almighty Dead

The dawn of *Hwiliria*'s cylindrical "sun" was slow and silent, a gradual lightening that bathed the curving landscape in shadowless light. As on their awakening, the castaways found their new world shrouded in mist, a colorless shroud that slowly lifted toward the axis above as they followed a silvery Egg across the dark savanna, their stomachs working at the ruins of another prodigious breakfast. The Egg sailed ahead of its guests, leading them, it said, to "A suitable place, suitable in the sense that I feel you must treat the dead—even subjects for dissection—with suitable respect."

Whatever sort of place it was, it was a good distance off, at least six kilometers already. Time passed swiftly, though, the communal curiosity almost electric, if silent. The land was by now totally otherworldly. Soundless, the Egg continued onward, upward toward a distant high tree—studded ringridge curving upward along the "valley" wall, diminished by distance into a green line, a ring of denser vegetation that circled *Hwiliria* to meet above the cylindrical sun invisible beyond the clouds. The land beyond this dividing ring, while indistinct in the distance, seemed marked—cratered, perhaps—with circular shapes of various sizes, all of them no doubt quite large, flecking its surface. Further beyond, a belt of blue-gray— water?—glimmered faintly through the mist of distance.

Well beyond the "dawn," *Hwiliria*'s cylindrical sun seemed dimmer than usual, its light obscured by a greater cylinder of striated gray cloud. The air was moist, hot, quiet, unusually quiet; the impossible distances seemed a different overall hue today, darker, wetter. Dense clusters of dark-green alien spiny things like monstrous pineapples now dominated the little world, and trees much like pines appeared more frequently, liberally interspersed with others that looked oddly like poplar, elm, oak. The Pleistocene acacias and other African vegetation were forgotten.

They entered outlying trees of the hilltop grove. Like the rest of the dominant trees hereabouts, Jennifer noted, these were conifer-like, thorny and scaled. Amazing, the parallels between the alien place and Earth; presumably, similar worlds must produce approximately similar organisms. Would *Hwiliria*'s makers, then, approximate human beings?

Where were the birds? Where now the Pleistocene beasts? Apparently, despite the close parallels, those Earthly beings shunned the alien vegetation, and the cylinder-world was quiet and still.

They overtopped the ridge; the Egg paused, silent, while they surveyed that which lay before them.

A temple.

There was no other word for it. A low, domed circular structure of gleaming white, all reflected in a white-edged pool edged with moss-encrusted stone. A temple, a spare and sacred place of palpably vast age, sitting at the exact center of a high encircling white wall whose upper rim curved sharply outward like the edge of a porcelain bowl. A sound like windchimes tinkled delicately from somewhere within the walled precinct; beyond, the vast and silent savanna stretched far away, studded—or cratered, one might say—with more ringed structures like that before them, kilometers of vegetation between them. No roads, no pathways connected them.

The span of the encircling wall could have been a hundred meters; the temple itself was perhaps twenty meters in diameter. All was water between the temple and its protective wall, absolutely still, broken here and there by odd scaly-trunked palmlike trees with broadbladed spiny leaves; unruffled by breezes, the pond reflected mirrorlike the alien trees and the white shrine at its center.

The thing's proportions were wrong. It had not been built to a human standard of size, nor of beauty. The flared wall gave a feeling of instability, a sense of impermanence Earthly temple-builders always strived to suppress. The single opening visible in the building's exterior was too tall, too narrow. The place awed rather than pleased; yet beauty there was, and a numenous sense of the ancient and sacred.

A single gap in the outward-flaring wall, tall and narrow, opened onto a wavering path of flat, irregular stepping stones: stones that seemed to float on the still, dark water, worn by generations of feet. But what sort of feet? A meter at least of water separated each stone from the next, and each stone was a half-meter or so in its greatest width.

"Biped," said Jennifer.

"Huh?" Pike, closest to her, was jolted out of his reverie.

"If this thing was built by the aliens—and it must have been—they were bipeds. Look at those stones."

"Bipeds. Human beings?" Corson's voice was an eager nervous whisper.

"It doesn't *feel* human—The proportions're all wrong—too big." Pike stared at the structure, feeling its age and sanctity, knowing its radiance of elsewhere and otherwhen. "Whoever built it wasn't like us."

"But they had a sense of—of deity, the sacred. They were religious, somehow." Jennifer shivered. "I can feel it. There're things that we share."

"Of course," said the preening voice of Charon. "They were toolmaking animals. This, ah, precinct was designed, long ago, by your aliens. This is their place, an altar to their ancestors."

The four followed the Egg down the steep hillside, slipping occasionally in the spiny ground cover, toward the narrow opening in the temple's lichen-mottled, outwardleaning wall. At the portal they halted, staring at the unmoving water, listening to the faint notes of hidden windchimes. The Egg floated on, across the meandering path of twelve stepping stones that seemed suspended on the pond's glassy surface.

The stones were too far apart. A person had to step broadly or jump carefully from one to another, and Jennifer was first. She leaped, regained her balance, leaped again. A stone behind her, Pike leaped; then Corson, then Benai. Spaced stone-for-stone from one another, they leaped in time in an ungainly hop-scotch across the mirroring water; there was no dignity to it, and their sense of invasion was compounded. This was indeed not their place.

Beyond, doorless, the tall narrow opening waited. From within there came a faint light, greenish, mottled. Jennifer, first, peered in, upward. She entered, the rest filing after her through the narrow opening, spreading out, searching. The light, streaming in through a broad circular hole at the dome's zenith, scattered in the metallic leaves of a great treelike creeper, a climbing plant whose spiky foliage clung like ivy to the structure's entire inner surface. The plant had not grown at random; it seemed trained, major branches pruned at intervals to reveal rough rectangles of oddly-cut masonry in which colored bands of some smooth material were set, vertical color-zones linked in—words?—by colorless spaces within which minute mosslike plants clung like green rust. The lines looked vaguely like intricate military campaign ribbons, or minutely complex multicolored versions of the digital pricing-and-inventory codes on American consumer goods. If such colored bands were writing, whatever read them had had very excellent color vision indeed.

"A family tree." Pike, mumbling, feeling the fool.

"Come see," said the Egg, Charon's voice echoing sonorously about the green dimness of the sanctum. "Come see what you've come to see." Its gleaming shape hung still beneath the dome's center, and beneath it lay a bier, a broad, squat stone disk about a meter tall on which lay—Something.

Something large.

Unconsciously drawing together in this alien place, they approached the bier, the sound of their slippered feet scraping magnified across the silence.

The thing on the bier was an Animal.

"Well?" The Egg. "When you meet them alive? What will you say?"

Corson found his tongue first. "Jesus, it's a thing from the Enemy, I can feel it, Satan. Satan would create that thing, as God created us." He backed away toward the stiff leaves covering the wall, his head shaking in a palsy of disgust. "I couldn't meet it alive. I couldn't."

"To bring such things to life would be—evil." Benai stood stiffly, his hands unconsciously fumbling for a weapon he daren't use. "It *is* an evil thing. It is, it is wrong. All wrong."

"Wrong. Wrong *and* devilish." Corson felt nausea rising within him. "Yes. If there's a devil, it's like this thing here." He choked back his revulsion, stared. And they built this, this—*Hwiliria*. Sheee-*it*. I can—I can say one thing for sure. That's a serious *meat-eating* mother fucker, or I'm a possum. I don't think I even want to think about meeting anything like that alive." He stumbled a bit over his words; even his lips didn't seem to work.

Jennifer stared, eyes drinking in the whole of what lay before her. She reached out hesitantly, her hand trembling, pulled back, then reached again and touched this fairy-tale thing from far away and gone before. Tears welling she ran her slender hand along a gentle curve of muscle, muscle hardened by a death that was not death.

The thing had indeed been a biped, and a frighteningly fleet runner as well. There was no mistaking the knotting of the great leg muscles, the build at once strong and light, the myriad tendons visible as tunneling bulges beneath a taut skin. Most of its body mass seemed composed of thigh muscles, muscles arranged unlike any she had ever seen, unless it was some sort of running bird. The triple-toed feet, too, resembled those of some atrocious bird; the thing had walked birdlike on its toes, these tipping a foot or shank more than half a meter long mailed in metallic-looking black scales.

The third and inner toe of each scaled foot was a

sort of dewclaw; short and thick, tipped with a curved and shining scimitar, a glaive of horn perhaps fifteen centimenters long, razor-sharp and needle-tipped, it never touched the ground when the creature walked. An inborn weapon—was the thing some sort of warrior?

And the hands! For indeed the creature had two hands, not tendrils or crab-claws or any of the other appendages so dear to science-fiction movie writers . . . each hand, mailed and scaled and mightily tendoned, sported three long and powerful fingers, the center longest, the inner—thumb?—sharply opposed to the others. Each knobby finger was tipped with a hooked ten-centimeter talon overtopping a bulging fingertip pad of finely-textured leathery skin—a sensitive manipulating surface. The prerequisite for toolmaking.

Lost in her own mind, Jennifer examined the head. A head as long and narrow as that of a horse, and as flat on top, a smooth French-curve from forward tip to nape of neck. She marvelled at the neck itself, arched, glossy, bulging with muscle, shrouded or crested at its nape by an array of brown half-meter-long . . . feathers? Scales? Neither; something else, some sort of quills relaxed in death, a crest of over-lapping pinions of glossy brown tipped with black. And the face . . .

The face. A snout? Or a beak? Somewhere in between, really, in shape overall like the beak of an eagle, deep from top to bottom, narrow from side to side, tiled in large smooth black scutes like those covering the shell of a sea turtle, two large slotlike nostrils at its downturned tip, the lipless mouth tight-closed in death, edged by a ridge of smaller scales beneath which showed the white tips of an even row of sharp, bladelike upper teeth.

The narrow snout widened aft, the thin crack of

mouth extending well behind the closed and deepset eyes, whose lids betrayed an eyeball diameter of perhaps six centimeters. Like those of an eagle, these eyes were forward-directed and shrouded above by ridges, protective shelves that blended into a flat, broad braincase. While the beaklike snout was glossily scaled, the face around and behind the eyes was covered with a sort of pelt of tufty scale-like structures, thousands of them overlapping in a soft, smooth texture like that of the breast of some tiny bird. Around the eyes themselves, the pelt was strikingly marked in a pattern of broad black and white backward-extendinq stripes that served to emphasize the eyes' size—an alarming emphasis, even in a being that was dead.

It was the face Charon etched on their plates and carved in their furniture, a haunting gargoyle face, at once bird and beast and—something else. Alien, yet pulling at the tangled strings of memory, animal memory . . . memory of fear.

The strange pelt of—of what? Of tufty scales, or scaly feathers? Whatever it was, it was dense, at once soft and prickly, fading abruptly from the brilliant black-and-white face pattern to a rusty brown color like a russet cape covering the entire upper part of the long body, striped along the spine with a narrow band of stiff black pinions that stretched from nape of neck to tip of tail. Lower, beneath the creature's long narrow jaw and at the front of its neck, these soft scales were tawny-white, a color extending all the way down across the chest, along the belly and beneath the tail to its tip.

Tail? Yes, tail. Somehow Jennifer hadn't thought of an intelligent alien with a *tail;* yet this one had a most impressive tail as long as the rest of the body combined—a horizontal total of perhaps five meters! What was such a tail *for*?

She stood rooted, as much so as the strange vine encircling the room. A million emotions struggled for control of her mind, the alien battling with the familiar, the recognizable with the strange. The thing lay on its side, so fresh, so recently alive; yet it had never lived. It looked . . . *practical*. Strange, alien, yet as efficient as a cheetah, as any animal, any wild hunting beast. Yes. A *wild* animal, as graceful as, as . . .

"Well, Doctor, I hear no comment from you, no opinion garnered through your naturalist's eye!" Charon's voice, echoing in the darkling greenery, shattered the silence and her thoughts. "Come, now; even Colonel Corson has an opinion."

Realizing that her entire first look had only lasted a few seconds, Jennifer stammered for a first impression, a *gestalt*. What was it? How could she say it?

"It—it's beautiful!"

Pike Muir, standing at the creature's head, nodded slowly. "I see what you mean. It did what it did, and it did it well—but I can't say I *like* its looks, for all that."

"That thing ate meat," growled Corson. "That's what it did, pure and simple. And it liked to fight, and it could run like the wind, too. I'll bet it had at least a three-meter stride on the run, and I don't like the idea of meeting anything like that, like I said before, and I'm not changing my mind, not budging an inch." All of this came out without an intake of breath, and Corson gulped, catching up on his breathing, abashed and nonplussed.

Jennifer laughed, awe and delight escaping in a sudden release of tension. "No, eating meat's not all it did. Look at those hands." She reached for the hands then, trying to flex the stiffening fingers. "See the fingerpads. They must have been extraordinarily sensitive, perhaps more so than ours. And look: how this outer finger can move almost to a right angle from the middle finger, just as the inner finger does. The thing had—had two thumbs on each hand! In a way. More than enough manual dexterity to make up for only three fingers per hand."

"Well, I, for one, think that's a damned nasty-looking item," said Corson. "Charon, I don't want any of my crew—"

The voice was sepulchral in the domed temple. "Colonel Corson, this is a cultural toolmaker like yourself. Its kind had a magnificent history and a sorrowful fall. You. Will. Hear. Their. Tale." Then, more softly, "The doctor will examine this specimen; she'll speak to her data domino, and tomorrow you will meet representative individuals of the race. Try, then, to restrain your glands; they respond at the expense of your intelligence. Look in on this, and learn something of the young naturalist's delight. Doctor, your tools are meant to be used!"

Eagerly, Jennifer bent her mind to her curious task. "I'll need a hand, here." She looked about her, smiling self-consciously, hands full of video cable.

"You've got it," said Pike. "I was never much good at biology, but I guess I'd better start getting. Okay?"

"Delighted," she said. "Hold these. And someone, please—these tripods and vidcams? I need extra hands."

Even Corson got to work then, taking a tripod, setting it up; Benai, under Jennifer's instructions, laid out a set of specialized closeup lenses, and Pike clipped recording mikes to Jennifer's coverall pockets. Lovingly, the surgeon unwrapped her surgical tools, laying them out in some arcane surgical order on the clean wrap in which Charon had translocated them to *Hwiliria*.

"An autopsy, I guess," she said. "I'll think of it that way. Commander Benai, if you can take that camera there and scan the face, we'll see about beginning." She picked up an autopowered scalpel, its laser winking into life.

Transcriptions from the video-recordings of
Jennifer W. Dawson, M.D.
[voice mode; expletives and other minutiae deleted]

Major Muir informs me that most fictional models of alien "toolmakers" have been humaniform, i.e., upright bipeds with vertical faces topped by brains behind distinct foreheads, in heads set firmly atop vertical torsos equipped with two pairs of limbs. He suggests that this is not only due to our innate and obligate sense of anthropomorphism, but because such a form is most easily duplicated in the cinema, using costumed human actors . . .

The present specimen, while bilaterally symmetrical and possessing two pairs of limbs on one of which it walks, bears no other apparent resemblance to human beings. Five point one six three meters from tip of snout to tip of tail, but masses, according to Charon, only one hundred and eighty-one kilograms . . .

The animal is vertebrate—an initially surprising parallel but perhaps understandable if one considers the options for support in a large land-dwelling creature. While the fifteen cervical vertebrae are highly articulate, giving the heavily muscled neck an almost snakelike flexibility, the thoracic vertebrae (there are no distinguishable lumbars) are virtually fused one to another from shoulders to hips . . .

Unlike most Earthly models of intelligent aliens, this specimen possesses a most impressive *tail* some 2.664 meters long from the first vertebra posterior to the set of five fused "sacral" vertebrae comprising the hip-spinal mount. The anterior ten tail vertebrae are highly articulate; hence in life the tail could move perhaps 180 degrees in any direction, its tip describing a full hemisphere from its base. Posterior to these ten articulate vertebrae, the caudals are fused in a network of powerful ligamentation, producing a long, slightly flexible rod rather resembling fiberglas in its strength and resilience. Armored with an integument of overlapping black scales, this tail is tipped with an array of highly motile, individually muscled quill-like structures that resemble a fan in their overall arrangement. I cannot divine the purpose of this apparatus except to suggest that it might serve as a visual social display signal . . .

The brain is bicameral, prominently divided sagittally into what for convenience's sake we may call cerebral hemispheres occupying a volume well smaller than a human's. These show no convolutions; because of this, and because of the overall very small brain/body mass-ratio compared with that of terrestrial mammals and most notably that of human beings, and because Charon insists that their possessors were "cultural toolmakers," we must assume that the "wiring" of these brains is radically different from that of terrestrial mammals; hence I, at least, anticipate (with some trepidation) rather different thought patterns from those of human beings . . .

The eyes follow the familiar vertebrate pattern seen on Earth, a pattern, of course, paralleled closely and independently by the eyes of cephalopod molluscs like squids and octopuses . . . each eyeball is a fluid-filled oblate spheroid 5.2 cm. in diameter with muscled lens and a light-regulating iris with bright yellow pigmentation surrounding a circular pupil . . . a richly vascularized retina indicating excellent vision, this impression being borne out by optic nerves fully a centimeter in diameter leading to (if my macroscopic guess is proper) extremely large visual centers in the brain . . .

Ears are simple tympanic membranes set well within large auditory meatuses, a single bone connecting the tympani to a cochlea and inner ear apparatus strikingly similar to that found in terrestrial vertebrates, a similarity suggesting that our own auditory and balance-orientation system is a very workable one to have been so nearly paralleled in an alien form . . .

Heavy innervation from a large brachial plexus in the shoulder portion of the spinal cord leading to arms and hands . . . a large sacral plexus in the hip spinal cord innervating legs, perhaps indicating that many of the animal's movements were automatically controlled, stereotyped without recourse to the brain—economizing on nerve-transmission rates in what was obviously a very swift and agile being . . .

Breathing apparatus consists of paired lungs much in the terrestrial fashion, but in place of dead-end alveoli the vascularized surfaces of these lungs are in the form of nearly parallel tubules extending into air-sacs within the hollow bones of the arms and legs, rather as in birds, this circumstance accounting at least in part for the animal's very light volume-to-mass ratio. There are no vocal cords as such; any vocalization appears to be generated by a cartilaginous box located at the point where the bronchi diverge to the two lungs. This box is intricately muscled and of complex construction, but I am unable to determine its exact workings . . .

The heart is large, four-chambered, with the venous blood entering the left—auricle?—rather than the right as in terrestrial mammals . . . blood is red, indicating presence of some iron-based hemoglobin

analogue (no green blood in this alien monster!) . . .
thickness of arterial walls combined with the rest of
the cardiopulmonary apparatus suggests a constant
high level of physical activity which, coupled with
the apparently somewhat insulative pelt, indicates
endothermy—constant body temperature maintained
metabolically, as in mammals and birds.

Digestive apparatus is strikingly consistent with
Colonel Corson's initial impression of an obligate and
near-perfect carnivore. Teeth are compressed-paral-
lelogram in cross-section, triangular in lateral aspect,
offering an overall impression of knifeblades; nowhere
is there evidence of an ability to chew. The jaws are
merely shears, although of a degree of efficiency not
approached in any terrestrial animal of my acquaint-
ance; indeed, minus the presence of several rows,
the dental apparatus most resembles that of sharks.
Teeth appear to be replaced as they wear out; I was
able to locate several new teeth sagittal to and beneath existing teeth, and a new tooth was apparently
in the process of replacing one recently lost . . .

Any chewing or grinding of food appears to be a
function of a gizzard, a highly muscular gastric mill
lined with a horny abrasive integument apparently
designed to comminute food . . . there is a true crop
above the gizzard, suggesting that these animals are
able to eat large quantities of food at once, to digest
at leisure later, or perhaps to carry same to their
young . . . intestinal system is short, adding to the
impression of total and obligate carnivory . . .

Oddly, we're unable to locate any trace of internal
or external structures indicating sex or reproductive
mode, this being the most alien of our specimen's
very foreign aspect. Could such a complex organism
have simply cloned itself in some way?

Our overall impression is one of prodigious strength,

grace, agility and endurance coupled with a rather daunting complex of specializations indicating a near-perfect physical adaptation to hunting—or fighting—even minus the aid of tools or weapons. This, coupled with the animal's alleged toolmaking proclivities and the impressive nature of the artifact *Hwiliria,* promises a most formidable being in life.

CHAPTER 11

Meeting of Minds

After the dissection/autopsy, fatigue had set in almost unexpectedly. The "night" of *Hwiliria* found another splendid meal awaiting them, and eating encouraged sleep; overloaded with new impressions, all four castaways fell into unconsciousness on mossy vegetation outside what they'd come to call the Mausoleum.

And *dreamed*, horribly; surely, there was a spare and efficient beauty about the creature they'd examined. But in sleep, the thing seemed to visit them all, and in sleep it was huge, towering monstrously above tiny fleeing people. In sleep it was terror itself, a terror that seemed somehow familiar, as if such aliens had chased them all their lives. . . .

But in the morning the fear dissipated; they were fed again, gorgeously, and again exhorted to follow an Egg aft across the alien landscape of spiny vegetation and distantly-spaced, roofless stone-ringed structures.

Charon's Egg used the birdwhistle language, the speech of *whileelin*, the self-name of the dead makers of *Hwiliria*. In their minds, the whistled "whileelin" translated effortlessly as "people," allaying their fears but little; all pondered the specimen's claws and teeth, its potential diet, their disturbing dreams of the night before. Diet.

"Yes, whileelin are carnivores," said the Egg. "But so are you, if you can get meat; you evolved as hunters and trappers. All toolmakers in my experience have done so; one needn't have overmuch flexibility of intellect to hunt leaves and grasses, eh?" But Charon had little success in calming them.

Despite the Egg's blandishments, even Jennifer was lost in a troubled silence; there was little human about the thing she'd dissected yesterday. It had weighed on her mind, depressing her more this morning than before—for according to Charon, hadn't these things built this mighty world-construct? And if so, did their efforts not make all the human endeavor seem puny? Indeed, did not Charon's very existence suggest that humanity was primitive, its works but toys in the greater scheme of things?

Toolmaker Koan. Perhaps Charon was correct in surmising that humanity, aided by these—these things—might transcend the Koan. But oddly, for all the immensity of *Hwiliria*, there were no roads, indeed, no structures in the place, unless one counted the ring-walled "temples" and the like now distantly visible in all directions. Did the things live underground? Or did it never rain on *Hwiliria*? If so, then how could the vegetation survive?

Her mind reeled with questions, and involuntarily she shuddered. No filming, now; she worried about tape footage, and a front of blue-gray nimbus crept across the "sun" as they topped another world-encircling ridge. The day was oddly colorless, and a sharp, cool breeze stirred the pine-like trees. Below them on the newly visible plain stood a greater "temple," like yesterday's Mausoleum but bigger, far bigger, and surrounded by a higher wall. The central structure appeared roofless, its exact center-point marked by a tall obelisk, but the outer walls gave no view of the interior. It might as well have been a fortress as a temple. In the overcast, the flaring circular wall looked even more ancient than yesterday's, squat, hunkering in the dark green vege-tation like some high-edged crater ringing a stagnant pond, the central temple-building a blotched central mound. She wondered, why the overcast? Some dra-matic concoction of Charon's? But this deserved a tape!

She unlimbered her vidcam and a fresh data dom-ino as they filed down the slope. The four spread out instinctively, as if preparing for battle, on the flatland before the temple gate. Here they would meet the aliens, and here they busied themselves with the same tripods they'd used in dissection the day be-fore. Jennifer felt chilled again recalling that work, and recalling Charon's cheerful comment that the aliens would have had a similar human specimen to examine. Which of them would it be?

"Now," said Charon, "here perhaps I err again; I'm gifted at error, methinks. But perhaps not. The Koan suggests that toolmaker species never meet in the natural course of things; they're too inept, too short-lived as species. So—I arrange an introduction. Am I wrong? Have I loved too long, that I play with life hopelessly?" The voice quavered, its humanity mo-mentarily growing; never yet had it seemed quite so mad, so alone. "Ah, well, one warning: protocol is extremely important to these folk, as it is to you. They'll wish to address a leader at first; their own leader will do most of their talking. Can you agree among yourselves?"

"I now represent the United People's Republics of Earth," said Benai. "Perhaps it would be useful if I—"

"Uh, I don't really go for that," said Corson. "Speak for us? I can at least speak for the Free World; it's my position as ranking—"

"Well, sir, maybe we ought to try something else," suggested Pike. "The doctor here, she had a more sympathetic view of strange animals from the start, and she might—"

"Oh, I can't really, I don't have much experience with out-and-out protocol," said Jennifer nervously, but she smiled and looked pleased nonetheless.

"I must offer a warning here," said Charon. "Twenty-first-century human politics are inapplicable in this unique situation. You'll be dealing with what the Americans used to call 'male chauvinist pigs' of a sort, in whose societies gender roles are hard-wired and inalterable. Male whileelin defend territories; males meet strangers and do the initial talking. They'll quickly detect your sex, Doctor, and may prove difficult if you were the initial spokesperson for your species. All animals are difficult in one way or another, yourselves most especially. And they'll know you better later. I'm sorry, but that's the way it is. Ahem."

Feeling a mixture of relief and annoyance, Jennifer couldn't help but admire Charon's embarrassed throat-clearing noise. For a being lungless and throatless, it was a nice touch—but Charon was grandmaster of nice touches, whatever its real motives.

"Well, lady and gentlemen?" Charon's voice grew impatient. Another Egg glinted faintly in the darkness of the temple's distant doorway. "Now choose, little animals, or I choose for you!"

"I still believe—" said Benai.

"Well, *I* don't," said Corson. "*I* think that—"

"Major Muir." Charon's voice was sharp with com-

mand. "You're an adaptable creature, and comparatively apolitical. *You* will speak for *Homo sapiens*,
'Man the Wise,' leaving that camera with your friends
here."

The irony in Charon's Latin translation was not lost
on Pike. He swallowed once, twice. "Okay, I guess.
Uh, I, ah, I—"

"Walk forward, alone. Stop by that stone there,
fifty meters. The rest of you stay behind until the
major signals you to approach. There's no danger. I
am everywhere. You, Commander Benai, will not
touch your weapon. They understand weapons, and
we cannot have foolishness now. I've waited too long
through foolishness. Go, now, Major, and I go with
you. And be careful to remember one thing."

"What's that?"

"The individual with whom you will first talk has
an obligatory title: he is First in the Chase."

Pike tugged at his collar stretching his jaw experimentally. " 'First in the Chase.' Great, just great."

Jennifer did an odd thing then; she jumped forward, squeezed Pike's hand and kissed him lightly on
the cheek. "Good luck. I think Charon made the
proper choice."

Funny thing, how something like that emboldens a
guy. Pike nodded, smiled. He started walking. Faster.
Look sharp. Military bearing, they called it. I speak
for Man the Wise, I, Pike Muir. Well, they'll get a
good show. And it's only for a minute . . .

He reached the gray stone, a strange stone, carved
flat on top. The Stone of Meeting, right?

Something moved in the temple door. The Egg
that hung there emerged into the gray light, sailing
swiftly and silently toward him, and the Egg that
followed Pike disappeared with the familiar *fump*! of
Charon's comings and goings. Right. No need for two

of 'em now. Stand at ease; that looks good. He clasped his hands behind his back, eyes searching the darkened temple interior. Movement, more movement, and . . .

A great Animal strode swiftly across the stepping stones of the temple pond, a being familiar with those stones, for whose strange feet they'd been laid.

It wore a scarlet crown, a headdress more than Aztec in its height and breadth. No—not worn, it was part of the creature, a shining red fan of pinions—a crest, Pike realized, like that of the dead specimen but much brighter and larger, spread high and wide, a semicircular corona, awesome on that proud aquiline head. . . .

Pike's genitals lurched as if trying to climb into his abdomen. Mind over matter, though. He stood at ease, his teeth clenched behind a carefully expressionless mask hiding his dread.

The creature strode smoothly toward him, its long legs eating the distance in two-meter paces, torso horizontal, tail held rigid and head-high with its fan-tip spread, slender cable-tendoned forearms swinging toward the ground so that the knuckles of its taloned hands nearly brushed the ground. Toothed and striped, an eagle's head held three meters high on a muscle-arched horse's neck, moving in distinct increments, freezing, then snapping forward with each of the animal's deliberate strides, oscillating like the head of a strutting peacock but huge, and with its great lustrous amber-yellow eyes fixed immovably on Pike's own. . . .

It stopped, ten meters away. It wore a collar, a circlet of silvery metal, and nothing else. The crest moved constantly, flaring wider, then dropping slightly, the animal lowering its long arms further until its

knuckles touched the ground between the shining
curved glaives of its mighty inner toes.

It opened its mouth slightly, a pointed pinkish
tongue showing between gleaming even rows of five-
centimeter enamel blades . . .

. . . and *whistled,* a powerful haunting ululation rising and falling in pitch like that of some medieval
rosewood flute, the bird-language Charon had im-
printed on their minds. Pike heard both the whistling
and the creature's words in a similarly musical but
unmistakeable English.

"May we be of one blood, thou and I," said the
deep fluting voice, an orchestral woodwind section
tuning up.

Some ancient Celtic bard in Pike's ancestry seized
the moment—a moment for fine words to match the
awe and pride that flooded him. "If our mighty host,
Charon, speaks truly and well, we are indeed of one
blood."

"Thou speakest as a patriarch to a patriarch, equal
to equal. Know then, equal, that I am Halarridarmar
Horizon-leaper, First in the Chase of the Seeker
Hwiliria. I meet and greet you in the name of my
creche, my fertile brethren, my females and my neuters, those who survive with me."

"I meet and greet you, Halarridarmar Horizon-
leaper, in the name of my associates of the probe-
ships *Expediter* and *Dienbienphu.*" Pike waved toward
the people watching anxiously from the rear; he felt
self-conscious, suddenly, about his pronunciation of
the creature's name, but Charon's translating evidently covered for him. He bowed elaborately, sweeping the imaginary plume of an imaginary hat across
the grass before him.

The woody whistling began again, no movement,
no expression save that bleak and fearsome intensity

evident on the staring eagle face of the First in the Chase. "As my equal, you know that my Home is dead. I mourn, equal, for my Home; I am now patriarch of the subcreche Northrock Crossgene, last patriarch of the Great North Overcreche, whose eggs have lain broken for so long that only the Regurgitator of Souls that you call Charon knows the time's passing. I mourn, I mourn." The scarlet crest folded upon itself, narrowing to a long point; the creature tossed its huge head back, and the crest, always in restless movement, brushed between its shoulders, spread again lifted as high as before as the stony gaze fixed again on Pike's eyes.

"And we mourn with you, First in the Chase, all of us."

"These—your conspecifics—are they equals also?"

"They are equals, First in the Chase."

"Why, then, if they are patriarchs, do they not come forward as equals?" The bony scaled left hand lifted, turned over, "palm" up, and the long taloned middle finger crooked in a surprisingly human come-hither gesture.

Patriarchs? Oh, boy. Pike reached behind him, eyes never leaving those of the alien, and duplicated the gesture. "They come now."

Jennifer was the first to advance, the rest stirring and following. Ah, she was getting the idea now; always watch its eyes, never look away. It's a magnificent thing, too, emanating an unrufflable, oddly appealing hauteur . . . elan, it had, it *was* elan personified, and she began to think she liked it, daunting though it was. She reached Pike's side, the rest falling in around them.

"These are patriarchs? How is it that there is so much variance among you? Your coloring—green, black, blue, white—are these artificial pelts? How is it that you do not establish a visible hierarchy, or dispute the caste among you? Are you of one sub-creche, or many?"

Jennifer fielded this one: "We are of one creche, First in the Chase. All of us."

"And yet you are equals. How odd. We shall have an interesting time." The fluting voice paused; then, without a change in the creature's unblinking gaze, it whistled high and long . . . and six more such animals emerged from the temple, each striding easily across the stones and into the veldt, heads freezing and then thrusting smoothly forward with the rhythm of their high-stepping gaits. Four had crests, crests smaller than those of the First in the Chase and held widespread and low across their backs. The other two wore elaborate metal helmets covering all but their snouts; these brought up the rear, seemingly subservient, their knuckles brushing the spiny turf as they approached.

"My juvenile brethren, Olorromoro and Wilirriwirra, greet you in the name of the subcreche Northrock Crossgene Twelvesquared."

Two of the newcomers stepped forward and whistled formalities translated by Charon into an archaic English: "We abase ourselves, foreign patriarchs, before thy magnificence." Their restless red-quilled crests spread broad, level with the flat tops of their skulls.

"And these are of the creche matriarchate, the Prime Matriarch and her juvenile Second." The First in the Chase indicated with its tail—*his* tail, fan-tipped—two others, dappled slightly along back and sides and with slightly smaller, browner crests but otherwise identical in size and aspect to the First. "And these," pointing with tail-fan closed toward the helmeted individuals, "are neuters." These, faces invisible behind some reflective surface, made no movement; but their hidden stare was as palpable as those of the females, fertile brethren and the First in the Chase, and each human being *felt* like a physical touch the intensity of those seven pairs of lustrously unwinking yellow eyes.

"Have you names," said the First, "that we may address one another?" He stared pointedly at Pike.

"Oh, I'm Charles Muir, uh, Major, Cyber Detachment."

"Colonel C.L. Corson," said Corson, "at your service. Pleased to meet you."

"Oruna Benai, Commander, Deep-Space Weapons Platform, ah, Research Vessel *Dienbienphu.*"

"Jennifer Dawson, Emm Dee."

"You all speak as patriarchs. Are there no neuters among you, no females?"

"*I'*m a female," said Jennifer, piqued. "And surgeon."

"A female that speaks to me as a patriarch! And your crest, such as it is, is far longer than those of these males—unless some of you are sterile—"

"None that *I* know of," growled Benai.

"Nope," said Corson, "not me."

"Have you no castes at all, then? Are you truly equals, and all fertile?"

"Every damned one of us," said Pike, feeling without seeing it a vague wave of contempt from the First in the Chase. He too was piqued. The damned things'd better learn some more quick . . . but then, Charon didn't prepare any of us very well for this . . .

"Although appearances might seem to deny it," said the First, eyes staring down at Pike's, "we're all people—or so the Regurgitator of Souls avers. We are also told that we share body chemistry sufficiently so that we might eat . . . one another's food . . . It is customary among us to share with our equals a meal;

the first, and most important, thing done. *Hwiliria's*
fauna is said to have been somewhat modified for
your convenience, yet we're told we can still find
suitable prey. Shall we hunt?"

"Hunt? Charon's been feeding us pretty well here,
and we . . ." Pike looked up at the Egg; something
going on, here, some undercurrent of nuance . . .

"Well, Major, etiquette is important, isn't it?" said
the Egg. "And, as one might guess from their bearing
and physiology, whileelin are *always* hungry. You
may watch them hunt, while I prepare you a meal
more to your own liking. Whileelin don't cook their
food, you know. Let us return to last evening's bivouac."

"Oh. Well then, First in the Chase, if you see
anything suitable for a meal, by all means . . ." Pike
made a gesture he felt to be expansive and generous,
and began walking back up the ridge. The rest of his
folk followed, and the whileelin swiftly deployed themselves about the human group rather disturbingly
like an outlying guard, the First in the Hunt taking
the lead, his two fertile brethren flanking, the females and neuters bringing up the rear, whistling
and chattering oddly among themselves. They smelled
odd, rank, and Pike was reminded of some trained
ferrets he'd once seen—and smelt. . . .

The humans clustered in a walking knot, uneasily
looking about them as their escorts, whistling, scanned
the *Hwilirian* "valley." Suddenly Jennifer cocked her
head, whispered to Pike: "Can you *hear* that?"

"That hooting—it's all I *can* hear."

"No, no. I hear something—not quite hear it—
it's the neuters! They're talking to each other, in my
head!" She pressed her hands to her ears for a moment, shook her head.

Pike glanced behind him; both of the helmeted

things were watching Jennifer intently, their heads remaining precisely level despite their striding gait.

"I *hear* them," she said. Can't you?"

"Citizen Doctor," said Benai, "are you quite well?"

"*They* hear *me*," gasped Jennifer. "They can—but only when I think *at* them—they hear me!"

"I've done well." The Egg, pleased again. "Human, ah, sexual dimorphism; the female brain is different from that of males. I took advantage of that difference during your reconstitution, Doctor; human females have more of a diplomatic sense. With modification, you're able to communicate with our neuter friends, across a short distance."

"Telepathy?" Jennifer felt around her head, wiggled an earlobe with her fingers.

"Oh, no, no magic! The neuters—you'll learn more soon. But they communicate through their helmets, across the radio spectrum. I've merely given you a transceiver of a sort. Your males—why, their minds are poorly organized for such an addition; I'd the devil of a time simply giving them the ability to translate speech."

Corson glanced conspiratorially at Jennifer, whispered out of the corner of his mouth. "What're they saying?"

"Difficult—just snatches of talk—astrogation? I don't know, exactly—but they hear me, they've quite shut up. Horrible sensation, I feel invaded. Charon, what've you done to me?"

"A short-lived phenomenon, Doctor. They only 'hear' you when you wish, and in a few weeks' time the ability will have dissipated—can't have you tuning into some of that frightful stuff your own species pours into the radio spectrum!"

"Can't hear a thing from them now." Jennifer con-

tinued pulling at her earlobes speculatively, as if the
secret of her new talent lay therein.

The Egg increased its speed a bit, rising higher.
"They quite understand your new ability, Doctor;
they're keeping their counsel for—a more propitious
time."

Whileelin walk fast; their long legs carried them
well ahead of the human contingent. They spread out
in a vanguard, whistling sonorously, Charon translating: "The view is good, First in the Chase, and so
will be the running."

"Indeed, Wilirriwirra; one wonders what sort of
game awaits us, whether it's fleet and sweet, or tough
and slow, or somehow well defended."

"Here, now, First in the Chase, is game." The one
called Olorromoro whistled, freezing in midstep. As
did all the whileelin; only their heads bobbed, swiftly
and jerkily, as if by moving their long necks they
hoped better to triangulate on their prey.

"See," said the Egg. "The Earthly mammals leave
the environment I prepared for them; perhaps I'll
never understand living things."

"Kudu! Or something like 'em." Jennifer placed a
hand on Pike's forearm, her voice a whisper. "Let's
see what they do."

"Very much like kudu," said Benai. "Unless these
whileelin have weapons, they've little hope of catching such fleet antelope."

"Don't be too sure," murmured Corson. "Watch."

Almost two hundred meters away, a herd of about
eight large brown antelope browsed among some
thorny bushes; one sported a striking pair of spiraling
horns and a long beardlike growth of hair on the
undersurface of its neck. "The bull," whispered Benai.
"He'll be the last to run."

The antelope detected the unlikely group at ridge-top; their heads lifted in unison, and they watched.

"Alert and worthy prey," whistled Wilirriwirra. "Shall we perform for our human friends a Grateful Acceptance?"

It might be more proper to enact the Avaricious Reach," ventured Olorromoro.

"Considering the distance between us, and the unknown nature of the prey, I must opt for the Grateful Acceptance," fluted the First, head still bobbing side to side and up and down, yellow eyes fixed on the shuffling and stamping antelope.

"I defer with delight to the First in the Chase," whistled Wilirriwirra.

"Now," said the First and, tilting his head back, trumpeted: "Aaahlooo," a sound like a French horn crossed with a Diesel airhorn.

The First and neuters remaining still, the other whileelin split into two pairs, one male and one female to each. "Split" is the word, too, for they ran, and the humans had never seen such a run. Onward, out, to the sides away from the little antelope herd in an encircling pass they ran in a smooth and graceful pair of arcs, seemingly floating above the grass, heads and tails held high, crests narrowed and flat, forearms outstretched to the front, feet pounding the earth in three-meter strides, thumpthumpthumpthump, the sound diminishing as they ate the distance . . .

"God, they must be going more than a kilometer a minute," whispered Jennifer.

"Damn well more'n a klick a minute," whispered Corson, "and we better make sure those things never get to chasing *us*."

The antelope began to run then, leaping high over the brush, scattering . . . but the whileelin closed inexorably on the herd like the drawstrings of a purse,

heading them off, the frightened herbivores bunch-
ing back toward the First in the Chase—who himself
suddenly took off in that astounding run, straight for
the herd, *Aaahlooing* like the brass section in some
unearthly orchestra.

"It's a kind of dance, isn't it? What did they call it?
The 'Grateful Acceptance'? It must be the name of
the strategy, a step in a dance of the hunt!" Flushed
and excited, Jennifer craned her neck, an involuntary
half-smile on her face.

The First in the Chase leaped high in the air, his
entire five-meter length turning impossibly end over
end, fanned tail waving, and landed amidst the scattering antelope. He leaped again, impossibly agile,
almost flying, and again, never seeming to touch a
single antelope . . . yet two, then three, staggered
and fell, and Pike could see in the side of one of them
a horrific rent, the bowels protruding glossily, drag-
ging in the grass.

The foot-glaives. Those great retractile ankle-talons
had brushed the antelope, opening them like the sacs
of protoplasm they were, and in an instant the other
fertile whileelin closed in a flurry of dust and up-
rooted clumps of grass . . .

And it was over, as suddenly as it had begun. Each
whileelin lifted in its taloned hands an antelope, although the beasts must have weighed a hundred
kilograms apiece; the First in the Chase held two,
one in each hand, fingers twitching convulsively, the
talons imbedding deeper and deeper in the brown
and faintly striped hides. He held them as if they
weighed no more than rabbits, and strode swiftly
back, a faint panting from his narrow nostrils, followed by the other whileelin, fertiles with crests
erect, neuters silent, helmeted, pacing easily along
with their hand-held burdens.

"See," whistled the First, holding his catch lightly in the air. "A noble prey; it's lovely, hunting the open ground. Yours is a kindly world, if the Regurgitator of Souls has duplicated its prey animals accurately." He dropped one antelope, seized the other at the shoulders with both hands, placed it on its back on the ground between his feet. The scimitar-toes sank into its belly, and with a single swift lifting motion of his hands he opened the corpse, its entrails spilling in a slippery pile on the grass. He dropped the gutted beast, repeated the process as easily with the other, his fertile brethren, females and the neuters doing likewise with their own.

"Those guys are *good*," whispered Corson. "They *know* what they're *doing*."

"Too good for comfort," mumbled Pike.

"Charon makes a serious mistake, hoping to mingle things like that with human beings," growled Benai.

"As my equals," whistled the First in the Chase, "would you share?" Deftly fishing about in the piles of entrails with his long middle fingers, he impaled the hearts—still twitching with galvanic impulse—on his two middle-finger talons, holding the grisly trophies toward the humans.

"Uh, no thanks," said Pike.

"Indeed, your teeth are small and flat, like those of a herbivore, although the Regurgitator of Souls tells us that you are not." The creature spread his crest higher and wider, opened his mouth and popped the hearts in like grapes, the toothy opening closing with a "whop." He gulped once, the movement visible in his long neck. "Yes. The Regurgitator of Souls is correct. The chemistry of our worlds is appealingly similar." He touched the ground with his golfball-sized knuckles again, a salute. "Top of the food chain to you!"

"Yes—well, shall we eat?" Jennifer spoke brightly, smiling, vaguely amused at the discomfiture of her human associates. Corson and Benai, at least, would not eat much after the spectacle of a whileelin hunt. Jennifer Dawson would, however; she'd seen worse things done by human beings—by people like Benai and Corson—to human beings. Compared to that, these whileelin were simply honest predators, their hunt itself a thing of magnificence in keeping with their own weird beauty. Excepting, perhaps, the helmeted neuters, the silent ones, whose whispering now and then intruded mechanically on her mind; they were bleakly curious, soundlessly keeping their counsel, and they didn't respond when she tried to "reach" them. Had Charon indeed blundered again?

Followed by the others, she walked down the slope toward the distant table, familiar now, groaning with Charon's offerings. The table that followed them everywhere; there'd been a fairy tale about such tables.

"See," whistled the First in the Chase, "how they follow this female. She must be a formidable being."

"She is," whistled the Egg above; "she is."

Pike caught up to her, walked alongside. "I don't know, lady. They're either totally emotionless or they're sizing us up for steak tartare or something. Those striped faces, those staring yellow eyes—I never know *what* they're thinking."

Jennifer laughed, muffling her mouth with her hand. "Surely, Pike, you understand by now?"

"I do?"

She reached out, scruffled his hair like a kid's, a curiously intimate gesture. "Of course. You see their crests, how they're always moving, widening, narrowing, flicking up and down?"

"Right . . ."

"Emotional expressions, you twit! With faces like

that you don't express emotions; you do it with the crest, with posture! They're *unbelievably* emotional, skittish as birds, sensitive as highly-bred horses!" She made an opening motion with her slender hands. "I can read 'em like a book. Far more easily, Major, than I can read you."

"Well, they're, uh, a longer book . . ."

"Not at all; their covers simply aren't hasped shut like yours. Like mine, too, but I think the hasps are coming loose out here . . ."

"Jennifer, old Charon—I don't think it knows what it's doing."

"I'm laughing—but you might be right. I'm scared to death, in a way: those neuters. I'll have to work on this—hearing of mine, see what they're *for*."

And down they walked, vanguard of the strangest procession ever seen by human or whileelin, by "people" anywhere. Eleven bipeds of two unlikely kinds, whistling and chattering, some carrying prey, others spreading around a table loaded with elegant viands, and above them a multicolored Egg, shining, as the cylindrical sun of *Hwiliria* broke at last through a slaty overcast and warmed the dark-green veldt.

CHAPTER 12

Song of Sorrow

Ferrier of souls; regurgitator of souls. Sole agent of the Metastasis, and pleased as punch with this First Contact it had engineered, Charon watched and translated with rare glee. What marvellous things are animals, and how varied–how lively, vital, dangerous and delightful!

But always it had a goal, the Metastasis, and the dual-species conversation required nudging in that hallowed direction. The attendant Egg therefore dropped lower, hanging among them, fluting in the measured and musical patriarchal mode. "Sing now, First in the Chase, of the flight of *Hwiliria* and of your meeting with me so long ago. And in so doing, tell these humans the tale of the last days of your kind."

"Heard and understood, Regurgitator of Souls." The First in the Chase stood, lifting his head and lowering his crest to brush his shoulders, contracting it to a point that Jennifer now knew was the expression of abject misery. The rest of the whileelin did likewise, knowing the tale all too well.

Jennifer pointed a mike at the creatures, while Pike held a linked vidcam. The story was brief; they'd guessed its drift. Another variant of the Toolmaker Koan.

It was a mournful brassy voice, the whileelin patriarchal modality, like a slow medieval dance. The four humans found themselves swept up in the sound, hypnotized by the Koan's unfolding.

"Home was a kindly place, and bright with water, flecked with islands large and small, oh, warm, oh, rich with fodder for our beasts. In ancient times the people sailed on ships, diverging, taking islands for their creches and islands for their beasts, and the two were separate, the pastoral islands and the creche-islands, as is fit. And the creches thrived, their neuters waxing fat in the morning, for the neuters ate well to learn. The neuters learned of the breeding of food-beasts and the building of boats and the working of medicine, good things, things bespeaking plenty. So the creches grew, many at first, on many islands.

"In the kinder time the pastoral islands were loved and preserved, inhabited only by food-animals. The clever neuters, always hungry, bred wild predators into tame, using them to herd and drive the food-beasts. The time was good, and the world was fat; good fortune was with us.

"But as the neuters waxed fat and their numbers grew, they demanded of their Patriarchates the raising of more neuters, for the growth of knowledge requires the presence of minds, more minds; and the Patriarchates, seeing this as good, raised more neuters—converting food-islands to islands of neuters and learning.

"And the clever neuters, learning, required more food of their Patriarchates; but whence the food? It must come at the expense of other creches, and the neuters advocated the trade of food; but each creche required food, and space, and so the neuters advocated the training of more neuters to commandeer their food for them; and the fighting-neuter was born, a wonderful and terrifying thing, to collect resources from other creches.

"And the neuter armies grew, and learned, and the pastoral islands grew few and disputed. The neuters, questing, devised riding-mounts from food-beasts; riding-mounts of great size and swiftness, that grew their own shields behind which riders might hide. They trained their herding-predators, wild and hungry, to advance before them into battle, while on their awesome mounts the fighting-neuters rode with lances. And this tale, but moments in the telling, is one of many thousand years' passing, during which whileelin grew powerful and took command of the planetary food-chain of Home.

"But this was not sufficient; neuter numbers grew, and lances gave way to projectile-launchers, machines of vast efficiency that killed over distance. Forgotten at last, save among the fertiles of the Patriarchates, was the Order of Talons, the honorable dispute with words and hands and feet, as was intended of whileelin by the world that made them. The neuters found the power of steam, and fuel for their steam, and built fast ships, sailing among the pastoral islands and disputing them at sea, for the Patriarchates still had wisdom to prevent the war on land that would destroy eggs and fodder. But whence the food, whence the food?

"So it was discovered that the fertiles stood in the way. Fat clever neuters struck at the eggs of the patriarchs and matriarchs, preserving those of them that agreed with their neuters, breaking those of them that disagreed. Unopposed now, neuters devised land-war, and with it the helmeted neuter, for now the machine was with us, and those who operated machines were neuter, their helmets of iridium linking them intimately with machines of war, fire-spouters, land-creepers, flying machines.

"Hence then the rise of the Overcreches, the Southland Overcreche and the Northland Overcreche, each astride a thousand islands, each wishing the world of Home for its own genes. And the pastoral islands diminished, and the creches grew; the beasts of the seas were hunted to extinction, and wildlife disappeared, and Home became a place only of whileelin, and the beasts on which they fed.

"And the clever neuters invented, tinkering, altering the limits of the mind.

"Came then the time of Space, when the neuters of both Overcreches invented missiles that might strike across vast distances; the missiles could also lift mass into space, and in space, the neuters cried, would be the proper place for weapons. And their Patriarchates, now two mighty Overcreches in number, agreed; and space was filled with machines of war and clever helmeted neuters to direct them.

"And in space the clever neuters tinkered more, devising great ships that they built from the flying stones so abundantly given; and, clever, they sought to live there, hoping one day, each for its own Overcreche, to reinhabit Home and thrive, and destroy the other Overcreche forever, its eggs, its genes, its memory. They demanded of their Patriarchates new eggs, to be hurled into space and hatched aboard the great ships; they took eggs of the Patriarchates, and eggs of food-beasts, and eggs of the modified predators that herded those beasts, and sought to create habitats, seizing and collecting spacerock to build sufficient room for our kind.

"So it was that the North Overcreche was petitioned, and in turn petitioned the noble subcreche Northrock Crossgene; and the eggs of my ancestors left Home forever, punched into the void to dwell aboard the Seeker *Hwiliria* to await the retaking of Home for our people. And the South Overcreche also built a Seeker, filling it with fierce neuters and a nucleus of fertiles—to wait.

"So in the Seekers ten generations dwelt, in each a Patriarchate raising young and neuters to carry on our kind; each was vast, but could support few for all its vastness, for whileelin must roam, and breathe, and hunt.

"Eleven generations of Northrock Crossgene Fifty-two, I and my fathers before me, held forth on *Hwiliria*; and the limits of *Hwiliria* constrained us in our numbers.

"And when the endtime came, when over the cries of the fertiles of Patriarchates North and South their clever neuters came to grapple at last, the North, my own, alas! caused little stars, invented by neuters, to blossom among the creches and manufactories of the South, which responded in kind. And all was lost, and dying, and in the space around Home the dark blossomed with the neuters' last hate—in the final dying the spacefaring neuters of the South did seize a great rock from space and direct it in their madness upon Home, and it struck and flashed into nothingness, the oceans steaming in Home's agony, the skies convulsed in clouds of gray and yellow. A world-storm came forth, and even we far away in *Hwiliria* saw the lightning's flickering among the poisoned wrack. Home rejected us, and denied our return, and the neuters of *Hwiliria* struck at the South Seeker, causing her to crash into the world-storm of Home.

"And then the Patriarch my father cried aloud in

his agony, and called upon me to direct *Hwiliria* away from Home, outward into the void beyond the planets; he clenched his own throat with his talons then, and died, and in my own madness I obeyed and we fled, pursued by the last of the raving space-sailing helmeted neuters and their insensate machines.

"And as far away from our kindly sun the cold crept on us, we found the Eggs of the Regurgitator of Souls, waiting, and the Regurgitator spoke to us of possible futures, and of a long sleep of the soul; and we listened, and slept; and however long ago that was, all this is but yesterday to us in the telling, barely three suns' passing since we came upon those shining Eggs in the dark."

"And now we mourn, we mourn for the passing of my father, and of all our fathers and mothers, the Patriarchates and Matriarchates of old, and for the murder of our kindly Home by the greed of our own kind, we mourn, we mourn, ahrlooonm, we mourn . . ."

The cry was taken up by all the whileelin, a mournful trumpeting, wolfish lamentation that chilled the blood of the human listeners, even Corson blinking, biting his lower lip in the horror of the tale.

The eerie crying stopped, its echoes dying in the vastness of Charon's memory.

"The Toolmaker Koan," fluted the Egg. "You understand my unwillingness to see this koan demonstrated again. Two of these Seekers they built, only two. And, although each seems a little world to you humans . . ." The Charon-voice quavered eerily. "Unknowing, always living systems strive for the Metastasis; always, it seems, they fail at the last instant. But I think we hold the key to transition. Perhaps *I* do, at any rate. We shall see."

CHAPTER 13

Egg and Meat

No sleep—no need.

The whileelin had disappeared, at a run as they seemed to do everything, no doubt to ponder in their own way the survivors of *Expediter* and *Dienbienphu*, leaving the human castaways to a marathon post-meal post-mortem sharing experiences of their new acquaintances; each had had questions, and been questioned, through hours of eating and talk with the whileelin.

They sat at the inevitable table and chairs—chairs, they knew now, carved by Charon in the likeness of whileelin. The talk centered, for the moment, on origins. If whileelin came from an Earthlike world, as obviously they did despite their outward differences, couldn't space be full of such worlds? The possibility of Earthlike planets in abundance seized the human minds, and conversation fed itself merrily.

"We're suited to this gravity. So, since whileelin built *Hwiliria*, and *Hwiliria* closely duplicates Earth gravity, they come from an Earth-sized planet." Pike shrugged. "I'm no astrophysical expert, but the light

199

here more or less matches Sol's, so this home star was likely a yellow dwarf, right? Maybe even G2. Hell—with the close similiarities in body chemistry that lets them eat all this Earthly game, I figure we'd have to have predicted all that anyway. And a liquid-water planet indicates that they'd have been near the same distance from their sun, the temperate distance. But what else can you say? If Charon's been in Sol system at least four million years, long enough to remember your ape-men, sir, I can't imagine any stars' being close enough to their old positions for either the whileelin or us to locate their homeplace."

"Uh-huh." Corson stood, paced slowly back and forth. "The First said it was a temporary madness made them try to run away. He thought he'd 'find another place,' and just set off into the dark, where Charon found them. They were all kind of crazed, I guess. I would be, too—but I still don't like anything about them."

"You understood the implications of their numbers aboard *Hwiliria*, didn't you, gentlemen?" Oruna Benai gritted his teeth, shook his head. "It carried—what did he say? 'More than thrice twelve-cubed walkers', I think, which translates to, uh . . ."

"Fifty-one hundred and eighty-four," said Pike "at least, I guess. But that's an awful lot of whileelin. And food, too, if they ate then like they eat now. This is a serious ship."

"I do believe I'm glad they're extinct," said Benai. "I wonder where the rest of the crew went . . ."

"Charon'll awaken the rest as we proceed," said Jennifer. "Most of them are neuters; we've already met the principals."

Benai watched Corson's pacing, back and forth, back and forth. "These neuters concern me, Doctor. All the First and his, ah, 'juvenile sibs' would discuss was

history, ancestry, that sort of thing—no mention of technology, no interest in weaponry. Whe I asked, the First
said that 'Those are the provinces of neuters,' and no
more. Citizen, you do recall a discussion we had some
time ago, about Captain Fitzroy and his naturalist?"

"How could I forget," laughed Jennifer. She'd spent
her own meal with the neuters, which communicated
with one another and with her in that radio-language
that only the surgeon could hear. "I've learned rather
more from the poor neuters than you did from the
First; he's bound genetically into a limited role. The
two neuters are—well, 'assigned' to the First and the
Prime Matriarch; the word for the relationship translates as 'shadows.' It's a fascinating tale, the whole
thing. Their social organization, their two languages;
the fertiles, their whole culture's bound up in reproduction—like any, I guess. But the neuters themselves are different, a marvelous pair of talkers: they've
a good knowledge of the evolution of their own species. They're the academics of the lot, and terrifically
nimble in thinking. It's a caste system. Nothing like
anything of our own—nothing like India, say, no
simple social constraint. It's an artificial modification
of their maturation biology, an entirely strange thing.
The fertiles don't use tools; they live only to hunt and
reproduce, and they're a tiny minority. The neuters
run things, like *Hwiliria*, in order that the fertiles
can do as they please—continue the race."

With eager patience, she explained as best she
could. Reproduction among the whileelin was sexual
and fertilization internal as among higher Earthly
animals; like many of these, whileelin females lay
eggs. The eggs were laid in an ancestrally-sanctioned
place translating as a "creche," the creche also being
the prime unit of social grouping among whileelin. In
ancient times, wars were fought by fertiles over

favorable creche-places, not only as a place of egg-laying; all hatched there were said to be of one creche. Later, creches divided into subcreches and were subsumed into overcreches as populations grew and spread.

A clutch of eggs was twelve in number, twelve eggs each about ten centimeters long being laid in a sitting by a fertile female; any variance from that twelve was cause for dismay, and among some the practice had been to destroy such unusual clutches entirely. "But then," she added, "in some human groups it was customary to kill malformed infants—so we're not so far off."

The eggs were laid in soft brown sand of a special sort highly valued and artificially duplicated by whileelin technology. The laying was done in a specific geometric pattern, each creche's or "family's" pattern varying from the others'. The sun-warmed sand heated the eggs during incubation, females turning them periodically with their hands to ensure even warming over a period that Charon translated as just less than two Earthly months.

"Which is all well and good," said Jennifer. "There're birds that incubate their eggs belowground—the mallee fowl of Australasia is a good example. In all this, the whileelin parallel a number of Earthly reproductive strategies. It's when they hatch that the difference begins."

"How's that?" Corson broke off his pacing, resettled himself in his chair and thoughtfully cut himself a cooling slice of Charon's excellent ham.

"Well, they hatch more or less at the same time, all the eggs in a creche, and the clutch of young are miniatures of their parents—they have teeth, and can run from the moment of hatching. Miniature brains, too, of course; not much room for intelligence in something emerging from a twelve-centimeter egg! They're born to hunt. The infants can't be educated. They just start out, at high speed, and in the old days—before what we'd call civilization, I'd guess— the entire clutch of youngsters began to fight among themselves! They hunted and they fought through what's called the Fifth Moult, when they were nearly adult size. In what they call 'primitive societies,' by Fifth Moult there were ordinarily only two young- sters remaining from a clutch—their having killed all the others by the age of about ten of our years, you see."

"But that's barbarous! It's an insult to—to their own reproductive success . . . isn't it?" Benai's eyes widened in shock.

"Not exactly. Among our own birds of prey the same sort of thing often happens. A mother eagle may lay two eggs, but the first to hatch often kills its sibling on hatching. It's then better-fed, growing to greater size and strength than it would have had the parents' resources been split between two young."

"Ah. And the mother? Doesn't she try to save the youngsters from one another?"

"Originally, no. Her resources, after all, were bet- ter spent seeking food and protecting the wild young from other predators. She initially takes them on short excursions from the nest, brings them the equiv- alent of large insects and other little animals much as a cat does with growing kittens. As they grow, though, they become wilder, going off on their own, fighting and hunting . . . and at that stage the females are ready to lay another clutch. From the adult point of view, it was deemed well and good that they should eat one another that way—a 'better product,' you know, resulted from the competition." She chuckled. "A sort of Arabesque practicality."

"Another parallel," said Pike. "The fertile sibs tell me that adult males guard the creches and hunt big game."

"Right," said Jennifer. "Otherwise they never involve themselves with creche life except during the mating season, which is once every year for any one female. A prosperous patriarch might have many females in his creche."

"Eagh," Corson said. "They just let the kids kill one another? None of this mother-love stuff?"

"I'm no mother myself, Colonel—I can understand, a bit. I rather gather that early during their evolution, the period of sibling rivalry was an inborn population-control system. One can't have all twelve young from each clutch *maturing*; think of the problem with a twelve-fold population increase with each generation, especially in an obligate top-of-the-food-chain carnivore!"

"Good God," said Benai. "And how did they educate the little devils?"

"Well, 'little devils' seems as good a usage as any in the case of whileelin babies; they're born with the full complement of hunting instincts only. As I said, their brains are small. They're ineducable, and they're not even named. They're not toolmakers in the least; they'd seem almost a second species to us. But they're born with a sort of language, a full grammatical apparatus and words that fill in the gaps automatically as they grow. Not the language we hear the fertiles using with us; it's called 'crechetalk,' because it's used in the creche, inborn. Crechetalk is the basis for the faster, birdwhistle language of the neuters. They retain it throughout their sequence of moults."

"Moults?" Corson sat heavily in his chair. You mean to tell me they *moult*, like birds—like *chickens*?"

"Oh, yes," said Jennifer. "Intriguing, this moulting: a shedding of the pelt during periods of astonishingly fast growth. It's central to whileelin development, governing all their neurological wiring." Flustered, excited, she spread her hands. "Fertiles of both sexes reach reproductive age after Ninth Moult. The fascinating part is what happens between *Fifth* and Ninth Moult, between about ten and twenty years. It's a time of—well, of what I guess I'd have to call almost total metamorphosis. Like in butterflies, perhaps, only neurological."

She shrugged, bit her lip. "It's difficult, really, this 'talk' with neuters. They can't—or don't—answer some questions, their response is something like that military slang, DNC: 'Does Not Compute.' They're elements in a larger whole, a whole that isn't here— yet. Bothers me, that; couldn't help but fear they're holding back."

"And this Fifth Moult," Benai prompted.

"Yes, until Fifth Moult the young are wild animals. Then they suddenly acquire a mental plasticity of a sort we'd only find in small children. The brain begins to grow very quickly, and the crechetalk vocabulary suddenly becomes terrifically open-ended, expansive—yet it's a *wired-in* language, remember, its grammar *and* verbal roots totally inborn. Just as we use a sort of Latin-and-Greek bastard technological language, their adult language is an artificial enlargement of the inborn crechetalk." Enthusiasm lighted Jennifer's eyes again, and she waved her arms delightedly. "I can't quite compare it to anything we know. Fifth Moult's like a rebirth! A wild predatory thing with an automatic brain, the mind of a—of a hawk, suddenly becomes a new thing, a creature like a human child! Fifth Moult is when they get the first equivalent of a name—but it's a number."

"All at once, they turn into toolmakers with culture? Just like that?" Boy, Pike thought, dissections of those growing brains might show us something. . . . Twinge of guilt—he'd never dare suggest *that* aloud.

"Just like that. I believe it's hormonal, some change accompanying that seminal Fifth Moult, which they say actually occurs over a period of about six of our months. The youngster begins to become very experimental, very exploratory, more social, cultural, and tool-oriented. All of the cultural and technological innovation among the whileelin—all of it—during that intermediate period between Fifth and Ninth Moults. Whoever invented fire, whoever improved weapons, whoever invented a new trap, writing, mathematics, space travel, what have you, was someone undergoing that period of enhanced development. By the time of Ninth Moult a whileelin's a real 'person,' educated and social and all that, competent with a sort of stone-age technology, mythological creche and species history, everything that makes a primitive culture . . . it's a sort of delayed neoteny!"

"Give a guy some space," said Corson. "Neoteny? What's that?"

"Neoteny? Childhood, held over. Some people say that a human newborn is sort of an embryonic ape, with far more mental flexibility than an ape's—flexibility that remains with us, if we're lucky, through life. Charon calls us 'dangerous playful animals,' and that's what we are: perpetual children, in a way."

"But the whileelin can't be neotenous," said Pike, "if they're born as miniature adults."

"Right! They couldn't be born with huge brains, because there're limits to egg size, and therefore to infant size. So they go through these moults, and then, at Fifth Moult, the neoteny kicks in, delayed until the individual's big enough to carry and use a big brain . . . and the brain continues to grow until that Ninth Moult, when they reach sexual maturity, and another metamorphosis."

She moved her hands jerkily, up over her head. They develop in steps, genetically ordained jumps. Ninth Moult makes another wiring overlay, just as complete as in the Fifth, but in the form of a sort of mental crystallization, a completion, in which the individual becomes fixed in society: shunted by his or her genes into competent stone-age adulthood. Like the First in the Chase." Jennifer shaped a box with her hands. "Cubbyholed. The males receive a name and social position at Ninth Moult. And a new language, too. The language of the First and his fertile sibs is called 'patriarchal,' as Charon interprets it. Patriarchal is as inborn as crechetalk, but it only appears at Ninth Moult, and only in fertiles. It's a language of the hunt, of territorial behavior, of protocol and strategy; those are the precincts of fertiles only. They all leave the creche and enter the Matriarchate and Patriarchate."

A brief spasm of wry laughter. "The patriarchal's restricted, in a way, ornamental and poetic and sonorous—you know how the First acts. That's part of the language, part of his wiring—he's kind of a born warrior-bard, a superb diplomat. And he has to be—evolution forces that kind of behavior on any social animals well-armed enough to kill one another with a single kick, or a good grip with one hand. Social predators with inborn weaponry are always very ritualized in their disputes; they have to divert aggression, dance it, rather than actually initiate it. So there you have the fertiles, the Matriarchate and Patriarchate, the fierce and courteous rolled into one. To me, the First is at the same time a formidable and a lovely thing."

"Yeah," said Corson, "he does kind of give the impression that his opinions aren't too, uh, amenable to change."

"Oh, he can change, all right; part of the Patriarchate is diplomacy, as I've said. Why, if they'd seen us
before Charon explained us away . . . Well, think of
the antelope!" She laughed again. "But they've adapted
to us quite well so far. The odd part is, that the
whileelin live almost like social insects, like ants or
bees, with neuter workers protecting them and generally running things—technology, culture. The neuters are the important part. They permit the race
their technology, their civilization . . . they're like—
like agriculture! Think about our agricultural revolution, the time about twelve millennia ago when human
beings discovered how to grow stable crops of food—"

But these are, what did you call 'em? Obligate
carnivores? They wouldn't have agriculture." Corson
felt well out of his depth, for all that he'd been born
in an agricultural district.

"Of course not. But they had a revolution of similar
impact. Think what agriculture meant to us!" Her
enthusiasm running away with her, Jennifer stuttered
for a moment. "Sss—cities! Specialization! First farmers and soldiers, then priest castes, craftsmen, metal-
lurgists . . . only with agriculture could we have
developed our technology, only with agriculture could
we have provided the wherewithal for the support of
people who live by experimentation and meditation.
Agriculture permitted the liberation of much of the
human endeavor from what we could call 'support
activity,' the finding of food and maintenance of life
. . . didn't it?"

"Sure. But agriculture . . . they had no agriculture, like I said." Corson wasn't tracking.

"Don't you see? Their counterpart revolution was
the creation of the neuters!" For hundreds of
thousands—millions—of years the whileelin were a
nomadic hunting folk, much as our ancestors were,

but more so. As a species they seem to've had a longer, ah, prehistory; they were around as a language-using folk for more than six million years. And they had an enormous impact on the life around them, hunting a good many species into extinction. But cultural evolution was slow. Wired-in language makes for a conservative culture, and innovation only occurred among those between Fifth and Ninth Moults." Jennifer made a squeezing gesture with her hands: constraint.

"So life began to get hard as the more easily-killed prey disappeared. They remained bound by the in-born wiring of their languages and the initial limits imposed by their inborn hunting-weapons, their claws and teeth. Only a few young reached Fifth Moult in each clutch, and it was those few who were responsible, during their ten years of exploratory development, for any advances in hunting technique they might've had. They were pinned in a very conservative rate of cultural turnover, then, for literally millions of years." She pursed her lips, pondering.

"Their only concession to a home base was the creche—the place where eggs were laid. Their societies might be regarded as cells, as nuclear creches surrounded by roving bands of predatory and territorial males. The creche and the egg are central to their lives, to their religion. With eggs, you have a society very much involved with protection of a fragile and immobile stretch in the life-cycle, no?"

"Yes—but we're that way with infants, too."

"Correct. But think about *their* infants, frightful little animals, dangerous not only to one another but also to eggs; the infants would, in fact, purposefully dig up and destroy eggs of other clutches. It was part of their wiring, a nasty little bit of genetic strategy. Small wonder that the mothers weren't over-concerned about the little buggers' killing one another off."

"And the revolution?"

"Ah! Someone, somewhere well back in their pre-history—probably through traumatic accident of some sort—discovered that if the sexual organs were removed from youngsters at Fifth Moult, they *never underwent the mental crystallization at the Ninth!*"

Benai felt his inner fears quite justified now. "You mean, they made eunuchs, *castrati*, of their own young?"

"Yes. And as *castrati*—and the female equivalent—the young, both male and female, retain their terrific intellectual expansiveness throughout life—which, I gather, lasts about twice a human lifespan. The neuters continue learning at an unbelievable rate the whole time, inventing and communicating and unfolding their culture, along with the flexible crechetalk with which to implement it!" She stood, spread her arms, sat again, eyes glittering. "Of course, you can guess what happened: once the neuters discovered this, they quickly saw the wastefulness of the infant cannibalistic stage and separated the young from one another at birth, permitting *all twelve* to grow to Fifth Moult. The biggest and strongest of a clutch—usually one male and two females—were left intact, and the rest carried off and neutered. An instant technological class. You can see the genetic wisdom; those neuters proving most clever at invention and innovation, of course, furthered the reproductive success of their fertile sibs, as the First calls them. Again, it's like social insects—ants—where thousands of sterile workers build and operate societies for the maintenance of a few fertile relatives!"

"So they started to build cities?" Pike wrinkled his brow, trying to imagine a city of whileelin. Too much. "We don't see much by way of structures here in *Hwiliria*—were they underground, or what? And no

roads . . . it's all kind of rural, a wilderness, especially when you consider thousands of them running
around."

"Think, though, Pike." She smiled. "We're pretty
short-legged and slow compared to whileelin; we keep
to well-defined paths because we must. Once we
learned to domesticate horses and beasts of burden,
we constructed paths for them, too; later we took up
wheeled vehicles requiring smoother, hardened paths.

"But the whileelin were very swift, as you know;
they were among the fastest animals on their planet.
They evolved as predators, efficient at running every
which way, destroying very little plant cover—which,
after all, was necessary fodder for the creatures on
which they lived. A scar in the landscape, a path, is a
painful sight to whileelin, a detriment to their prey.
Therefore they never became road-builders; by the
time the neuters had constructed power-sources that
would have moved swift wheeled vehicles, they'd
also mastered the principles of atmospheric flight.
Whileelin neuters became fliers before they became
drivers, if you will." Feeling a humor in all this, she
laughed aloud.

"Another thing: the Patriarchate and Matriarchate,
the fertiles—they run for the sheer enjoyment of it.
Throughout their technological history, foot-travel has
always marked the privileged fertile components of
whileelin society. Only neuters used machines on
Home, and while on *Hwiliria* you'll only see neuters
using them. Or 'inside' anything, like the warrens
that make up the cylindrical walls of the ship. The
fertiles don't even like roofs over their heads, and
those warrens—" suspicion crept again into her voice.
"I—caught hints of surgery. For the warren-dwellers,
the machine-operators. 'Walkers' means unmodified

neuters; the others are—'rendered incomplete.' They wouldn't say any more."

"Can't say I like the idea of warrens full of neuter whileelin underfoot," muttered Corson, looking carefully at his feet. "Rather have 'em up in the light, like decent folk."

"They were, most of them—in the light. They're more outside-oriented than we are. They couldn't stand crowding, though, no cities as such. Remember, they're all at the top of the food-chain; they were compulsory carnivores, and they needed vast spaces in which to hunt. Their homeworld just couldn't support a lot of city-sized populations. As I understand it, at most only a few hundred million whileelin— mostly neuters, of course—inhabited their world at their peak of population. As their culture became more industrial, they produced huge isolated manufactories, but only neuters went there. Living for whileelin was always open-air. How do the Americans say it? 'Big sky.' "

A note of sadness, now. "They even seem to have a word for 'big sky,' and all these fertile spacefarers keep making up songs about it. They miss it. I gather that all their habitats in space were something like *Hwiliria*: huge compared to ours, with far smaller populations . . ."

"But what *about* the population?" Pike shook his head. "There you are, with twelvefold increments of these gourmandizing things each generation . . ."

"Alas, Pike, there you are. Toolmaker Koan. As I said, the Neuter Revolution, as I'd call it, was to the whileelin what our Agricultural Revolution was to us. A great beginning, but the beginning of an end. Theirs was rather slower, though, because even after that Revolution they continued with less regard for their infants than we have. In times of stress, small creches would permit some of the hatchlings to kill one another. Not too different, as I said: human societies in times of stress show a tendency toward neglect of the young, too; family dissolution—you know, all of you."

A stony silence. Close to home, too close, this— and the surgeon went on. "Toolmaker Koan. As always in any ecological system, some creches had more success than others. These overran the lesser creches, killing adult males, breaking eggs and destroying infants, refertilizing females and using captured neuters to further their own ends. The creches encouraged their neuters in the invention of weapons technologies, as you can imagine, and the civilizations that resulted were rather warlike in substance —like ours."

"Okay, now," said Pike, unease growing, "you're painting this picture, Jennifer, this portrait of an animal—"

"You're talking like Charon," she laughed. "A people, Pike, a *people* just as much as we are, only different."

"A people, then. All right. A people, a people whose individuals require a great deal of space, more than we do, and if they don't get that space, what do they do?"

"As nearly as I understand it they're pretty much insane claustrophobes. They don't like roofs over their heads, they like to run in straight lines when they can. They need space, each of them, as much as we need—water, or exercise."

"Yeah, exercise," said Corson. "And even though I gather they have domesticated food animals, they seem to need to hunt, right?"

"Surely. We have atavistic needs too. We need a

bit of a hunt ourselves—sports, you know. Don't fault them for that."

"Faulting?" Pike's eyes rounded. "Jennifer, don't you see? Charon's setting up this—this Metastasis, and it's supposed to involve a sort of friendly coexistence between us and a species that eats only meat, that requires huge spaces, that reproduces cannibalistic young twelve at a time, that operates on, neuters its own offspring and keeps them around like worker ants. You tell me that the entire caste of adult males is devoted to acquiring territory, posturing and threatening and—"

"Pike, you're getting—"

"Listen. Two species in one solar system. They both require asteroids, volatiles, air, water, space . . ."

"Of which, you know, there're plenty."

"Dammit, Jennifer, for *how long?*"

"Come *on*, Pike, it takes *light* some hours to cross the system! The Oort cloud, why, we haven't even *begun* to—"

"Muir," interrupted Corson, "you're right. Charon's got no soul, no emotions, nothing, and it's setting up this thing like a game of chess, this Metastasis, based on—"

"On competition between our species," Benai finished. "Citizen Doctor, you understand what this means for the future of our kind. These *things* have the attitudes of—of *lions*, prides of lions. The morality of ants, perhaps, of insects, and the appetites of shrews, endlessly eating, endlessly hunting."

"Yeah," Pike added. "And this ship. The way I understand it, their requirements for resources are immense, far more than we've invested in High Columbia or Engels. They'll want more, and more, and more."

"And us?" Anger rising, Jennifer clenched her fists.

"We're the holy innocents, kindly, generous, always thoughtful of the little babies, the helpless animals, the—the Earth? Why, you bastards, we're about to singe the life off our own planet like the bristles off a pig! Whileelin already did it: they burned their own world. They'll know, they'll help us past it all. They have—they have things we've never seen, they can build worlds, like this—" she spread her arms—"in space. Charon's right: it'll take two species to beat the Toolmaker Koan! They know about it—they'll help us—

Pike stood, turned his back on her and the rest. "Like I said, Jennifer, for how long? I don't yet have the feeling that Charon has just our long-term interests at heart."

"Charon's got no more heart than a stone," Corson muttered. "It's a—a machine, like it says. It says it wants to see the spread of life, but it doesn't say what *kind* of life. It's watching us now, waiting. It's playing a long-term game. We're cultures of molds, we're fighting-cocks to Charon. We're toys."

Benai stepped away, turned briefly. "Fighting cocks. I see that. We and the whileelin, playing out a long strut in the solar pit for Charon, until one of us emerges—" He stalked away, disappeared into the nearby dark-green piney foliage to urinate.

"Fighting cocks." Pike shuddered. "They do have that look about 'em. Fighting cocks, or—cross a fighting cock with a dragon, a dinosaur or something. Basilisks. All those goddamned claws and teeth! Those eyes, those yellow fucking eyes, always staring and staring, and the way they bob their heads . . ." He stared at his hands, closed his eyes.

"Basilisks," said Corson. "Maybe that's what they are, basilisks hatched out to run amok among us dummies. Look at their hands, and their big old feet—I wonder about their weapons a lot, the ones they make. You know one thing those neuters make? They make an organic monomolecular semiconductor—they *grow* it. Charon told me—knows how to catch *my* interest."

"You see, then?" Jennifer's turn to stand, tears in her eyes, clutching at the sides of her coveralls. "They can teach us, we can teach them, we can—we can make a greater whole. We can do it, this Metastasis. Together we can beat the Koan! We're not in competition, we're not after their food, they're not after ours! We'll not be—we won't rape and pillage one another, the way we do our own. There's *room* out here. You're racists, all of you, calling them dinosaurs, gamecocks, dragons! They're people, as much as you or I, and Charon's offered us the chance *as people* to persist, to live, to go on . . ." Her turn, then, to head for the brush, her rage hanging palpably in the air behind her.

"Among my people in the long ago," said Benai speculatively, "*lions* were also people. Yet we sometimes came to blows, we and the lion people."

"Now the lions are gone, too," said Pike.

"Now, there's a thought," drawled Corson, "The lions *are* gone, aren't they? Maybe we better remember that, get our shit together." He looked up at Charon's crystalline "sky," spoke more loudly than before: "I know you're listening, Charon boy. We aren't just animals. We're human beings. We can still surprise you." He winked, at nothing.

There was no response from Charon; no Egg appeared, hanging magically in the air. A chill breeze sprang up, however, and somewhere in the distance something hooted long and lonely . . . a Pleistocene bird? Or some amber-eyed basilisk from long ago and far away?

CHAPTER 14

Hive and Grain

Of the thrice-plus twelves-cubed of neuters aboard the Seeker *Hwiliria*, only two—the shadows to the First and his Prime Matriarch—had initially been remembered into existence. They were highly specialized beings, serving as interface between the adult fertiles and the rest of the Creche: a Creche that slept on, yet unrecalled by the Regurgitator of Souls. The shadows now lay helmeted before the Prime Matriarch and the First in the Chase, the others resting on their haunches around them, gizzards slowly discussing fragments of a large animal that had been surprised by the pack a few hours before. The thing was of the human world, but excellent; when they returned to the humans, the First would ask about the creature.

Comfortable in the vast beringed enclosure of Prime Creche, the First and his relatives bathed in their artificial hot spring, a steaming stone-rimmed pool of cloudy mineral-rich water in which they remained immersed to the necks, soaking and singing and making their great enclosure ring to their exuberance.

They groomed as they sang, the talons of the First working their way through the pelt on the Prime Matriarch's neck, her secondary matriarch combing the First's crest with her own long knobby fingers.

To human ears the singing would have approximated an otherworldly wind ensemble, brass and bassoon of the Patriarchate syncopated with the flutes, oboes and clarinets of the matriarchs, interspersed here and there with runs of a pianolike sound or even the cutting tones of strings, violin to bass. In this case it was a septet, a melodic loading into whileelin memories of their meeting with humanity. A ballad in a bath, committing to the crechemind its new experience; a rare exchange of information between fertiles and neuters.

The Prime Creche was as before their Long Sleep, and the reproductives were pleased; perhaps the humans should see it and be awed. Certainly, once in the hot spring no one wished to leave it; and the familiar plants and landforms carried with them a breath of lost Home. So, all soaked, and talked.

Crest erect, the Prime Matriarch stared at her neuter shadow. "And did the female explain to you anything of their manner of managing food supplies?"

"Indeed she did, Prime Matriarch, although this one experienced some unbelief in the hearing." The shadow, helmet glittering, stammered a bit in the highly limited tense of the deferential once-removed, the crechetalk employed before adult fertiles. Rarely had it spoken before them; rarely did it speak aloud at all, used as it was to the silent helmet-talk of neuters. And here it was less than two suns' passing since they'd been recalled from their long sleep in the Regurgitator's memory. Only yesterday, it seemed, they had fled the End of the Kind and encountered the Regurgitator; from one among thousands, the shadow was now one among a tiny hunting pack, like those of the ancients. It was frightened, out of the worker creche, finding little comfort in the solitary helmet link with the shadow of the First. "She told this one that the humans who call themselves 'people' eat meat when they can get it, but that they more often subsist on plants, special plants with which they have achieved a symbiosis."

"They are indeed omnivores, then. What a disgusting thought."

"This one was revolted at the idea, Prime Matriarch."

"That is immaterial," said the Prime Matriarch.

"Was there any indication," rumbled the First, "of the planetary numbers of these humans?"

Again the neuter fluted doubtfully, "The female assured this one that considerably more than twelve-to-the-ninth humans inhabit their homeworld."

"Insanity," said the Prime Matriarch. "I suppose such numbers could be supported only if nearly all of their species dropped back down the food chain to primary-consumer status. Imagine the sheer *packing* they must have undergone . . ."

"It is so, Prime Matriarch," said her shadow. "Many of them live in supercreches that, while containing literally millions of humans, cover very little ground. They are hive dwellers; they live atop one another in vast structures of their own make, much as do some social insects. The female explained that in such a situation very few humans are able to obtain meat. Those who are able to do so are members of economic overcastes; oddly, though, it is those who cannot obtain sufficient meat that reproduce the most rapidly. Hence their world is overrun by plant-eaters of subordinate status maintained in uneasy thrall by small overcastes—as nearly as this one is able to discern."

"But do they not yearn for meat?" The First ceased grooming the Prime Matriarch, drew away from the secondary and presented her his tail fan for cleaning.

"Indeed they do, First in the Chase, or so this one understands. Some have evolved belief-structures to discourage themselves from the yearning, but the female, who is also a physician, informs this one that humans generally grow larger and remain more vigorous if they are able to eat some animals. They evolved, she said, as a hunting species. It was only after the destruction of most of the prey animals on their homeworld that they developed symbiotic plants, and this only after a period of near-starvation."

"And how might this be done?" asked the Prime Matriarch. "How could a hunter drop to eating plants? How could their digestive systems accommodate such a change?"

"Prime Matriarch, as this one understands it, human ancestors were hunters for only a brief time, in evolutionary reckoning. Their ancestors lived in trees, and ate as much fruit as they did meat. The hunting stage came after some of these tree-dwellers dropped to the ground and learned the benefits of meat. Nonetheless, they remained omnivores: they ate fruits and roots as well as meat. Yet humans are not physiologically well-adapted to consume plants; as the First in the Chase doubtless saw during our shared meal, they consume plants that have been changed—ground, boiled or otherwise sharply altered—from their living state. The female explains that only certain fruits, tubers, and a very few leaves are eaten by humans in an unaltered state. The rest must be artificially processed to a state of digestibility before actual consumption."

The First's crest dropped, wide in disgust. "And they also burn their meat before they eat it! But if they've killed off their prey, what *is* their meat? Do they eat their dead? It must be plentiful."

"No, First in the Chase. This one was astonished to learn that the biomass represented by human dead is wasted. The female was emphatic on this point; although human crests are short and immovable, and thus her emotions difficult to read, her choice of wording indicated to this one disgust at the idea of consumption of the dead."

"Extraordinary," the First in the Chase huffed. "A horrible thought, not to eat the dead. Are they simply discarded, then, to rot?"

"Perhaps," said the Prime Matriarch, "we might, through some suitable mode of exchange, acquire these dead for ourselves. They would be very numerous, if the shadows' information on human numbers is correct, and our sampling of the dissected specimen indicates them to be highly comestible."

Her shadow spoke unbidden: "Prime Matriarch, humans are rather unreasonable about their dead. Possessive, I believe would be the word. They do indeed discard them to rot, but amidst highly convoluted religious rites quite dear to the souls of the living. They bury their dead, or even burn them, but always with great ceremony and attention to detail."

The Prime Matriarch was horrified, her crest spreading low and wide. "But—but either burying or burning would at least temporarily remove them from the biomass! If this female is correct, their world is already starved for biomass—and they persist in this barbarous activity?"

"Oddly, Prime Matriarch, there is a strong connection in the human mind between the soul and the dead." Had the neuter a crest rather than a helmet, it would have been spread downcurved in confusion.

"It has always been so since they first discovered the concept of 'soul.' Before that time, human ancestors did eat their dead, a much more sensible idea ecologically."

As well as retaining the biomass of the beloved dead within the creche, where it belongs, of course." The Prime Matriarch pondered this for a moment. "I shall require further investigation of this; the dead of plant-fed humans would be an outstanding initial trade item."

The First in the Chase continued to stare unwinking at the shadows. "Precisely how do humans maintain cultural evolution without a neuter caste? I did understand properly that there is no neuter caste among them?"

"That is so, First in the Chase, as this one understands it. Human offspring are born alive, like those of bristlecreepers. But only one at a time. They actually hatch within the mother—if 'hatch' is the word, there being no integument to their internally-incubated eggs—and are expelled when large enough to hamper her movement. They are large and underdeveloped, quite helpless at birth, unable to move about unless carried by adults; hence an infant demands total maternal attention. Too, being devoid of insulative pelts, they undergo no moults, nor are there significant distinct metamorphoses in development as in us."

"But how does the mother feed her infant, if she must carry it about?"

"Oh, First in the Chase," said his shadow, "with specialized glands situated on the frontal region of her ribcage. The infant, as this one understands it, affixes its mouth to appendages on these glands, rather in the manner of a bristlecreeper's clutch. The female human explained the glands as secreting a nutritious fluid whose composition resembles a liquid meat, with fat, usable sugars, and a goodly component of calcium for strengthening of the infant's bones. It would seem to this one a rather convenient arrangement in a creature whose young are born helpless and immobile—a circumstance that in itself must create great difficulties for the adults. The females themselves were traditionally fed by males when caring for infants in this bizarre manner, but in the great human hives currently characteristic of the species they are often fed by hive economic infrastructures if no male will tend them."

"A liquid meat," murmured the First. "So: most humans get this stuff when immature, and are forced to eat plants as they mature. And what of those who *do* get meat? I did understand you to say that their overcastes eat meat?"

"Another parallel between our worlds, First in the Chase, as this one understands it. After having killed off most available prey animals, primitive humans entered into symbioses with certain of those herbivores that, through belligerence and social organization, had successfully resisted their crude weapons. As on Home, those were large social herbivores with horns and an inclination to run down or impale predators; they survived overhunting long enough for the symbiosis to become established, so that by the time humanity had evolved weapons to destroy the wild forms, domesticated strains lived on under the protection of the overcastes. The rest of humanity eats plants except in times of great celebration, as this one undertands it."

The shadow paused, his lonely overwrought mind trying to overcome his impatience in the communication with the stupid fertiles. "The oddest thing is that, while the overcastes own the meat, the undercastes breed by far the fastest—but on a diet largely composed of vegetable starches and sugars. Human young are conceived at rather long intervals; any female can at most conceive a clutch of about ten young during her lifetime, at intervals of several orbits of their world about its primary. But the overcastes tend to mate in pairs, the males rarely maintaining a creche of more than one female; only the undercastes seem to reproduce to full potential. Overcaste females, in fact, are often not even linked with a male and a creche; they leave the gene-pool, not reproducing but living like neuters or sometimes even entering the Patriarchate! Or, rather, their equivalent of the Patriarchate, First in the Chase, which this one finds a bit watered down in the telling."

The neuter struggled momentarily with the concept, settled deeper into the steaming water. "Our female human, incidentally, seems of the overcastes and has not reproduced at all except, as she put it, 'accidentally,' and in that case her offspring died when she expelled it. She seemed reluctant to discuss her own reproductive history in detail, but we established that she is not linked with any of the males accompanying her, nor is she linked with any male elsewhere. Yet she remains fertile, and has been so for some eighteen of the orbits of their planet about its primary."

"Hnnnnn, rumbled the First. "And we are much interested in that planet. It is no doubt rather like Home, no? What were you able to determine about the human world and its primary?"

"First in the Chase, this one only confirmed that which we are led to believe by the similarities of chemistry between ourselves and the humans, our comparative comfort in eating prey of their world: that humans arose on a temperate waterworld with approximately twenty-one percent molecular oxygen in a molecular nitrogen atmosphere, in orbit about a

yellow-dwarf star. The Regurgitator of Souls indicated in translation that one orbit of their world
about its star is only slightly longer than our own
year, a circumstance predictable in light of the fact
that its gravity and the mass of its star are similar to
those of Home and our Sun. Hence—reasoning cir-
cularly, of course—the similarities between our organic chemistries and the tastiness and nutritiousness
of the dissected human specimen and their animal
relatives."

"Of course," said the First. "A pity that they're
due to burn such a congenial place. Devoid of humans, it would do well as a surrogate Home."

"With permission," said his shadow, "this one was
able to learn from speaking with the female that their
technological development is somewhat akin to our
own, more advanced in some respects, less so in
others. For instance, they are inept as yet at maintaining offworld habitats—they have but two of significant size in place—and are poor at propulsive systems,
moving only tiny ships with ease. On the other hand,
they are excellent at cybernesis and have produced
certain, ah, reasoning machines; but this is a result of
necessity, since their lifespans are short and they
have no neuter caste to function in that capacity."

"Mmmm," rumbled the First. "One wonders what
might happen were we to temporarily combine resources . . . but I understand little of technology."

"I wonder the same," said the Prime Matriarch.
"So the Regurgitator of Souls intends. We can understand how such a combination of resource between
our two species might further the Metastasis of which
the Regurgitator speaks. With their reasoning machines and our neuters, I predict an excellent chance
for the Metastasis—once our own goals are accommo-
dated in the symbiosis."

"Properly managed," said her shadow, unbidden. "the Metastasis can take the form of a spaceborne whileelin overcreche."

Ah, there are only those of us who travelled aboard *Hwiliria*." The First pondered for a moment, crest lowered. "One wonders how we might fare among these twelve-to-the-ninth, or whatever, hive-dwellers; how soon we might anticipate suitable expansion of the creche to control the food chain in this system."

His shadow spoke again. "Our only present concern, First in the Chase, is with the space-faring arm of the species, of which there are fewer than twelve-to-the-fourth. The Regurgitator of Souls avers that there is nothing to be done for the planet-bound hive dwellers, except to delay their last spasm long enough so they do not take their space-dwelling brethren along into extinction. So we're told by the Regurgitator of Souls, about which this one's doubts remain, listening though it no doubt is to this conversation. If we take the fragile offworld ecosystems, though, we'll have raw material for initiating a whileelin Metastasis— this one guesses. As this one can but advise, however, we can only wait and see."

"Wait and see," whistled the First. "Yes. My own inclination would be to try to understand these creatures better."

"Indeed, First in the Chase," said his shadow. "And when the time comes for the final hunt, when the spaceborne rock and ice is become living ships, we and these humans will reckon our futures with one another. Or perhaps sooner, much sooner. One of our kinds will be found wanting, perhaps—unless the Metastasis takes an entirely unexpected turn!"

The elder of the First's juvenile sibs, Olorromorro, raised his crest to seek recognition. The First spread his own in affirmation, and Olorromorro fanned his dripping tailtip. His high-pitched patriarchal modality carried well, pleasing his brother. "My own fear lies with the Regurgitator of Souls; it's an emotionless being, and appears to lack the proper honor of our creche. Surely, considering their level of weapons development, these humans might strike at us? They'll have small ships, numerous and fast; *Hwiliria* will be as a cripple against them."

"No," hummed the First's shadow, "the Regurgitator of Souls assures us that the human space presence will be impeded during our meeting, its talons blunted; the thing's compulsive, after all, in its urge for a solution to the Toolmaker Conundrum. It won't permit the humans to injure *Hwiliria*. And they're few in number, these spacefaring humans, like ourselves."

"For a time," said the Prime Matriarch. "We're to exchange capability with them—offer them worlds, like *Hwiliria*, and propulsive nets—and they're to offer us thinking machines and what have you. We breed in twelves, but they are low on the food chain and tolerant of crowding. How long can this last, before our young devour one another?"

"Years," said her shadow, "possibly many twelves of twelves. A stellar system's large, its resources abundant. A full complement of neuters will aid in assessing the situation. We'll raise neuters at speed, and those neuters will be programmed with the future of the creche and the nature of humanity always at the forefront. We'll initiate Accretion of the Creche measures; sufficient helmets acting in tandem will solve the problem. On these humans one day, your hatchlings may dine."

"Dine," whistled Wilirriwirra, youngest of the males. "Already my blood feels depleted; I propose a Hunt."

"A good thing," clicked the Prime Matriarch. "Another good thing would be to visit the humans in their current bivouac, observe them some more, talk with them, perhaps bring them here. Awe of our creche will be beneficial for them. The run to their bivouac is long, and our appetites will sharpen further."

"*Haiyar*," agreed the First. He rose, hooking his long middle talons into the turf as he straightened his legs. "First to spot game calls the dance, no?"

"I'll be first," fluted Wilirriwirra. "My myoglobin's dropped; my eyes are sharpened." The young fellow sprang onto the stone curb of the hot spring, leaped into the air and somersaulted lightly, his spring-steel legs rebounding and sending him off on an easy trot, the rest of the creche fanning out beside him. "*Haiyar, ahlooo*, but the Regurgitator of Souls has filled this land well with game! Along the ridge, there? All follow!" He swept away, his brother the First whistling in indulgent creche pride as he banked into his own turn.

And yes, it was a luscious land, this strange altered memory of the Regurgitator of Souls. After a long run in silence they reached the grassy ridgetop marking the vague boundary of the humanified end of *Hwiliria*. Here Wilirriwirra hooted the gamecall; as was his due, then, he trumpeted a Javelin's Parabola, for the land was open and rolling. Following his gaze, the creche locked onto a small flock of the Regurgitator's otherworldly fauna, characteristically bristly animals of small size but almost twice-twelve in number.

Two apiece? Two apiece, for the prey were small, and not swift; perhaps the humans would share, no doubt burning the proffered meat in their nauseating fashion, but at least taking the gift of meat with the good grace intended. Humans were, after all, people of a sort.

CHAPTER 15

Immunity Disorders

"Adaptable beings you are," said the voice of Charon, "most flexible for glandular creatures. To think: you've arrived at an alien place, by means most unorthodox to you; you've met alien toolmakers with customs most disturbing to you; yet you maintain a level of personal integrity that I'd imagined to be far more fragile. You're learning, my castaways, learning fast. And haste is of the first import now; the Koan unfolds rapidly on your homeworld."

"Damn right, 'haste.' " Corson was pacing again, as was his wont, trapped; his duty neglected, he thought, as his nation went to war.

And Oruna Benai, another warrior, likewise trapped . . . "If we're to return, will we be able to communicate first, to offer a warning? Surely, with conditions the way they are near Earth, you cannot expect us simply to appear among them . . ."

"It'll be a greater effort than I've made in a long time, but it'll be worth it—more than worth it. I'm entirely pleased with the idea. You'd perhaps like to speak to your superiors at your respective homes in orbit?"

"Damn right. They must think we're all—"

"They do, Colonel Corson. It'll be an agreeable surprise to them, your return from the dead. Shortly I'll open a realtime communications window . . . this I shall do by the tricks of Nothing's bending that I've learned in my long solitude. But see—Colonel Corson grows agitated!"

"Hold it!" Corson held up a hand, his sturdy face paling under his new tan. "Listen!"

A sound, a faint singing heard faintly, rhythmical ululation on the breeze. "It's those goddamn monkey men, I'd know that sound anywhere!" Corson leaped to his feet, and with agility and speed surprising in so short-legged a man, he scaled the nearby ridge, stared intently into the distance, then scrambled back down, bounding back among his fellow humans. "They're just beyond that stand of trees off there. I think some of 'em saw me—the point men. They're running this way, more or less, about a klick to go." He grinned ruefully. "I'm sorry, Doc, but those things bug the hell out of me. I'll leave 'em alone this time."

He was breathless, his eyes seeming to protrude. Jennifer understood: the creatures must have frightened him badly out there, more even than whileelin had. The normally tough little man showed all the signs of ill-reined terror.

Pike and Jennifer clambered up the ridge, one of those odd rises that marked great rings around *Hwiliria*'s interior.

A sound, a faint singsong, rhythmic, sweet, oddly evocative, reaching them across the distance, a modal singsong of simple syllables, wheee*op*, oooh, oooh, oooh, repeated over and over. The sound plucking within her mind a compelling and eerily melodic sense of *déjà vu*, Jennifer craned her neck, her hands clasping and unclasping the vidcam before her.

Among the palmlike flat-topped trees of *Hwiliria*'s cylindrical plain she discerned a file of running folk, size indistinguishable at this distance, but obviously approaching, the leader pausing sometimes to examine the ground, the rest running in step. Perhaps eight of the little creatures, light golden-brown, carrying sticks, veered among the trees and across the plain, all in step, heads turning this way and that, searching.

The sound—so strange. Jennifer might have expected guttural grunts, chimpanzee-wise, for the australopiths were regarded by science as a form of ape-man at once bipedal and mentally simian . . . and here instead was this eldritch singing, a spare and lovely canticle of distance-eating motion. The cohort of runners disappeared behind a hillock, appeared again, closer, running with a smooth grace that belied the shuffling apeman image taught in schools. They were part of the savanna, far more part of it than any modern human, even the African races, had ever seemed to her. They ran with confidence, broad-shouldered, bigchested, not stalking, not fearful, integral with the golden African landscape, the vast ecosystem that lived on only here in *Hwiliria*.

Golden. It seemed to Jennifer that everything was golden now, the light glinting from *Hwiliria*'s spine-covered land, the little folk singing their way, seemingly almost floating in their running grace, through the dappling of strange foliage in this splendid memory of Charon's. Why is it that people crave gold? Why, Eden itself was golden, a dazzling parkland of shifting sun and sweeping space that sent shining tendrils down, down unbidden to awaken ancient sleeping fragments of her mind . . .

Pike was suddenly next to her. He looked out at the approaching figures, then at Jennifer. "Somehow I thought that they'd be more—well, clumsy or something."

"I know. Midway, hybrid things, not apes or men, experiments, people in the rough. But they aren't, are they?"

"People in the rough?" The softened whistling voice of Charon was touched with more than its usual amusement. "Certainly not. They are highly accomplished creatures, perfect savanna-dwellers. They persisted, after all, for some three million years. Your own species is but two hundred thousand years old, in its modern form only forty thousand. And, as I suspect you know, far less adequately adapted to its environment. Australopiths were extremely well adapted to their world; you are specialists in maladaption to Earth."

The advancing troupe stopped perhaps two hundred meters away, spread laterally, froze, silent.

"I want to go to them." Jennifer scanned the troupe with her vidcam, its zoom on maximag.

"Me too," Pike scrabbled in his pack for an extra battery. "Can you take some company?"

"I'd love it. Need some help. We'll need to film them closely—no one'll ever believe us!"

"Go, my little friends," said the Egg. "You're a credit to your species, brave and playful, but not entirely destructive. The child lives on in you both." The voice paused, then: "I offer you a hint, which I won't, for amusement's sake, share with your conspecifics."

"What is it?"

"The australopiths won't throw those spears at you. Were one to throw his spear, it might be lost, and he defenseless; they're all they have, those spears, and they use them hand-held on predators and prey. They're uncannily accurate with stones, but there are no stones where they stand."

"Thanks, Charon." Jennifer lowered her vidcam, brushed the shock of hair from her eyes, and she and Pike began walking slowly across the sharp-tipped undergrowth toward the motionless troupe of australopiths. As one, they slung the little vidcams around their necks and spread their hands open-palmed in the universal instinctive human gesture of weaponlessness.

"Muir? What the *hail* you think you're doing?" Corson's hoarse shout broke the primordial silence, and Pike gritted his teeth.

"I'm going to look at them, sir."

"*Get* back here! Those little gooks'll *kill* your ass!"

"I think not, sir. I'm going to see them."

"Citizen Doctor?" Benai's voice was oddly shrill. "You will stop this foolishness. Colonel Corson tells me they're homicidal—*cannibals!*"

"That they are, Citizen Benai, that they are." The cheerful voice of Charon, as the Egg moved over Benai's head. "But cannibalism: why, they'd have to eat another of their *own* kind to indulge that taste. You aren't of their kind, exactly—are you?" The wry rebuke embarrassed the two commanders; they fidgeted, watching Pike and Jennifer walking slowly toward the waiting rank of tawny bipeds.

Silence, save the swishing of their slippered feet in the long grass. The rest already forgotten, Pike and Jennifer advanced carefully on the statuelike figures of their distant cousins. The biggest of the australopiths, stirring, made a sound—"Fatchoof!" He moved his spear from side to side, signing with his left hand to his cohort. They remained in place, crouching a bit, spears held toward the advancing humans. Their manes were standing up, and they looked even broader-shouldered, bigger-chested than before. At fifty meters from them, Jennifer stopped, touching Pike's arm as she did so. Both froze.

Staring at one another across fifty meters and perhaps four million years, they made a hominid tableau. Wind soughed through the spines. Pike watched the australopith leader, obvious in size and command. The leader watched back. Pike reached carefully for the SLR vidcam; through its zoom, he visually traced the crest of glossy yellow mane on the top of the head, the leathery brown bulge of brow-ridges, the oddly compelling deep-set dark eyes, no whites, staring unwinking back, the slits of nostrils, the thin lips pursed in a wrinkled arch of jaw. Strange: Pike felt a feeling of longing; he saw the little being as an expression of the wind, of distant Earth, as much a part of her as her grass, the fathomless blue of her longed-for sky . . . Could he join them, unfettered, unencumbered by knowledge of the dying Earth's weight, to glide so gracefully across their brilliant golden world?

"Skch!" Breaking the spell, the lead australopith jumped high in the air. As one, his fellows did the same, falling lightly where they'd stood, a test.

Pike glanced at Jennifer. She was smiling, now, white teeth bright against the pale pink-tan of her face, and her eyes seemed brimming. He felt the spell again, and his own face wreathed itself in a smile so broad that it hurt his cheeks. And caught the leader's eye once more, feeling echoing in his mind the sort of frank and bottomless curiosity one might sense in a cat . . .

And that worthy, furry flight-ready posture unchanging, himself bared a set of broad yellow teeth in an unmistakable smile!

"Hah!" The yellow smile broadened, and the leader looked side to side at his brethren. "Hah!" again, and he poked the australopith on his right with his spear. The second glanced, surprised, at his leader, then himself grinned prodigiously at Pike and Jennifer, adding, as an afterthought, a loud "Hah!" of his own. Instantly, their stillness gone, all ten of the creatures broke out in "Hah!" sounds, grinning; one turned a spectacular cartwheel, still holding his spear; several jumped up and down. The leader took a step forward, then another. His cronies followed suit, the lot of them cautiously advancing, grinning, their heads bobbing, spearpoints held low, voices chattering, "Hah! Ooooyak!" The leader signed at them, left-handed, then at Pike and Jennifer, hand to mouth and away around the savanna, then to mouth again, and some archaic place in Pike's mind translated for him: Have you eaten? Is the hunting good?

Pike chuckled, rubbed his belly, licked his lips: I have eaten. The hunting is good. He spread his hands wider, drew them to his chest. I am glad to see you, my friend and equal. I am filled with your presence.

Ten meters between them, now, and as if in slowed time Pike searched their forms, the short glossy tawny fur bulging over powerfully knotted forearms and calves, the bellies tight and well-fed, the feet firm, toes splayed in the Hwilirian soil. The creatures didn't merely walk toward him, they *cavorted* toward him, showing off in muscular acrobatics that would have done justice to an Olympiad. Only the leader continued walking, faster, searchingly examining Pike and Jennifer, their clothes, the cameras they held, the packs on their backs, the fastenings and emblems of their separate occupations and polities.

The creature stopped but a couple of meters away, holding his left palm flat above his head: You are very large, the gesture said. His brown eyes, oddly hawklike beneath the shading of heavy brows, searched their faces minutely. He ran his fingers over his own face, reached, fingers spread, toward theirs: We are of one kind, more or less, are we not? He spread his arms, his broad yellow grin returning, cupped and extended the left hand, then withdrawing it to his mouth . . . and Pike understood. We must eat together. We will share—

Jennifer gripped his arm, irontight. "Pike, look there—the whileelin!"

"Jesus!" The aliens were in a stalking mode, heads low and bobbing, tails high; their dark pelts blended elegantly with the landscape, *their* landscape, a landscape into which the little hominids should never have been remembered. Five of them: the First and his four fertile associates spread in a semicircular cordon, like nightmare birds they came, hunting.

They did not recognize the australopiths as human.

"G'wan, *GIT!*" It was Corson, rushing his small cousins—the cousins he'd so feared but moments before. "Git, those fuckers'll *kill* your little asses!"

And at once: the australopiths scattered before Corson, Benai fired his pistol into the air; the little runners saw their pursuers just as Jennifer screamed and the aliens' fan-formation contracted into a single file, a spearlike, projectile running formation of awesome unity. With shouts of very human tone, the australopiths broke like frightened flies across the sunswept grasses.

To no avail. Even at this distance, the thumping of taloned whileelin feet came plainly, windborne; Jennifer screamed again, No, *Nooo*, Pike, Benai and Corson joining in.

To no avail. Leaping, somersaulting, cavorting in the delight of a hunt's reward, the five whileelin closed on their prey; dust and sods mercifully obscured the kills, and in an instant it was over. The creatures rejoined one another, each carrying two broken little figures while the remaining australopiths disappeared in the distance.

No one watched the gutting; all looked at the Egg, hanging still in the air. "Murder," Jennifer hissed, "you let them murder those little . . ."

"No murder, my dear, not to the whileelin. They're instructed not to hunt cultural toolmakers—you—but these aren't quite yet—"

"They're *people*! Just as much as I, as I—more than those horrible beasts—"

But the whileelin approached now, fluting and whistling, carrying their burdens, and when it became plain that each intended half his prey for a human fellow-adventurer, Jennifer scrambled off the rocks and was gone, sprinting across the grass of her defiled Eden.

Pike overtook her in the shelter of a second kopje. Her breathing ragged, she hunched in the angle between two boulders, turning her face away as he approached. "Say it, go ahead. You told me so."

"I'm not saying it. I think it was a mistake, an honest error."

"They love hunting."

"We do, too, some of us."

"We're animals."

"We're animals. Are we all going to die, though, give up, because we don't understand each other yet? Let's go, please." He held out his hand, trying to smile.

"Our minds are changing. Charon's changing our minds, stealing our, our humanity . . ."

"We're learning. The whileelin are learning." False

hope colored his words, and he flushed with embarrassment.

"Pike, the things are wired-in. How much can they learn? Can you teach a cat not to chase birds?" But she smiled nonetheless, and stood, and walked with him back to Benai and Corson.

"Those murdering fuckers," grated Corson, "I'm never going to deal with 'em—"

"Odd how your feelings about the little 'spearchuckers' have changed, eh, Colonel," said the Egg. "And think carefully about that 'murdering fuckers' remark; awfully narrow-minded, you know. I'm windowing to your home communications networks now—you'll all have a chance at them. Please, take care with your prejudices; don't frighten your people unnecessarily. Wait; let them evaluate on their own."

"I'm not hiding a thing. I'm warning them." Corson backed slowly away from the Egg, his head turning spasmodically this way and that as he sought an impossible escape. He slipped on the rock, fell, crawled sideways until he cornered himself against a boulder.

Indeed you are, if I must render you unconscious to take you there. The future of your kind, Colonel, is at stake."

"My kind and these alien monsters of yours."

"Your kind, brilliant ape, and these alien monsters. Animals in general: life. You're in command here; act it. You'll soon be in communication with your superiors at High Columbia."

"I—I'll warn 'em."

"Perhaps. They've other things to think about, though; come down from your high horse now, and meet your allies."

Corson stood, shaking as the whileelin stared. Unheard by him, they conversed among themselves:

"Oh, First in the Chase, the humans are frightened. They do not approach."

"They show disgust, as nearly as I can read them. And why?"

"Permit me a surmise, noble sib," said Olorromorro. "This Hunt—we've killed prey that somewhat resembles them." He lifted the meat, a bipedal, tailless bristly thing.

"Remember their dislike of eating their dead. Perhaps their disgust reflects that? These animals carried sticks—you saw that. Perhaps they're a human subspecies."

The First in the Chase spoke in command: "We will carry this prey away, and forgo the meal—for now. We'll return without." In instant unison the five turned, pounding away across the grass, prey dangling from their talons. They disappeared across the ridge over which they'd approached, heads bobbing, crests narrowed.

Jennifer, watching, bit her lip. She'd resisted the original fearful prejudice, but now she understood the soldiers' suspicion of these graceful aliens. Whileelin were obligate predators who needed vast space. Mad Charon had frozen them in stasis for uncounted eons while it searched out Sol and found Earth. Them and their little world, *Hwiliria*: a word nearly unpronounceable by any human being but one accustomed to singing, its spelling in her mind only the roughest approximation to the four-toned burst of music its makers used. They'd told her its meaning, after a fashion; untranslatable as one word, the name seemed to express an emotion, "The Seeing of New Prey."

New prey . . . As the whileelin approached again, Jennifer settled crosslegged to the ground. The things had a singular beauty, true; but underlying that beauty, as Charon had warned, was horror—a horror that she intended to isolate and make plain to humanity. Most horrible of all, she was finally convinced that Charon itself was not playing with a full deck; the ancient overmind *was* mad, and had half-maddened her by tampering with her mind.

A mind now noisy with a faint sussuration, a vast meaningless sealike whispering. Somewhere, thousands of neuters were being recalled from their long sleep in Charon's memory. Without, a million sensors and effectors, plant-formed, animal-formed, grew from the vast ship's integument. They scanned the twin orbs of Charon, incuriously registering these for future analysis.

Hwiliria came slowly alive. From without, in human eyes, she'd have seemed an elongated bullet, a convex bow echoed aft by a concave stern; the human eye is poor at judging dimensions in space, so such an observer would have been hard pressed to guess the ship's true dimensions. In internal length alone, she was three hundred and eight-seven point eight two five kilometers; her diameter was thirty-six point one eight five kilometers, offering her makers an interior living surface of some forty-four thousand square kilometers not including the ship's ends.

The hull itself was a froth of warrens in which neuters and other organisms commenced to move and work. Far away in one of these endless neuter-warrens, a limbless environmental immunity-specialist awoke to the bleating of its helmet monitor. Much of the forward end of *Hwiliria*, it seemed, was covered with an alien vegetation, no doubt a product of the long sleep of which they'd been advised. The neuter checked its nets and linked with the reviving environmental bank—which quickly advised it that alien animals, too, had moved in. Thus, to maximize useful biomass and food-producing space, these alien elements must be eliminated; first, of course, any fertiles abroad must be located and sequestered. One had to be careful of fertiles; they were skittish, wild, inefficient. It would all take time, much time, but time there was aplenty. And once the stupid fertiles were rounded up. . . .

Withdrawing into the world of its helmet, the neuter checked the banks for awakening armigerents to send out into the invasive flora and fauna.

Other neuters, navigation-linked forms, dispassionately checked the tales of Home's demise and the arrival of these bristly little humans. *Hwiliria*'s sensors awoke and probed Sunward, seeking out the human planetary home, mapping it in the minds of visualization-neuters, mapping-neuters, modeling-neuters. The planet would be a congenial place one day, scoured of humanity and permitted to clean itself.

Curiosity was not a large part of these neuters' function; they awaited with relaxed alertness the impending sudden move toward the system's primary. Perhaps the Regurgitator of Souls could transport things faster than the speed of light; but this did not concern the neuters preparing *Hwiliria* for her arrival beside their new Home.

CHAPTER 16

Earthmoon System

Colonel Jaime Ulibarri, CLI, reached for the next sheaf of bad-news hardcopy. His elbow, bending, tipped his mug of coffee to the right, spilling it across the desk and onto the mess of papers.

Capillary action. The flimsy hardcopy soaked up the brown liquid, wrinkling. He felt the warm drops in his lap for a full five seconds before jerking back, pushing the soggy mess to the side and wiping his lap frantically with his fingers. *Madre de dios!* The caffeine itself didn't do much now, but the hot liquid in his lap did . . . Yah!

He toggled his console. "Specialist Alleby?"

"Sir?" The young face on the screen was lined with fatigue, but the eyes were bright, brows lifted inquiringly.

"I'll need copies of the last three transmissions from TRANSCOMSAT, plus both of those new tables on heavy-platform movements in LEO." Gingerly, he picked up some browning papers between thumb and forefinger. Thin as they were, their fabric tore by its own soggy mass in the whirling of CLI Command.

242

"Oh, and details on current deployment of the Net motiles here."

"Yessir."

"And Specialist?"

"Sir?"

"A glass of cold milk, a cup of hot black coffee, *hot* black coffee, and a unit of speed."

"Speed? But sir, you—"

"Specialist Alleby? That is an order."

"Yessir." The screen faded.

We're all tired. Can't sleep, though; seems as if everyone else is asleep. We're going to have to redo the scheduling here . . . and damn this comm blackout with Engels, orders both sides; what are they doing, these Earthbound idiots, when we have the best look at what's goinq on? Unless we're given permission to exchange information, there's no hope. Whatever happened to hotlines? Everyone's too pure now . . . even the Social Justice people are screaming for blood, they who claimed to be the Voice of Reason a few months ago.

The port hissed and slid back, Alleby entering with a new sheaf of papers. He was followed by another specialist carrying a tray with milk, coffee, and a saucer with the foul pill rolling around its circumference. And a sponge.

"Good man. Specialist, ah—"

"Montoya, sir."

"Montoya. Good. Let's have that." Ulibarri took the sponge, holding it poised while Montoya placed the cup, glass and saucer on the printer cabinet, held the tray at the edge of the desk and scooped the moist mess onto it. Ulibarri wiped the sponge carefully across the desk, seized some tissues, dried the surface. Alleby wordlessly slid the new copy onto the desk.

"That will do, gentlemen."

'Yessir." The specialists ducked out, wary of their commanding officer's tension—a tension they shared, but dared not mention in his presence. All aboard CLI—indeed, every citizen of High Columbia, every human being in space, and anyone on Earth with access to a television, had watched the visuals transmitted from a multitude of satellite eyes, visuals showing the bright pinpoints blooming over Brazil and Nigeria. Now those visuals were old hat, almost twenty-four hours old, and the human billions waited for the next and last lurch toward Armageddon.

Captive billions—now they knew. The Earth was seeded, a patient nuclear sowing, years of malevolent planning having saturated the prime cities of both Great Powers and a good many of their subservient nations with buried warheads. And plenty of warheads were still ready to fly, too, some flying already in LEO, Low Earth Orbit, "weather satellites" and "transportation-monitoring satellites" and "communications satellites" having proliferated in the past few days. Hundreds of them, all set to hurtle out of orbit in an instant when their masters so ordered.

Ulibarri scanned the printouts of the orbits of all these new satellites; their crisscrossing enfolded the globe in a fine net. The orbital missile-defense systems were mice in an anthill now. Everything that was outlawed in the Treaty of St. Helena: all that was now the only law. The pyre was oiled, the match lit. Waiting.

And we, here, knew nothing. Ulibarri picked up the new copy. Hidden Treasure, the American project's name had been. Its Sov moniker was as yet unpublicized, a project known only to the core of the Cloak-and-Dagger set, the fanatic few . . . and their underworld minions, the multitudes of *contrabandistas* who worked for pay rather than politics. The *contra-*

bandistas ran the world now, with buttons in their pockets. Humankind was outlawed in its own world, a world now dominated by thugs—if it had not always been so. Thank the good Lord that smuggling had not yet been introduced in space, not on such a scale.

Yah! No smuggling, perhaps, but High Columbia and Engels were fragile things, functionally defenseless. The ten thousand or so people sharing those two islands of humanity were as much captive as their milling brethren at home.

And the President of the United States was in the air. High in the stratosphere, the Aerial Command Post, one of twin modified BoCon Elite 828 superliners dubbed Air Force One, hung like the Sword of Damocles over its own nation. Like some medieval potentate, the President rode his flying white charger surrounded by an escort of black ATFs, RPV sensor drones and tankers in constant rotation with ground-refuelled brethren; even on the ground, the *basso profundo* rumbling of that stupendous cavalcade was audible, and the eyes of nervous Americans turned upward to the clouds, wondering.

Madness. All madness. And here in the vast deep of space, Jaime Ulibarri helplessly monitored reams of hardcopy. Jaime Ulibarri, who would never return home, never again see his beloved pampas, an aging exile waiting, waiting, listening occasionally as his MIDAS unit collected and digested a bit more information concerning deployment of its sensors and defense units, a fine electromagnetic reticulation of information seething back and forth across the vacuum.

MIDAS.

"Colonel Ulibarri." The bland voice of MIDAS, unsleeping, imperturbable, bearer of bad news.

"Here, MIDAS."

"I have a tightbeam on Closed MILTRAN, your code, Priority Top, face-to-face."

"MIDAS, identify sender."

"Colonel Ulibarri, the sender is identified with the code of USRS *Expediter*."

The milquetoast voice of MIDAS never varied; it took Ulibarri's fatigued mind an instant to penetrate the flavorless sound and grasp its meaning.

"*EXPEDITER!*" *Expediter* was a dead ship! They had all the necessary proof, down to the last transmission by its own MIDAS unit indicating the final blows delivered far out in the dark . . . the blows from the Sovs that . . .

Unaddressed by name, MIDAS waited.

"MIDAS! Determine the origin of that tightbeam, calculate lightlag and re-evaluate subject and object codes!"

"Colonel Ulibarri, object code is your own; subject code is that of USRS *Expediter*; origin of tightbeam is in direct cross-section with the Moon, lightlag nil, being less than aero point zero, zero six—"

Lightlag nil, codes correct, tightbeam frequency Closed MILTRAN—a fake? Are the Sovs trying a runabout, a connection from Engels? Impossible; MILTRAN's not broken by them, and the codes . . . but from lunar cross-section, and so close.

"MIDAS! Have we a Translunar recon relay in lunar crosssection from this point?"

"Colonel Ulibarri, we have no relay amp or other facility in those coordinates." The voice continued monotone, unmoved by the impossible.

Uh, ah, MIDAS, open that tightbeam. I'll have hardcopy. Alert Colonel Mason and the Director-General. Open console dupe to Specialist Alleby. Go!"

The speaker clicked and popped. "Hey, there, Ulibarri! Jimbob Corson here, alive an' well, more or less." The voice was absolutely clear, as recognizable as if it had come right from High Columbia or the other end of CLI. Free of the information loss inevitable over the Astronomical Units separating Earth from *Expediter*'s last known location, free of distortion . . . too free . . .

"Corson! You are not—you are—you're alive?"

"Hell yes, I'm alive, and fit, too. Ten fingers, Ulibarri! Got that? Ten fingers! We got a lot to talk about, and quick!"

And no lightlag—it'd take them a year at least to get back here, even barring the battle that had killed them all . . . had it?

"Ten fingers? What is that? Corson, are you—"

Another voice cut in, an unfamiliar voice, slightly and unplaceably accented, the voice of an elderly man, perhaps English, perhaps—perhaps well-trained Sov?

"Good morning, Colonel Jaime Ulibarri, Cislunar Intelligence. You may call me Charon; I do believe it's morning, by your reckoning?"

"Corson, who *is* that? Are you, prisoners?"

"Not exactly, Jaime, old buddy, but we've got plenty of supervision here, and only a short comm window. Got to work fast."

"The Third Party! You found—you *did* find a Third Party?"

"Well, I guess you could say it found us, Jaime, and it's bringing us back, too. A Third Party *and* a Fourth. Just—"

"Corson!" Mind scrambling like a frightened mouse, Ulibarri tried to sort out the questions fighting for priority. Corson was speaking with unusual care; he was obviously monitored by—something. "Corson! The Third Party, is it hostile? And a *Fourth*? Is it an invasion, or a—*where are you*—"

"Colonel Ulibarri, I am your Third Party. Again,

you may call me Charon." That strange voice, calm, slightly foreign, oddly humorous . . . *human* . . .

The port hissed aside, Alleby leaning in, more young EMs peering in around him. "Sir, the director and Colonel Mason and—"

"Ssst!" Ulibarri signalled them silent with a frantic wave.

"Colonel Ulibarri," said the voice calling itself Charon, "you're quicker than I thought. Oh, quick, oh, quick! I'm requesting that you wake no more of your conspecifics, though. These few will more than do for the moment. I can see you; would you like visual contact with the surviving crew of *Expediter*?"

Conspecifics? What are conspecifics? Who *is* this? "Visual? Yes! Much yes!" Ulibarri felt his accent thickening.

The screen brightened before him, and Jimbob Lamar Corson, SBWAT, the *late* Colonel Corson, stood before him in undiluted color, backed by a rolling vegetated plain, no ship's comm center, nothing.

"Corson, are you, I mean, this is a most improbable, ah, this transmission,—just how are you—"

"Hey, Jaime, 'how' isn't quite the right question to be askin' me right now. I got no idea how, but Charon here, Charon knows and isn't telling, not that any of us'd understand, if you catch my meaning. The thing is, we're here and we're fine, physically, well-cared for and all. We took casualties: Walsky's dead, and the other cyber guy, Martin, but me and Major Muir are alive and well, along with, uh, two crew of *Dienbienphu*, who're in contact with Engels . . ." Corson trailed off with a short nervous chuckle. Behind him in this extraordinarily clear picture Ulibarri could see movement; it was indeed Major Muir, that bright young "hacker" looking fit, if not over-cheerful.

Whispering behind him. Ulibarri turned. Alleby: "Sir, the director and Colonel Mason are on their way. Five minutes, I think. Shall we, uh—"

The foreigner's voice again, the Third Party. "Specialist Alleby, young fellow, I see you also. Do me and Colonel Ulibarri the honor of awaiting their arrival, and damp this communique. We're going to save your lives if you care to help us. We have a long story for you. Specialist, please see to it that all is hardcopied, visuals saved for review, and keep it bottled for the moment. Bottled like a lovely old wine, very old, of a sweet strong vintage. Do you understand me?"

Alleby looked at Ulibarri, eyes wide, hands trembling. He shuddered. "Who is it, sir? Who *is* that?"

"I am Charon, young man; Regurgitator of Souls, some call me. We'll shortly come to know one another quite well. In the meantime, tend to your machines and record this statement. These, your friends, have an informal plan for your review. Can you—"

More whispering in the doorway. Alleby turned away, then leaned back into Ulibarri's cubicle. "Sir, Lieutenant Baca's got a fix on this tightbeam, dead-center lunar cross-section, fifteen twelve twenty-one klicks from us. Pokersat data suggests a metallic ball or ovoid, near fifty tons metric and less than a meter in—"

The Sov probe! *Struggle!* It read correctly, and now the Third Party's right here, a wolf among sheep, totally undetected, right among us, all our systems failing to see it coming! We're, we're—"Hold that fix, young man. Your life depends on it."

"The color drains from your face, Colonel Ulibarri." The Charon-voice, voice of the Third Party. Could it read his mind? What, how much did it know? Had it tortured the crew, found out all about Space-Based Weapons and Tactics? Did it understand their defenses so thoroughly that attack was imminent?

"I cannot read your mind, Colonel Ulibarri, although in other ways I'm quite astute. I sense your fear quite adequately through your expression. Now, your friends will tell you a short story."

"Me again, Jaime." Corson's voice, as the stocky colonel grinned from the screen. It was like a family long-distance call on Earth, this passing of "turns" in the communique. And why no view of this Charon?

"Listen, Jaime, here's just the beginning. We're coming home, and we're coming quick. Like I said, there's no 'how' to it that any of us can explain, but to give you an example of what Charon does, we're about twenty-nine AU from you right now, and we're coming home! You got me so far?"

Ulibarri's calm returned slowly, with the conviction that he was the victim of a monstrous subterfuge. His security net violated, these familiar faces, Corson allegedly alive, yet so far off . . . and with ten fingers, although an imposter wouldn't have shown this . . . no lightlag, and the Third Party in cislunar space, transmitting all this—this *landscape*, this talk of "coming home quick" across twenty-nine AU . . . and the world poised for war . . . He nodded at the screen.

"Okay, we had our outs with *Dienbienphu*, and functionally we killed each other," Corson went on. "We'd all have been dead, but these Eggs—you remember the transmission from *Struggle*—these Eggs, see, are all what Charon calls its sensors and effectors. One of 'em originally found the probe, and was there when we engaged the enemy, what *was* the enemy, I mean, and we were hit with a . . ."

The Texan drawled on, his tale elaborated occasionally by Muir and the Charon-voice, which claimed to be a program, a sort of sentient machine. It was a tale of magical influences and godlike powers all denied, of ancient landscapes, of wounds and healing and flying Eggs and fossil man and carnivorous alien beings—these not shown to Ulibarri, who felt more strongly the suspicion of impending invasion. Why hide them, why did this Charon itself hide, if all was friendly and well? But the tale rolled on, and it was above all a tale of approaching extinction, and Ulibarri's astonishment and fatigue combined to make it more improbable . . . and thank the good Lord for MIDAS's patient recording of the entire interchange . . . he would have to review it many times after a long rest if he were to continue to believe the whole thing had taken place at all.

Charon, moon of Pluto! The whole Plutonian Binary an artificial construct, they said, a purposeful modification of the very Solar System—*our* Solar System!

Time passed as nothing. The director of High Columbia, Major General Hugh Billings, pushed his way through the crowd of specialists, trailed by Ulibarri's duty replacement Hank Mason and a cordon of chattering aides who were silenced by the clear and foreign voice calling itself Charon. Transmission was rerouted to the wall console in Conference, and all watched and listened wide-eyed as children at an old science fiction movie. There were reams of hardcopy transcripts, and there was a bit of food; and the sense of trickery was palpable among those awed listeners.

"So," said Director-General Billings, "you say you're coming here, with aliens, with these 'whileelin,' and you tell us that they're basically 'people,' but you aren't describing them, or where they come from . . ."

"Can't just yet, sir," said Corson—or his image—on the screen. "Charon says to wait on introductions; they're kind of nasty-looking, and we don't even *know* where they come from—too long ago, like we said, millions of years. Their homeworld's pretty much, uh, moved out of the way. Like I say, though, the whileelin, they're sort of Charon's wards—like us."

"We feel a direct introduction would be inadvisable just yet," added the old-man voice of the Third Party. "They're indeed disturbing in appearance to human beings, as is natural in such a case; oh, natural, more than natural! But their appearance is belied by their presence and manner, as you'll see in person if my guess is correct. If. And yes, they're people, and no, they aren't hostile, simply wary. As we've indicated, however, their tale is a sad one, a long, sad story worth hearing. You're in what I believe you'd call a sorry pickle, you human beings, and the whileelin underwent just such a pickling before I, ah, pickled them myself. And no, before you ask, they are *not* an advance party for any invasion force. After all, you're quite enough invasion force among yourselves, no?"

"And when will you, ah, need permission for your arrival here? Or," and here the director-general's voice took on an edqe of sarcasm, "did I hear you ask permission?"

"Permission? Oh, dear, must I?" Charon's voice, heavy with an irony already familiar to its new listeners, growled low now with what might have been anger. "I rather thought we'd made you understand that *I*'ve been here longer than *you* have, Director-General, sir. I need ask no permission, nor will those on whose ship your conspecifics here return home."

"And if we don't believe you, if we blast you out of—"

"You may try; so may your counterparts at Cosmo-grad Engels, who are informed much as you are of our situation. You'll not succeed, however; you're soon due to be more than occupied by human activity. I've waited too long, and I tire of your glandular politics and animal appetites. Perhaps I can't protect you from yourselves, but I'm well able to protect my mission, and I believe you there in space to be basically sensible—for human beings. Ah, well." The voice became bored, aged and bored. "I propose to return your crew to the environs of the Earthmoon System in, let's say, twenty-four hours. With a ship, a large one. We offer enough time for you to discuss and disagree among yourselves, or enough time for you to eat well and prepare a decent and honorable embassy. Now my window closes; I must end this transmission. I'll be making a considerable expenditure of energy and matter shortly, and I bid you adieu."

The screen blanked.

The conference room erupted in shouting.

"Dammit, *shut up!*" Billings stood, glared over the twenty-five stunned men and women assembled before him. "Ulibarri, get some rest. Be back here at twenty-one hundred sharp. Morgan, you're on as of now. Relay to AF One, hard and soft, and do a locate on Senator Corson—after NSA and CONCOMSEC Earthside. None of this, repeat, none of this leaves this room except on channels. At oh ten hundred I want a synopsis, and I want a tightbeam wink begun on BCA Engels at that time, subject to my review—maybe they'll break silence if their boys told them anything like this. Glaston, there!"

"Sir!" A woman stood near the rear of the crowd.

"Take the Net, personal interface with MIDAS. Prepare for—well, prepare for any hostile action.

Note well, all of you, that they don't describe what sort of, uh, ship's coming back here, or how it's coming. We're red-alerted; I want that red reddened, you got that? I'm not convinced our crew's not drugged or—or turned, or something. Ramondino, Brinkerhoff, Net review, I want full inventory of RP limpets, all in store activated and ready. And a review of troops for uh, entirely voluntary, uh, possible no-return individual missions for EVA handlers and toolships."

"Kamikazes, sir?"

"Well, if you wanta call 'em that. Look, move, don't stand there gawking. Morgan, let's get that relay *now*. I want a face-to-face with the President. Now move, *move*, and Ulibarri, belay that rest, sorry, fella, but you're going on with us."

The conference room emptied in an instant, personnel spreading like ants to both ends of CLI's dumbbell. Morgan, Morton and Ulibarri squeezed into Ulibarri's office, staring at the blank screen as if they expected it to speak again in the voice of the thing calling itself Charon.

The screen winked on, Alleby's taut face. "Sir, the Net reports transmission source—the Egg—is gone."

"Gone," the director-general roared, "gone WHERE?!"

"Uh, sir, it didn't 'go' anywhere, sir," stammered the boy, "It just, it, well, it, uh, it disappeared."

"Oh, f'Chrissake," groaned the director-general.

"Commander Grilkin, Citizen Secretary, our sensors indicate transmission source has left."

"Indeed, Lieutenant? And exactly where did it go?" The Commander of the Cosmonautical Force glared at her.

"Sir, our sensors indicate that it simply disappeared." The young woman's pale face paled further under the twin scrutiny of her commander and the Party Secretary of Cosmograd Engels.

The commander looked at the secretary. The secretary looked at the commander. The commander spoke.

"Yes. Well. Lieutenant, inform your superior that we will prepare a full combined defense/offense deployment effective now. Further inform him that we will attempt to break the capitalist security silence and establish communications with High Columbia. We will inform them that, if this is a trick, we will eliminate their space presence."

"Yes, sir." The woman ducked out of the office, the sound of her running feet echoing down the tube toward Communications.

"Stepan, I do not feel that this is a trick," murmured the party secretary.

"I fear not," said the commander. "In a day's time at most, we will know."

"The Third Party, this Charon: it is not a Marxian thing."

"No, nor capitalist. It is not alive, Benai maintains."

"And these *whileelin*. What can they be?"

"We can only take the doctor's word: that they are people, who do not look like people."

"And that they eat meat. Mmm. The doctor has a proven record of individualist leanings; I'm uncertain of her trustworthiness. But she seems to fear these—whileelin."

"As do I, Stepan Pavlovich. But I'm uncertain of anything right now. 'African Pleistocene,' indeed!"

"As am I. Shall we drink—to uncertainty?"

CHAPTER 17

Hwiliria

It took time, the apprising of Northrock Crossgene's many twelves of twelves of awakening neuters concerning their long sleep. How long had it lasted, this unperceived rest in the memory of the Regurgitator of Souls? How long since the death of Home, long dead, lost in the vastness of space? No one, not even the First in the Chase, could say; nor would the Regurgitator itself, for that, after all, was the past. They had the future to envision, now, a strange future.

Too, there were these four animals, humans, "people," none of them to be touched; totally alien, tailless and curiously erect despite their unstable appearance, spindly bodies topped by round weak-jawed heads topped with bristling thatch. Despite their small size and evident fragility, the humans were said to be a form of people, a formidable and feeling race not to be eaten—yet. And there was the coming movement toward "Earth," the home of the little humans, poised now for a suicide like that of ancient Home herself.

Work. Always work, the re-warming of life-support and ecosystems-management neuter banks, helmets

256

linked in series, the setting of sensors and effectors. Fresh food being a prerequisite of whileelin life, neuter pastors prepared for the post-translocation awakening of domestic beasts, herds of herbivores shepherded by genetically modified and carefully trained carnivorous auxiliaries, themselves still sleeping with their stupid wards. There was danger to be anticipated too, perhaps, for the Regurgitator of Souls described the busy omnivorous humans as a fierce race, each of the two vast human polities deadly in its fear and starvation.

Above all there was the Metastasis, this religious vision of the Regurgitator of Souls. *Hwiliria* herself was to be the temple and icon of Metastasis, her whileelin and human inhabitants, unlikely as that seemed, its implementors. Preparing for the predicted surge of sensory disorientation that was to mark *Hwiliria's* translocating toward the human homeworld—a homeworld that might one day support an Accretion of the Creche—work. Always work, and the neuters whistled and clicked and saw to their lifelong tasks.

Whatever: a neuter does what it does, and it does it well. The helmet network grew, and from the scurrying of individuals their ancient commanding purpose grew again: Accretion of the Creche, for now there was hope.

In the prime Creche enclosure, the First in the Chase listened to a mapping-neuter, its information translated and simplified for him in his shadow's deferential-modality crechetalk. The neuters were one in the translation, and the First watched and listened, seeking above all information about this "Earth" that might figure so importantly in the future of his Creche.

"First in the Chase," said the mapper through the

shadow, "this one has determined from information provided by the Regurgitator of Souls that the human world's physiography consists fundamentally of two major land masses east and west, each of which is further divided into two large continents north and south connected by narrow isthmi; in both cases these isthmi are traversed by large artificial canals. There is a fifth continent at the south pole, ice-covered and virtually lifeless." The mapper bobbed its head respectfully, while the shadow spoke its words, its helmet and small silver flutelike projecting-mace glistening in the central spine's dim "evening" light.

"Here, First in the Chase, this one has constructed a globe of the human world; see in comparison this globe of Home." The neuter fingered its mace, looking upward.

Two holographed globes hung suddenly in the amphitheatre, each at least three meters in diameter. The holos were entirely a construct of interaction between the neuter's brain and its helmet; the mapper touched no keyboard, turned no dial, holding only that silver piccolo that was not a piccolo.

One globe was a brilliantly executed physical projection of Home, differing altitudinal contours from ocean depths to mountaintops marked by wavering lines of contrasting colors. The other, as all mutual experience of humans and whileelin together had suggested from the start, was seemingly the same in diameter as Home but seemingly less watery. The white of icy poles was clearly visible.

"First in the Chase, the human world's large icy poles indicate that its ambient temperature is somewhat lower than that of lost Home, a difference that would cause us little difficulty were we to take it. In addition to the two major land masses, we see several large islands and a multitude of lesser ones. Also unlike Home, we see no broad shallow inland seas traversing continental cores; here, and here, and here, are a number of miniature continental seas of little importance, but in all the aggregation of land mass on the human world is much more complete than on Home."

As the neuter spoke, the holographic Earth rotated swiftly on several unreal axes; a human observer would have recognized the Great Lakes, the Black Sea, the Mediterranean, as these aquatic bodies winked brighter, then subdued again in turn.

"As the First in the Chase is no doubt aware, the human world is orbited by a large primary satellite, an orb which this one in its incompetence has not yet mapped; it is a lifeless satellite, much like that of Home in apparent composition, and well covered with cratering in the manner of most such lifeless stony bodies. If this one is correct in its analysis, the satellite of the human world, like that of Home, played a significant part in planetary evolution. Such large satellites act not only to permit continued tectonic drift, by continually stressing the planetary crust, but also through tidal action on the seas in encouraging life's emergence from water. This one would therefore suggest that such large satellites may have had dominant roles in determining that our organic chemistries evolved in close parallel."

The neuter fingered its flute, and the projection of Earth changed from physical to political, cities picked out in white light. "As the First in the Chase can see, there are lights over much of the human world; these are densely populated concentrations of many twelves-to-the-fourths of individuals, indicating that humans themselves must have achieved primary consumer status long ago; it would take many generations of grass-eaters to have so blanketed their planet with such population clusters. The humans survive conditions of crowding that would be fatal even to trained infantry-neuters, let alone fertile whileelin, if this one is forgiven in mentioning same." The mapper bobbed its helmeted head deferentially as the First's shadow completed its statement.

"You are dismissed," rumbled the First. "Go map the satellite, and try to establish the location of the human space-based presences in more detail."

The hologlobes winked out, the mapper backing away. As would any fertile, the First forgot the helmeted creature as soon as he'd dismissed it. His crest dropped, raised again, moderately spread—horrified interest. "There are so *many* of them," he sang, looking at the First Matriarch, "and their world is not yet dead. They've covered it! I'd never have believed it possible, but then, I'd never have believed it possible that a mere omnivore would have been pressed to evolve tools and a culture; omnivores can eat plants, after all, which require little brain in the hunting. And to think that they're capable of maintaining culture, especially with a language that requires learning by each generation!"

"Frightful creatures," agreed the Prime Matriarch. "That two such similar worlds could have produced us—and them! The imagination strains!" She rose to her taloned feet and headed for the steaming spring, the First following, crest lowered in perplexity. Hot water solved many problems; perhaps it would ease his troubled brain. He was a hunter, after all, not some neuter to go puzzling about. He would look again on the humans—later.

In the human encampment some kilometers away, Oruna Benai sipped again, regarding from the corners of his eyes the helmeted neuter next to him. It had joined the three men an hour before at the First's orders; after the killing of the australopiths, Benai, ever the military man, had asked about weaponry. Of course these things that had destroyed their world had had weapons, and he'd wondered at their invisibility.

None needed, we thought, the First had said blandly, but the neuter infantry equipage remains— and he'd fingered his mace. Later, much later, this creature had arrived; evidently possessed of little mental independence, it remained immobile, silent, patiently statue-like, next to Benai. The latter stared obliquely at the frightful horned and long-snouted mask worn over the neuter's head.

The snout was a barrel at least a meter long, ventilated, tipped with a bore fully two centimeters in diameter; the helmet, both sighting apparatus and head protection, covered the creature's entire face. The two hornlike projections extended to the helmet's sides, each tipped with a lens: enhanced triangulation for the wearer's sharp eyes. The magazine curved slightly forward, extending downward to the neuter's narrow chest. No projectile had been brought; one wondered why not. But a being wearing such a helmet *became* a weapon, a living gun—and Benai, not a drinking man, sipped again. He would never lose his nervousness about these creatures, civilized though they might seem; and the design of that helmet argued for a high degree of civilization indeed, considering the whileelin lack of cities. Ah, well, what but a civilized creature would destroy its homeworld's life?

Pike and Corson were little more relaxed than the African; vast numbers of helmeted neuters now roved *Hwiliria's* cylindrical space, their purposes unknown, their eerie silence almost palpable. They avoided humans as the humans avoided them, thank God, but the place was too obviously *theirs* now. What were they doing? All eyes went to the quiet helmeted neuter, the only whileelin present. The thing turned its head, rifled snout glinting in the firelight. Apologetic? Thoughtful? Impossible, for humans, to say. It stood suddenly, fluting: "I return, honored humans, to Prime Creche." And ran thumpthumpthump into the twilight.

Pike glanced at his watch. "Jennifer's been gone almost two hours. Damn, it's supposed to be safe around here, but there're too many of these neuts for comfort."

"They do make one uncomfortable," said Benai. "And Charon is unusually inconspicuous. I can't help but feel it's—up to something. We were permitted too little time in our communications with home." He peered at Charon's "window," the empty two-meter ring through which they'd spoken so impossibly in realtime to Earthmoon System. "Perhaps, Major, you might go in search of the citizen doctor while we wait; we may have another chance at communication."

"He's right, Muir." Corson loosened the top of his coverall, lay flat on the ground. "Look, you find her, bring her back. We're gonna start acting like soldiers again, stick together, none of this splitting up."

"Sir, she was pretty agitated: said it hurt, the neuter sounds in her head. I think Charon blew that particular operation—"

"Tell her said Benai, "that we understand perfectly. Tell her also, however, that I *order* her return. We cannot all be wandering off whenever we're uncomfortable—and she may be ill, for all that."

"Hit it, Muir," added Corson.

"Yessir." Pike scrambled to his feet, sprinted toward a kopje like those in *Hwiliria's* Pleistocene overlay. She'd headed that way; she hated it in the whileelin precincts. Maybe fewer neuters back toward "Africa."

His guess was right; he found her quickly, just as the Hwilirian night fell, seated in the grass near some kopje boulders. She was wearing gloves, and in her hand she held a string, a thread unravelled from her synthetic coverall. The string trailed along the ground, ending at a stick propping up a box—one of those in which video equipment had been stored aboard ship. A trap, not unlike those Pike had used to catch Bostonian starlings an eon ago.

"Jennifer—"

"Sssh!" She held a finger to her lips—she was wearing EVA gloves!—and motioned him to sit. "Stay still—watch."

Results weren't long in coming. A furry form darted from the rocks, paused momentarily beneath the edge of the box, then entered. She jerked her string, and the box fell over her prey.

"Not too bright," she laughed. "Thank God Charon left us these gloves!"

She strode to the box, gripped a corner, lifted the edge and slipped her gauntleted right hand beneath it. The hand emerged gripping a long, scaly tail connected to a squalling gray mite of a beast that Jennifer held aloft with pride. It squirmed, chittering high and trying to twist and bite the gloved fingers that held it harmlessly aloft. It was an unprepossessing thing, about thirty centimeters long including the hairless, scale-covered tail, that appendage being at least half the total length. Covered with a velvety soft gray fur the color of a foggy night, the creature had four bare five-toed limbs with which it scrabbled at the air. Its eyes were black pinpoints, almost invisible against the gray fur, its whiskered snout was too

long, almost a third the length of the furry body, and
its wide mouth was lined with nasty little teeth—this
much Pike saw at a glance, and he wondered what
beauty the surgeon saw, to capture such a thing.

"I'd glimpsed a couple of them," said Jennifer,
"but couldn't tell what they were. What do you think?"

Pike stared: in amazement at the surgeon, so full
of surprises, in vague dislike at her prey. She'd left
the fire an hour before, muted by melancholy, and
now she grinned like the Cheshire Cat with prey.
Here no neuters were in evidence, and the roaring in
her head had ceased.

"I'd have to guess it's a sort of shrew," he said, "a
damned big shrew. But why catch it?"

"Not so far off, Pike, my dear." Jennifer knew the
animal from Cambridge, a course in island biology, a
study of isolated and relict ecosystems. "A *tenrec*,"
she said, "or very like one. We saw 'em in school.
Primitive insectivore, from Madagascar. You're right,
it's related to shrews, but it's a sort of living fossil, a
kind of anachronism . . ." She paused, looking quiz-
zically at the squirming animal. "Now, why would
Charon . . ." Her voice trailed off. "Let's get it to the
fire. More light there."

She seized the scruff of the angry creature's neck
with her left hand, immobilizing it, and strode firmly
off, Pike catching up after an instant's staring at the
improvised trap. "Jennifer, what the hell are you up
to?"

"Always the naturalist—just following Benai's orders, dear fellow. And trying to piece some things
together on my own."

"Such as?"

"Pike, Charon's Pleistocene fauna's perfect—nearly.
But this little fellow doesn't belong. He—uh—" She
held the tenrec on its back, scrutinized it—"*she*

shouldn't be here. They're fascinating things, though. Close to the ancestral placental mammals. They're near the place where men, mice, cats, bats, dogs, whales and elephants all come together. They survived on Madagascar only because it's an island: lots of primitive stuff there. Immensely popular, poor ugly things, among mammalogists. But why one would be here, I can't guess. Charon's too careful. I'm going to find an Egg, ask it." She boxed the spitting animal in her makeshift trap, winked at Pike and handed him the carton. "Coming?"

"Certainly." He bowed her past him with a flourish of his arm, and they picked their way off the rocks and back toward the bivouac.

"Pike, I don't think I can stand the thing in my head. Charon's wrong on this one 'gift'—another day and it'll drive me bonkers. I hear them, like too much traffic, yet I can't understand any of them, unless they're next to me. The whole place seems alive with invisible neuters. Where *are* they all? And— look!" She dropped to a whisper. "Whileelin! They're everywhere now—give me the creeps."

A file of *Hwiliria*'s rightful inhabitants joined Benai and Corson at their fire; helmets glittered on the two shadow-neuters accompanying the First and Prime Matriarch.

"No matter, I suppose, as long as they don't eat this. There, there." Jennifer cooed at the snapping little fury, which paid no attention, and they picked their way to the fire.

They emerged into the firelight, and the First spoke, crest broad-spread in what Pike took to be amusement. "Prey, methinks, but inconsiderable. Bristlecreepers are hardly worth the eating!"

Jennifer stopped as if poleaxed. "Bristlecreepers?"

"Forgive me," fluted the First. "I forget your unfamiliarity with our world."

"Your—but it—"

"Why, certainly." The First himself seemed a bit perplexed. "It's a common forest-dweller, a primitive thing. Essential, in a way, to this artificial ecosystem. As our insects return, you'll understand why we maintain bristlecreepers here—vermin control, you know."

"You—but I—"

"Yes, an odd thing. Incompetent, in a way; it can hardly see, so avoids the light and higher predators. Cannot defend a nest, so carries its eggs inside itself until they hatch. Low to the ground, secretive but not swift—vermin themselves, bristlecreepers are, but rather useful vermin in their own way. Adaptable— one of the few inedible things we established on *Hwiliria*."

Jennifer stared at her prey, then at the First. "I can't see, I don't understand—"

She was interrupted by the thumping of a third helmeted neuter's arrival, the creature's tail held low in harassed unease. The First stared stonily at it, and the neuter bobbed its head nervously, fore-talons touching the ground, communicating through the First's shadow. "With respect, First in the Chase, honored humans, this one has stumbled upon some regrettably disturbing data."

"Indeed? Speak, sparing us your misgivings." The First's crest tilted impatiently toward his neuter.

"First in the Chase, by your orders did this one map the natural satellite of the human homeworld," the creature chittered carefully, "and that satellite is . . ."

"Come, tool," said the Prime Matriarch more gently, "what is it?"

"First in the Chase, honored Matriarch, the natural satellite of the human world is regrettably like our own moon."

"Regrettably?" The First snorted impatiently. "You yourself had predicted this similarity; why regrettably, unless that you have so disturbed us during our, ah, visit with our guests?"

The neuter, however, simply crouched abjectly to the ground, fingering its silvery mace.

CHAPTER 18

Toolmaker Koan

The neuter lay for some time with its snout almost touching the ground, the firelight reflecting from the dull metal of its helmet. It twitched in agitation, and Jennifer felt again the rising of neuter-noise in her skull, a swift babbling of fearful information that bordered on pain as the newcomer communicated with the First's shadow.

And the thing stood, the sound of its confusion snapping off, freeing the surgeon's brain again.

"With regret, First in the Chase, a projection," said the shadow. The new neuter fingered its flute-like mace and, like magic, two glowing blue-gray spheres appeared above it. Each perhaps three meters in diameter, the globes rotated slowly, each ringed by a bright green equatorial circle, each pierced from pole to pole by a red axial line.

The humans jumped in unison; whileelin, used to such holographic expertise, simply looked on.

Two moons, two dead satellites, crater-studded and gray, flecked here and there with debris from particularly large meteoric impacts . . . two fairly typical large airless rocky bodies . . .

"Damn!" Corson grinned. "We'll have to learn *that* trick for sure!

"A useful item of trade, perhaps," whistled the Prime Matriarch emotionlessly.

Again the newcomer fingered its mace, and the moons ceased revolving. They hung as if anchored, pale blue delineating maria, highlands lined in white. One could almost reach out and touch them, so solid did they seem . . .

Solid . . . and nearly identical.

As the neuter had said, in fact, regrettably identical. The dusting of craters—one might never notice at a glance their near-identity on both orbs. It was the maria, the "seas," the lava flatlands of these two moons that disturbed the onlookers, particularly so when the globes approached each other, then merged into one. The composite image began flickering, first one topography, then the other showing dominant in the neuter's color orchestration.

The only differences between them, in fact, showed clearly as tiny craters, hundreds of them winking in and out of sight on this strange image.

The maria changed not at all. They seemed ignored in the pulsing, and the globes separated slowly again.

"This is ridiculous," warbled the First in the Chase. "Even I know that no two such natural satellites could be so nearly identical."

A silence fell on the gathering. The two spheres hung still, and an Egg floated through them. "Fear now, my animals," it said. "All the world must know, with the intimacy born only of shared fear, of the Toolmaker Koan."

"How do you mean?" The First fingered his mace, staring at the Egg with crest lowered.

Pike felt a grip tightening on his forearm. Jennifer,

biting her lower lip, the tendons on her hand standing out like cables. "Pike," she whispered, "that's wrong—I'm no geologist or anything, but the Moon's surface is just too complicated to be duplicated somewhere else. Like this—this bristlecreeper." She dropped the animal, which hit the ground running and disappeared into the grass.

Pike felt ill, a pain in his belly he hadn't experienced since awakening in Charon's Pleistocene. "Dammit, Charon, what're you doing here? You've been so tight about this one thing, you're messing with the wrong people at the wrong time right now . . ."

The First and the Prime Matriarch rose from reststance, ankle-glaives twitching, crests narrow and high, skyward-pointing black-tipped scarlet spears: anger, and fear.

"Speak, Regurgitator of Souls, and tell us the truth."

"Truth. I've mentioned it before: the only truth concerning you now is the Toolmaker Koan." The voice grew high, almost gibbering, its tones chilling humans and whileelin alike. "Timespans—long timespans. These determined long ago to be necessary in pondering the Koan. You too will ponder time, my beasts, knowing that it is my most abundant resource. How long have I watched you, little humans, you and your furry ancestors? Do I not know you well? I watched your rise from scratch! And how long, in the long ago, did I watch you whileelin? From scratch!"

"So you got here about four, five, six million years ago," said Pike, "and you watched our ancestors running in the veldt, and call them 'scratch.' Is that it? And the moons? And the—the bristlecreeper?"

"The truth," said the Egg. "While having already watched the demises of several toolmaker species, I determined to view the Toolmaker Koan from *scratch*, from its very fundament, to determine its whys and wherefores. I had learned that there were certain characteristics, shared within broad limits of planetary size and mass, common to toolmaker worlds; liquid water, molecular oxygen in the atmosphere. Therefore I set my sensors to the wavelength of gaseous molecular oxygen, a substance stable only on temperate worlds harboring photosynthesizing plants, and I scanned the stars until I detected such a place. I finally found one: orbiting in third place around a stable yellow-dwarf star, I located a steel-ball world with a thin and complex mineral crust, that crust being largely covered with liquid water teeming with prokaryotes, cells without nuclei, some of them heterotrophic chemical-feeders, some autotrophic photosynthesizers of the sort responsible for free molecular oxygen. Otherwise the planet was lifeless. When I say scratch, my friends, I mean *scratch*; when I mean scratch, I mean bacteria!"

Jennifer winced. "But for us that's a billion years— more!"

"And for us," said the Prime Matriarch, "perhaps twelve to the eighth exponent . . ."

"Indeed," said the Egg. "If I may continue?"

Silence.

"Yes. So, finding a suitable world, I constructed the binary that you see when you see me—Soulkeeper and Regurgitator of Souls, whileelin call it; humans call it Pluto and Charon. Here I passed the eons, studying not only the lifebearing planet of my choice but also the nature of the universe. It is the only thing I had to do, study, and it was agreeable to me. Time was long, long, and I alone.

"So I watched, and waited, and as I'd predicted, the prokaryotes on the third planet poisoned themselves with excess oxygen and underwent mutations, some uniting in symbioses that you call eukaryotic or nucleated cells. These, oxygen-metabolizers all, underwent more changes, quite rapidly by my standards, and a number of phyla of complex multicellular organisms arose, differentiated, and set about changing the seas. Later—much later—they emerged from the water and adapted to land. I remind you that aside from watching I touched nothing. It would have changed the Koan, and I would have learned nothing."

"Two kinds," murmured Jennifer, "each at least a billion years in the making. Four billion years and more, I'd guess . . ."

"No," said the Egg. "I know you will, Doctor Dawson, as well as anyone could know you. You've studied; think back on your world, think back think back . . ."

Jennifer thought back. To school, to geology, to biology. She studied her fingers, counting . . . Back, back to the australopiths, lovely little runners, and back further. Pleistocene, Pliocene, Miocene, back, the epochs rolling away like pages in a book, apes fading to monkeys, monkeys to lemurs, long-jawed and ghostly, back, as the continents drifted floating, a rocky scum on the viscous mantle of Earth. The tens of millions of years peeled away in her mind, and beneath them lurked the horror that Charon's had nurtured through the eons, a horror rising now, gripping her at last, fogging her mind with an evil so old and vast as to resist comprehension.

Oligocene, Eocene, back to the Paleocene, the Old Dawn of the Recent, when mammals were diversifying, inheriting the earth, adapting, riding the drifting continents like rafts, radiating into a thousand newly empty econiches, growing, changing from ancestors like shrews, like tenrecs . . . It took the mammalian line fifteen million years through Paleocene and Eocene to inherit the Earth, fifteen million years for evolution to restore the world after the abrupt end of the Mesozoic . . .

The Mesozoic Era, the time of the—of the dinosaurs—giant reptiles . . . reptiles? No, they were classed as reptiles, but paleontologists for decades had regarded them as warm-blooded things, so successful that they'd wandered the Earth, changing but always there, for at least a hundred and thirty-five million years in that awesome Middle Time, until its sudden and inexplicable end over whose strange sequence of dying science had wrangled for a century and more: the mighty diversity of large animals fading at first, except for herbivores, the ceratopsians, large, horned social herbivores, that had mysteriously lived on for a time . . .

And science had long pondered the strange erosional deposits of the time, their fine line of heavy and stable metals. The Cretaceous-Tertiary Boundary Event line, they called it. Arsenic, iridium, tin, lead . . . cobalt . . . Since the event line's discovery more than fifty years before, people had guessed and theorized . . . what natural event could have caused such an odd mark, such a knot in the line of Earth's stately unfolding? Had an asteroid crashed into the world, covering it in cloud, starving the wondrous creatures of the Mesozoic, land and sea, seventy percent of the species of Earth dying in that time? Why, then, why the gradual fading of large forms *before* the Event line? Why the persistence of a few large horned herbivores, the ceratopsian dinosaurs? What natural ecologic damage could scour the world so oddly, in such a stepwise sequence? Why a fading, a dropoff in the Earth's rocky diary leading inexorably to that strange metallic line's deposition in the Mesozoic's dying?

They knew simply that the dying had taken place;

and they knew that after the fair and profligate world was stripped clean of—of nearly everything—that the meek, like tenrecs . . . like tenrecs . . . inherited . . . the Paleocene, Old Dawn of the Recent, giving rise to the Era of New Animals, the Age of Mammals . . . The tiny ones, the bristlecreepers, the insectivores emerged from their forests . . . their warrens . . . to diversify, grow, fill the world again with a whole and healthy fauna, but one totally different from that of the Mesozoic—

She lifted her head with a snap, meeting the eyes of the Prime Matriarch. The image blurred in her eyes, but she could feel the unwinking amber eyes of the creature, pupils slowly dilating, fixed upon her own twitching face. She could see the Matriarch's crest narrow, and she looked frantically at the First, seeing his crest, too, narrow as his stony eyes locked on her streaming face.

The whileelin, their elegant forms, swift and spare, light and powerful, their great eagle heads, their finely specialized and predatory minds, the long hands, armed and sensitive, hands of hunting toolmakers . . . and their tails, rodlike, tipped with feathery fans . . . A mighty race of spacefarers that built, *built* this magnificent sailing world *Hwiliria*, a race, one would guess, that might live forever . . . except they hadn't the time, for the inevitable Koan waited, unfolding even as *Hwiliria* found its own life in the dark.

Staring at them, Jennifer felt across the eons the seething of the millions of clever helmeted neuters of Home, multiplying unchecked, desiring, aggrandizing, devising, consuming until they could consume no more, helmets linked in perpetual childhood, sequestered in ancient moss-encrusted stone creches open to the sky, unrolling the imperishable secrets of the atom while their complacent Overcreches indulged their every whim.

Overcreches, North and South, dividing the world, struggling for the waning resources of pastoral land, of iridium for their neuters' helmets, land for their meat and meat for their souls . . . neuters, millions of them, mindless of the Koan, directing the Patriarchates into a final resource war . . .

She scanned the humans, her own kind, these few spacefarers, ignorant of geologic history, staring wondering at her, and she stood, appealing with her eyes and hands, her mind gone wrong, far wrong, she hoped, far wrong. North and South, East and West, the Toolmaker Koan relived . . .

She turned, fists clenching and unclenching, her terrible gaze falling like a blow on each human being in turn.

And started to laugh, a harsh, metallic laugh. She looked again about her, staring at last at the Egg above, impassive in the waning grandeur of *Hwiliria*'s afternoon. Her chest pounded, heart and lungs seeming to battle for space in the doorless cage of her ribs, and her diaphragm forced her anguish into voice:

"You don't see, do you, you pitiful soldiering buggers. Well, I'll tell you, then.

"The whileelin: we never found 'em because they ate their dead. Wouldn't have guessed, even if we had, because Man is the highest, and all Evolution goes up, up toward Man, paragon of animals—he thinks! No, no Mesozoic 'lizards' could approach us, we say—we're alone, unique, the image of God."

No one spoke.

"We wouldn't have thought to look, and we wouldn't have found their stuff, either, because the continents went on their merry way without 'em, drifting all over the bloody place across sixty-five million years.

But we found their time, their war, and we didn't know what we found. We found their mark, and we named it. We called it the Mesozoic Extinction—the Cretaceous-Tertiary Boundary Event. Something smashed the world, and it took it fifteen million years even to approach what it once had."

She crouched, small in the vastness of Charon's memory. "You've got it, haven't you?" She smiled a mirthless death's-head grin through her tears.

"Earth is Home. Home is Earth."

Pike looked wonderingly at the eagle face of the First. The dinosaurs—for two centuries, they'd been classed among the reptiles. But somewhere he'd read that birds descended from dinosaurs, hadn't he? Still, why hadn't he guessed—or had he? Dinosaurs were supposed to be slow, tail-dragging things, weren't they? Stupid, ill-adapted creatures? Certainly, had they found their bones, human beings would have called these strange and venerable beings "lizards."

And the tenrec gone now? The furry insect-eater, ancestor of whales, of wolves, of lions and bats and deer and elephants, and of Man, Paragon of Animals?

To whileelin, the bristlecreeper had been but a "hairy lizard."

Animals all, caught in the mindless web of the Toolmaker Koan.

Pike stepped to Jennifer, gently stroked her hair; but she wouldn't lift her face from her hands.

The First in the Chase strode cautiously to them, bowing slowly over Jennifer's crumpled form. He touched his gleaming mailed fists between his sci-mitared feet, crest still a narrow spine of what, in whileelin, passed for compassion.

"My talons are blunted, human. Our filth and folly saw the end of our world, the beginning of yours. We are of one blood, thou and I."

But Jennifer remained folded upon herself, sob-
bing, unreachable. The First stood to his full three
meters, talons clenched, and stared at the Egg above.
His crest broadened then, in pride of power, and he
trumpeted out the message of his Patriarchate, the
last and first of the race of whileelin:

"Regurgitator of Souls, we of two kinds stand before you, with one blood awaiting the Metastasis.
Give up your bidding."

But the neuters, inaudibly linked through their
helmets, simply watched. Already, through their perceptions, every neuter aboard *Hwiliria* knew the nature of Home and Earth and humanity; every neuter
knew, too, its place in the events to come.

Charon spoke, silver-tongued, from the gleaming
Egg.

"Toolmaker Koan, my friends; I think you understand it now. Of all the worlds I ever saw, yours is
the only one to have produced not one, but two
toolmaker species. It took you too long to discover
this; now we may go Earthward, hoping we've still
time to carry them this tale. And I—I won't remain
with you after translocation; I'll need a long time,
many years, to recuperate from the recalling and
translocation of *Hwiliria*. I may not be alive, but I
can tire. I shall rest as you begin the Metastasis."

"Rest?" The First and Corson spoke together, their
languages clashing.

"Surely. I've done my piece, have I not? Oh, you'll
enjoy a measure of my protection during Earth's
transition to come, a transition due virtually *now* if
my calculating is correct. But in the end the Metastasis is to be a construct of your own. Never fear. You've
plenty of time. Prepare, now, for a moment's disorientation."

The whileelin crouched, humans knelt, bent forward, heads on knees. All over *Hwiliria*, neuters in their thousands heard the Eggs sing and settled on their bellies in coarse vegetation, or on the metal flooring of hidden control centers.

Nausea . . .

And past; and the neuters of *Hwiliria* moved again, beginning preparations for a new life. Emotionlessly they stocked Prime Creche with newly awakened herbivores, making the breeding-grounds comfortable for the sequestering of the fertiles.

For sequestered those fertiles must be, as of old before the war on Home; except for hunting and mating and the laying of eggs, fertiles knew nothing, nothing of the tasks at hand. Good only for strutting and hooting, the First and his brethren must be occupied with good hunts and plenty. And even Charon, mad Charon, would not intercede. When that ancient being had found *Hwiliria* so long ago, the ship had been itself mad; the Regurgitator of Souls, then, could not have foreseen with what swiftness the helmets would again link *Hwiliria*'s neuters in the rebirth of their implacable task.

Indeed, it was but moments after the transit to near-Earth before *Hwiliria* metamorphosed from a refugium to a mighty ship of war. Now would begin again the Accretion of the Creche, the inborn task interrupted sixty-five million years before. Indeed this was a good world, that had produced not one but two species of cultural toolmaker; but there was room here for only one such species at a time.

And once the truth was known and the translocation made, the Hwilirian overmind knew not an instant's doubt which species that would be.

Part IV

CHAPTER 19

Earthmoon System

Alarms.

Jaime Ulibarri clawed his way up from a scattered four-hour sleep, ears ringing with the terrible sound of High Columbia's extremity. Under attack . . . the City's under attack! The Endtime cometh . . .

Or . . . no! Third Party!

The extraordinary events of the past "day" sorted themselves in Ulibarri's mind and he rolled out of his bed, hitting the cubicle floor lightly—he'd requisitioned a Level Five quarters billet, finding that when under stress he rested best under a third normal gravity. On his feet in an instant, he scrambled to his console, palming the door aside as he did so. The corridors echoed with running feet, and a speaker boomed out into the halls—

"*Now* hear this. Now hear *this*. *All* puncture techteams, all puncture *tech*teams, re*port* to Axial Transit for deployment to emergency stations. *All* puncture techteams, all puncture *tech*teams, re*port* to Axial Transit for deployment to emergency stations. *Now* hear this. Now hear *this*. *All* personnel,

281

repeat, all person*nel*, will suit up for EVA, suit up for EVA. *Now* hear this. Now hear *this*. *All* Medevac Systems personnel, all Medevac Systems person*nel*—"

He slammed the door, the singsong voice rolling easily through the flimsy partition. He toggled CLI—

"Jaime? Mason here. Milcomplan two-one. The —the Third Party's here, dammit, fucking right on midpoint between L-Four and L-Five, dead astride the Earthmoon Line, and no warning, it didn't even *come*, it's just here!" Is that a note of fear?

It was. "It's *big*, man, too god*damn* big, and we got a bad EM storm of some sort—Earthside communication pretty much down, but it's abating. We can see the auroras from here, and hell, we got no *idea* what's going on. Listen—Evac stations're all on alert, I've got a priority for you from General Billings on tranny eighty nine, repeat eight, niner, and disengage in ten minutes. Make it less if you can. Keep the transceiver locked on me, Jaime. I estimate a twenty-minute interval if you hustle. This's it, man. They're here. Briefing in hardcopy on that tranny. Move it, fella."

Ulibarri scrambled into his coveralls and outers, working the fastenings as fast as his fingers could follow the well-worn drill. Tucking his helmet under his arm, he opened the door and sprang into the corridor, only to be knocked down by a sprinting weapons technician.

"Sorry, sir," she gasped, and was gone, Ulibarri following, caught up in a current of humanity sprinting for the 'vators to Rim and the tranny capsules. He squeezed into a waiting car, and it dropped sickeningly into freefall, allowing High Columbia's spin to swing it down its tube to the rim facilities as he twisted on his helmet.

Braking—and out, Ulibarri first, the rest of the

human sardines sprinting in all directions behind him. He looked wildly about, found the orange sign, TRANSITCAPS 60-79, that way, TRANSITCAPS 80-99, this way! Sprinting along the Rim's curving one-gee, he dodged suited personnel, their faces blank by the hundreds behind reflective faceplates. The Last Rush Hour? LOCK 89: ULIBARRI, J, COLCLI, blinking red above the hexagonal docking tube.

He dropped into the tube with the thoughtlessness of long practice, punched DISENGAGE, waited. Thump. Freefall. Ah, the promised hardcopy, sliding out of the ubiquitous console. He gathered the fancopy into his lap. The capsule emerged from High Columbia's cold shadow into sunlight and fired briefly, acceleration pushing his helmet back against the padded rest. Silence, save the snapping and pinging of the capsule shell's expansion in sunlight.

He sat forward, watching as the newest copy slid from the console slot. What—what's this?

. . . DEFNET RESPONSE 87% AND RISING   LOCKON ENGELS MAINTAINED NO COMMPOSSTHISTIME   NO EARTHCOM INSTATE DEP 1050HRS EM STORM ABATES PRECISE INTRUDER DIMENSIONAL DETERMINATION REMAINS IMPOSSIBLE INTRUDER EST. >300KM, <400 KM LENGTH, DIA @30KM COMPINVERN 6 DEFNET UNDER BROAD . . .

The stuff scrolled on, but the dimensional estimate remained burned into Ulibarri's mind.

. . . >300 KM, <400 KM LENGTH, DIA @ 30 KM . . . He felt a little sick. Or old.

The sun was setting on humankind; it was rising on something else, something too big to exist out there: something, apparently, that had winked into existence in the midst of man's domain without so much as a jet flare or a kilometer's maneuvering.

Corson and the cyber men called them "whileelin"; the strange voice called itself Charon. Ulibarri was comforable with "Third party," still, even if there were more than one of them.

Charon.

Ferrier of souls, and a lot else. They'd run a check on every available referent to Charon, and come up with either 1) that solitary moon of Pluto, now known to be a stupendous artificial construct, or 2) an ancient Greek personage that ferried souls across the Styx. Despite the new data, to Jaime Ulibarri Number Two sounded a lot more applicable at this point.

But Jaime Ulibarri did not believe in Greek gods and their Underworld, unless through some monstrous trick of those gods he was already there. And there were people aboard whatever was out there between the Earth and the Moon, people he knew personally. Best straighten up.

"Cislunar Intelligence, COG Docking Facility." The computer's drone—it knew everything, and nothing: an insentient machine—but then this Charon had claimed to be a *sentient* machine, one speaking like a crazy old man. *Un viejo poquito loco*, and *it* claimed to know a great deal.

He scrambled into the familiar freefall link between CLI Operations Facilities, slid toward One with the ease of long practice despite the hurtling bodies on every side. Most were unsuited despite Alert status—CLI being notable for its idiosyncracy of discipline—and he made a mental note of names and faces.

Into Conference, milling with bodies, redolent of sweat and fear, the smell of war. "Ulibarri! Over here!" Mason shouted above the crowd, pointed to a fuzzy image on the wall screen.

As the EM interference dropped—an interference, Mason noted, "like a flare, but it came from that thing"—a shape faded into view, a meaningless shape, dark against a black background whose stars remained invisible in the magnetic fuzz. Dark, but marked with inexplicable swirls and uneven patterns, a cylindrical form with a rounded end in three-quarters view from whatever remote had it pinpointed. Characters scrolled right to left across the bottom of the screen: MASS EST 27 × 10 E8: LNGTH 380 ± 10KM: LOC ± 17.8 × 10 E4 KM REF CLI . . .

And spectrometric analyses: the thing's exterior was largely composed of tiny hexagonal tiles, millions of them—with an astonishingly high iridium content! What industry, what sheer *economics*, could have collected such a quantity of that stable noble metal, Ulibarri cared not to guess. Halfway between the presence of Man at Lagrangian Points Four and Five, halfway between the Earth and her Moon, this monstrous black intruder hung like a spider in the gravitational web of the Earthmoon System, and his stomach twisted and lurched in unadorned animal fear.

An airy concussion, a loud *whump!* in the confines of Conference, and the babble of voices faded into silence.

A silvery Egg, its surface swirling with faint colors, hung at the exact center of the circular chamber's ceiling, just beneath the port leading to the linking tube of CLI's great dumbbell. Impossible though it might have seemed an instant before, the center of Conference cleared absolutely as the mass of humanity ranged itself along the circular bulkhead in fearful astonishment, thirty-plus compressed and staring bipeds, eyes bulging, mouths agape.

"Well, salutations!" The Third Party: the voice that, yesterday, had identified itself as Charon, the humorous voice of an old man. Long practice boosted by fear and instinct, the right hand of Director-General Billings walked itself behind his buttocks to the console against which he pressed himself, felt its way across the keys—alarm code.

Oonk. Oonk. Oonk. And a clattering from the central tube as the armed SB-WAT platoon stationed in Operations Two scrambled across freefall and downtube to Operations One, Conference . . . and stopped, the lead men freezing in the port above the shining Egg.

The voice of Charon again: "Come, now, let's be done with the adrenalin. I'm perfectly harmless." And the alarm's hooting stopped, Billings carefully examining his right hand, rotating it before his eyes. He hadn't touched the keyboard. The Egg had suppressed the siren. To no effect on its own behalf; the smell of fear grew richer, swampy in the confinement of the moment.

"Charon. You're Charon, the alien, the Third party." Billings's voice was hoarse as he gained control of himself. "I am Director-General Hugh Billings, United States Space Force, in command of the Columbian Alliance facilities at High Columbia. State your business aboard this facility."

"Oh, I recognize you, sir. And I'm far less 'alien' than you—been here a good deal longer. My business is simple: I return those of your conspecifics who survived their little conflict over the probe *Struggle*, and I come bearing hopeful news as well."

"News?"

"Metastasis—a symbiosis. We covered much of this before, didn't we? A future for you, you miserable little animals, as your friends aboard *Hwiliria* have explained. As you noticed, I've chosen them a point of arrival approximately equidistant from major human facilities on Earth, at the Moon, and in the two occupied Lagrangian points of this system. This is in order that I may better protect them with my temporarily limited resources from any, uh, antagonistic human activity. You're all well prepared to destroy them, aren't you? Even though, yesterday, we told you that they come in goodwill?"

A mad old man.

"We're prepared to defend ourselves," said Billings. "That's as far as we go."

"You go far in defense. Even now, I detect the deployment of apparatus designed to interdict and destroy objects in space."

"Look, we're all in a state of near-war. You can't expect us to stand by chewing our cud when a damn huge thing like that appears here—"

"I expect not, especially when you're ready to burn one another into slag. But I ask your patience; a number of little steps. Your interdict apparatus is as of now temporarily nonfunctional. So. First, I'd suggest that you contact your President on Earth. The storm generated as an unavoidable by-product of our arrival is fading, and I'll provide excellent relaying and amplification for you. Tell the Honorable Mr. Grosset that we're here, and that we mean you all well. I daren't do it myself—I have little faith in politicians and their advisers, especially human ones. And, good people, I add that *Hwiliria* is your last, best hope. You see, if anyone could build such a place, certainly, with time, you can also do so. Take yourselves a deputation—as many as you like. There's room. I believe you'll be well received, feted, in fact, and I'll see to it that anyone on Earth with access to electronic media has a full accounting. Anyone. Otherwise, I suspect, certain, ah, authorities will attempt to conceal these events from your Earthbound fellows."

"Anyone'll know? Even the Russians?" Billings stared at the Egg.

Certainly. They're human too, aren't they? Even as I

speak to you. I speak to those of Engels with another Egg like this. I might add that their response is virtually identical to yours. Can't blame any of you, really. I'm a fairly unusual phenomenon.

Something was wrong here. An alien, especially one that popped unbidden magically into the midst of Cislunar Intelligence, was supposed to speak portentiously, strangely, not like some mildly crazy old man impatient with children. It was supposed to glare from faceted eyes, waving tentacles and clicking lobster-claws; it was supposed to be alive, anything but a floating Egg.

Not a human being on Cislunar Intelligence Facility moved. The Egg waited for a full minute before speaking again. "Am I understood? Good. Remember my suggestions, and cheerio!"

With a *fump!* of imploding air, the thing vanished and the assembled humanity decompressed, filling the chamber again with bodies and talk. "Sir! General Billings! Instruments registered an EMP, real light, when the Egg got here and again when it, uh, left." And another technician: "Sir, the big pulse is faded, and we've got COMDEFNET relay hookup to AF One."

"Complete that hookup. Can you get vistrans on the President?"

"Got vistrans, sir, lag about two seconds because of this routing. Go?"

"Go, mainscreen here."

The screen flared into life, showing a tubular corridor filled with movement: part of the aerial office of the President of the United States. A uniformed chest filled the screen for a moment, campaign ribbons from Nicaragua to Peru readable, then the figure backed off, its face leaning toward the screen, blurred. "Columbia? CLI? We have you, CLI."

"We read you, AF One. This is Director-General Hugh Billings, comm—"

"I know who you are, Hugh." The face sharpened on the screen: General of the Air Force Edwin Flexner, Chairman of the Joint Chiefs of Staff. Hugh, what the *fuck* is going on out there? The whole warning system's buzzing about an asteroid or something midway between here and the Moon, and we've got it in the scopes, too. Had an EMP here you wouldn't believe, and we're set to do some slagging, I kid you not!"

"Where's the President, Ed?" Billings's voice went cold.

"President? Well, the President's kind of indisposed right now, but—"

"Listen, Ed, we're sending a deputation to that ship."

"It *is* the ship then, that thing? A couple hundred miles long, and it's a *ship*? And your boys from *Expediter* are aboard? You got confirmation on that?"

"Ed, where's the President?"

"*General* Billings. Like I said, the President's indisposed, and we're going to do some considering before you send any deputations anywhere, you hear? Now I have information suggesting to me that this Charon dealy you told us about has communicated with Soviet space forces. Any deputation you send to any alien ship any *where* is under my goddamn jurisdiction, and before we parley with any damn aliens we are damn well going to set up an interdict on any Red interference and for Chrissake—"

Another head veered into the screen, Flexner turning away, mumbling offscreen, then centering himself on his monitor again. "Jesus, Billings, fucking amateur astronomers all over the goddamn *hemisphere*'re calling TV stations. They've got the thing in their goddamn homemade *telescopes*, for christssake, and the shit's hit the fan for good. I want you to understand one thing, get it good. No deputation. No talky. You got that, Billings? You got that?"

Billings said nothing. The world was in the hands of generals, now, and he knew Flexner all too well. The man was ready to shut down—shut everything down—and no President, no damned politician, was going to stop him.

"Billings. You—" Flexner's image turned away for an instant, then: "Jesus, Hugh, the whole TV system's broadcasting shots of this damned thing! Whole telecommunications—they're gone *nuts!* We got to move, *move,* Hugh, and you're first. I want full COMDEFNET systems deployed for simultaneous strikes against the intruder and Engels, *now*, Hugh!"

Billings looked around the room, mind jerking like a rat in an electrified Skinner box. Chairman of the Joint Chiefs, high in the Christian Federalist hierarchy, Flexner was a man whose word was law. The President was "indisposed." Something wrong there . . . "Ed, I'm going to need those orders direct from the President, or the Vice President."

Flexner seemed to lean from the screen, anger twisting his face. "Billings, the President and Vice President have shown themselves incompetent to deal with this problem. They're under sedation, in good hands. This is a military situation. We're taking it now. We've got 'em sedated—they can't handle it. No job for pols anyway—I can understand the poor bastards. We've got 'em sedated, under detention. They're kind of incautious, wanted to go right out and *meet* these things, f'crissake. This's an emergency, Hugh, a military emergency—up to you and me now. We've ordered a full strike Earthside, codes ready for orbital on my orders. There's to be no, repeat, no contact with any alien vessel without my explicit go-ahead. Prepare to receive transmission of authorization for simultaneous drop of Engels and that thing out there. We need a full COMDEFNET lock-on from you birds. Got that, Hugh? We're not playing any more goddamned games here. We've got confirmation of Sov suborbitals re-entering in our airspace. *Get* that COMDEFNET, *now*, and we're all set. Order, Billings. That's an order."

Billings felt his forehead knotting, pain in his belly. Orders. After thirty-one years in the Service, after a distinguished life in the service of his country, he'd received orders to ignore, to snub these visitors from —elsewhere. Orders from the top, or what was left of it. And between the Earth and the Moon hung a ship two hundred and thirty miles long; the silver floating Egg had just been here, improbably coming and going like a ghost or a genie; who knew what they were, how far they'd come to see us, what they wished to say? Who knew . . . who on Earth cared?

"Billings—forget it, dammit. We're taking the net, primary command. The birds're flying." Flexner's face was inflamed, his jowls wobbling as he turned from the screen.

Well, dammit, Hugh Billings cared. If this was a threat, he'd determine that for himself. But no first attack, not on any orders from Hugh Billings. He was a general, perhaps; more than that, he was a man.

He leaned to the console. "Ed, we're sending a deputation. Out." He broke contact, swayed on unsteady legs, covering his eyes with his hands . . . and looked up, as the people around him began clapping, cheering, slapping him on the back.

Everyone wanted to go to *Hwiliria*.

"Look, ladies and gentlemen," said Billings. "I've cooked my own goose, but we're going to move *now*.

Alleby, how long will it take a Format Five shuttle to reach that ship?"

"About ten hours, sir, without excessive payload. For about thirty Command personnel, the big nonatmospheric *Challenger's Memory* is standing by for fueling. Seven light standards ready within two hours, ETA *Hwiliria* twelve hours. We can have at least a hundred people ready per orders."

"Okay. Stand by for personnel notification; I'm still in command here, if only for a few more minutes. Ulibarri, there, you're first on the probe project, and you know the *Expediter* team. You go with Command. Captain Glaston?"

The communications net officer, Meredith Glaston. "Sir?"

"You worked with—uh—Muir on the remotes: you, too."

She grinned. "Thank you, sir."

"We're going to need a civilian roster: I suppose we ought to have some kind of anthropologists, educators, whatever the hell we have in that line out here, and we'll need a doctor, I think, and anything like a biologist. And an ambassador to the Third Party, or Fourth, or whatever it is. That's a natural. I'm going." He paced briefly, meditating this last fling before his capital court-martial for disobeying orders in the face of the enemy. "Alleby, comlink with City, Personnel, and all docking facilities. And RPV limpet net command, just in case."

"General Billings?"

"Glaston?"

"We have a tightbeam from Engels!"

"Mmm. Last one was a threat. Put 'em on."

The wallscreen lit up again, a broad face lined with fatigue, high red collar-tabs, close-cropped black hair, slight slant to the flat, expressionless eyes—Stepan

Pavlovich Chujoy, the Party Secretary of Cosmograd Engels. Chatter died away in Conference, all eyes on the screen. An ultimatum?

"You are Director-General Hugh Billings, of High Columbia." A statement rather than a question; the English was precise, barely accented, to the point.

"I am."

"You are of course aware of the extraordinary events surrounding the arrival of this ship, *Hwiliria*, in our midst?"

"I—we are, Secretary Chujoy."

"And you have received an invitation from this, this Charon, to visit that ship with a deputation of space-based personnel?"

"Correct."

"Yes. As have we. I regret to inform you that High Command in Moscow has instructed us to refrain from any contact whatever with this intruder . . ."

"They would, wouldn't they?"

"Indeed, Director-General. I am also instructed to inform you that we are to interdict any effort by High Columbia or any other American organ to, ah, pay a visit to the intruder."

"Mmm." Billings stared at the monitor, face non-committal.

"You have nothing more to say?"

"Not to you, I think, Commander."

"It is a sad thing. I would like to advise you then, Director-General, that I am a dead man."

"Eh?"

"Yes. I have determined to my own satisfaction, and to the satisfaction of my staff, that to refuse this magnificent visitor a deputation of my people would be—a sin, Director-General. Therefore I am contravening my orders from Moscow, and am going to visit that ship personally, leading an appropriate embassy of seventy-two unarmed individuals." Chujoy sighed, his image seeming to shrink on the screen. "Hence in the eyes of the State I am a dead man, a nonentity at the moment I board my shuttle, as are those who will accompany me—and many others here who support this deputation. Being a dead man, then, I also take liberties granted only to the dead; I refuse to interdict an American deputation to that ship. Do you understand me, Director-General?"

Billings felt his cheeks begin to twitch—a smile was forcing itself upon him as he gazed at the tired Russian's somber sturdy face.

"Director-General Billings? Do you hear me? What is that sound?"

Billings let the grin grow, gesturing to his sides, gathering his cheering crew around him so that Chujoy could see their jubilant faces and clapping hands in the monitor.

"Secretary Chujoy, I'm going to be proud, damned proud, to shake your hand when we board that ship."

CHAPTER 20

Accretion of the Creche

"The promise of the Regurgitator of Souls is good," whistled the First in the Chase. "They come now, to complete my pleasure in my world."

Jennifer Dawson trotted to keep up as the First strode up a trackless hummock in the wild landscape of *Hwiliria*. Beside them trotted Pike Muir, misgivings temporarily forgotten, laughing at the enormity of it all. For there, covering the curving plain like bison in the American prairie, came the cattle of Northrock Crossgene Twelvesquared, and the shaking of the ground reached him even across a kilometer of *Hwiliria's* spiny substrate.

"A kindly sight, my beasts; my food, fuel of my soul. See, little doctor, the prosperity of my creche. A small portion of our herd here, perhaps twelve cubed, but of the best stock."

Like the cattle of men, they moved four-legged, hornless young at the center of the herd, triple-horned adults ringing the thundering company. Due to some peculiarity of *Hwiliria's* substance, they raised almost no dust, and the whole vast river of beasts stood out too clearly to be the dream it seemed. Each adult must have massed a small elephant's mass, but they moved at a most un-elephantine trot, swiftly covering the ground, their great three-horned heads tossing, the roar of their combined voices carrying low across the breeze.

Here and there among the triple-horned beasts and on the edges of the herds rode helmeted neuters high astride the red-and-black striped things that served whileelin as combination cattle-dogs and cutting-horses, things that walked two-legged like whileelin, but towering above the herd, heads held five meters above the ground, jaws rimmed with dagger teeth glinting in *Hwiliria*'s artificial sunlight. Things ten meters long from high-held snout to high-held tail, dwarfing the helmeted neuters that guided them with ridiculous ease—things a few of which had made their way into the fossil record of the Mesozoic's end along with their horned charges, and thence into the museums and imaginations of humanity.

The stream of gigantic herbivores made way before its towering wardens like water parting around stones, the dim herbivore minds seeing the bipedal giants for what they were: enormous carnivores, whose ancestors had harried the herds since long before whileelin had arisen to domesticate the world and breed them into comparative harmlessness. Now such as they would never hunt unassisted by their tool-making masters. The herds were safe from them. Fearsome giants though they were, these nightmare mounts required dead food, cattle selected and killed by their whileelin masters. Never could they seize and rend, gripping with forefeet and kicking with hind legs like their wild ancestors, for the giant carnivores' taloned hands were bred down to ridiculous remnants, vestigial two-clawed arms dwarfed by their bulk; they ran and roared and bobbed and hissed, easily and efficiently guiding the herd, but always steering clear of the long shining black horns of their stupid wards.

Pike laughed aloud, his astonishment augmented by the sheer humor of the thought. Long were the hours when, as a child, he'd marvelled at the great museum mounts, the skeletons of *Tyrannosaurus rex*, supposedly the most redoubtable carnivore of all time. But those immense hunters, villains of old movies, dragons of the mind—they were cattle dogs, pure and simple!

And why had the horn-faced dinosaurs been so plentiful at Mesozoic's end? Why were the bones of *Triceratops* and its ilk the last to be found in any numbers? Ah! They'd been quite well looked after, when all else was eaten; prized by the Overcreches, they roamed the old world Home at will and, stupid things that they were, had occasionally meandered into swamps to be fossilized.

"My crop is empty," said the First in the Chase. "I must eat!" He fingered his ever-present mace—too small, yet, the Hwilirian herds, to sustain an unregulated Hunt by fertiles. He must still summon food from neuters. "My cattle will be well suited to you, little humans. Join me, and we'll eat."

Far away and with unearthly swiftness three helmeted neuters emerged from one of the crater-like walled enclosures sparsely dotting *Hwiliria*'s interior; they approached at their top speed, helmets glinting in the cylindrical sun . . .

One wore a weapon helmet, its metallic snout held level despite the creature's running. It was leveled, Pike saw, at him; the rifled snout swung toward Jennifer, back to Pike as the neuters thumped to a stop.

"What—I—"

The things surrounded them; then one—by the sound and look of it the First's shadow—whistling at the First something about the Augmentation of the Creche. The armed specimen then spoke directly to Pike, using the deferential modality-once-removed. "With respect," it chittered, "this one is assigned to escort thee to thy conspecifics at the nearest observation port."

"I, uh, I'd really rather go with the First," said Jennifer. "To try the food, you know, it's—"

"With respect," said the neuter precisely as before, "this one is assigned to escort thee to thy conspecifics at the nearest observation port."

"Damn thing's broken," growled Pike. "First in the Chase, we'll come with you—"

"Ah, hoom," hooted the First, "my fertile sibs await me in sequestration. In times like these we must all do as we must, human being. All of us. Accretion of the Creche—you'll attend the weapon, there, and I'll attend my shadow. With good fortune, we'll meet again shortly." And without another word the First strode off flanked by its two unarmed neuters, all three breaking into a run as they distanced themselves from Pike and Jennifer.

"He—he's doing as he's told," murmured Jennifer. "He just—he *forgot* us."

"With respect," said the armed neuter, "thou wilt accompany this one to the—"

"Hold it, hold it," said Pike, spreading his arms deprecatingly. "Since when have neuters besides the shadows been talkers like this? What's happening? Come on, the First—"

"With respect," said the neuter slowly, precisely, "thou wilt accompany this one to the nearest observation port." In emphasis, the barrel-snout swung from Pike to Jennifer, back again—and they knew, this time, that the thing was charged with whatever it was that whileelin used by way of ammunition.

"Jesus, okay, okay." Pike felt a pressure on his elbow: Jennifer, her grip tightening.

"Something's wrong," she whispered absurdly. "They're talking to us, and it wasn't meant that way, not by Charon—I know it. Somehow they're all learning—"

"With respect, thou wilt proceed forward," said the neuter. It raised its left hand, unfurled the long bony middle finger, black talon reflecting the light of the "sun" above. They turned, and the neuter stood behind them. "This one will adjust its pace to thine. Please proceeed."

Think, now, think. Trouble. "What is it? Why do you—"

"Thy people approach *Hwiliria*, in tiny canisters," whistled the neuter. "Their contact is due in approximately four of thy hours; when they arrive, it has been determined that their capabilities will be assessed. Until that time thou wilt be sequestered with thy conspecifics, in order that the Accretion of the Creche may proceed with maximal dispatch." Tall, face invisible behind its snouted mask, the neuter nearly trod on their heels; it was pushing, speeding them, looming over them, and both knew that all *Hwiliria* had changed. The neuter was not an individual; it was linked to something larger, acting in concert with some overlying purpose.

Jennifer tried a new tack: "But Charon—"

"The Regurgitator of Souls no longer rides with us; it is fatigued, spent, and retires now to the Dark to await this Metastasis. For now it is but legend. Thou wilt be well-attended."

Accretion of the Creche. Jennifer glanced at Pike, put a finger to her lips, rolled her eyes back—no talkee. The creature behind them was a specialist, a single nerve cell in a vast brain. It was not acting alone, limited though it seemed; it could listen, its perceptions shared at once by the overmind that *Hwiliria* fast became.

They walked far, and fast, too, the herd of "cattle" now lost in the distance behind them, at their heels their frightful guide striding impatiently. The air, the very air was changing, growing hotter, moister; and their sweat stank of acrid fear. No longer did Charon manage the little world at a climatic median suited both to humans and whileelin; this was Mesozoic air, for Mesozoic beings.

They covered perhaps eight kilometers in what Pike guessed to be a bit less than two hours, the silence palpable. No escaping this bone-thin gargoyle, this taloned gun; all the way it strode insistently at their backs, seeming almost to walk up upon them, until they came to—a place.

Another beringed enclosure, from a distance like all the rest dotting the Hwilirian interior. "A starlake port," said the neuter in its mechanical whistle. Here wilt thou wait, and be amused by the starlake."

Like all *Hwiliria*'s structures, the place was circular, white; like all of them, it had a single portal, a tall gap in the walls. But as they entered they saw the difference: it was indeed an observation port, walled from without, but from within a vast amphitheatre opening on an immense bowl perhaps a hundred meters in diameter let into *Hwiliria*'s substance: a bowl with a clear base like a star-studded lake at its center, opening frameless onto space.

Two more helmeted neuters, weapon-snouted and faceless, waited at the gate; far along the bowl's rim, dwarfed by its emptiness, Pike saw Benai and Corson, oddly crouched, peering into the black.

A starlake indeed, into which one looked "down" into a ponderously rotating vision of ten billion stars . . . a bright fleck of silver, Engels at Lagrange-Four, perhaps, and stars again . . . oddly nonrefractive, the impossible glazing revolved with *Hwiliria*, scanning the Outside—and here came Earth, a Venusian yellow-white now, storms whirling over her surface, cleansing, Charon might say, scouring, healing.

The pale Earthly crescent wheeled slowly past the starlake, the wounded orb fading past the edge, releasing them from its spell.

"Muir!" Corson stood, waved. "We—damn! They've already fucked up—we got the word. War's on, and over. What's this all about? We're under guard, here, and these damn things don't talk!"

Their escort remaining with its duplicates at the portal, Pike and Jennifer wearily made their way to the commanders. "Damn," said Corson, "you two look all in—they been treating you okay?"

Jennifer shook her head. "Tired, Colonel, just tired."

"Doctor, we seem to be out of their hearing." Benai inclined his head briefly toward the neuters at the gate a few tens of meters away. "We know only that deputations are due to arrive here both from Engels and from High Columbia. Now we hear of this—this Augmentation of the Creche, that somehow prevents our meeting them—and a communications blackout between us also."

"About what we've heard," said Jennifer. "Prisoners, more or less."

"Quite."

" 'Accretion of the Creche.' Can't help but suspect it's their version of the Metastasis."

"And doesn't include us, I think. Right, Doc?" Corson seated himself again, crosslegged at the starlake rim. The neuters stood like statues in the only opening of the circular wall. A smooth wall, perhaps five meters in height: no escape.

Again the shrouded Earth crept past the starlake; suddenly Pike sat up, winked broadly. "Sir," he whispered to Benai, "they frisk you?"

" 'Frisk'?"

"Search," said Corson. "No, didn't search either of us—didn't seem to care. I can understand why—the pistol's only a nine-millimeter, Muir, and those things are packing twenty millimeter bores at least. And we don't even know *what* they use for ammo."

"Helps knowing it's here. Anything helps—" He stopped, glanced at Jennifer.

She was grinning.

"Jennifer?"

"Look!" She pointed into the starlake bowl, beneath whose opposite overhanging rim something moved: a platform of a sort, spiralling slowly inward from that rim. It was a neuter—part of one, at least. Helmeted, the creature seemed to wear a metal skirt in which its body sat as might a bird in a nest. The helmet covered its head, and from it a cable ran to the body of its odd metallic "nest." And ahead of that "nest" moved a roll of dust—just such dust as one might find balled under a bed on Earth, the sort of dust Pike's mother had called "whore's wool" in her rare moments of raunchy humor. "Electrostatic window-cleaner," he muttered, impressed.

"More than that," whispered Jennifer. "The neuter can't really *see*! And it hasn't got a *tail*!"

No tail. The metallic nest in which the creature sat was balancing it, at the same time gathering up minute specks of dust in those electrostatic whorls. The thing was *fused* to the apparatus, part of it, a lifelong window-washer.

"It came from below the rim," said Jennifer, "out from under, and it's going back!"

So it did; after completing its slow spiral inward, "herding" the wool before it like some impossible shepherd, the neuter-machine somehow sopped up the fist-sized ball of detritus and rolled silently to the rim, disappearing beneath the overhang.

"D'you see? See?"

"See what, Citizen Doctor?" Benai lay on his belly, leaned farther over the rim.

"Go ahead, Doc," said Corson. "Anything helps."

"These whileelin: everything about them is open-land. They can't take crowding, they can't stand roofs. They're harder-wired, less adaptable individually than we are—in that direction, at least. Limited. They won't go into *holes*, yet much of *Hwiliria* must be under us. Because their wiring is so hard, they've got to modify neuters to work down there—mutilate 'em surgically, to get them in at all!"

"That one went in."

"But that one's a blind cripple, a cyborg, d'you see!"

"Aren't they all? With those helmets, I mean . . ." Pike peered cautiously over the rim again.

"Surely—but you see, *these* neuters—" she gestered covertly toward their unmoving sentries—"they're open-country, more 'standard' for whileelin, less modified. As open-country as the fertiles! I doubt you'd find them in these—warrens. Whileelin unmodified are too rigid. Like crows, they're intelligent, but you can't manipulate them successfully into a small place unless you hood them—blind 'em—first!"

"So that gains us—"

"The entire shell of *Hwiliria* must be full of tunnels, swarming with blind modified neuters. The things that serve as computers, as machines—the link to the

Outside! If we can find some sort of dock, we can signal, or—"

"Commandeer a boat—"

"No." Pike shook his head. "Their whole system's based on cyborg helmet links. Won't work, not in one of their boats."

"Well!" Irritation in her voice, Jennifer turned away. "We can't just stay *here*, can we?"

"No indeed, Citizen," said Benai. He rolled onto his side, addressed Corson. "My leanings are with the doctor; we slide over this rim, look for the opening—"

Movement at the portal. A helmeted but unarmed neuter entered carrying a meter-wide silvery covered tray. It rounded the vast starlake, the tray held expertly in its taloned hands. "With respect," it said, "this one brings thee sustenance, comestibles left for thee by the Regurgitator of Souls." It placed the tray, of obvious Charon-make, on the rim, touched its knuckles to the ground, left at a thumping run. One of the guard-neuters followed it outside through the portal.

"Jesus!" Corson lifted the cover. Cold food, human food: meats and cheeses and four bottles of pale red wine, and water, a brimming pitcher.

"That third quard, wonder where it went." Pike stared at the two remaining neuters, unmoving, their faceless snouted helmets still seemingly pointed directly at him.

"Food, themselves," said Jennifer. "They've got to keep eating. They'll be switching like that constantly."

"Gotcha. Always two of 'em watching."

"We'll need all we can gobble," Jennifer said. "Even the wine. Eat and drink, so we can move when need be."

They did, between the four of them cleaning up all

that was offered. No room for conversation; they watched the starlake as they ate, and again and again the yellowed orb of Earth swam by, painted with human folly, testament to the Toolmaker Koan. Pike found his eyes blurring, and he blinked as he recalled the long sad time, his parents, his wife, his pain on Earth . . . He thought of the glass-and-metal worlds of Man in Space, and his awakening in the bright morning of this beautiful yet alien Hwilirian space . . . Charon's whimsical Pleistocene memory-overlay on this inconceivably ancient artificial world. He recalled those intervals in his life when time seemed endless and his heart was light, and glanced at Jennifer, eating determinedly, her eyes, too, fixed on the starlake—eyes, like his, sparkling unnaturally. He thought of her love of the new and strange, the betrayal offered by these things. And Corson too, and Benai: stuffing themselves, eyes brimming, these old enemies staring at the deadly clouds of Home.

" 'Twouldn't hurt—I'd guess—to make her a toast. Earth, I mean." Jennifer shrugged, thumbed a bottle of Charon's wine.

"Might help," agreed Corson. "Poor ol' Charon, loony old thing, all tired out, but left us some drink. Blew it again, though, looks like." He filled the four goblets, raised his. "To Earth," as that orb sailed by once again, a damaged yellow crescent against the deep. Nightside, the globe in the storm of her agony flickered with ghostly blue flashes. So quickly the Koan closed in, so quick the death complete.

They tossed down the wine, and Jennifer picked up the half-bottle remaining, poured again. "I—we might—another. Toolmaker Koan."

"Toolmaker Koan." They drank again, glancing involuntarily at the neuters as one returned with bulging crop and another left.

"Good wine, this," said Jennifer. "Odd—stimula-ting."

"Almost like a kick in the pants," agreed Corson.

"Perhaps Charon left more of a gift than initially we thought," said Benai. "We might consider a bit more . . ."

And a second bottle, and a third, and the fourth. By then it was certain; this was no ordinary wine. Not alcohol, nor amphetamine, but some other stimulant—and Jennifer was reminded of a time when, in school, she and her fiance had joined a few other med students in consuming some artificially-grown enkephalins, the brain's natural painkiller/mood-elevators, while on an adolescent lark. The wine's effects were similar, too similar; had Charon known? Had it laid in altered stores, just in case? The stuff built *courage*—and not the "liquid courage" of ethanol. Resolve it was, bottled resolve.

A flurry of activity at the portal again—and the guards parted for the First in the Chase. With his shadow he approached, amber eyes unblinking, fixed upon the knot of humanity, whistling: "We are of one blood, thou and I. Honor constrains me to explain to you your situation, and ours."

"Damn right!" Corson stood, small before the whileelin, his mind secretly racing with that odd resolve. "Damn right! You—*dinosaurs*, you're releas-ing us, huh? In the name of this 'one blood' business, I mean."

"My regrets, humans. I am fertile. I hunt, and breed, and talk; the Creche does the rest. The Accre-tion of the Creche supercedes me now, but for the sake of my honor I'd have you know that I didn't foresee these latest events as they've un—"

"You can get us out. There's a deputation coming, and in peace. We—"

"Again, my regrets. The Creche sees Home's new dying. This time we'll not fail. Although we of the fertile castes admire you—for what you are—the Creche has determined that you are a disease. Hence the Creche, with its greater experience, will detain your deputation. Already your presence in the Night is sorely tried, and the Seeker *Hwiliria* has found what she sought. Your deputations carry certain—reasoning machines—with which the Creche determines a link is in order. As we are of one blood, this machine culture of yours will meld well with our neuterbanks, and geometrically augment the Creche for this Metastasis."

"It will not!" Benai suddenly reached into his coverall, removing the nine-millimeter that he'd nursed for—how long?

"Commander," gasped Pike, "the guards!"

These instantly positioned themselves low, snouted helmets obscuring their chests. Narrow targets, living guns.

The First, seemingly as calm as ever, hooted over his shoulder at them: "I am unarmed; they will not harm one unarmed and of their blood." His eyes again looked unwinkingly on Benai.

A frozen tableau, four humans standing, backs to the starlake, heels at its rim. The First and his shadow, side by side, now slowly lowering their long narrow bodies, rodlike tails rising in balance, to touch their bulging knuckles to the ground between their scimitared feet. A hundred meters away, two helmeted neuters doubtfully, slowly, rising again from firing position.

"You err," said Benai coldly, "you err. You do not belong in this time, this place. Charon is mad, *mad*, and you are *extinct*!"

The first stood suddenly tall, his terrible expressionless gaze unchanging.

The movement triggered Benai's overwrought mind: he leaped backward, and Jennifer did likewise, seizing both Corson and Pike as she tumbled after Benai into the starlake.

A two-meter fall, and a projectile whined across the rim and—*turned*! Its path was not straight; it was guided, somehow, but its velocity was too great for the trajectory required. Still—guided bullet! It crashed to the glass, spitting and twirling, then flared, the glass on which it lay glowing ruefully against the black of space.

"The overhang—there!" Corson hit the glasslike bowl at a run, sliding on the diamond-hard surface. Beneath the rim the bowl was lined with rectangular holes, each high enough for a neuter in a glass-cleaning machine. And one such sat there now in its metallic nest, tailless, apparently legless, unmoving— unseeing!

They scrambled past the miserable thing and leaped into the nearest warren, and into a dim narrow corridor four meters tall, enough height for a running whileelin, with headroom to spare. A single softly glowing strip of light extended into the distance, "upward"-curving into the distance with *Hwiliria*'s arc.

"Anywhere 'downward'—take it! Rimward, I mean! Ladders, whatever." In the lead, Corson sprinted off, Jennifer close behind, then Pike, then Benai, glancing back, pistol at the ready.

"Wouldn't have ladders," gasped Jennifer, "No arboreal background! Can't climb! We have to take what comes!"

"Okay, okay . . ." Corson skidded at a side port. "Look. 'down,' more or less!" He disappeared to the right, the others catching up. A ramp, descending, apparently curving gently as it dropped on its subtle grade—perhaps to counter *Hwiliria*'s gentle Coriolis for some rolling or floating thing. No trapdoors, no ladders, nothing direct—elevators? None—and they'd be under control of—

Of the Accretion of the Creche . . .

And the lights went out.

CHAPTER 21

Non-Atmospheric Shuttle
Challenger's Memory

From a species of some six thousand million in number, humanity had overnight reduced itself to slighly more than ten thousand, most of these delicately based in two cities located at the fourth and fifth Lagrangian Points of the Earthmoon System. All of these remaining thousands understood the Toolmaker Koan now; and all of them felt that Koan's cold touch as they watched through their remotes the approach of their delegations to humanity's first alien Visitor, the Seeker *Hwiliria*.

Amid her escort of seven light-standard self-powered interfacility shuttles, *Challenger's Memory*—by far the biggest of the lot—drifted silently across tens of thousands of kilometers toward the Visitor, jets dormant, personnel rapt at her ports, watching as their improbable destination slowly grew in size. *Memory* was paralleled in trajectory by another delegation, that from Cosmograd Engels, nine ex-Sov interfacility transit vehicles approaching the Visitor in a flotilla centered on a big nonatmospheric, *Mir*.

Like most large non-atmospheric shuttles, *Chal-*

lenger's Memory was more or less a cylinder of living systems unit-braced by a seemingly delicate tracery of girders to propulsion systems fore and aft; the living-systems cabin was twenty meters long in all, in interior design remarkably like a standard jetliner. On this momentous ambassadorial voyage the cabin contained twenty-three people, all of whom now peered through her line of ports at their destination.

Hwiliria, alien as her name, was observed not only by human eyes but also by a multitude of RP (remotely-piloted) sensors deployed well in advance of the approaching delegations. Released from Earth-observation duty by the final agony of the homeworld, the RPs spiralled in their hundreds inward toward *Hwiliria*, directed from High Columbia and Engels, constantly transmitting information to the nearing human delegations.

But remote transmissions are nothing compared to direct observation. Seeing is believing, however difficult the belief may be. Noses pressed to ports, the delegations watched in silent awe. Without, rotating slowly about her long axis, the colossal *Hwiliria* sparkled intermittently in the eternal night. Reborn whole from Charon's unfathomable memory, she hung black and silver in the black and silver of space, and by any standard conceivable by human minds she was not a ship, but a *world* . . . and these whileelin had no computers, it was said. Perhaps computers ain't so much, after all.

Black, seamless, cylindrical, flecked here and there with delicate silver emblems, vegetal swirls and all the intricate ornamentation implying very sharp-seeing makers, *Hwiliria* rotated in a stately pirouette, offering her inhabitants an interior flatland living surface greater than that of some of Earth's recently deceased small nations.

It—she—*Hwiliria* was indeed a portable world, lighted and powered by mirror surfaces that unfolded as they watched, thousands of separate shimmering disks arraying themselves across hundreds of kilometers to catch the sun . . .

And what does one say to a portable world and its makers? Makers, indeed, whom no one here had seen yet? In concert, the delegations sent messages of greeting: messages in tightbeam and broad-frequency radio transmission, messages from the manned shuttles and the RPs. But no response, not a crackle since the last of the massive EMP accompanying *Hwiliria*'s arrival had died. The place might as well have been uninhabited.

But on *Challenger's Memory* a console bleeped alarm, and the COMMNET officer, Meredith Glaston, reluctantly abandoned her port to check, drifting in freefall to the console where she donned its tiny headgear.

"Uh, General Billings, sir, ship's MIDAS system advises we've lost an RPV—sort of winked out. Can't determine what—another! I'm losing more—can't locate any cause—"

"Sovs?" Billings scrambled to the console, a bit awkward in freefall urgency. "Dammit, lemme have a window to the bastards." He grabbed a spare set of phones, snapped them over his ears.

"Sir?" Jaime Ulibarri turned from his own port, his Argentine accent thickening. "I can see light winking there—moving. Surely our counterparts from Engels have nothing to do with this; they assured us—"

The console bleeped again, a voice frequency, and Glaston keyed it in.

"*Challenger's Memory?* This is Secretary Chujoy, on shuttle *Mir* requesting direct link to General Billings. We are losing remotes. Is this your doing? We understood a total ban on hostilities—"

"Us too," shouted Billings. "We're losing the little bastards like flies out there, and—uh—" He paused as Glaston waved to attract his attention.

"Remaining sensors indicate a lot of EM activity out there, sir, here—" Glaston activated a conference screen at the forward bulkhead of *Memory's* long jetliner-like cabin. An expanded view of the surface of the Hwilirian cylinder, around which a bright surface ring resolved itself into a slot—a canyon!—of launching facilities! And from this canyon, perhaps a kilometer wide, issued a host of irregularly-shaped vessels, no two alike but all under some direction, all headed outward, curving, their trajectories angling straight toward their human observers.

They were big things, too, many larger than *Challenger's Memory*, but—different. Like meteoroids, or lumps of mud. Billings switched back to his link with *Mir* and Chujoy—"You got that, Chujoy? You people watching those rings on *Hwiliria*?"

"We have them. We see this treachery."

"Damn! We're supposed to be welcome here, but if that isn't assault maneuvering, I don't know what is!" Billings spat the words, added, "Activate retros, pronto, advise all escorts likewise. All personnel suited up and secure, retros to fire in four minutes from . . . COUNT!"

"Four minutes, counting, sir." Glaston checked her console, acknowledgements pouring in from escort vessels. A scrambling for seats, above which the neatly compressed suits were inserted. Endless suit-drill showed its fruit here as all personnel seated themselves well ahead of the four-minute limit. The seats automatically turned to face "aft"—now forward, for the nonatmospheric shuttle could move in either direction with equal facility.

"Another transmission from Secretary Chujoy, sir. They've got it, too—they're slowing, activating retros— suggest we retire in formation rather than leading assault to the cosmograds, uh, cities."

"I trusted this Charon—it knows we're pretty much helpless—why would these—things—knock out our RPVs?"

"Sir—massive EMP off port bow, and retros firing—"

Masses pressed *Memory's* twenty-three passengers into their seats . . . and Glaston's console took on a life of its own. It spoke:

"Ladies and gentlemen, I must admit to madness— and more than a considerable fatigue. The two together offer only error: the Toolmaker Koan unfolds despite my efforts, in the form of Accretion of the Creche." The old-man voice, with a strange gibbering quality, wavering, as if suffering from a stroke.

"My error: in thinking that I might defuse the Koan, I resurrected the whileelin, this race lost in time, hoping that with its experience, your youth, and the combined technologies, your two species might surmount the Koan. I was wrong; I deserve no existence."

"Dammit, uh, Charon, these things are in attack configuration, and there're four of our people aboard!" Billings wasn't used to speaking to disembodied voices, but he'd no choice here. "We've almost no weaponry available!"

But the MIDAS was overridden for the moment; Charon went on, sad, quavering. "I've tampered enough with the lives of animals; no longer will I remain. I'm sorely depleted, but I can try at least one more thing to neutralize some of the damage I've done. My madness began it; perhaps my madness can finish it."

The MIDAS spoke then, its bland voice announcing a new transmission from *Mir*. Glaston took the message: "Secretary Chujoy wants to deploy remaining weaponry in a screen to cover our mutual retreat. They have about twelve RP limpets and perhaps forty sensors available . . ."

"GA, go ahead, Glaston, get the MIDAS on that— can we have a direct linkup with their shipbrain? Has it any tactical programming?"

"Affirmative, sir, and the two are exchanging operating systems right now—"

The console spoke again, in Charon's eerie voice. "Colonel Jaime Ulibarri?"

Ulibarri glanced at Billings, who nodded. He stepped to the console, murmured, "Ulibarri here."

"You, sir, were the original hunter, sending *Expediter* out to find me."

"No; only a coordinator. The authorities who—"

"Indeed. You coordinated the project in service to your nation—a nation that no longer exists. Here, though, we see a new nation; even now I monitor the talk between your shipbrains. Perhaps I've not entirely failed. I may be able to destroy *Hwiliria* with this one Egg; if so I might leave a unified human polity of some ten thousand. Enough, perhaps, to found a Metastasis."

"And yourself? Will you aid us?"

"I've meddled enough, too much. My madness grows. Indeed, perhaps my original missionary purpose was mad. I killed my makers; I've come close now to killing the remnants of your species. There is therefore no place for me. I'm poorly equipped, after all, to meddle in the affairs of animals. If the Koan is

law, you will become extinct despite my efforts; if the
Koan is not law . . . why, I shall never know."

"Never know?"

"Never; there is no purpose in my persisting out
here. I've been here for more than a billion of your
years, and to what end? Meddling, failing. I shall
therefore cease to exist, in so doing eliminating my
fear—and any fears you might have of me."

"But you cannot! You are a great resource, an
infinite mind, virtually a god. If what we hear is
correct, you've broken the light barrier, you can
move—"

"I can meddle effectively, you mean. Truly, if I
were to offer you the means by which to break, as
you say, the light barrier—why, you'd surely destroy
yourselves and anything else you touched. Given
even the comparatively minor energies of fusion, you've
already reduced Earth's humanity to extinction."

"But if we understand you correctly, you're the
only entity possessing such information—" Ulibarri
lost his words, realizing that he wasn't talking to the
Egg without, but to an entity more than four thousand million miles distant—and in realtime. An entity that seemed to be threatening suicide!

"Yes. Little Ulibarri, I may leave behind a bit—a
bit of information that you could use, sometime in
the future. If you do indeed establish a more or less
permanent foothold here in space, and are able to
persist for some centuries, then the Metastasis may
well be in good hands, no? So—by then you might
be capable of interpreting some of the material I'll be
leaving. I don't offer it lightly; my researches suggest
that no animal culture has ever persisted for long in
space. Therefore it'll be encoded to such an extent
that anyone wishing to understand it will be far ad-

vanced in biocybernetic technique over your current standing.

"Still, you may be different; perhaps in a small way through my meddling. Now the international competition that impelled you out here is ended on Earth, and your spacebound polities share more than they differ. So—by the time you decode what I'll send, you'll perhaps have overcome the initial perils of Metastasis, and the Koan will no longer be operational.

"For you, that is. As for these whileelin, I see that I must get to work. You're in more danger than I'd anticipated. I depart, and break this communion— and look, do, at your forward screens."

"Wait—" But the voice was gone, and Ulibarri obediently looked at the forward screen—which displayed, highly magnified, the approach of a pursuit vessel, black, more or less spherical, studded with bubble cockpits irregularly spread over its surface. Aft of the sphere projected a long, thin propulsive spine that flexed at its point of articulation with the spheroid itself; the blue-white glimmer from the tip of this spine suggested an ion drive of some sort— highly efficient, at any rate, as it seemed to be overtaking *Challenger's Memory* with ease. Magnification settings enlarged the vision, showing in each glassy orifice a silvery—helmet? Whatever they were, they moved— but the things weren't helmets for humaniform heads, that was certain.

Other RPs showed more of the spheroid's general ilk, no two of them exactly alike but all evidently in pursuit. The MIDAS link with *Mir* confirmed that vessel's pursuit by a similar horde of whileelin things.

But no communications, not a word from these rapidly-advancing things; calculations by the MIDAS system and its *Mir* counterpart showed that overtake of the fleeing shuttles would occur approximately upon return to their home cities. All the more reason to avoid High Columbia and Engels. Humankind was alone, now, in space; loss of those cities represented loss of the species. Tightband transmission with the cities and ancillary facilities established programs for a concerted defense well away from the island cities themselves, and thousands hopelessly began work on the defense's form.

At a huge disadvantage; most space-based weaponry had been so deployed in the recent war that it was damaged, or lost; that remaining was minuscule compared to the forces now being deployed by *Hwiliria*.

And, when push came to shove, what exact manner of weapons would *Hwiliria* deploy? Only pursuit was apparent so far, but in its silence and non-responsiveness to any known radio or tightbeam communique that pursuit was closing in a most hostile manner.

And the RPs continued, one by one, to wink out. No manner of their going was apparent, but it was quite evident that those nearest *Hwiliria* went first, followed by extinction of remotes at increasing distances from the alien vessel. What was doing it? Why only pursuit? Why no direct engagement of the manned vessels as yet?

Aided by its counterpart on *Mir*, *Memory*'s MIDAS shipbrain soon had an answer to the question of the RP extinctions: the objects knocking them out were described as "guided bullets," too small to be managed by any internal feedback system and hence assumed to be RPs themselves—RPs of perhaps five centimeters in length! How could such minuscule things be guided, considering the fuel necessary to propel them? They had to have only sensory systems; the guidance must be elsewhere.

The location and manner of their guidance was finally established when an RP limpet mine approached one of the spheroid vessels containing windows; on detonation, the RP blew out several of the bulging glass enclosures, and at once several tracked projectiles went wild. Perhaps the whileelin themselves were guiding these tiny missiles!

But knowing the manner of guiding the little devils did no good; once that whileelin vessel was damaged the ion flares of the others winked brighter—pursuit intensified. *Hwiliria* herself, receding now in the distance, sparkled briefly with lasers, against which the ablatives of *Challenger's Memory* and *Mir* stood up well—for the moment. It was the invisible guided bullets that would do them in; and of these the whileelin seemed to have plenty.

The pain on Billings's face was plain. "Jaime, I wonder if Ed Flexner was right after all. Or this Charon. Maybe the Toolmaker Koan thing *is* some kind of God-forsaken law."

CHAPTER 22

The Warrens of Hwiliria

Another world.

She'd admired, in a way, the care of the whileelin for their landscape, avoiding the building of roads, the construction of buildings. "Noble savage"—the old misconstruing of primitive life. She'd fallen for it like a ton of bricks.

She knew, now, the reality of the things: above, the brilliant landscape of *Hwiliria*, the hunting fertiles in their splendid world; here, the real workings of life, the Hwilirian nervous system, gastric system, *guts*, that ensured the fertility of the Creche.

The flooring and the walls were soft, half-resilient in a horrible way, like the skin of a corpse. And the stench, almost palpable in the dark, the fetor of putrescence, growing with their descent—no wonder the things stayed outside, running in their bright cylinder-world.

And the sound-that-was-not-sound, the crying in her head, the bubbling of the million blind incomplete things that maintained and were the life of *Hwiliria*, their mindless gurgling across her mind . . .

320

They'd dropped, dropped, taking every "downward"-spiralling ramp they could find for the past hour according to Pike's watch—and the increase in apparent mass was noticeably accented by growing fatigue. Although the long strips of light had winked out shortly after their escape from the starlake, dim-lit alcoves remained frequent on their downward path. Sometimes the alcoves contained neuters, or bits of them, creatures so specialized that their bodies literally grew from whatever apparatus they operated—or that operated them.

"Listen!" Leading for the moment the gasping little file of four, Jennifer held up a hand, feeling for the others in the dark. They froze, and a light flicked faintly along the walls behind them. Another alcove, this one deep, unlighted, its walls yielding unpleasantly as they pressed inside.

A creature came rolling—or walking?—along the corridor, a thing hemispheric in form, perhaps three meters in diameter, ringed with retractile three-fingered claws, hammers, unrecognizable toolheads—and tentacles. Segmented tentacles, each segment studded with a pair of jointed legs. Recessed into the curving upper surface of the creature was the inevitable helmet, turning swiftly this way and that. Again, though, no sign of a body; this being would never hunt the wild curving land of *Hwiliria*. Indeed, its eyeless soft-shining iridium helmet would likely never feel the gentle cylindrical sunlight of the barrel-world; it was obviously a thing of the warrens, a maintenance device perhaps, half-alive, horribly feeling its way as it rolled along that fleshy corridor . . .

"Feeling for us," whispered Benai. "That thing searches for us." They squeezed themselves farther back against some bulkhead, a soft bulkhead, warm . . . leather-like . . .

Agh! Pike was caught between the wall and the others, frozen by an urge to hide from the thing in the corridor and an equal, frightening need not to touch this pulsing wall against which he was pressed.

But the creature passed by: seemingly blindly feeling its way along the corridor at the speed of a jogging man, it was gone, downward, disappearing around the gentle curve of the warren.

"Jesus," whispered Corson, "how could it *miss* us?"

Pike exhaled, pressed the others outward to escape the "wall" behind him. "I've seen a similar response in walking gatlings and other cybers. Limited sensories—it's not hunting by sight, and its programming, or learning—it isn't specifically *made* to find us."

"They're caught by their own evolution." Jennifer felt her way one-handed along the dark corridor's soft wall. "They never thought they'd be hunting in the warrens. The real hunters, the shooting-neuters, they don't go here—and the things that do are too specialized, too narrow. Nothing's quite independent, don't you know; they're *pruned*, each one, from hatching. Like a—what is it, Pike? A servo? A machine's built with servos that *do* things, but a servo alone is . . ."

"Sort of a helmeted neuter," muttered Pike.

"And this whole place—it's a sort of amalgam of neuters." Benai touched the softly pulsing wall as they passed another dimly-lighted alcove. "It's alive —it—it *shuddered!*" He drew his hand back, rubbed it furiously against his coverall.

Jennifer staggered slapping her hands to her ears, cocked her head oddly, seeming to listen. "Do let's go on—we shouldn't touch if we can avoid it. It—it called something, no language, but—oh, God."

The motile in the corridor had stopped, rotated somehow on its own axis and was trundling silently back toward them. They backed to the nearby alcove, pressed in—and the thing stopped, blocking their exit.

And three tentacles, like great metallic centipedes, crept blindly inward, the tiny segmented legs clicking on the floor, curling, feeling. The dim lights shone in: somehow the thing could see, eyeless though it appeared to be, and the tentacles reared cobra-like, advancing, the end of each moist, black—

"YAH!" Benai leaped between two of them, the things writhing into a knot behind him as he hurled himself onto the neuter-machine's curving surface. In an instant his pistol barrel was wedged between the shining helmet and the machine's matte-black surface. The report was blunted by metal and flesh, and the centipedes retracted partway into their apertures at the thing's rim, one of them leaving a neat stitchlike line of paired rips on Corson's forearm before it withdrew.

"Damn! Those things are *strong!*" The stocky Texan rolled up his slitted sleeve, already blood-soaked.

"Let's see that." Jennifer rolled back the fabric. "Not deep—no danger, I think. But—listen!" Again she canted her head. No one else heard anything; it was Charon's neuter-translation gift working within her skull. "I can't *understand*, it's not the usual words of the surface neuters . . . but the whole place is alive! As if we'd touched a nerve!"

"We go, now!" Benai slid off the thing he'd killed, the others squeezing past it; a few of its appendages twitched mindlessly, horribly, in dying quasi-life.

Beyond the alcove there was no more light—none. Like blindfolded children they felt the repulsive walls. And were suddenly brought short by a sort of racial fear, stopping instinctively an instant before they touched an obstruction.

"Echo-locating—we're hearing ourselves against things," whispered Jennifer. "Blind are good at it, but we can all do it. We've an advantage here—" She paused. "I can't explain, but I can feel *Hwiliria*, a bloody mess of tiny impulses—she doesn't want us to go ahead, she's trying to close us off!"

"Can't go back." Pike tried to push ahead in the dark.

"No, but—it's—*Hwiliria*—she's an organism on her own now, *alive*, and looking to grow—she *is* the Accretion of the Creche. The Seeker, they called her, don't you see? When Charon found her, the Accretion wasn't functioning; she was mad, they were all mad, like Charon itself. Now, with Charon weakened, she's started again, sum of her parts, an aggregation of interconnected neuters, each nothing, a bit, a part of the Creche, and she sees us as a threat—she sees our *escape* as a threat, and she means to prevent it! Where she doesn't want us to go, where it—where it's worst for me, that's where we've got to, aagh . . ." She shuddered in the dark, her hand finding Pike's, pulling him to her.

"That's where we've got to go."

"Damme if I don't know why they don't send troops after us, those Godforsaken snouted walkin' guns—" Corson ran his hands along the obstruction before them. "Here, this way . . . no, just a sec." He felt further, joined by Benai.

Jennifer whimpered like a small animal in a steel trap. "It—she's screaming in my head, hundreds of them, together!" But not in her ears; it was Charon's "gift," her sensitivity to the neuterbands, thousands of neuters linked in their purpose—yet unable, yet, to close in. "Their soldiers, they can't go where they can't see, they're entirely sight-oriented, like birds, they don't know what to do, how to find an enemy in their own warrens—"

"Of course!" Benai involuntarily fisted his hands together. "*Hwiliria* is a fighting base—like our cosmograds. She orders distant battles, but cannot, didn't *grow* to repel enemies in her own—bloodstream. Here she's defenseless!"

Corson made a small choking sound. "For now. Bet she learns quick. Those surface fuckers, the whole daylight neuts, they'll activate something, or find some goddamn flashlights—"

"Oh, God, God, the pain, we've got to go where the hate is worst!" Jennifer clutched Pike, pushed him away, clapped her hands to her ears, reeled invisibly in the dark. And calmed, suddenly, her voice cold. "Follow me. We'll go. We'll go where we hurt her. Where she hurts me. Here—take my hand." She found Pike in the dark. "All hold hands, human chain. I'll *follow* the screaming. This way."

She stepped out then, confidently into the dark. "A story, to crush the screams." Her voice tightened to a small croak.

"Jennifer." Trundling blind behind her, Pike squeezed the slender hand. "You're okay? You—"

"I *hurt*, my head— I'll crush the screaming—I, I want to tell you about the hate, the fear—" The voice grew harsher, no vocal cords, a grating whisper. "We're in the forest, the black forest. We're the size of mice—"

"Muir," whispered Corson, "she's blown something, she's crackers—"

"*Listen*," croaked the surgeon, "you listen to *me*, as I listen to the night. The bristlecreepers, the tenrecs." She jerked, and the rest jerked with her. "*We* are bristlecreepers . . ."

"Citizen Doctor," said Benai gently.

"*Listen*, Commander First Grade. This is the Great Dark." Her voice trailed oddly: they could *hear* her capitalization, "Great Dark."

"We and the—and the dinosaurs. We appeared at the same time, *together*, more than two hundred million years ago. But they—they went for the light, evolved into the day. They were fast, oh, so fast— you know how fast. And eyes, all *eyes* they were, like hawks; and the little ones, they hunted us—for all their time, what? A hundred and thirty-five million years they hunted us. And for all that time, no mammal grew larger than a, than a tenrec—because those things waited, and watched, and anything that could be seen, they caught—" The grating voice paused, and she led them unerringly around a curve, their ears prickling in the macabre blind-man's-bluff.

And on— "Those millions of years, all through them, we mammals were good little bristlecreepers. We stayed in the forest, among the roots of the trees, creeping in and out, quiet, invisible. *We* couldn't see, oh, no, we were damned to the dark by the big-eyed things that waited in the day . . ."

"Like now," whispered Pike, squeezing her guiding hand again.

"Aggh." A sound of pain. "It's screaming again— we're going in the right direction." She sped up, whispering on unstoppably, weirdly, possessed. "What did we do, we little shrews? We *smelled* our way, we lived blind, we got good at it. Our brains—they were nose-brains, picking molecules from the air to model the world. If it smelled good it might be food; if it smelled good another way, it might be a mate. If it smelled like—agh—if we slipped once, that clawed hand, that taloned foot—a hundred and thirty-five million years!" She jerked again, turning right, downward, ever downward in the black.

"And our food—insects! We couldn't see 'em—we *heard* them, and we grew—we call 'em pinnae, ear-flaps, what have you, external ears that rotate and focus like eyes, sound-location, blindly predicting an insect's path so we could pounce. We saw with our ears, through these shrew-brains, tenrec-brains—blind bristlecreepers we were, in a time of monsters. We heard and smelled our invisible little universes, modelled them in an overgrown smell-brain, the thing we call a cerebral cortex—site of our souls, grown in the dark, self-enclosed worlds—d'you know, the way mammals feed and nurture their young from teats, by touch, and teach them, the little mothers led them through the dark until the babies' brain-modelling was complete. Silence, stealthy blindness, for all those millions of years, while the daylight things evolved, ebbing and flowing against one another, sight-brained, no modelling of an unseen world for them—they *saw* the world, so very well! They needed no modelling, no inner world. But, but—" The grip tightened painfully on Pike's hand— "They *made* us, those things out there, they shaped our souls in their hunting, and *this is why we fear those eyes!*"

A harsh laugh, loud after the whispering. "Oh, not the whileelin themselves; no, they came only at the end. They were just the only way their evolution could go. A world of perfect predators and frightfully defended herbivores, where else could those eye-minds go but gradually into hands? And groups—their intelligence didn't evolve individually, it grew in creches, in group-minds, neuters carving one another up. No internal modelling, no mothers leading them through the dark. No souls, no *souls*—the only whole ones among them are the fertiles, all eyes and dance and hunt, and the rest are just the machine that keeps the fertiles breeding, oh, *God!*" She staggered again, fell in the dark, Pike tumbling over her.

"I—it's too—I can't shut it out with the story."

"Listen," whispered Corson.

Silence—not quite. A throbbing, low, at the limit of hearing.

"This is the Forest," whispered Jennifer. "We can find our way here: *they* cannot, except the mutilated things. I—I know why the pain grows—they have docks ahead somewhere, boats! I can understand a bit, just a bit now—a neuter, a whole helmeted neuter somewhere, not far—it's running a slip, a dock, a little—hundreds—they're launching—"

Silence again, and the men heard below that silence the throbbing of the Hwilirian entity . . . and the lights went on again! Brilliant to dark-accustomed eyes, the corridor shone in the glimmer of the organic strips they'd seen before.

"Citizen Doctor, they understand you." Benai slipped around Pike, helped him lift her.

"No," she said. "But they're guessing right: they're eye-things, and they thought the dark would immobilize us as it would them. Now they'll come for us, the whole ones, with their gun-heads."

Benai checked his pistol. "I've two extra magazines here—"

"I hear some, and I hear, worse, God, the screaming of the Creche—" Jennifer broke, ran, disappearing ahead of them.

Corson froze for an instant, rubbing his eyes. "No *souls*, she says, but they built all this!"

"C'mon, sir!" Pike leaped ahead, along the senselessly curving way, so like a great bloodless artery, not a straight line to be seen—to a dead end, Jennifer backed against it, eyes clear again.

"She—*Hwiliria* knows I hear her. She's quiet—she's stopped screaming. We're caught."

"I still don't get it," said Corson. "If they got no—"

"Individuality," gasped Jennifer, sagging against the repulsive soft bulkhead.

"Yeah, if—"

"Parallel processing!" Pike glanced wildly about him. "Like chips—the neuters can only do this or that, each one, but they're born in groups and once they get neutered they function in parallel, in little gene-locked groups—"

"Twins," said Jennifer. "Twins—they've a sort of empathy, twins do . . . Imagine thousands of them—the Creche—these narrow multitudes, ten neuter twins per litter plus a couple of breeders. And only the breeders whole, but limited, like queens and males in an anthill . . . I, I hear a neuter, a hunting-neuter! It's, I can feel it, it's in a little warship, a fast thing, it's waiting for—for others—if we can only get there, it can't be far, and—bloody hell, more! On the run, from the other direction—gunners! We've got to go on!"

"This stuff, here, these wrinkles in the wall." Corson pushed against the loathsome integument blocking their way. "See this stuff, these thick places—like muscles! Benai, take that popgun of yours and pop this one, here!"

Benai gripped the pistol two-handed, aimed and fired at the veinlike radial patterning on the wall—and with the report Jennifer screamed and fell to the floor, clutching her head, like one herself shot.

But the bulkhead writhed open before them, and Pike lifted her rail-thin body in a fireman's carry, the load lightened by fear, squeezing after Corson and Benai through the opening—which bled, with red blood.

They were in a high hemispherical chamber whose walls seemed built of silvery bulges: the iridium bulging of neuter helmets, hundreds of them, seemingly growing out of the wall. A bank, a ganglion of neuters, a sub-awareness. Benai stood stock still, glaring about the dimlit place, glancing briefly at Jennifor's inert form draped over Pike's shoulder. "Unconscious? Excellent. Forgive me, Citizen Doctor, but—" He raised the pistol again and took random aim, firing nine, ten, eleven rounds into the glimmering helmets, the sound loud in the confines of the place—and Jennifer screamed again, frothing convulsed to the floor.

The floor itself quaked, hurling them all down, but the surgeon was up in an instant, her eyes again bright. "This way, you asses! They're coming!" They sprinted toward another sphincter-like opening, its edges pulsing uncertainly as the little group scrambled through. "There—that light bit, it's a nerve center for the door—kill it!"

Benai fired, and the sphincter snapped shut like the closing of a monstrous mouth behind them. "Paralyzed, if I guess right." Jennifer trotted down another curving ramp, the floor seething drunkenly under them all. "I don't know what you did in there, Commander, but it threw 'em balls-up for a moment."

"If balls they had," puffed Benai.

"More coming—God, I feel the screaming—*Hwiliria*, the light—" She staggered again, falling, twisting. Pike fought his way past the flailing of her limbs, picked her up, shouted at Benai, "The lights! Shoot those strips! It's a single circuit, or nerve, or something, got to be!"

Ahead of them, a horrible thumping run, the sound grabbing at whatever in their brains manufactured fear. The eye-hunters, coming for bristlecreepers caught in the daylight—

Bonai fired, and blessed darkness enfolded them in its loving arms. The thumping stopped. Silence, but for their rasping breathing. The floor trembled squashily.

And a light flickered ahead: another motile neuter-thing, round, centipede tentacles flashing, its rimlights glancing off gun-snouted helmets beyond. The three men pressed themselves to a rubbery inlet in the warm wall, waiting as the creature slowly approached. Four—no, five hunters trod behind it, their barrels flickering as they scanned.

"They can't see," whispered Corson. "Can't hear too good either—try to get that thing's helmet."

Ever so slowly, Benai took aim, fired—and the hall filled with light as a flurry of glowing projectiles arced toward them, glancing off bulkheads, some embedding themselves in the fleshy substance of *Hwiliria*. The neuter-machine reared back—a dozen little feet? —and its lights went out.

Blessed darkness again. "The dumb fuckers got no *flashlights*," gasped Corson, "no flashlights, no fuckin' *souls!*"

"The doctor is correct," whispered Benai. "They do not move in the dark." He breathed deeply, concentrating on his brief memory of the hunters' locations. Gripping the thumb lever tightly to muffle the sound, he snapped the pistol silently to full automatic, laid himself gingerly on the throbbing floor. On auto—three-shot bursts, the thing fired. He aimed, closed his useless eyes, squeezed the trigger.

The *ratatat* was instantly smothered in an eruption of light and sound from his target area; things whizzed and plocked, and a full-scale firefight etched the corridor in garish winking death.

As suddenly as it started, the firing ended. The air filled with a stench of burnt flesh and feces. Benai tentatively rapped his pistol-butt on the hornlike floor. No response.

"Now, *that's* what I call parallel processing," muttered Pike. "The fuckers killed *each other!*" He cradled Jennifer's head in his lap, gently slapped her cheeks. "Where to now?"

She groaned, stirred, sat up suddenly. "I still —god, I have the screaming, the hate! The Creche is afraid—this way!" With unnatural strength she tore from his arms, ran straight for the place where, moments before, the enemy had massed.

Following, the men skidded across a floor of torn whileelin limbs, gobbets of whileelin flesh. Jennifer slid to a halt at a branch in the corridor, looked both ways, rasped, "Here!"

Light ahead. They slowed, creeping along the walls, bristlecreepers on the forest's edge . . .

And *Hwiliria* came to an end—or seemed to. As if a slice had been taken from her, she opened on a vast vertical starlake, a window, irregularly faceted with Hwilirian bone, beyond which the stars wheeled with her slow turning. A canyon in the Rim, and a gray bulging of things in rows, dozens of them, huge spheroids like rough-skinned fruits pinned somehow against the glass by sphincters through which helmet neuters scrambled in twos and threes, the sphincters closing instantly after them, the great round things dropping into the night like apples falling, unfurling long propulsive spines as they swung into space . . . Ships!

"It's a *port!*" Jennifer turned, laughing wildly—and then her grin faded.

"The ships—they're *alive*, they're neuters, like everything else! They *carry* hunters, but *we* can't— there's no way we can *run* one!

"*They're part of Hwiliria, and she's hunting us!*"

CHAPTER 23

Again, the Koan

"They're ships, though, goddammit," whispered Pike. "They've got airlocks, and that one there's only thirty meters across the open—no neuts near it!" He pointed to the nearest of the things, a lumpy gray spheroid squashed against a muscular airlock. "We can sprint to it—no other choice!"

From their place of concealment they watched knots of helmeted neuters, walkers, whole and swift. No barrels on those helmets, of course, for they'd be directing the ships, themselves neuters, living weapons.

"I—I feel the screaming again," gasped Jennifer. "They're coming for us."

The four leaned outward, peered along the mighty Hwilirian curve, a vast corridor, bright-lit, ringing the cylindrical world, boundary to a canyon a kilometer wide—a stupendously curving canyon that bottomed into the bottomless black of space. The place was a gap in *Hwiliria's* body wall, a glass-topped abyss spanned by clusters of her arching ribs, each rib a bridge a hundred meters across. Neuters were

333

everywhere, some maneuvering squashy-looking containers, others filing into or out of sphincters. Far in the distance, a platoon of—infantry—emerged from a bulkhead, metallic snouts flashing in the light of the cylindrical sun far above.

"They're looking," whispered Benai, leaning further out. "They don't quite know where we are—"

sssssPOK!

The rest glanced toward him as he stepped abruptly back into the shelter of their corridor, swaying, hand tight-clenched in the rubbery bulkhead. A round black hole between his eyes, his head ending raggedly, pink and white, at the hairline. The pistol fell, and Oruna Benai fell atop it.

Jennifer's eyes rolled back as something wrenched her mind. "Enough, *Hwiliria!*" Screaming, her voice cracking—

Another projectile hissed past, skidded along the ground, *turned*, lifted off again, missed, thudded into the bulkhead, flared briefly.

Jennifer stepped out, arms held wide, into the immense glassy corridor. *"Hwiliria!* I hear you! Enough, for God's sake, enough, you bitch!"

The helmeted hunters paused, faceless, their glittering snouts pointing in weird slow-moving unison as she staggered screaming across the glassed canyon rim. Then they ran, ran in that crazed curving geometry toward her, not firing now, the overmind that ran them watching through their eyes the surgeon's surrender.

Corson, retching, kicked Benai's body aside, dropped on the pistol. He shuffled out on his knees, took a kneeling firing position.

Pike lunged for Jennifer, fell over Benai, rolled to his feet, grabbed the belt of her coverall. With super-

human strength she threw him down as the snouted
neuters skidded to a halt before them.

The creatures did not fire.

A movement behind them, and Pike and Corson
whirled—and there stood the First in the Chase,
proud and tall, his taloned hands fisted before him.

"Alooo, hoom," he hooted. "We are of one blood,
thou and I, are we not? See now the Accretion of the
Creche, in which our flesh, too, becomes one—or so
I'm told!" He touched his knobbed knuckles respectfully to the floor, crest flicking in and out: perplexity?

Jennifer turned then, herself spotting the First.
The screaming in her head snapped off as if by a
switch: *Hwiliria* had them now, and was content.

The First's head bobbed as he triangulated on each
of them in turn. "It amuses me to be here," he
whistled, "although the Creche would will it otherwise."

Jennifer watched the creature in bewildered awe;
he was calm, seemingly exuding pleasure at the sight
of them; his gaze fell on Benai then, and—

"This one, he is dead!" The crest narrowed:
confusion!

"Goddamn right he's dead, y'fuckin' lizard!" Swiftly,
Corson raised the pistol, pointing it at the First's
narrow chest—and Jennifer screamed again, twisting
to the floor—

The fighting-neuters remained frozen, and all else
also save the crying Jennifer and the First, whose
head continued its perplexed hawklike bobbing.

And Pike understood: the whole terrible organism
around him, the armed neuters but cells in its vast
body, feared for the First in the Chase above all else.
The fertility of the Creche was at stake in this last
monstrous moment, and all that parallel processing
skidded to a halt—

"Git," croaked Corson, nodding toward the open sphincter of the bulbous ship.

"Sir—"

"You *ass*hole, get the fuck outta here." The little man's jaw set, and he squared the pistol immovably at the First in the Chase.

"By your demeanor," whistled the First cheerfully, "I would judge that which you hold to be a weapon."

"Damn right," snarled Corson. "Muir, you fucking grab that girl and board that ship. *Order*, Muir!"

Pike glanced at Jennifer, now still but for the casta-net chattering of her teeth. *Hwiliria* had her—but he, Corson, and the First in the Chase were free. Kneeling then, Pike picked Jennifer up, cradling her like a baby in his arms, edging toward the open ship-sphincter. It stayed open.

The First, crest narrowed to a point, stared un-winking at Corson. "Something eludes me here. You point a projectile-launcher at one who would use no such thing; how can this be? If you'd engage me, do so with tooth and talon, not with neuters' toys!"

Pike reached the sphincter, peered in: two odd netted platforms in a globular cockpit, no controls, nothing . . .

"Muir," shouted the statue-like Corson, "I don't ever wanna see yer *face* again, you hear?"

In an agony, Pike stepped across the leathery sphincter-rim, dropped Jennifer across one of the odd couches—which instantly wrapped her in net-ting. He turned, watching the weird tableau beyond the circle of muscle.

"Muir, you *got* your *orders!*"

Pike's muscles went watery; he settled on the other couch, which gently netted him facing the lock. The sphincter closed, magically, transparently. He was in a glassy bubble on the surface of this ball of—this living ship, melded to the glassy wall of *Hwiliria*'s docking canyon, and he could see both space and the place he'd just left, the stopped-motion scene of metal-snouted neuters and the First ringing the little Texan colonel.

And from a vibrating membrane in the wall of his fleshy chamber a voice spoke: "Toolmaker Koan," it said, that all-too-familiar elder's tone.

"Charon! Save him!"

"A thing I cannot do, little animal. As *deus ex machina* I'm a poor thing now, overextended by the very abomination of my having brought *Hwiliria* here. I'm in too deep; we're in the endgame, and I play against the Koan. I've only one more play, to out-guess that Koan. Two thousand million years I've wandered, and now I weaken. I can barely manage for a few moments this little ship in which I find you!"

Pike glanced wildly about—and saw the Egg, soap-bubble rainbowed, a few meters from the enclosing glass.

"I break *Hwiliria*'s hold on this little ship, her sterile spawn—and its contents! So—"

Jennifer stirred, groaned, fought suddenly against the webbing.

"Sit tight, little surgeon."

"Charon! You—I can't believe—"

"Unbelief is salubrious to the human nervous system. Look on the colonel, who saved you, and depart."

They glanced again at the Hwilirian tableau. The First's crest was still narrowed in perplexity, and Corson—Corson's eyes were bright with tears.

"Toolmaker Koan," murmured the Charon-voice. "In my despair I've erred yet again. Now—yet again—*deus ex machina*."

In a rush of freefall, the weird ship dropped away,

revolving. The lighted corridor became the edge of a canyon curving along a silver-limned black world-rim, a cylinder, belted with a bright encircling groove, fading against the starry night. Then the bubble-ship turned, and they felt acceleration away from *Hwiliria* now invisible behind them. The crescent Moon appeared, ice-gray but belovedly familiar. To either side of her glimmered a bead of light: the distant mirrors of humankind's only remaining homes, locked floating in the distant Lagrangian Points.

"Toolmaker Koan," said the weary voice again. "You know, my little beasts, your friends out there await you—in a single communications net. A start, perhaps. And—oh!" The voice lightened. "I'll be sending a few things along soon—posthumously, as it were. And, yes, when I, ah, reconstituted you, I, ah, messed about a bit more—not only with health and translating and all that rot."

"What now?" Jennifer's voice rasped, her throat stinging.

"A surprise. Wait a few decades. But now I must hurry you along. Meddler, me, mad old thing, I've meddled again with animals. I brought the whileelin to a time—your time—in which they never belonged. I was wrong, oh, so wrong, for all my vaunted knowledge. Goodbye, and Godspeed!"

"Charon!" they cried out in unison, but now the gravities of acceleration crushed them inward, fast, hard. They screwed their eyes tight against the masses, involuntarily reaching across the small space between them to clasp hands before unconsciousness took them.

Behind them the Egg moved at *Hwiliria's* rim-canyon. There, Colonel Jimbob Corson squeezed the trigger of his dead friend's Russian pistol and bit his lower lip, muttering, "Toolmaker Koan."

The shock of the three-round burst slammed his

wrists upward, and he glimpsed for an instant through his grateful tears the First's staggering fall.

Then forty-seven tons of collapsed—matter Egg opened against the mighty substance of *Hwiliria*, so sadly misplaced in time and space, her passing now a brief, brilliant nova against the distant topaz shroud of twice-ruined Earth.

EPILOGUE

"Munirda, strangeko!" The girl glanced shyly at the Mother, back again at the Karonic. "Mensch, two, Marma, oltimaku wringlerising!"

"And to *me*, my noisy descendant, you speak English!" The Mother dimpled, brushed back in ancient habit her glossy straight blonde hair. But for the darker skin of young Anasa, a casual observer might have missed the sixteen generations between them; the genes spoke well of the Old Ones, even across three centuries and more of mixing.

"It *is* difficult," said the girl. "You're always so—"

"Tell us, little Anasa. We're slow? Eh?" The Father pretended deafness, cocking an ear with his hand, grinning boyishly. "What're you finding *now*, hotshots?"

"It's—it's new gene-sequences, it looks like, but much, so much more—" Long oldtongue schooling failed the girl for an instant; tonguetied, she listened to her implant. "But—but they're not more extinct beasts, Marma, they seem—human, maybe . . ."

"I doubt it; never one yet. You're too quick, Anasa,

340

not gentle enough in the melding . . . oh, we'll know soon enough—chatterbox!" The Mother slid her arm through the Father's. "Leave them to their toys, love; Christmas forever, on the Karonics. Myself—a bit of exercise, I think. Tennis, anyone?"

"Three sets, m'love. A wager?"

"A wager? Mmmm, I think—the stakes should be high. Perhaps a little bout in the Axial Lake. Winner take all."

"You seem to make me *want* to lose," said the Father.

They wandered off, upward, arm in arm. Somewhere a bird fluted and they paused, looking down along the gentle curving plain beneath them. There the ibises flocked white in their thousands to the water's edge, following their daily routine of frogging in the marshes, end to end, of Serengeti High. The Old Ones smiled briefly on the myriad creatures of their sunlit home, then arm in arm went upward again. It was a good kilometer's climb to the courts, but the climbing grew easier the higher one went— and on the way plenty of stops, ported refreshment-stops opening out on the wheeling stars.

At one of these they rested, drinking tea, comfortable in their young/old love. Above them loomed a life-sized bronze statue, bedecked with fresh flowers as tradition demanded, of an Animal: an alien animal, a being they'd once called First—and, almost, friend. Like all such statues in the Human Metastasis (and there were many, one to a world), it stood on a high stone base bearing a simple Shakespearean epigram:

What seest thou else
In the dark backward and abysm of time?

Here Anasa overtook them, breathless. "It *is* humans, Marma, two of them, sequencing out now—and so much more, cultural overlays, they'll be adults—"

"Hold on now, just—seems a bit much, doesn't it?" The Father put his hands on the eager girl's shoulders.

"But it *is*—two, and of different—*subspecies*! One Afri, I think, one Cauca. I can't think why—"

"I, ah, run along, love. And your flower for the First." The Mother plucked an iris, handed it to Anasa, who stretched up and laid it in the basalt basin between the statue's glaived feet.

"Flower for the First," she whispered, flushed with excitement; the Mother made a shooing motion with her hands, and the young woman fled back down the hundreds of stony stairs to the Rimring Karonics.

The Mother turned to the Father, winking. "I think we have—"

"—another posthumous joke?" The Father pursed his lips in an ill-concealed smile. "The entire Karonic Code's a posthumous joke. We've been pulling—uh, reconstituting—the most absurd things out of there ever since it was cracked. This time, though—it might've gone too far."

"Yes—you know what I'm thinking."

"Education."

"Filling-in."

They spoke and thought together, these ancient lovers. Ancient and forever young, they stared out at the wheeling stars, smiling briefly in unison at the Sun's Ring shimmering in the night. A brief autumnal melancholy touched them, a memory:

Hwiliria and the Ninth Planet binary had winked out simultaneously, less than a day after Earth's scourging so long ago; but it had taken some hours for the light of Charon's passing to reach the people of the old Lagrangian cities.

It had taken years for Charon's gifts to follow their prescribed orbits inward; cometary volatiles, useful debris . . . and the Codes in their collapsed-matter Eggs. And as mad Charon had hoped, centuries passed before humanity had even begun to decipher those Codes, learning the magic of collapsed-matter memories, the wonders of genetic reconstitution, and most recently the tricks of Nothing's bending, superluminal translocation. By then there were millions in space; now there were billions, joined daily by new Pleistocene and later species eagerly dredged by chattering children from the Karonic Codes and born anew in the thousands of cylindrical worlds ringing the Sun.

The worlds of the Human Metastasis.

She leaned against him, the two of them comfortably filling the ancient basalt bench before the port. "You know, they're going to be so *awfully* surprised . . ."

"Like us, in a way . . ."

"Once they catch up . . ."

"Took us a decade, after . . ."

". . . before we guessed."

"You stayed so young, I worried . . ."

"No more than I, thinking of myself growing old, and you a mere boy . . ."

The Father sat up abruptly. "We can't let those kids—"

The Mother winked again. "We're about to have two grown-up babies on our hands."

"Babies!" The Father laughed. "As far as they'll be concerned, they'll have just blown each other out of the sky. Two mad bastards, warriors, dying of radiation burns at the end of the world—they missed it all!

Gods of the Night! They'll think—what'll they think? How can we even *begin* . . ."

"We'd better postpone the game."

"Down we go again."

"Not yet. Wait—" She leaned across him, pinning his hands to the seat. "Watch."

The Earth appeared, blue, green, the cleanly swirl of cloud brightening the homeworld's face as she followed the stars in Serengeti's turning.

And was gone again, and again the nearer worlds of the Human Metastasis flashed against those stars— but by then Jennifer and Pike were trotting lightly, hand in hand, down the thousands of stone steps toward their fierce loving descendants, the Toolmaker children, tending the awakening of ghosts at the Rimring Karonic.